BOAT LOAD OF TROUBLE

A Novel

A Slop Bucket Mystery Series
Volume I

By John Shivers

LAUREL
Mountain
PRESS

Clayton, Georgia

Laurel Mountain Press
PO Box 2218, Clayton, Georgia 30525
www.laurelbooks.com

This book is work of fiction. Names, characters, places and
incidents either are the product of the author's imagination
or are used fictitiously. Any resemblance to actual events,
locales, or persons, living or dead, is coincidental and beyond
the intent of either the author or the publisher.

Printed in the United States of America

ISBN: 978-1516893621

Dedicated to...

With each book I've written, I've been able to recognize and say thank you to the many people who have supported and encouraged my efforts. Without some of them, my books would truly never have seen publication.

As this book was nearing completion, I realized there is one person I've never mentioned. It's an oversight that's going to be rectified with the publication of **Boat Load of Trouble**; I just regret that she died just a few short months before publication happened.

I think sometimes we don't realize how just a few words can provide a lifetime of inspiration and motivation. It was late May 1968, just a couple of days before my graduation from Calhoun High School, when my journalism instructor asked what my plans were for the future. While my dream was to become a publishing writer, I seriously doubted my ability to make that happen, so I answered, "I'm not sure."

She looked at me as only she could, then she quietly uttered the words that made all the difference. "If you don't go into some field of writing," she said, "it will break my heart." She didn't know it then... I didn't know it then, but those 14 words were what I needed to hear. Her encouragement gave me the chance to believe that dreams could come true. She believed in me, and I can never thank her enough.

Mary Lou Hobgood
Boat Load of Trouble is dedicated to you,
with my deepest appreciation.

And, as always, I can't finish any book without telling Elizabeth, my partner in crime as well as in life, how much I love her and appreciate the constant support she showers on me.

Other Books by John Shivers

Create My Soul Anew Trilogy

Hear My Cry
Paths of Judgment
Lift Up Mine Eyes

Renew A Right Spirit Trilogy

Broken Spirit
Merry Heart
His Mercy Endureth

Repossessed

Author's Notes

I've never quite understood how I first became hooked on mystery stories. But hooked I was, by about 1957 or 1958. Whether my interest was seeded by the "Perry Mason" TV series, based on the books by Erle Stanley Gardner, or merely cultivated and fertilized by the adventures of Perry, Paul and Della, I may never know.

Fast forward through the years, and my horizons broadened, along with my love of the mystery genre. I've played armchair PI with more mystery authors than I can count. If the word "mystery" was on the book's cover or in the title, I had to read that book. Along about 1960, I paid a whopping thirty-five cents for Gardner's "Mystery of the Buried Clock." That was the first Perry Mason book I ever purchased, and today, after a lifetime of searching and accumulation, I have almost every title in the series. And I'm still on the lookout.

The first book I ever wrote was a mystery, if you want to call 150 pages of notebook paper covered with childish scrawls of green ink a book. I was 11 and had just vowed to become a novelist. To seal the deal, I began to pen my own whodunit, just to prove that I could.

While I have thoroughly enjoyed writing the seven inspirational fiction books that I have in print so far, and have been tremendously fulfilled and blessed by all that has gone into those books, I still dreamed of trying my hand at writing mystery. With the completion of the manuscript for **Boat Load of Trouble**, that dream has been realized. A second title to continue Mags' story is already underway. But I'm not abandoning inspirational fiction. My eighth book in that genre is tentatively scheduled for release in late 2015. In the years ahead, I'm looking forward to straddling the fence to write in both genre. Writing is my God-given talent and I'm excited to cultivate and refine that talent in more than one direction.

I hope you'll enjoy Mags Gordon's trial by fire as she earns her PI license in the school of hard knocks. In order to save new her life and her livelihood, she must do things she never even considered in her old life. She really does have a full boat load of trouble.

Chapter One

HAVE YOU CHECKED HIS VITAL SIGNS?

The last thing Mags Gordon expected when she stepped on board the *One True Love* that balmy spring morning was a man's obviously dead body, lying in a sticky pool of blood. The second surprise came when she recognized the recently departed as her billionaire client from hell.

Her heart went into her throat and she grabbed the bulkhead wall to steady herself, even as her hastily-eaten breakfast backed up in her throat. *This is so not good.*

With bird calls and the melody of water rippling in circles from mountain bass breaking the lake's surface in dramatic displays of acrobatics, Mags ran her fingers through the tightly-curled cap of red and silver-gray hair crowning her head. Some action was required of her and suddenly, she wasn't certain she was up to the task. After all, she'd never found a dead body before.

Then she realized how Annie Darling must have felt in "Death on Demand", when that miserable Elliot Morgan was murdered, and poor Annie was accused of doing the deed.

Mags dug in her oversized purse and finally located her cell phone. Thank goodness there was one notch of a signal! Many places on the conjoined lakes where she peddled waterfront real estate were forever out of range.

With shaking hands she punched the three numbers to summon help. "This is Mags... er, Margaret Gordon," she said, when the 911 operator answered. "I've just found a man's body on my boat. I'm afraid he's dead."

"How can you be certain, Mrs. Gordon? Have you checked his vital signs?"

"Trust me," she replied, somewhat irked. "He's dead all right. He's a sickly gray white, and he's bled enough to stock a blood bank." She thought for a second. "And, no, I haven't touched the body."

"Are you qualified to make a medical diagnosis?"

Mags was about to get sideways with the woman whose monotone voice was neither helpful nor friendly.

"Look. I may not be a doctor, but you aren't here to see what I see, either! Would you please just send help?"

"They're en-route. Don't leave until they arrive."

"But you don't even know where I am."

"Yes ma'am, you're at the Davis Marina. I got a GPS coordinate from your cell phone signal. They'll be there shortly and the sheriff will want to talk with you."

"I'm sure he will," Mags answered, dreading the drill that awaited her. Sheriff Malcolm Wiley had never forgiven her for taking his good friend and her now ex-husband, Franklin, to the proverbial cleaners.

Never mind how the sheriff felt about her. It was her boat. This man was her client. It wasn't any secret after all these weeks, after so many defaulted contracts, that he wasn't her favorite buyer. In fact, so far, he wasn't a buyer at all; just a most obnoxious looker. She didn't need Miss Marple to tell her that she was prime suspect number one.

Mags prided herself on her arm's length friendship with so many fictional amateur detectives. There were even a few guys in the bunch, because Margaret Streetwood Gordon had read thousands of whodunits since discovering Erle Stanley Gardner's Perry Mason, when she was only eight years old.

But she never thought she'd find herself in the middle of a murder. How would Nancy Drew handle this?

Before she could peer into her favorite girl sleuth's deductive brain, the sound of approaching sirens could be heard in the distance. An ambulance swung around the curve and into view, followed by not one but two sheriff's vehicles.

The next few minutes were a blur as Mags showed officers where the body of one Horace J. Humphries lay sprawled in an unsightly position of demise. Once the EMT's discovered the industrialist was indeed as dead as Mags had known him to be, they reloaded their gear and turned things over to the deputies.

It was a sight she would never forget. Not only would she never make a commission from the bozo, she'd probably have to buy a new boat. Once word got around, no one was going to want to view property from a boat where someone had been murdered.

Mags had given the officer in charge all the information she had, which wasn't much, considering she hadn't seen the disagreeable Mr. Humphries since the day before. "Thank you, ma'am," the uniformed officer replied. "You'd best wait on the dock while we process the crime scene. And Mrs. Gordon?"

"Yes?"

"Please don't leave. Sheriff Wiley is on his way, and he gave orders that we were to detain you until he arrived."

Orders, huh? Great. The day was just getting better and better.

She didn't have long to wait.

"Okay, Mrs. Gordon," the burly, bald-headed man in tan and brown ordered a few minutes later. "Tell me what happened and don't leave out anything." His voice was both foreign and formal, very unlike the relationship she had known with him for so long. The sheriff had strode onto the dock with such purpose and presence, Mags was certain she felt the wooden platform tremble. Or maybe it was just her knees?

"That's just it, Malcolm. There's nothing to tell." She wagged her head like she thought a good shake might reset her brain, and bring some sense to a situation she couldn't explain. Or understand.

"Mr. Humphries was in the office yesterday morning, shortly before ten o'clock. When he left, he said he wouldn't be back until the middle of next week." She shuddered as she recalled the man's threatening last words. The ones he muttered right after he wagged his finger in her face, and challenged her to find him a suitable property "this time!" But she didn't share that part.

"And...?"

"Last night he called me at home, insisting that we look at a certain house this morning, and we agreed to meet here at the boat."

"That's IT?"

The sheriff clearly expected more drama than he was getting. "That's it. I swear. I didn't see him again until I boarded this morning, and found him between me and the wheelhouse." She extended her arms and turned her hands palms up. "End of story."

"He's obviously been dead for several hours," the sheriff observed. "We'll have to wait for the autopsy to know exactly when."

Mags knew what was coming next.

"So where were you last night?"

"At "The Slop Bucket", of course," she responded, feeling more than a little trapped. "Where do you think I was?"

"I don't know, Margaret. I don't know you at all anymore; not since you swindled my best friend out of his boat, and the lodge that's been in his family for half a century."

"Franklin cheated on me. Remember?" She choked as she recalled discovering that he'd brought women to The Slop Bucket to wine and dine, and charm them out of their pants. The vision of what had been haunted her. "You know where to find me," she charged. "I'm outta here."

"You don't leave town," the lawman barked. "We aren't through talking, and I want you where I can find you easy."

Mags knew what he really wanted was to be able to find her easily, but she chose not to correct his grammar. It wasn't just the sight of his bulk straining the seams on the brown uniform that intimidated her. If she was honest, and she usually tried to be above-board, she had never truly liked Malcolm Wiley. Now that she and Franklin were divorced, she simply didn't trust the man who had been her ex-husband's best friend since childhood. It would, she knew, be a most interesting next few days.

"I have no intention of leaving town," she informed him through clenched teeth. "But I am going back to my office, because I still have a business to run."

Without waiting for the response she was sure was forthcoming, Mags turned and walked as fast as she could, without breaking into a record-breaking sprint, anxious to put dead bodies and one overbearing sheriff behind her.

Once behind the wheel of her Jeep Cherokee, it wasn't until she heard the automatic door locks engage that she realized how frightened she had been, and how vulnerable she still felt. All she could think about was getting back to the security of the lakeside office she rented in town. She kept her speed under the depressed limit posted throughout the marina but, as soon as she hit the public road, safely out of sight of the gaggle of officers that now swarmed over her boat like ants over a forgotten bread crust, her foot became very heavy.

"Don't leave the office, Carole," Mags advised her office manager. "You're not gonna believe what's happened." As she drove back toward the small mountain town of Crabapple Cove, Mags had monitored her cell phone display until it registered a viable signal. Pulling to the side of the road, she was desperate to hear a friendly voice and, at that moment, she preferred to talk to Carole Pickett. Not only was the woman her employee, but the two had become close friends in the short time they had worked together.

"Horace J. Humphries is dead. I heard it about half an hour ago and I've been frantic to reach you," Carole informed her.

"I've been in and out of range. But how did you hear it so soon?" She consulted her vehicle's dash clock. "I only found his body about forty-five minutes ago."

"You found his body! Oh my gosh. Tell me you didn't. Really?"

"Sorry, friend. I wish I hadn't, but I'm the one who literally stumbled over his corpse. How did you hear the news so quickly?"

"Maudeann at the "Eat and Greet" told me when I stopped in to grab a cup of tea."

Carole finished filling in the blanks. "And Maudeann got the information from her sister Jeanann, who's married to Malcolm's Chief Deputy Larry Gowens, who has been in constant contact with his boss." Mags wondered how she could have underestimated the grapevine that thrived in the small town she now called home, and how Carole could say all of that without taking a breather.

"So did your sources also tell you who killed our client?"

"There's speculation, but I don't think you want to talk about it."

"In other words, they think I did it." A cold chill so massive it caused her to momentarily lose control of the Jeep invaded her body. She fought to wrestle the steering wheel, while her mind was processing a kaleidoscope of emotions and possibilities. "Well, just for the record, I didn't do it," she professed. "But something tells me it's going to be up to me to prove that I didn't kill that despicable little man. I'm on my way."

As she navigated the twisting curves that led to town, Mags mentally reviewed her dealings with the wealthy gentleman with the New York accent, who had shown such financial possibilities for her fledgling real estate agency. In death, he would still provide PR possibilities she could never hope to purchase. Unfortunately, the advertisement quality would be negative instead of positive.

Sight of the four block-long business district encouraged her somewhat. This was normal and, right at that moment, normal was what she needed. Mags headed straight for her office that overlooked the lake, and nosed her vehicle into its regular parking slot.

"You look like hell," her employee volunteered, as Mags entered the reception area of the little building that had once been the town's police department.

"You try discovering a dead body first thing in the morning and see how you look." She settled her tote bag on the edge of her desk. "It'll throw you off course, I guarantee."

"I guess it was pretty bad?"

Mags ran her fingers through her hair more to keep them occupied than for styling purposes. "Bad, I could have handled. This goes so much deeper than bad, and I don't know where to begin."

"Telling me exactly what happened would be a good place to start," Carole suggested. "Maybe I can see something you're overlooking, because you're still in a state of shock." She held out a large Styrofoam cup. "I ran down and grabbed another cup of tea. Just the way you like it." She flashed her boss a blinding smile. "Sit right down here and sip your tea while you spill your guts."

"Eeeeewwww," Mags replied. "That doesn't sound like anything I'd like to do. But I get your drift." She settled back against the cushions on the sofa across from Carole's desk. After a long and fortifying slug of the hot, amber liquid, heavily laced with sugar and lemon, Mags took a deep breath. "Okay. Here goes. I had an appointment to meet our client at the boat this morning. He called me late last night demanding to see the Wilkinson property. I offered to show it to him the other day, only he was too busy. Yet at ten o'clock last night, he was insistent that he had to see it this morning."

For the next few minutes Mags toured her friend through the events of the morning, trying desperately to remember each and every tidbit of information.

"Now," Mags said, as she shifted position, "you know everything that I do. Which means that neither of us knows enough to make a difference."

"Maybe we do and maybe we don't," Carole argued. "We know that you didn't kill him." The wicked grin that was her trademark illuminated the woman's face that others called pixie-ish. "If you'd told me he'd been strangled, I might've had to suspect you. But you can't even stand to cut a raw piece of meat, so there's no way you'd have had anything to do with blood. Nope, you didn't do it."

Mags had to laugh. The mental image of her hands around the swarthy-skinned little man's throat was clearly visible in her imagination. How many times had she visualized her long, slender fingers tightening around his airway in order to stifle his belittling tirades.

"You're right," she finally agreed. "I didn't do it, though Lord knows I was tempted. More than once." She pointed a finger at her friend and noticed that her nail polish was chipping. "So how about you? He made your life miserable as well. Did you kill him?"

"Me? Are you serious?"

"We'd be burying our heads in the sand to think that they won't look at you as well. Can you prove where you were last night? I was in bed. Alone. Anybody making pillow talk with you?"

"Now you know the answer to that one just as well as I do. So I guess we've got problems?"

Mags didn't answer immediately, as her eyes traveled about the room that surrounded her. At that moment, it truly was an oasis and a safe haven. Its walls of sea breeze aquamarine, adorned with framed work by area artists, her favorite African violets, and the overstuffed loveseats and comfortable club chairs gave the space a homey feel. The furniture had been in the family sitting room of the sprawling mansion in Atlanta's tony Buckhead suburb. Besides her clothes and her books, the flowered-chintz pieces had been all she had taken from the house. From Franklin's house. He was rarely ever in the cozy, inviting room, and she didn't associate the upholstered pieces with the man who had betrayed her so cruelly.

"Mags. You okay?"

The sound of her assistant's voice brought her back from the pain of the past, into the discomfort of the present. "Yeah, I'm fine. I was just remembering…"

"Look, boss lady. You've got to let go of Franklin's betrayal. It happened and there's nothing you can do to change the past."

"I was just thinking how he's going to chortle when he finds out about this. He'll say it serves me right for ripping him off."

"But he's the one that slept with your friends. That's friends with an 's'. Plural. He slept with your friends in your bed. It doesn't get much lower than that. Besides, he may not find out."

"Fat chance. Malcolm Wiley has probably already called him. And that's the other thing that bothers me. There's no way the good sheriff is going to conduct a thorough and unbiased investigation. He's too intent on avenging the wrong he thinks I inflicted on his best friend."

"Ol' Malcolm better take a long, hard look at himself before he starts pointing fingers. There are those of us who have known him all his life."

"You mean Malcolm has a past?"

"He does. Want the 'Reader's Digest' version?"

"Yes!" Then Mags thought about what she'd just said. "No. I don't want to know anything more than I do right now. I'm already on information overload."

"Well you can't just sit here and do nothing. You're right about your chances for a complete investigation."

As if to illustrate her resolve, Mags rose from where she had been sprawled. "I'm not going to sit here and do nothing. We're going to investigate this deal ourselves."

"But we're not detectives."

"Neither is Malcolm." She waved her hands about her face. "I know, that was below the belt. We may not be detectives, but we do have common sense. Besides, we don't have anything to lose."

"So how do we begin?" Mags began to pace the small room, barking questions as they came to her and, in many cases, answering herself. "How much do we really know about HJH?" Early in their association with the elusive businessman, the two women had adopted the three-letter abbreviation instead of saying his entire name. "I'd say we really know very little." Mags looked at Carole for confirmation.

The office manager scratched her head and looked hard at the painting on the wall across from her desk. "You know, that's one of my favorite pieces. I love to sit here and look at it." She appeared to mentally wipe her mind clean. "But as for HJH, you're right. Outside of the fact that he told us how much money he had to spend, we really don't know anything."

"My point entirely. And before we leave here today, we're going to know everything there is to know about this creep who bloodied up my boat."

"So what's our first step?"

"Pull his file. We need to read everything in it. There should be some leads to help us get started. One of us may see something the other misses."

Breaking only for sandwiches they had delivered in, Mags and Carol worked until the sun began to fall behind Razor Ridge Mountain.

"Well," Mags observed as they were closing down the office, "we know a lot more than we did. I'm just not sure we understand all that we know."

"The one thing that comes through loud and clear," Carole said, "is that HJH wasn't exactly all that he represented himself to be."

"But why? What was his reason for being here if he was some kind of con man?" Mags massaged the back of her neck and felt the knots that had taken up residence. It had been a long time since she'd experienced the neck pain that mysteriously disappeared the day she walked out of the Fulton County Courthouse with her divorce decree in hand.

"He wasn't on the up-and-up. That's for sure. But who was the intended victim? Us or some hapless property owner?"

Mags mentally jogged through the meager results of their sleuthing. She wondered what take Paul Drake, who had been Perry Mason's right-hand PI, would make of their findings.

Carole's assessment that Mr. Humphries definitely hadn't been on the up-and-up was on point. For starters, while he had claimed

New York ties, nothing in the file substantiated that he had ever been up north. Calls placed to the few numbers listed on his new client information form reached disconnected phones. The two numbers that were answered by a live person denied any knowledge of Horace J. Humphries. Even when Carole described the gnomish-looking man, neither of the individuals on the other end recognized him.

It was a mystery, to be certain. Mags had paid particular attention to the more than fourteen properties she'd shown the unpleasant client, but could find no common theme, no connecting thread there, either.

"Other than the fact that everything he saw was priced at two million dollars and up, there's nothing else in common. Even the properties he put under contract and then defaulted on, there's no connection there. I'm stumped," Mags confessed.

Carole had agreed and, as they locked the front door and walked together to the end of the gravel walk inside the yellow picket fence, she patted her employer on the shoulder. "Go on home. There's nothing more we can do until we can unravel some of these threads. Tomorrow is another day."

Mags hated to concede defeat, but she also had to admit she didn't know which way to turn. "You're right, of course. We'll take a fresh start in the morning."

The two had separated and were walking toward their respective vehicles. "Mags?" Carole called out. "Hold up." She reversed course and made long strides toward her employer. "Do you think it's safe for you to be at The Slop Bucket alone? Should I go home and pack a bag and meet you at your house?"

Mags had to contain herself to keep from laughing. "Why would I be in danger? It was HJH who got killed." She attempted a grin. "What would you pack? A gown and gun?"

"You're making fun of all this. You could be in danger as well, and The Slop Bucket is so remote." The worried frown on her friend's normally cheerful face paid testimony to Carole's true feelings.

"Thanks for being concerned. But I don't feel like I'm next on the hit list. I'll be fine."

Carole's face clearly said she didn't believe her boss and, that she didn't know what else she could do. "Call me once you're inside and have the door locked. Be sure to check all the doors."

Mags laughed. "Yes, mother, I'll be extra careful. And I will call you." She hugged the other woman. "Thanks for being concerned."

The two separated again.

"And be sure to arm the security system," Carole called back over her shoulder. "Do it as soon as you're inside."

As she drove home, Mags replayed Carole's concerns in her mind. While she had initially dismissed any possibility that a killer might be gunning for her, she had to admit on second thought, that the possibility was very disconcerting. Yet she still couldn't identify why anyone should want to waste her. She grinned, as she realized her love of murder mysteries was influencing her speech. *Waste, indeed!*

As she entered the mountain cove where her ex-husband's family lodge was located, Mags once again found the peace that always met her at one special curve in the road. What the place did for her emotions was one of the main reasons she'd chosen the lodge over the Atlanta house. She really felt more at home in the simple setting and, if it bent Franklin's butt out of shape in the process, so much the better. She had painted the master bedroom and replaced all the furniture, most especially the mattress where Franklin had done the dirty deeds. She had no intention of sleeping where she had been betrayed.

"I'm inside. All the doors are locked, and the alarm is set. I'll knock it up to highest security when I go to bed," she promised Carole, when she called to check in.

"I hope you searched the place inside out, before you locked all the doors," Carole said. "Wouldn't want to lock yourself in with a murderer."

Mags had to admit to herself that she hadn't even considered that possibility. The prospect of being chased by an unknown person intent on doing harm, and having a locked door seal her fate, wasn't at all attractive. Still, and with only a slight twinge of conscience, she lied. "Of course I checked. What do you take me for? Besides, Delilah wouldn't let anyone in here." She looked across the room to where an aging Welsh corgi rested on her favorite bed. The two were close companions, and the dog's tan, black and white coat was regal against the bright red of the rug.

The women chatted for a few more minutes and, when Carole finally decided her friend was safe enough, they ended the call.

Mags had just finished a frozen chicken pot pie and a freshly-prepared green salad, with the TV to keep her from dining alone, when she heard the sound of tires crunching the gravel in the driveway. Delilah raised her head to deliver one lone "woof" and Mags' guard went up. She shoved the dirty dishes aside and sprinted for the window near the front door, wishing all the while that she had some kind of weapon at hand. But then she had to acknowledge, she probably wouldn't know how to use it effectively. Unless it was a baseball bat. She'd been quite good on the diamond during her high school days. But that had also been almost forty years back. Maybe she'd lost her knack for hitting home runs.

As she held her breath, wondering what to do for the best, a strident knocking assaulted the front door. She ignored it. It happened again, only more intense this time. Still, she stood, frozen and unable to respond.

"Margaret! It's me. Malcolm. Open this door!" The order was delivered in harsh, no nonsense tones. But why was Malcolm there? Why didn't he call first? Why should he expect to be admitted, coming unannounced like this? And why was he calling her Margaret, not Mags? She was full of questions with very few answers. Still, she wasn't comfortable with the whole situation. Was she being set-up?

"I know you're in there. My men tailed you home."

At that moment, much preferring to take her chances with an armed murderer and a locked door, Mags quietly slid the safety chain into its channel. It was something she had forgotten to do earlier. She cracked open the door as far as the chain would allow.

The sheriff's belligerent face peered at her through the two-inch wide space."

"Open the door, Margaret! Now!"

She cringed inwardly from the force of his verbal assault, but Mags was determined not to allow the sheriff to see how intimidated she actually was. "I'm opening it, Malcolm. Keep your pants on. You could have called first and I'd have been expecting you."

Without waiting for a further invitation, the lawman sprang as soon as the door was free. "Yeah. I could have called and you could have conveniently left before I got here. You try to do somebody a favor and this is the thanks you get."

A favor. What favor?

The dog, as if she sensed her master's discomfort, growled, low and gruff, but made no move toward aggression.

"Now I've got some questions, but because we're…

His demands were cut short when, out of nowhere, a whistle so shrill it made both of them grab for their ears, began to shatter the mountain calm. Mags knew immediately that she'd opened the door, totally forgetting about the armed security system. She ran to the control panel and began punching buttons. Between her fractured nerves and trembling hands, and how long it had been since she'd actually used the system, it was necessary to enter the code several times before the deafening sound was silenced.

"What the hell…?" the sheriff demanded. "Is this your idea of a joke?"

"I forgot to disable the alarm before I opened the door," she informed him. "I wasn't expecting company tonight. You know…"

The ringing of a telephone interrupted. "That'll be the monitoring service. Excuse me." She grabbed the phone next to her favorite chair. "Hello?"

The man on the other end informed her that they had logged a security breach.

"I didn't disarm the system before I opened the front door." She gave the sheriff a black look. "I had an unexpected visitor."

When she was asked for her security password, Mags saw a problem. She wasn't comfortable giving it out where the sheriff could overhear, since she had changed it after the divorce, so that Franklin couldn't physically violate her sense of security. She had no children to worry about, so she hadn't given the new code to anyone. Not even Carole.

"Just a moment," she told her caller. "Excuse me, Malcolm." "She stepped into the next room and she supplied the necessary information. "I'm sorry," she told the caller. "Nothing's wrong here, I just wasn't comfortable giving the password where it could be overheard."

"You were smart there, Mrs. Gordon. Have a good evening."

"Thank you. I'll try to remember next time to kill the system before I open the door."

The kind gentleman on the other end laughed. "It happens. More than you know. Goodnight."

Mags returned to the great room where her visitor was waiting, although not very patiently, if body language was any indication. "Sorry, Malcolm. Now, where were we?"

"We need to talk," he said without preamble. "A dead man's been found on your boat. Normally I'd take you down to the jail to ask my questions. But since we've known each other for so long…"

He grinned but for some reason, Mags wasn't reassured. His eyes told a different story.

"Since we've been in and out of each other's lives for so long, I wanted to try to help you out a little." There was that grin again. "After all, what are friends for? You know, you're in an awkward situation here."

As he spoke, Mags could see him looking around the room where he'd visited so many times over the previous fifty years.

"I didn't kill him, Malcolm. And I don't know who did." She indicated the sofa. "So have a seat and we'll get started, although I've told you everything I know."

When the lawman made no move to sit, Mags made the uncomfortable decision to remain standing as well. She had no intention of allowing him to tower over her physically or emotionally. But she also knew that hiding her panic would be more difficult if she had to stand.

For the next few minutes, the sheriff rehashed their earlier conversation, and Mags supplied the same answers. Her accuser was more than a little peeved that none of what she said had changed. "I'm trying to help you, Margaret, but it sounds like you have your answers memorized."

"They're not memorized, they're the truth, Malcolm. Why can't you just accept that someone else murdered Mr. Humphries? I'd have been a fool to kill the client that would pay me well over a hundred thousand in commissions."

"From what I hear, that dude was breaking contracts right and left. You weren't going to make anything and, a lot of folks hereabouts are real angry." He was still taller than she was, and his face was impossible to read. "Can you prove you didn't kill him?"

"Can you prove I did?"

"Is it going to come down to that?"

"Look, Malcolm. This is my house, like it or not. I've got a deed to it and I'm paying the taxes. You intruded on my evening, so if you don't believe me, then we have nothing further to discuss."

"I could arrest you for resisting an officer and interfering with an investigation." He regarded her with a puzzled look. "I thought I could help you…"

"If you don't believe me, you'll never be able to help me," Mags told him, surprised at the strength she felt in those words.

"Maybe I should take you in after all." The words, hard and clipped, hinted at the anger that blazed openly behind his dark eyes. "Back at the jail we can interrogate you by the book."

"You'd like that, wouldn't you, Malcolm? Why I'll bet the cell door wouldn't be latched good before you and Franklin would sour down on a freshly-opened bottle of Canadian Mist on the rocks."

"You leave Franklin out of this."

"And you leave me out of this. I didn't kill that man and I will fight you tooth and toenail. You will NOT pin this on me, I don't care how angry you are because your good friend Franklin got caught with his pants down. In fact, if the rumors around town are to be believed, I wouldn't doubt your pants hit the floor in this house a few times as well.

Mags had never heard any such rumors and, out of anger tinged with fear, she was simply making a shot in the dark, hoping to handicap her opponent. From the panicked expression that crossed the sheriff's face, however, she saw she'd obviously hit closer to the truth than she had intended.

"You talk that out in town and I'll put you so far under the jail you'll never see daylight," the sheriff snarled. "I can break you, Margaret. And I will. Do we understand each other? You leave me out of this!"

"I can break you, too, Malcolm. You make one move to arrest me and I'll have an attorney on your neck so fast you won't know what hit you."

"Who? The same shyster that helped you rob Franklin?"

"Never you mind who it will be. But keep harassing me and you'll find out."

Appearing far more courageous than she felt, Mags pushed the sheriff's arm. "I think it's time you left." So much for him helping her. "I've told you everything I know about Mr. Humphries, and I've given you my word that I didn't kill him. I don't think we have anything else to talk about. I'd like for you to go. Now."

"You're making a big mistake, Margaret. I can be your best friend or your worst enemy. Take your choice."

"Malcolm, you've never been my best friend and, before I'd place you in that exalted position, I'd rather have you as my worst enemy. At least then I'd have no unrealistic expectations."

"You're cutting your own throat."

"I'll take that chance. Now please leave." She grasped his elbow and began to propel him toward the doorway.

He resisted her efforts, but only minimally, Mags thought. Otherwise she'd never have been able to move someone so large with so little effort. Still, it gave her a sense of triumph to see the distance to the door decreasing. When she finally had him in the doorway, Mags said, "I've told you everything I know, Malcolm. Please don't bother me any further with this matter. I did not kill that man and I don't know who did."

"You sound awfully sure of yourself."

"When you're innocent, it's not difficult to be sure. Goodnight."

"Would you still be so sure if it turned out that Horace J. Humphries wasn't his real name?"

Mags felt the blow from his words. "What do you mean not his real name?"

"Just a question I needed to ask. That's one of the rumors going around town. Kind of like the ones about me getting laid here at The Slop Bucket. You can't make assumptions on the strength of rumors, you know."

Margaret was stunned to the point she couldn't immediately respond. How could HJH's name been something else? Or was the sheriff making a stab in the dark, just like she had, in order to throw her off?"

"Good night, Margaret. Rest well. We'll be talking. That's a promise." The benediction was delivered in a taunting voice, accented by a sarcastic smirk on his usually belligerent face. "Surely there's no mistake about his identity. I mean, what would be the point?"

Indeed, what would be the point, Mags wondered as she secured the door and re-armed the security system? Why would someone arrive in Crabapple Cove under an assumed name, and attempt to purchase real estate? Or did he really intend to buy anything? Six defaulted contracts for such asinine reasons as the style of the trim work or the shape of the swimming pool certainly didn't indicate seriousness.

Yet, as she settled into her bed that night, there was one thing she knew for certain: whether his name was Horace J. Humphries or not, there was more to the recently departed than any of them realized. So just who was the dead man?

She and Carole had their work cut out for them the next morning, but it was almost dawn before Mags ever settled down to sleep. Instead of rest, her mind was occupied by all that she knew about the dead man. Fighting equally hard for brain space was her understanding that the unknown man, who now lay a corpse, was even more of an enigma in death than he had been in life. Despite the sheriff's last words, she was still primary suspect number one. Not exactly the best way to get a restful night's sleep. But a night's sleep was the only way to get to the next day, and Mags finally surrendered consciousness just before the first daylight shined.

Chapter Two

WHAT WAS HIS MOTIVE?

Mags was nursing a mug of hot tea and waiting for her order of stuffed French toast and a fresh fruit cup, when the first volley was fired.

"You've put us on the map, you know," a voice behind her said, accusation hanging heavy from every word. "We're going to be lousy with the press."

"Yeah," a second voice said. "And you've put everyone in this town in danger. You encouraged that nasty little man to look for property here. He wasn't our kind. You should have known that, and now he's been killed."

"Probably a Mafia hit-man and there's no telling who else he'll kill while he's here," the first voice charged. "There's not a one of us who's safe in our beds."

It wasn't necessary for Mags to turn around to discover the identities of her harassers. From their voices and their manners, she knew it was Claude and Beatrice Adams, the town's unofficial naysayers. Never mind what it was, the two over-the-hill hippies were against it, and were always very vocal in their protestations.

"Look, you two," Mags answered through gritted teeth. "There are people who don't think you're right to live here either. As for this being a Mafia hit, where did you ever get such a ridiculous idea?"

It was Beatrice who answered. With her two waist-length, dirty blond ponytails swinging for emphasis, she allowed her face to invade Mags' personal space. "He was shot 'execution-style' so that means it was a Mafia gunman. Everybody knows that's how those type people take out their victims."

"That's crazy. Besides, who told you it was an execution-style killing?"

"Harrumph," the old hippie maven protested, as she punctuated her beliefs with an upward jab of her right shoulder. "Don't you ever watch TV? Ever body knows that's how Mafia people take care of business." She winked her heavily-rouged right eye at Mags. "If it's on TV, then that's how it is."

Mags chose to ignore the reference to the accuracy of television programming. "But how do you know it was an execution?"

"Malcolm said so. He was here earlier."

Mags was instantly thankful that she'd overslept. Otherwise, she might have encountered her nemesis. That was not how she wanted to start her day. "He said it was an execution?"

"He didn't say it was an execution. He said it was... how'd he put that, Claude?" Beatrice rubbed her right temple. "Now I remember... he said "it had all the appearances of an execution-style killing. And that man's dead, ain't he?" The old woman finished her announcement with the satisfied air of one who rests comfortably on her self-bestowed laurels. Mags knew she'd only be wasting time and energy, and elected to let them believe what they wanted. Besides, if Malcolm considered the killing to actually be an execution, did that mean it would take the heat off her? Could it have been Mafia related?

"But he was killed on your boat," Claude volunteered, obviously unable to tolerate Beatrice getting all the attention. "So did you take out a contract on that feller?"

"Certainly not," Mags protested and promptly abandoned her

intent to stay out of the fray. "I don't know why he died on my boat, but I had nothing to do with it."

"He was killed," Beatrice pointed out. "He didn't just die. He was killed execution-style. Malcolm said…"

"Yes, I know," Mags agreed, anxious to get beyond the conversation. She turned to signal Maudeann, who had taken her order. "Can I get my food to go, please? I'm running late." It was obvious the overweight server of undetermined age resented the last-minute change, but Mags wasn't worried. She had much larger problems to solve.

"I know what Sheriff Wiley said," she explained, in what she prayed was a pleasant, untroubled manner. "He was killed, he didn't just die. And I'm so very sorry he did, but I didn't have anything to do with his death." She was especially sorry he had died on board her boat. It was most inconvenient. So far.

"It looks mighty suspicious if you ask me," Claude announced. "Why on your boat if you weren't involved? You haven't been living here that long. You sure you didn't come from… from… where's that place the TV says the Mafia is, Beatrice?"

"New Jersey. The Mafia's in New Jersey. Remember 'The Sopranos'?"

Mags groaned inwardly at the reference to a once-popular television show about members of an organized crime family. As if television script writers were the final authority, but try convincing the two resident agitators otherwise.

"Yeah, New Jersey." Claude squinted closely at Mags as he asked, "You sure you didn't come here from New Jersey?"

"Now Mr. Adams, you know that Franklin Gordon is my ex-husband. I've been coming here for the past thirty-odd years. Year before last I moved here permanently."

"Yeah, but when you weren't here, were you in New Jersey? You do talk kinda funny. Don't she, Beatrice?"

His wife didn't answer, but instead continued to study Mags closely, as if looking to inspect her pores.

Mags spotted the server headed her way with take-out container in hand and gave silent thanks. Escape wasn't happening a minute too soon. "I lived in Atlanta, Mr. Adams. In fact, I've never even been to New Jersey."

"Here we go," Maudeann interrupted, handing Mags her breakfast. "I've already put this on your account, so you're ready to go. Here's some fresh tea and I dropped in more lemon wedges."

Mags nodded at her detractors, grabbed the big, bulky cup, and prepared to make her retreat. "Thanks, Maudeann." She rewarded the server with a grateful smile. "Folks," she said, looking straight at the elderly couple. "Work calls. It's been good talking to you."

Back at the office, Carole had already opened for business and was sorting the day's mail, when Mags barreled through the door.

"Whoa, boss lady. Is there a bear on your tail?" While the remark was made primarily in jest, both ladies knew that bear sightings in the small mountain town were not uncommon.

"I'd rather it were a bear," Mags groused, as she deposited the food container on her desk, and unloaded her tote bag without spilling anything. "A bear would be preferable to Claude and Beatrice Adams. Two bears, even."

Carole was tending to the plants in the office. "What are those two nutcases up to now?" She gently pruned a dead leaf from one of Mag's favorite African violets. "You know, they deserve each other. It would be a crime to poison two relationships."

"I was going to eat at the diner this morning, but I decided to get my food to go." She indicated the opened container of bread and syrup and whipped cream. "Umm… this is sooo good. I needed a sugar fix." To emphasize her satisfaction with the food, she forked a generous bite to her mouth before continuing.

"According to Claude and Beatrice, HJH was killed 'execution-style'." She raised both her hands to indicate quotation marks. "What's more, they're quoting Malcolm as their source. Now those two old coots have decided the Mafia is involved and that I'm somehow involved with the Mafia."

"That would be hilarious under any other circumstances. Surely you put them straight?"

Mags cut into her sweet breakfast again and savored the satisfaction before responding. "Carole, you, of all people should know that no one can straighten out the mary jane royalty of the 1960s." She was referring to a property line dispute the couple had waged with Carole's father for several years. Despite a court ruling that the line was correct, the Adams' continued to move the surveyor's corner pins whenever the mood hit them. "But yes, I did attempt to set the record straight, since others were hearing the conversation."

"Do they understand that Mountain Magic Realty by Mags isn't the Mafia's north Georgia branch office?"

"What do you think?"

Something outside the window had caught Carole's attention, and it was a moment before she responded. "I think we're in trouble. Look."

Mags abandoned the last few bites of her breakfast and joined her friend at the window. What she saw made her heart go cold. In the few minutes since she'd raced from the Eat and Greet to the office, the whole of Main Street had sprouted a crop of news media vehicles, satellite trucks, and even a couple of luxurious RV's.

Claude and Beatrice were right! The couple had forecast that the media was about to descend on Crabapple Cove. As much as it hurt Mags to give the obnoxious duo credit, it concerned her even more that they might also have been in the know on how HJH was killed. Could there be a contract killer out there?

"Looks like we're going to be on TV," Carole observed, but there was no joy in her prediction.

"Whether we want to or not," Mags finished for her. "I'm wondering how we're going to be able to get any work done. And we've got plenty to do."

Carole's expression was one of confusion. "We don't have one single closing scheduled this week. What do we have to do?"

"Detective work."

"But we hit a brick wall yesterday. I went back over all my notes last night. There's nothing we missed."

"Listen. I need to talk to you before this town explodes. Malcolm came to see me last night." She remembered the encounter with too much clarity. "At first he tried to be all sweet and concerned. Then he got obnoxious, but he did drop one piece of information." She scratched her head. "Only I don't know if he was baiting me or not."

"Baiting you?"

"I'll tell you about that in a minute. He hinted that Horace J. Humphries wasn't our client's real name."

"That makes no sense. How was he going to buy property under an assumed name? You know how many forms of identification we have to document."

"I hear what you're saying, but I also know what Malcolm said." She proceeded to give a quick overview of the previous evening's visit, all the while keeping one eye trained on the front door. She knew it was only a matter of time before their peace was shattered.

"You actually accused Malcolm of using The Slop Bucket as a love nest?"

Mags blushed. "He made me mad. I don't have any evidence to indicate that he's ever been unfaithful to Shirley. And certainly not at the lodge."

"Well then, you're the only one in town who doesn't know how he's treated that poor wife of his, although I'm about to lose patience with her. She's giving doormats a bad name."

"You mean he has been unfaithful?"

"Consistently. The man cannot keep his zipper up."

"And Shirley knows?"

"Absolutely. She's even left him a couple of times, but it doesn't seem to faze him."

"How did I not ever know this? He and Shirley have been in and out of my life for..." She stopped to calculate. "I first met them when Franklin and I were dating."

"He's never made it any secret. Shirley just holds her head up and keeps smiling." Carole's expression was quizzical. "Your accusation that he had used your house for his sexual escapades was really a shot in the dark?"

"Of course it was!"

"Rumors around town were that he and Franklin used to take their women there at the same time and swap up."

Mags felt the entire room whirling and tilting, and she had to grab hold of her desk to keep from falling. "I swear, I had no idea. When he made me mad last night, that thought popped into my head. Before I could stop myself, I said it."

Carole came over to put her arms around her employer. "You were dead on the money. The Slop Bucket has seen more than it's fair share of sex down through the years." She kneaded Mags' neck and shoulders. "Malcolm would take women there even when Franklin wasn't here. The whole town knew it. I mean, how would it look for the high sheriff to be checking into a motel with a different woman on his arm every time?"

For the first time since she'd come to the mountain hideaway, Mags didn't feel at all secure. The mental image of Malcolm just making himself at home in her house was unsettling at best. Then a horrible possibility presented itself.

"Carole! How did Malcolm get in when Franklin wasn't here? Don't tell me that piece of slime has a key to my house!"

"I really don't know," her assistant confessed. "I never thought about it, but how else could he have gotten in?"

Mags was going hot and cold, vacillating between rage and fear. "I've got to get the locks changed today or I'll never be able to close my eyes in that house again." Then it hit her. "He could have come in last night if I hadn't opened the door."

"I'll call Peter Tompkins right now and get him out there." Carole began to hit the phone keys. "Get the best locksets you can buy and get them all keyed alike," she told the handyman the agency used for minor repairs. "Change out every exterior lock in the place." She went quiet while he confirmed the order. "It has to be done today, Peter. Before dark. Please?"

Mags was still holding on to the desk, trying to get her bearings.

"Peter said he'd get out there right after lunch. He'll come back by here when he's finished to drop off your new keys."

"Thanks, friend. That was a curve I never saw coming. I changed out the security code to make it more difficult for Franklin, if he ever got the urge to visit me uninvited. But it never occurred to me that I needed to change the locks."

"It's handled. Don't worry about it."

"When I think what could…"

"Then don't think about it," Carole encouraged. "But do talk to me about Malcolm's news blast that HJH had another name." She massaged her chin. "That could be why we couldn't track him down yesterday."

"I guess that makes sense." Mags felt totally deflated. It had been, she decided, one heck of a twenty-four hours since a pool of congealed blood and the dead man next to it turned her life upside down.

"It does," Carole agreed. "So how do we find out… uh oh, Mags. Here's that trouble. That starts with T and that rhymes with P. The press is about to invade us."

Mags, already weary even though it wasn't yet ten o'clock, raised her head to follow Carole's extended finger. What she saw totally paralyzed her, cemented her to the floor where she stood.

Members of the media were descending en masse on the office, each one determined to be the first one to confront the woman on whose boat a man had been killed. They had plenty of questions, Mags suspected. She wasn't nearly as confident about her answers.

The remainder of the morning was unreal. Carole was finally forced to step in and demand that all the reporters and their camera technicians vacate the tiny building. "Mrs. Gordon will come outside," she assured them. "It's simply too crowded in here."

With poor graces and much complaint, the reporters, some twenty strong, almost took the doorway out of the building as they jostled for front row positions. Finally, however, everyone had their equipment repositioned and the inquisition began. Mags answered all their questions as honestly as she knew how. Still, it seemed all too inadequate, if the demeanor of the inquisitors was any indication.

"Yes," she told them, the murder scene was her boat, the *One True Love*.

"No," she assured them, she didn't have any idea who might have killed Mr. Humphries. It certainly hadn't been her. This she stressed several times.

The inquiries continued rapid fire, some quite sensible Mags thought. Others, she couldn't help but wonder how the questioner had sense enough to get out of the rain. Like the man who asked if "Mags" was short for Margaret. When she explained that it was actually a nickname from a childhood love of magazines, she could tell he hadn't understood. But then, what did her unusual handle have to do with a man being murdered?

One woman in particular, an anchor that Mags recognized from one of the major Atlanta TV stations, had been particularly biting and baiting, and determined to hog the time. Suddenly, her biting turned brutal.

"Mrs. Gordon," the willowy blond inquired, as she shoved a microphone into Mags' face, "Is it true that the boat on which Mr. Humphries met his demise is the same boat you stole from your husband in a bitter divorce action?"

Margaret recoiled, feeling as if she had been physically slapped. While the circumstances of how she acquired the twenty-eight foot cruiser had never been secret, Mags was at a loss to understand how they were pertinent to the murder. With anger rising like sap in her veins, she said just that. "Ms. Woodson, while I fail to understand how my acquisition of the *One True Love* has any bearing on this case, I can assure you there was no stealing involved." She shoved her hands through her hair and wished she could pull it out. "The boat was awarded to me, by a judge, as part of the divorce settlement, and I have the legal documents to prove it." Then, unable to contain the venom the question had unleashed, she added, "I believe you recently became divorced yourself, so I'm certain you're familiar with the process."

When the other woman responded physically to the verbal blow she never saw coming, Mags was heartened to see that her volley had hit home. It was also the moment that she decided she'd had enough. "Now if you'll excuse me, I have a business to run." Without waiting for a response, she turned, grabbed Carole by the hand and dragged her back into the office. "Lock the door," she ordered. "I don't want them thinking they can just waltz back in here."

"We're probably safe, at least for a while." Carole consulted the clock on the wall. "The broadcast folks will need all the time they have, between now and Noon, to get their stuff edited and ready to air."

"That's what I need, too. Some air. But I don't dare go outside. Not right now anyway."

Instead, Mags finished explaining about the sheriff's visit the night before and the two women talked at length about Malcolm's veiled suggestion that HJH might have been someone else entirely.

"The more I think about it, given what we uncovered yesterday, I'm beginning to think the sheriff might be right."

"You mean what we didn't uncover, don't you? I couldn't find a trace of that man anywhere. It was like he didn't exist."

"That's because he probably doesn't. At least not under the name we have."

"But why? What was his motive? It just doesn't make any sense?"

"When we find out who he really was, we'll find also find out why."

"So what's our game plan?"

Mags pulled the client folder from her desk drawer. One by one, she began sifting the papers in it. She would study a document, then put it aside. Carole's face mirrored the curiosity she felt, but she sat quietly at her desk, waiting.

Finally, Mags spoke. We have to investigate each of these phone numbers he gave us, particularly those that have been disconnected. We need to know who had them when they were working numbers." She scratched her chin. "I mean, did he make these numbers up out of thin air? Obviously some of them did exist once. If we can find out who once had them, we might just get a handle on this."

"Or we could ask Malcolm."

Mags' answer to her assistant was a glare that would have curdled fresh milk.

"I'll get right on it," Carole vowed. "Now what are we going to do for lunch?"

"I'm not going out in that mess, but knock your socks off."

"No. I mean, what do we want to eat? I'm not about to venture any farther than the back door, when I have the food brought in."

"That means the Eat and Greet, because they're the only place that delivers."

"Nope. Pick a place. Any place. I'll get my neighbor to go pick it up."

"That's genius, Carole. The media won't recognize him. They'll just think he's a customer." She looked around the office that was empty, save for the two of them. "And customers are something we're short on right now. There hasn't been a single walk-in since all of this started."

Carole didn't answer, but the stricken expression on her face spoke for her.

The two quickly made their food selections and Carole put the wheels in motion. A few minutes later, at the stroke of twelve Noon, the small TV in the corner of the reception area was tuned to Atlanta's most popular channel. The duo wasn't disappointed. Gloria Woodson was shown standing in front of the small, gingerbread-trimmed real estate office. She began to tell the station's viewers all about a murder in paradise.

When the segment was finished, Mags had to admit that the facts had been fairly accurate. The anchor's delivery, her voice intonation and the varying speeds with which the woman spoke, lent undue emphasis to some aspects of the case, she thought. Carole had been flipping between channels to see how other stations were presenting the story.

"Is it just me," Mags asked, when finally the TV was silent, "or did you feel like each crew was talking about a different incident?"

"You're right. The way each of them chose to present the story really did give it a different personality," she said with a grimace. "So much for objectivity."

A soft knock at the back door interrupted. Their visitor, an older, gray-haired man sporting an Ernest Hemmingway beard and two plastic bags of food, looked to be sure no one was behind him, then ducked inside.

Carol kissed their delivery man and relieved him of the bags. "Thanks, Hank. I owe you. We just didn't feel like we could handle all the press."

"You couldn't have. Town is swarming. They're going into every store asking questions."

Mags buried her head in her hands. "People will really hate me now," she moaned. "Claude and Beatrice Adams will be the least of my worries."

Their guest moved to Mags' desk where he patted her shoulder. "Don't be so hard on yourself. It'll blow over in a few days. You wait and see. Inside of a week, it'll all be forgotten."

Mags looked up, grateful for the show of support. "You're a love, Hank. I just hope your crystal ball is plugged up to full juice today. A few more days of this kind of business will put me out of business."

After he had gone, Carole made quick work of serving the salads they had ordered, and while they ate, the two planned how they would attack the afternoon's investigation. Mags was just forking into the last bite of steak in her salad, when the phone rang. Carole answered it, then nodded at her. "It's for you. Martin Hancock at the

Georgia Real Estate Commission."

A momentary worry crossed her mind, then she remembered, "Oh, he's probably calling about that continuing education course I've got to take." She grabbed up the phone on her desk and punched the blinking button. "Hello, Martin. It's good to hear from you."

Only as it turned out, Mags would quickly decide, it might not have been quite so good after all.

"Good afternoon, Mags. I hope you have a few minutes to talk."

Mags knew immediately that something was up. She and the executive director had been on a casual, friendly, first-name basis for several years, even prior to her divorce. That he hadn't engaged in small talk first was very telling.

"Yes, of course I have time. For you, I'll make time." She hesitated, then throwing caution to the wind, she asked, "Is something wrong? You sound so terribly formal."

"That's because this is a formal matter, I'm afraid. May I go on?"

"Why, yes… of course." Mags couldn't decide if her fear was going to overcome curiosity or visa versa.

"We received a call this morning, an anonymous call, I should say, delivering some very disturbing news." He hesitated. "The person wouldn't identify himself, and we didn't give the matter much credence, until we heard the Noon newscasts."

Mags felt her body go limp. This was about HJH and it didn't sound good.

"The caller asked if we knew that one of our licensees had stolen a client's life."

"But… but…" Mags found herself incapable of doing anything more than sputtering. The impact of what she was hearing was more than she could process.

Her caller continued, "As I said, we almost considered it a prank call, until we happened to hear the news broadcast and learned that, indeed, one of your clients was dead."

Anger was rising in Mags for the second time that day. "He was killed. On board my boat, but I didn't kill him," she vowed. "He was already dead when I got there."

"Well, I certainly hope so, for your sake." Then his tone changed and her caller was more like the person she knew. "Felons aren't allowed to hold real estate licenses, you know."

Which means I'd be out of business, Mags told herself. Not that she'd be able to sell much property from a prison cell anyway.

"How could this have happened, Mags? You've worked so hard to build your agency."

"There's more going on here than either of us can understand," she explained. "This hasn't been broadcast, but it appears this man was an imposter, possibly even a con artist."

"But how could that be?"

"Believe me, Martin, I'm telling you all that I know."

"When we heard all this, I simply couldn't believe you'd be a party to murder. Still..." There was a pregnant pause. "Still... sometimes we're wrong."

"I promise you that I am innocent," she assured her caller. "I didn't kill that man, but I am determined to find out who did."

"I believe you," he assured her. "Unfortunately, we will have to monitor the situation and, should you be arrested for this man's murder, I'll have no choice but to suspend your broker's license."

"Suspend...?"

"Just until such time as you're either acquitted or convicted."

Mags knew that she would be bankrupt and out of business long before a verdict could be rendered either way. "I understand," she said at last, not trusting her emotions to say any more.

"Thank you, Mags. Trust me, the commission really hopes you're cleared in all of this, but we have our sworn responsibilities and we will do our duty."

"I do understand, Martin. Give my love to Marjorie." Mags laid the handset back in it cradle and put her hands to each side of her head, as if by doing so, she could keep herself and her world from exploding into bits and pieces.

"What is wrong," Carole demanded. "You're positively white."

"The Real Estate Commission found out about HJH."

"So?"

"He said someone called this morning to give them a tip that I had murdered a client."

"Who was the caller?"

"That's just it, he refused to identify himself."

"So what does this mean? Surely they aren't acting strictly on the basis of an anonymous tip. That's absurd."

"They haven't taken any action. Yet. But if Malcolm should suddenly charge me with murder, my broker's license would be suspended, pending the outcome of the case."

Carole's face was a study in concern. "Which means…"

"Which means you'd be looking for a new job, because Mountain Magic Realty by Mags would have lost its magic wand. I'd be bankrupt and in jail, and you'd be unemployed."

"We can't let that happen."

"Yeah. I think that's a foregone conclusion. So how do we stop this nightmare? This call to the commission convinces me that somebody is up to no good. But who? And why? WHY?"

"Like you said earlier, when we find out who HJH really was, we'll have all these other answers as well." She flashed her boss a two-thumbs-up gesture. "I'm about to start tracking down phone numbers."

The two women spent the remainder of the afternoon working, uninterrupted, except for stopping to discourage and dismiss several more media members who attempted to gain entrance to the office and, to accept the new keys when the handyman came by. As the sun set on the end of the second day, Mags left the office both exhausted and discouraged. Neither of them had been able to discover anything new and, with every brick wall they hit in search of information, their options for finding the answers they desperately needed continued to dwindle.

Mags cranked her SUV and headed to the tranquility of The Slop Bucket, wondering exactly what life in prison might be like.

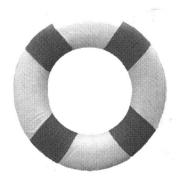

Chapter Three

TAKE A BUTTON; SEW A VEST ON IT

The next few days assumed a frightful similarity. No customers, no phone calls, and no business, unless she counted the business the press continued to try and inflict upon her.

When the county coroner's inquest ruled that death had been at close range, delivered by two bullets from a small caliber pistol, one such as a lady might easily handle, the attention from the press ramped up significantly. Further pointing the finger of suspicion at Mags was the finding that the shooter had been within two feet of the victim and, from all indications, the victim had known his killer. As for why he had been killed on board Mags' boat, unless one chose to believe the obvious conclusion, no one could say.

"In other words," Mags said to Carole as the two of them left the county courthouse, "that jury did everything except say, 'Mr. Humphries' murderer is Margaret Gordon'." She wrung her hands. "I mean, why would I have been stupid enough to kill somebody on my own boat? It doesn't make any sense."

Carole shook her head. "It makes sense to Malcolm."

"Yeah, but we all know that ol' Malcolm has a private dog in this hunt."

"You know it and I know it. Most everybody else, the press included, isn't aware of that little tidbit. I agree, it doesn't look good for you. But there's still too many unanswered questions."

"I couldn't agree more. But we're at the end of the road. Nothing we've done to try and uncover who HJH really was, has produced anything except frustration."

"Then we just have to try harder."

Mags looked about her as she and her friend walked the three blocks to the office. The depth of blue in the sky was in direct proportion to the beauty of the blooming trees and flowers that dotted the mountainsides. It was what Mags had identified many years before, as the perfect mountain day. Only this day was anything but perfection and, she wondered, what would it be like to see the world from inside a prison cell?

"I mean look at this whole deal," Carole continued. "Even the coroner had to admit they don't know who HJH was."

Mags had been stunned during the testimony portion of the inquest to learn that even law enforcement had not been able to trace the man's real identity. Even more shocking to her was that no one had claimed the body.

"I can't believe HJH... or whatever his name really is, hasn't had someone realize that he's missing. Looks like somebody would be concerned."

"Maybe they don't know where he is," Carole suggested. "Since the authorities don't know his real name, they probably also don't know how to contact his next of kin."

"But as much as this whole mess has been spread across the news, including a physical description, you'd think somebody would pick up on the possibility that the dead man might belong to them."

"You'd think. At least I don't feel so bad now that we haven't been able to get any leads. Even the real detectives haven't had any luck."

"Shoot," Mags said, "sometimes the real detectives are too concerned with themselves to solve a crime. Otherwise, why would sleuths like Agatha Raisin and Goldy Schulz or even reticent Constable Hamish McBeth be able to solve so many murders?"

Carole couldn't stop laughing. "Those are fictional detectives, Mags. The authors of those books can make anything happen." She hugged her employer to her. "You been reading too many whodunits, girlfriend."

"Says you."

Carole immediately sobered. "Unfortunately, we don't have a fiction writer to fix the ending of this story your way, so we'll have to do it ourselves."

"I'll be Nancy Drew and you can be Bess Marvin."

"Get serious, Mags. This is your business and maybe your life we're talking about. Forget how Miss Seeton found little Lady McSporran, because I'm certainly not Mike Shayne or Sam Spade."

They had reached the office gate, when Mags turned to face her employee. When she spoke, all play was missing. "Look, Carole. I know all these detectives are the creation of someone's imagination. But like you said, this is my life that hangs in the balance. If I stop and think about it too much, I'll go crazy."

"In other words you want me to make like Gertie, Perry Mason's receptionist, and take a button and sew a vest on it?"

Mags grinned. "You got it!"

With the morning lost to the inquest, Mags and Carole planned to renew their sleuthing in earnest as soon as they returned to the office. Other people had different plans. For starters, they had no more than opened the gate into the office lawn, when reporters and cameras appeared from out of nowhere. The two spent the next hour fending off the best efforts of the media, who seemed hell-bent on making a couple of mountains out of something that wasn't even a full-fledged molehill.

No sooner had the press been satisfied and on their way to create the stories for that day's newscasts and publications, when the bulk of Sheriff Malcolm Wiley filled the office door, and blocked out all the afternoon sun.

Mags worried what the sheriff was about, but she also wondered what she had ever done to anyone, up to and including her ex-husband, to deserve the way her life was going lately.

"Come in, Sheriff. To what do we owe the pleasure?" Mags was tempted to add inflection when she said his name, but resisted the urgings of the wicked little man on her left shoulder.

As if in response, the linebacker of a lawman waded on in to the reception area, dwarfing the space and making the furniture and accessories look like something out of a child's playhouse. Mags was almost afraid to invite him to sit, for fear he'd break something. But if his facial expression was any measure of his mission, the lawman wouldn't notice the lack of the social niceties, she decided.

"Need to talk to the both of you," he announced. "Now."

"We're right here. Talk away."

The sheriff seemed to fortify his bulk as he spoke. "As you gathered from the inquest this morning, I've got a two investigations on my hands. Somebody murdered this fellow, and I'm gonna find out who, if it's the last thing I ever do." As if for emphasis, he slammed his hand down on Carole's desk, upsetting her pen caddy and strewing papers onto the floor. He appeared not to notice.

"In fact, I'm willing to tell you that I'm more concerned about who killed him, than I am about who the guy really is." He looked hard at Mags, then slowly swung his gaze to Carole, who fidgeted uncomfortably. "At the end of the day, it doesn't matter what name he's known by. A man is dead."

"So how does this involve the both of us?" Mags asked cautiously, careful not to give the sheriff any ammunition he didn't already have. "I've already told you I had nothing to do with the man's death. End of story."

"Is it?"

"Malcolm…" She hesitated when he held up his hand stop-sign fashion, then forged ahead. "You can take it or leave it, but if you leave it, there's the door." She indicated the entrance he'd used a few minutes earlier. "Believe it or not, we have work to do here. Either get to the point or get out."

"You know, Margaret. You really could use an attitude adjustment and I'm just the one who can give it to you." His face was almost black. "I had thought for old time's sake that I'd cut you some slack."

Mags was bristling because, if other rumors she'd heard were true, the good sheriff wasn't above roughing up a lady if she got in his way. She had no intention of being the next notch on his stupid stick.

"Because we do go back so far, Malcolm, I'm going to do you a big favor and forget you ever made that statement. I don't really think you want to follow through on that offer, because then I'd be forced to make a few adjustments myself." She stared him down, even though he was looming over her. "Get my drift?"

Dealing with her ex-husband during the down-and-dirty divorce two years earlier had taught her to fight like a man. Otherwise, she knew, she would have never survived.

As she watched, Mags saw a number of emotions wash across her adversary's face, and knew she was skating on thin ice. Probably it was time to at least pretend to cooperate. "What is this all about? You must have had some reason for coming here."

"I need to ask both of you some questions and, since each of you has already denied killing Mr. Humphries, or whoever the hell he was, I'm going to skip over that question and ask one you haven't heard before."

Mags felt the hair on the back of her neck rise, but when she heard the question, relaxation flooded her entire body.

"So here it is, ladies. Do either of you own a small caliber pistol?"

Mags really allowed herself to chill, because she didn't own any type gun and, she was confident Carole didn't either. "Of course not, Malc... Sheriff. I don't even know how to use a gun, so of course I don't own one. And neither does Carole, so you need to look elsewhere for your murderer."

"Uh, Mags...?" Carole's face wore the oddest expression, Mags thought. "I do own a pistol. Not that I've ever shot it, but I do have a gun. If the Sheriff had bothered to check, he'd already know. It's registered and lawful."

Mags, who was watching the sheriff's face as Carole spoke, was certain she interpreted a "gotcha" expression. The hair on her neck resumed its alert posc, and Mags began to suspect that she and Carole had been set up.

"I didn't know..." Mags offered, unsure of exactly how to respond.

"To be honest with you," Carole explained, "I'd forgotten. My dad gave it to me when I started working here, right after those real estate agents in Atlanta were killed in their office in broad daylight."

"So you admit that you do own a pistol? What kind is it?"

Mags suspected Malcolm had known before he ever entered the door that Carole owned a gun. Furthermore, she concluded, he also knew the make and caliber. He was on a fishing expedition and if Carole wasn't careful, she was about to be the catch of the day.

"Good grief, Malcolm, do I look like I'd know one gun from the other? That's why I hid it as soon as I got it. I'm absolutely terrified of guns."

"Then why did you accept it from your father?"

Carole rewarded the sheriff with her most tolerant smile. "Sheriff Wiley, you know my dad. Can you see him letting me refuse? He was the one who registered it."

"So you took it, hid it, and never fired it? Not even once?"

Carole was perfectly relaxed, Mags interpreted, and she allowed herself to drop her guard. It appeared Malcolm was looking for the easiest way out of doing his job.

"That's the long and the short of it, Sheriff. I've never even seen it since the day I stashed it. Good grief, can you imagine me with a gun?"

"So you can show me this gun, in its hiding place, where it's been since... since when?"

Carole massaged her temple. "Let's see... we opened this office twenty-two months ago, and it was only a month or two later that those women in Atlanta were murdered. So I'd say about a year and a half ago, give or take."

"And you haven't seen or handled the gun since then?"

"That's right. That's what I told you."

"Then I'd like to see that gun as soon as possible. How long will it take you to get it?"

Relief flooded the office manager's face. "Oh, that's an easy one. It's right over here in the cabinet." She moved toward a wall of built-in cabinetry at one end of the reception area. "I wanted it out of my hands as quickly as possible and I stashed it in here, where I wouldn't have to worry about anyone getting hold of it."

"Then I'll be happy to relieve you of the burden," the sheriff suggested. "I'll take it back to the station and keep it for you."

"Why thank you, Sheriff Wiley." She was digging in the back of a top cabinet. "Now I know I put that gun right here in this corner. It was in still in the box it came in." Carole straightened and bunched her brow muscles. "It's been so long…" Her face brightened. "I know… I'll bet I put it in this cabinet." She opened another door and began to search."

Mags felt the hair on her neck go absolutely stiff with dread. She knew what was coming.

"Well, it's not in this cupboard, either," Carole announced. "Now this doesn't make any sense. I haven't touched that gun since the day I put it here, and no one was around when I hid it." She shot Mags a look of helpless panic. "Even Mags didn't know it was here, so how could it be gone?"

The sheriff lumbered across the small room to see for himself and opened several doors and looked inside. He ran his hands around and, when it appeared that he was satisfied, he turned back to face the ladies. With a smirk on his face he said, his voice dropping a couple of octaves, "So, you put the gun in one of these cabinets and no one but you knew it was there. Am I saying this correctly?"

Mags could see where things were going. "Carole, you don't have to answer his questions."

"Without taking his gaze off the other woman, the sheriff snarled, "Shut up, Margaret. You read too many mysteries. She'll do what I tell her to do... Or else!"

Mags tried desperately using both body language, eye movements and even a moment of mental telepathy to communicate to Carole that she should button her lip. Nothing worked.

"That's exactly what I'm telling you, Sheriff. I put the gun in there the day my dad brought it to me. I've not seen it since."

"You and Margaret are the only people here on a daily basis?"

"You know that. There are no other employees or agents." Her face brightened. "But then there are the clients. We've had a good many of them, thank goodness."

"So you're suggesting that one of the clients removed the gun from its hiding place?"

"Well... well, yes! I mean, who else could have taken it?"

"Maybe we were broken in on and the burglar took the gun," Mags suggested.

The man in brown, with a revolver strapped on his hip, swung his gaze to Margaret. "You had a burglary occur and you never reported it to my office? What did they take besides the gun? How'd they get in?" He looked around the comfortably-appointed room. "Doesn't appear they did any damage. You want to try that one again?"

Mags knew enough to realize just how critical everything was getting. "Carole, I think we'd..."

"I think you'd better stop trying to control what your friend says," the sheriff interrupted. His twitching facial muscles underscored for Mags just how dogmatic he could be. At that point, she had no doubt how little regard he had for women.

"Now, for the last time, SHUT UP! I'm conducting this inquiry." He swung his attention back to Carole who, Mags noted with despair, had turned a sickly shade of white, and was looking very green around the edges.

"Ms. Pickett," he said, addressing the now panic-stricken woman formally, "I am at this moment declaring that you are a person of interest in this investigation. In fact..." and he paused, "you are my number one person of interest."

Carole was clutching the chair in front of her to keep from falling and, when Mags made a move to support her friend, the sheriff waved her off with his hand. She asked, "Am I... am I going... are you arresting me? I didn't kill that man!" She kneaded the chair back. "I swear I didn't." Her voice had become a whisper and Mags had to listen carefully to hear what she was saying.

"No, you're not under arrest. At least not right now. But you will not leave town for any reason. I can promise that you and I are going to have further conversation." He turned and regarded Mags, much as one would view litter along the roadside. "The next time we talk, Margaret Gordon won't be present."

Mags got his message loud and clear.

Carole, by this point, was crying softly. "But I keep telling you, I didn't kill that man. How can you suspect me? We've known each other forever."

"That's right, Malcolm. You've known Carole for years. She's no murderer."

"Then perhaps you knew about that gun, you took it from its hiding place and killed Humphries, planning to implicate your friend here." He grinned. "Perhaps I should tell you that you're also a person of interest, Margaret. But right now, my money's on Ms. Pickett, I'm almost sad to say."

Mags had had her fill of Malcolm Wiley for one day.

"Simply because Carole's gun is missing doesn't make either of us the murderer. You're going to have to have something more than that." Mags defied his warning looks and moved to her friend's side, where she put her hand on Carole's shoulder. "It'll be okay. We're going to fight this. Malcolm's just pulling his intimidation tactics, and I don't intend to fall for them."

"But where could my gun be?" Carole mumbled through the tears that continued making tracks on her cheeks. "I put it there and quite frankly, I forgot about it." Her pleading, up-turned eyes told Mags just how vulnerable her friend was at that moment. Her heart ached that she couldn't put the matter to rest.

"Look, Malcolm. So Carole's gun is missing? How does that implicate her in this investigation? I'm sure she's not the only one in town who owns a pistol."

The sheriff relaxed his stance and leaned against the edge of the reception desk. "You'd be surprised at how many people in this county own firearms. The permit files at the office consume several drawers of space. Carole's permit is one of them." He grinned. "But Carole is the only one that I know at this point, who can't produce her gun." He paused, again. "And Carole's missing gun matches the caliber of the bullets we removed from Mr. Humphries' body."

Mags was stunned. She felt Carole's nails dig into her arm.

"Good try, Margaret." There was that sickening smirk of a grin again. "Produce Carole's gun. We'll test it. You've read enough mysteries to know the drill. If it doesn't match..."

"Then Carole and I are in the clear."

"Not in the clear, exactly. Just not at the very top of the suspect list."

"If Carole's gun proves not to be the murder weapon, why wouldn't that prove our innocence?"

Obviously relishing his role, the sheriff said, "Just because you didn't use Carole's gun to kill Mr. Humphries, or whoever he is, doesn't mean you didn't use a different gun. Good day, ladies. We'll be talking again. Remember..." He turned as he started through the doorway. Once again his face wore his trademark bulldog look. "Remember, either one of you leave town, I'll have you picked up and I'll put you where you can't leave."

"Don't threaten us, Malcolm!"

"Don't test me, Margaret. You'll lose." With that, he was gone.

The two women sat, saying nothing, just looking at each other, as if neither of them could grasp what had just happened. Mags noted that Carole's eyes were huge and suspected, if she could find a mirror, that hers were equally large.

"What do we do?" Carole wailed. "I didn't kill that miserable little man and I'm sure you didn't either."

"Unfortunately, Malcolm doesn't agree with you." At the look of alarm on her friend's face, Mags was quick to explain, "I'm with you, but Malcolm holds the trump card."

Unable to sit still any longer, Mags made her way to the wall of cabinets left over from the days when the big room had been operations central for the town's three-person police department. She began to open doors, looking and reaching and probing.

"What are you doing?"

"There are twelve doors here. You only searched three of the cabinets. Like you said, it's been a long time since you hid the gun. Maybe you simply forgot where you hid it."

"The sheriff already looked in some of the other cabinets."

"But he didn't look in all of them. Come on. Help me. We're going to take everything out of each cabinet.

Forty-five minutes later, when the last compartment had been emptied and its contents replaced, Mags had to concede defeat. *At least for the moment!*

The two traumatized friends returned to their chairs, too spent, too confused to even know what to do next. "Are you one hundred and ten percent certain you hid the gun in those cabinets. Could you have put it somewhere else in the building?"

"Look around, Mags. This place isn't big as a minute. There's no other logical place to hide the gun, or anything else. Unless maybe under the bathroom sinks or in the toilet tanks."

Her friend made a valid point. There was no place else. Mags had to admit that someone, at some point in time, had managed to breech the office security and steal the gun that no one else knew about. But who? And why just the gun?

"It's beginning to look like this whole deal was a carefully-designed set-up," she told Carole, who was still sitting at her desk with her head in her hands. "Someone is out to ruin me and they don't care who gets hurt in the process."

"But who?"

"I don't know. Not yet, anyway. But I will find out. I just wish we had someone on our side."

As Mags spoke, the office front door opened to admit an older woman. When Mags heard the door's familiar creak, and looked up, the first thing she realized was that they had failed to lock the door behind the sheriff. Then she recognized their visitor as Ernestine Shelby, a long-time, well-known crime reporter for a major Atlanta daily newspaper. Would the press never leave them alone?

"Good afternoon," their visitor announced. "I'm Ernestine..."

"Yes, Ms. Shelby, I recognize you, but I'm afraid we have nothing to say. In fact, we failed to relock the door after the sheriff left, so it's just by chance that you were even able to get in."

The visitor smiled. "Sometimes things happen because they are meant to be." Seeing that Mags was about to interrupt, she waved her hand. "Please, just hear me out."

"Very well."

"I've been following the details of this case. When you cover crime as many years as I have, you develop a sixth sense, if you will, especially when everything isn't what it appears to be. That's what I feel like is happening here."

"And you would do what to follow up on that feeling?"

"Interview you. Write articles about all that's gone down here in the last few days. Articles that point out some of the inconsistencies, the facts that don't support each other."

"In other words, you'd raise reasonable doubt and bring pressure to re-examine aspects of the case?"

"More or less. Are you ladies on board?"

Mags knew of the newswoman's reputation. She was hard-nosed, but she was also an award-winning journalist.

"You know what, Carole? I don't think we have a whole lot to lose. You in?"

Her friend had raised her head to listen to the exchange between Mags and the reporter. She didn't say anything at first, but finally, when Mags had begun to wonder if she would ever respond, Carole whispered. "I didn't kill that man and I don't want to go to jail. Let's do it."

"What do we do first," Mags asked their guest, who was already unpacking her tape recorder and note pad.

"First, lock the door so that we aren't interrupted. Then get ready to get turned inside out by your toenails."

"Pardon?"

"This is going to be long and possibly painful, because I've got a lot of questions to ask. If we're lucky, you'll have the answers!"

Chapter Four

HARRUMPH! YOU OWE ME!

Things were looking up, Mags assured herself. The sun was shining, a comfortable breeze licked at the edges of the morning heat, and she was in the mountains, where special music always played in her head. The previous evening's interview with Ernestine Shelby would be published soon in the Atlanta newspaper, and the tide would turn; she and Carole would no longer be "persons of interest." Mags felt it in her bones and, as she navigated the curving roads from The Slop Bucket, the beleaguered real estate broker adopted that positive attitude as her mantra for the day. Not only would it get better, it already was better.

Her new outlook on life lasted until about ten seconds after she dropped her purse and tote bag on her desk.

"It's for you," Carole called across the room, holding the phone high above her head. Mags got the distinct impression her office manager was trying to put as much distance as possible between herself and the caller.

"This is Mags Gordon. How may I help you?" Based on Carole's behavior, she braced herself and waited for a response. She didn't have to wait very long, but that didn't mean she was prepared for the ambush that slapped her up side of the head.

"You can tear up my listing contract, that's what you can do. Then you can cut me a check for two million dollars, because that's how much you cost me." The voice was that of a woman; a very unhappy woman whom Mags couldn't immediately identify.

"I beg your pardon?"

"You heard me. If you think you're getting away with this scam, you've got another think coming." The woman's voice was rapidly becoming more screech and less coherent. In an accomplishment born out of desperation, Mags finally recognized her caller. *Doreen McAlister.* That the person on the other end of the phone was angry came across loud and clear. What Mags didn't understand was why, so she asked.

"Doreen. DOREEN!" She attempted to break through the avalanche of venom that assaulted her ear. "Hold up just a second. Please... tell me what I've done to deserve this kind of treatment." And why, she wondered, *would I be cutting you a check for two million? Like I've got it!*

"You cost me a sale, and you know it. I don't intend to walk away from that kind of money."

Now Mags was truly confused. Before she responded, she mentally reviewed all her dealings with the elderly woman, who had once been a famous cabaret singer. Outside of the listing contract for Doreen's sprawling lakefront lodge, Mags could think of no other contractual connection.

"How did I cost you a sale? Your house hasn't had any offers."

"Oh, yes, there have been offers, Missy. You're not weaseling out of this one like you have with all those others folks. Word gets around, you know."

Mags felt the quicksand of confusion claiming her, and struggled to keep her head above water. Literally and figuratively. "There's no offer that I know anything about, Doreen."

"That's because the offer didn't come from you."

"But I'm your agent. All offers have to come through me." Mags was juggling the phone against her shoulder, while she executed a poor attempt at running her fingers through her hair.

"You didn't have to bring me the offer, because that nice Mr. Humphries brought it himself."

Mags rocked on her heels, feeling that she'd been sucker-punched by a Sherman tank. "But Doreen, there's no way Mr. Humphries could legally make an offer himself." Then she corrected herself. "More importantly, there's no way you could legally accept any offer he made. You have a contract with me."

"Harrumph!"

She sounds like my grandmother, Mags thought. She hadn't liked the sound when she was a child, and she certainly didn't care for it today.

"We have a legal contract, Doreen. A legally binding contract." She began to count the African violet blooms coloring the windowsill in an effort to hold her emotions. "Did Mr. Humphries make you a written offer? Something that you signed?" Her voice, she realized, had become almost a shrill as her caller's. Mags could feel the room twirling around her and, when Carole's waving arm caught her attention, the floor tilted even further.

Standing in the doorway, with a deer-in-the-headlight expression plastered across their confused faces, were a man and woman who were obviously from out of town. *Clients!* The first prospects they'd had in what seemed to Mags like weeks, and she knew she had to contain herself and do damage control.

Clutching the phone to her chest, Mags flashed what she prayed would pass for a legitimate smile, not the smirk of a kid caught in the act, and said to the couple, "Good morning. Please come in. Carole will help you and I'll be free in just a moment."

Without waiting for an answer, she fled toward the back door and didn't remove the phone from her cleavage until she was safely outside. Her caller was still screeching.

"Now you listen to me, Doreen." Mags hoped she was being firm enough, because she already knew the older woman took few prisoners. "I'll be glad to come by your house later today, so that we can talk about this. But you're not going to call me on the phone and rake me over the coals this way." She braced herself against the building. "I simply won't tolerate it. Do we understand each other?"

Not even a split second elapsed before Mags had her answer. "You can come by if you want to. I'll be here all day. Just be sure you bring my check or don't come."

"I don't owe you any money, Doreen. What's more, I don't understand how you think that I do."

The sound of exasperated air escaping was the initial response. Then, in a pace and tone that clearly indicated she thought she was explaining things to an idiot, Doreen picked up the conversation. "It's like this. Mr. Humphries looked at my house. He liked it. He called me after you showed it to him, and told me he wanted to buy it. He was calling to tell me himself, because he said you didn't know the first thing about selling real estate."

"He what!"

"Now, after all that's happened, I think he was right," Doreen finished with a satisfied squawk in her voice.

Mags grabbed for the building again. HJH was more of a jerk than either she or Carole had realized, and he was literally pulling the rug out from under her in every direction. "What Mr. Humphries thought about my real estate skills are neither here nor there, Doreen. The law says that you and I have a binding, legal contract, and Mr. Humphries was totally out of line to approach you directly." Mags knew this was not the time to divulge that Doreen's guaranteed buyer had later looked at three more properties, and had wanted to buy all of them.

"You're not going to scam me," Doreen screamed. "My lawyer says an oral contract is just as binding as a written one. That's what I had with Mr. Humphries."

"Legally you didn't have anything with him," Mags charged. "There's no way an oral agreement is going to trump a written contract."

"Harrumph! Legally there was no way you should have killed

him, either. But you did, and you cost me a sale."

Mags had to find the steps and sit down. Her caller had pulled out the final stop.

"I did not kill Mr. Humphries, Doreen! I don't understand why you would think that I did."

"You killed him," she crowed, "because he was going to buy my house and knock you out of a commission."

"But I didn't know that until just now, when you told me."

"Oh… well whether you knew it or not, you owe me two million dollars because Mr. Humphries was going to buy my house and now he's dead." She hesitated. "He was found dead on your boat, wasn't he?"

Mags watched fluffy white clouds scuttling across the sky. In the distance, pontoon boats crawled like crickets across the lake's surface, and the voices of many visitors' echoed from Main Street. She was fighting a losing battle. Not that she intended to cave, and certainly she didn't plan on cutting a check for Doreen. No, this battle would have to be fought, and won, but in a different way.

"I'm sorry, Doreen. I've got an appointment this morning and I've already kept the other party waiting." She hesitated; then plunged ahead. "You and I will talk about this later."

"Later? Like when?"

"When I get a chance, Doreen. That's the best answer I've got right now."

"You're going to try to cheat me out of my money, aren't you? You're going to try to scam me!"

"I can promise you I'm not trying to pull a fast one," Mags assured the upset client. Neither did she intend to roll over and play dead, but better not to mention that right now, either.

"I'll sue you, Margaret Gordon. I promise, I'll see you in court," Doreen screamed so loudly that Mags dropped the phone.

You may at that, Margaret said to herself. To the angry woman on the phone she simply said, "I'm sorry, Doreen. I've got to go. I'll call you." Then she punched the disconnect button with a little more force than the engineers probably envisioned necessary to terminate a call.

Mags stopped to gather her thoughts and to try and calm her nerves before stepping back into the office. There were clients waiting, something that had been in short supply for the past few days. These people had already been traumatized once. It wouldn't do to frighten them further.

"Hello," she greeted the couple, who were relaxing in the waiting area, each with a glass of iced tea in hand. "I'm sorry I couldn't help you when you first arrived." She made it a point to smile as broadly as her facial muscles would allow, and hoped the pain she felt didn't mean she was coming across as a fraud.

"That's alright," the woman said, as she struggled to rise. "Carole has been taking good care of us."

Mags shook hands with the woman and then with the man, who introduced themselves as Sandra and Tony Edwards from Ft. Lauderdale, Florida. "So, tell me, what brings you to Crabapple Cove?"

Over the next few minutes she learned they were actively seeking to retire to the area. "You couldn't find a better place to call home."

"There's just something about this place," Tony replied. "We've looked in several areas of the mountains, but this little place just has that extra 'something'."

The conversation went on for several minutes, while Mags took note of their likes and dislikes, their demands and their wishes. Once she had a good grasp on their needs, she moved to her computer and began to pull up property listings. Soon the trio was clustered around the monitor, as Mags flipped from one home to another. In the end, they had identified six places to tour.

"Enjoy your lunch," Mags called out as the couple descended the steps. "The Eat and Greet has a great menu."

"We'll be meet you at one o'clock," they promised. "We're anxious to find something on this trip."

Mags returned to her chair and dropped into it as if her legs had been pulled from beneath her. "I'm wiped out and it's not even noon," she told Carole.

"More than that, you're in a real pickle."

"You've lost me. We've got a customer, and I'm going to do my best to find them a house. We need the commission."

"And you're going to show property how?"

"That's a dumb question. You know I always show property by...." Her voice trailed off as the reality of Carole's question struck home. "I don't have my boat. Oh, my gosh! What can I do?"

"I guess you'll have to call the sheriff and throw yourself on his mercy."

"He'll love that, alright."

Mags began to pace the floor, which was no easy task given the small space available. The feeling of being trapped inside the office traffic pattern felt closely akin to the tight spot she was in over the *One True Love.*

In the end, while trying to recapture how positive she had felt earlier in the morning, Mags dialed the sheriff's phone number.

"Yeah, what is it, Margaret? And if it's another theory or sob story, I'm not buying today."

"No, Malcolm..., er, Sheriff, it's nothing like that. I need to get my boat. I've got clients in from out of town wanting to see property."

"You want the *One True Love?*

"That's right. It's my boat. Surely you've finished processing it by now."

"Are you insinuating we're slow?"

This wasn't going well. Mags gritted her teeth and tried again.

"Nothing like that. I just figured you'd be finished with the boat and I could get it back."

"Sorry, that boat is a crime scene and until we know more about this whole picture than we know now, the *One True Love* is impounded."

Mags felt the pressure valve blow. What's more, it felt so good.

"You listen to me, Malcolm Wiley. You've scoured that boat inside and out and you've got photos. What possible need is there for you to hold my boat?"

"The law says I can and I am."

"There's no way you can let me use it this afternoon? These people are ready to buy something."

"Don't you have a vehicle? Use it."

"You know I've got an SUV. But I advertise that I show property by boat, and that's what these people are expecting."

"Sorry. Wish I could help."

Mags had never heard a more insincere statement, and had to resist telling the sheriff exactly how she felt. Unfortunately, she also understood, the clock was ticking.

"Very well, Malcolm. How long will it be before I can get the use of the *One True Love*?"

"That'll be up to the judge."

"Why would the judge be a part of the picture?"

"Because I'm handing it off to him to make that call."

"You're telling me that I'm going to have to petition the court to get my property?"

"That's about how it sizes up."

"Gee, thanks, Malcolm. You're all heart today."

Mags had one eye on the clock and, with the other, was checking out the phone book for boat rentals. With less than an hour until the couple from Florida would expect to board the *One True Love*, Mags knew that time wasn't on her side.

"Okay, Malcolm. I see how this is going to play out, so I'll see you in court." Literally.

She ended the call and immediately punched in the number for the marina where she docked her boat. In a matter of minutes, she had secured the rental of a small ski boat large enough to accommodate three. As she was leaving the office to meet her clients, Mags remembered the promise she'd made to the sheriff. "If you don't do anything else this afternoon," she said to Carole, "please call Grant Lewis and ask him to file whatever is necessary for me to petition the judge to get my boat back." I'll show Malcolm he's not going to bulldoze me!

Her clients pulled into the marina parking area right on her heels and, as soon as Mags had signed the papers and gotten the keys to the rental boat, the three loaded up. Lifejackets on, Mags set about familiarizing herself. The instrument panel was totally foreign, and it took a few minutes for her to get ready to crank and cruise.

"I'm sorry for the delay. My boat isn't available, so we're going to use this one instead." She turned to the controls and, in a couple of minutes, Mags was piloting the ski boat toward the middle of Lake Germany, setting course for the first listing. "There's really no better way to view listings around here than by boat," she explained. "We've got some great properties to see."

"I guess it must have been rough finding that dead man on your boat? We really hope you didn't kill him," Sandra giggled. Rather nervously, too, Mags thought.

The questions came totally out of the blue and caught Mags in the gut. Her knees threatened to buckle. It took all of her concentration to hold the boat on course and still acknowledge the query.

"It was very upsetting. And, no, I didn't kill him." Margaret hoped she didn't come across as someone who might push this couple into the lake. "You're safe, I promise."

"The server where we ate lunch told us all about the murder, and how you found the body." When she described the woman, Mags knew exactly who had been talking behind her back. She made a mental note to properly thank Maudeann for meddling in her business.

With great effort, although she got the vibes that more salacious details would be welcome, Mags changed the subject. The first property was in sight, and she used that excuse to direct her clients' attention elsewhere. Anywhere but on Horace J. Humphries and how he had made his final departure.

The remainder of the afternoon was spent cruising among the coves and inlets, touring one home, then another. The conversation revolved around views and gourmet kitchens, bedrooms and bathrooms and still more views.

It was a weary Mags who headed back out onto the lake as the sun was beginning to drop. Six properties in five hours was a little much, but busy and occupied clients made for fewer nosy, personal questions.

"Have I totally confused you?" she asked the couple, who were huddled together in the rear of the boat. "We were moving pretty fast back there, so don't be shy about asking questions."

"The third house, the one with the turret, intrigued me," Sandra confessed. "I really liked the kitchen in that house."

"Yeah, but..." the husband rebutted. Mags tuned them out and concentrated instead on crossing the large lake back to the marina. She had listened to the same debates more times than she could count, and she'd shown enough property to understand that such conversation was normal for this stage in the house-hunting process. It was actually a good sign, but it didn't pay to start drawing up contracts just yet.

"If there are any of the houses you'd like to see again tomorrow, just let me know. We'll be back at the marina in just a couple of minutes."

Mags concentrated on maneuvering her way through the flotilla crowding the harbor, and she soon brought the boat back to its mooring.

"That was very interesting," Sandra said, after they were all back on the dock. "I don't think we've ever bought a house by boat."

"It really is the best way to see the property, and it's much faster than driving all these winding roads. We couldn't have seen but two, maybe three places today if we'd gone by car." Mags knew the boat gave her a marketing advantage, and she didn't mind giving credit where it was due.

They bid each other farewell and Mags cautioned them, "Property is selling well. If you liked any of those places today, other people will also. Don't delay and lose your dream house."

The couple agreed they'd call the next morning and Mags accepted that promise, knowing there was a fifty-fifty chance she'd just wasted her entire afternoon, and more than a few dollars in fuel. Still, it was one of the gambles of the game.

In the marina office she settled up for the boat, and was soon behind the steering wheel of her land yacht, headed away from the lake. It was already past time for Carole to close the office, and it would be out of the way to go all the way back to town, then back to The Slop Bucket. There was nothing she needed from the office, so she pointed her Jeep in the direction of home.

Once inside, Mags stopped to play with Delilah, the corgi that had come to her as a puppy, and was now her constant partner in this new life. The dog's muzzle that had once been almost auburn in color was now streaked with white, but the happiness she gave Mags was ageless.

Her evening meal of grilled steak and baked potato that Mags enjoyed on the lodge's screened-in porch hit the spot. Somehow she had missed lunch, she realized. The view of high mountain peaks spread before her was so much eye candy she didn't even need dessert. Instead, she grabbed her phone and punched in Carole's number.

"Hey, I was about to call you. How'd it go?"

"We don't have a contract if that's what you mean, but they're definitely interested." She paused and cleared her plate from the wrought iron table. "But I'm not the only agent in town, either."

"So why would they go to another agent?"

Mags scratched Delilah's ears and took some pleasure in how relaxed her dog became. Would that she could so easily find relaxation. "Because they know about HJH. Maudeann gave them all the juicy details over lunch."

"And took great pleasure in it, I'm certain."

"No doubt."

"So you think they'll bolt to someone else?"

"It wouldn't surprise me. It's happened before and we didn't have a corpse in the mix."

"I think you're borrowing trouble. I had a good bit of time to talk with those folks while you were on the phone with Doreen. They seem pretty solid."

Mags fondled the dog's ears again. "You may be right and maybe I'm wrong. I guess tomorrow will show us."

"Probably. So what, exactly, was Doreen screeching about? We never got a chance to talk."

Mags brought her up to speed, concluding with their client's threat to sue. Which made her think about the sheriff's refusal to release her boat. "Did you get my lawyer?"

"He'll be filing the petition to the court tomorrow morning. Said there was no reason for Malcolm to continue holding your boat hostage except out of spite."

"He's right."

The two were pondering the where's and why's of HJH's devious ways, when Mags' call-waiting function beeped. She checked the display. "I've got a call coming through," she said hurriedly, " only I don't recognize the number."

"Perhaps it's your clients from this afternoon. Maybe they decided not to sleep on it."

"That's probably it. Let me go before they hang up."

"Bye..."

"Hello, this is Mags Gordon." Only the voice she heard was not that of either of her clients, but was instead the long-familiar and still loathsome voice of her ex-husband.

"Hi, Mags. How are things going?"

Franklin! Immediately her antenna snapped to attention and she felt her guard go up. He must have a new cell number. Mags knew she'd need to block it from her phone.

"Why are you calling me? I told you in court I never wanted to see your face or hear your voice again."

"Aw, Mags. Can't we at least be friends?"

"Franklin, we never were friends before. Why would I want to start now?"

"You know, Margaret. We could have made a go of our marriage, if it hadn't been for your lousy attitude and your biting tongue."

"Thank you for that assessment. But don't short yourself. Your outside activities didn't help matters. So why are you calling?"

"I heard about your little unfortunate experience, and I was worried. I know that must have been very upsetting."

Franklin had never before shown any concern for Mags or her needs, and she found this sudden change of attitude both phony and suspicious. She told herself that the leopard didn't change its spots, with no offense meant to the leopard.

As she listened to the man who had consumed thirty of the best years of her life, she could hear Mrs. Jeffries' voice in the background, cautioning Inspector Witherspoon to question anything that was out of character. Mags was inclined to believe that the erstwhile Victorian British housekeeper and amateur sleuth knew her stuff. Accordingly, she attacked head-on.

"You've never been the least bit concerned about me, so your worries are way too late and highly suspicious besides."

"I'm sorry you feel that way," he said quietly. "That's what I get for putting my feelings out there, where you can trample on them again."

Mags heard his words, but she also realized there was no sense of legitimacy about them. Instead, she visualized herself playing the violin with the expertise of a virtuoso.

"Yeah, right. Franklin, you're just as full of it now as you were the day we divorced. Why don't you quit while you're ahead?"

"Margaret. Please…"

"Look, Franklin. I don't need your sympathy or your concern. And if I did, I'd do what I did all those years we were married. I'd look to someone else to get what you were too selfish to give me."

"What about the *One True Love*?"

"What about it?"

"Can you sell real estate from a boat where a man was murdered?"

Mags thought the question strange. Why should Franklin be concerned about the boat's continued viability? She chose not to challenge him. Instead, she said, "I don't see why that should make any difference. I didn't kill him."

"Maybe you should consider buying something newer and smaller. You know… better on fuel."

The light bulb flamed on and shot fire down Mags' back. Suddenly Franklin's true agenda had been revealed, although she was certain he didn't realize she'd picked up on his scheme.

"That would be an expensive solution to something that really isn't a problem," she told him.

"You could sell the *One True Love*," he persisted, "and use the money to buy the new boat. That way you wouldn't spend so much out of pocket."

"You're right. That's a good idea, and I would sell if the deal was right."

"You really need to think about it."

Mags visualized Franklin's mouth watering at the prospect of recovering his beloved boat, his very real one true love.

"They can handle it for you at the marina. People come in there every day looking to buy a boat."

"That's a good idea. Except for one thing."

"Oh?"

"Yeah. I'd have to be sure they understood that she wasn't for sale to you for any amount of money." The sharp intake of breath from the other side of the conversation told her the message had been received. "And if someone acting as your blind agent bought it, I'd have to sue everyone involved in the transaction."

"You know, Margaret. There's a label for you. It's called bitch."

"Thank you, Franklin. That's the highest compliment you've ever paid me."

"Excuse me?"

"You never thought I had sense enough even to dress myself. That I've been elevated in your estimation to 'bitch' tells me I'm finally being taken seriously." Her voice took on a frigid edge. "Remember what I said, Franklin. I don't buy your concern, and you're not going to buy MY boat. I'll sink it first."

"You wouldn't!"

"Push me far enough and you can watch what I'll do. Evidently you didn't learn your lesson the last time we faced a judge."

"Not all judges are wimps like that one. One of these days you're liable to find yourself in front of a judge who knows right from wrong, and isn't afraid to rule that way."

"And your point is?"

"You got lucky before, but that won't always be the case."

"Are you threatening me?"

"Take it any way you want."

"The way I'm going to take it is, 'Good night and don't call me again, or you may be facing that judge yourself!'"

"Bitch!"

"That's right. I know you for what you are, and now you know me. Goodnight, Franklin."

As she clicked the button to end the call, he was still ranting. The last thing she heard was, "You'll regret this. I'll see that..."

Mags had no doubt of Franklin's capabilities. She did wonder what he would do to avenge his injured ego. Whatever it was, she knew she needed to be on guard. And just what was that crack about a judge down the road somewhere?

Chapter Five
I'M CHARGING YOU WITH MURDER

B y ten o'clock the next morning, Carole's assessment of the previous days' clients had proven accurate. As Mags drew up a sales contract for one of the homes she'd shown the couple, she was only too glad to mentally declare her office manager's judgment spot on. She made a note to tell her so after the clients left.

"Congratulations," she told them, as they shook hands. "I'll call the seller in just a few minutes and with any luck at all, we'll have an answer before the day is out."

"What do you think our chances are?" Tony Edwards asked. "We didn't make a full-price offer."

Mags forced her face into a smile, one of the professional tricks of the trade: smile even though you don't feel like it. "This house has been on the market for almost two hundred days. He's had no offers." She waved the contracts in the air. "This is a fair offer, and I will do my best to make the seller see it that way." To herself, she acknowledged that the seller was a very stubborn man. Still, seventy-five thousand less than a one point nine million dollar asking price was a drop in the bucket.

"We're adopting a positive attitude," Sandra told her. "While we wait for the good word, we're going out and get better acquainted with our new home town."

Mags bid the couple goodbye, promising to call as soon as she knew anything. Then, true to her word, she consulted her files for the seller's cell phone number.

"That's less than the asking price," the elderly gentleman informed her, after Mags delivered the offer." I told you I wouldn't bend."

"Seventy-five thousand is nothing," she informed him. "Very few houses sell for the full asking price, and after more than six months on the market and no offers, I'd caution you to think twice before you turn this down."

"You're not threatening me, are you?"

"Certainly not," Mags replied, already weary of the conversation. "But I do know what's going on around here when it comes to real estate. I'm only trying to give you my best guidance, but it's your call. Just tell me what you want to do."

"I'll have to talk to Eunice before I can give you an answer. She's at the beauty shop this morning."

Mags understood that Eunice was his wife, and it made sense he'd want to include her. She prayed his better half had the vision to understand what a good offer this was. She also knew the couple was no longer able to travel from their south Florida home, and that they desperately needed to sell the mountain getaway.

"Call me after you and Eunice talk," she told him. "This couple is leaving in the morning, and they'd like to have an answer today."

"Underpaying me and then they want to rush me for an answer. That's a fine howdy-do," the old man said, and the tremor in his voice verified his elderly status. "They always take advantage of old people."

"In the first place, Mr. Lawrence, these people don't have a clue how old you are. And in the second place, this is as good as a full price offer. But if you can't give me an answer today, then you can't."

The seller promised to call by mid-afternoon, and Mags bid him goodbye. She and Carole spent the rest of the morning reviewing listings, and putting together the agency's ad for the quarterly real estate magazine. Carole e-mailed the details to the publisher just before lunch, just minutes before the deadline.

"Tell you what," Mags suggested. "This deal is going to be made. Let's live dangerously and celebrate early. Lunch is on me at the Eat and Greet."

"You're on. Just let me put the phone on automatic and we can be on our way." She turned toward her desk, as the phone in question rang. She looked at Mags and grinned. "Speak of the devil." She grabbed the handset. "Mountain Magic Realty by Mags. This is Carole." As she listened to the caller on the other end, her mouth began to smile, one that didn't stop until the corners were almost touching her ears. "Just a moment, Mr. Lawrence. Here's Mags."

"Yes, Mr. Lawrence. I wasn't expecting to hear from you so quickly."

"Eunice got home before I was expecting her. When I told her about the offer, she reamed me out for griping about seventy-five thousand dollars. So I'm calling to say you've got a deal."

"That's great," Mags crowed. "I really do think you've made the right decision."

"We do, too," her elderly client confessed. "But there is one thing…"

Uh-oh, why is there always something, Mags asked herself? "And what would that be, Mr. Lawrence?"

"How quick do these people want the house?"

Mags wondered if he was in a bind for the money. "We put a forty-five day closing in the contract. I'll have to ask them if we can shave a few days off that mark."

"No… no… no. You misunderstand. We're hoping they might need a few more days. Eunice called our son to tell him we have a buyer, and he wants to bring the entire family back to Crabapple Cove for one last visit."

"When would that be?"

"Not for five or six weeks, but then he wants to stay for a couple of weeks."

Mags rubbed her chin. "Tell you what, Mr. Lawrence, I'll speak to the buyers and feel them out. They haven't indicated that they're in a bind to move. I got the impression they were more concerned with knowing they had bought something, before they left to go home."

"If you could work it out, we'd be very grateful."

"Let me talk with them, and I'll get back to you this afternoon." She put the phone back on its base, hit the button to arm the answering service, and motioned to Carole to head for the door while they could still get away. In a matter of minutes they were seated in the café and had given their orders.

"I need to call the Edwards." She dialed the number and was quickly rewarded by the sound of Tony's voice. "You've just bought yourself a house," she informed her client. In the background, she could hear Sandra's excited reaction. "There is one thing I need to ask you, and this is your call to make." She explained the seller's request and the reason for it.

"That's not a problem, we can be flexible about moving, and if that gives these people a chance for one last visit, then we should do that."

"You understand this wasn't a condition of the sellers' acceptance," Mags clarified. "It's just a request they made, and you're under no obligation to grant it."

"We understand, but it's the right thing to do. As long as we can be in by the first of October, we'll be fine."

Mags ended the call after arranging to meet with her clients later that afternoon to finish signing papers. When their food was served, she ate with a light heart and a clear conscience. It was going to be a good day.

Carole was the first to spot the three lawmen headed their way. "Don't look now," she told Mags, whose back was toward the door. "Here comes trouble. I guess Malcolm's heard that Mr. Lewis filed for the release of the *One True Love*."

In a matter of seconds the sheriff himself and two uniformed deputies were blocking their table. "Carole Pickett, we need you to come with us."

Carole's face drained of all its color; Mags dropped her fork. It made a terrible clatter against the laminate table top.

"Malcolm, what is this nonsense? Sit back down, Carole."

"Stay out of this, Margaret. This is official business and I can arrest you for obstructing justice and interfering with an officer."

"But... what? Why?" Carole mumbled, as she again attempted to stand, only the two deputies were blocking her way.

The sheriff reached for her hand and helped Carole to exit the booth.

"Malcolm, I demand to know what's going on here. Where are you taking Carole?"

It wasn't so much what he said, but the sheriff's body language, that told Mags he wasn't paying any attention to her, or to anything she had to say. She pulled on his shirt sleeve. "Malcolm, I asked you a question and I demand an answer."

"You don't have any grounds to demand anything, Margaret. And, as a matter of fact, be certain you don't leave town. I may need you where I can get hold of you on short notice."

"Are you arresting me?"

"You? Not now. Not yet, anyway. Her?" He motioned with his thumb to where a shocked-looking Carole stood between the two deputies. "Her? She's another story." He pulled a piece of paper from his pocket. "Carole Pickett, this is a warrant for your arrest and I'm here to charge you with murdering one Horace J. Humphries."

Carole screamed and collapsed on the floor, where the deputies attempted to revive her and get her back on her feet.

"Have you lost your ever loving mind? Carole's no more guilty of murder than I am!" Mags charged, jumping to her feet and thrusting herself between the deputies and her friend. "Carole. It's Mags. It'll be okay. I'll get you out of this."

"Don't speak too loudly, or too quick," Malcolm advised in a voice that Mags didn't recognize. "We're arresting her because her gun was found, hidden, on board the *One True Love*."

"How do you know it's her gun?" Mags began to silently question how a gun had made its way onto her boat, and quickly decided it had been planted there. But by whom? The murderer was the most likely suspect, and that person wasn't Carole. Of that she was certain.

The sheriff held up his hand and began to lift one finger at a time as he spoke. "First, the serial number matches the number on her gun permit. Second, ballistics determined that the bullets that killed Mr. Humphries were fired from this gun. And third, Carole's fingerprints are on the gun."

"Well of course her prints are on the gun. It's her gun!"

"Which is why we're arresting her." He turned and grinned at Mags, although she detected yet another gleam of "gotcha" in his eyes. The sheriff was really racking up the points. "As soon as we can connect you directly with that gun, we'll be back to get you," the sheriff promised.

With that, he turned to Carole, recited her rights, and motioned to the deputies to escort the prisoner from the premises. "Remember, Margaret. Don't leave town. Don't ask to leave town. I'm watching you."

Mags stood numb and dumbstruck, unable to know exactly what to do. As her head cleared, and she once again became familiar with her surroundings, she discovered a café full of people with their mouths hanging open. Then, she realized, as if on cue, the conversation among the diners began again, only this time all fingers were pointed her way. She knew she had to get out of there. Not wanting to wait for their server to bring the check, she dropped a twenty and a ten on the table and made a hasty retreat, before someone attacked her with questions she wasn't prepared to answer.

Back at the office, totally oblivious to the bright sunshiny day outside, Mags locked the door and pulled all the blinds, plunging the room into semi-darkness. Suddenly, the lighting in the office matched the mood in her heart. Only she wasn't sure if she felt so defeated because Carole had been charged with murder, or because the sheriff had threatened that she was next. Either way, she needed a lawyer. And quick.

It didn't take long for the town's grapevine to swing into overdrive mode. By the time she finished her conversation with the appointments secretary for a major Atlanta law firm, securing an appointment for the next morning, the siege had begun. If it wasn't people knocking on the door demanding to know if it was true that Carole killed a man, they were calling on the phone.

"No," Mags told more than one nosy neighbor, "Carole didn't kill anyone. The sheriff has arrested an innocent woman." Before the day was over, however, Mags herself was inclined to commit several murders. She even visualized doing the deed. More troubling, however, were the other phone calls that came totally out of the blue. Phone calls that threatened her very financial security.

"But Mrs. Cooper," she had pleaded, "I can assure you, Carole is as innocent as you are in this matter. The last thing you want to do is cancel your listing contract. Don't forget we've got that couple who are very interested."

"Believe me, Mrs. Gordon, this gives me no pleasure whatsoever. But I cannot and will not be associated with an agency where murder has occurred."

"But Mr. Humphries was just a client. He wasn't a partner or even a business associate. Just a client."

"Nevertheless, he was murdered on board your boat, and now your employee has been arrested for his murder. I just can't do business with you under these circumstances."

"Very well, Mrs. Cooper," Mags conceded with poor grace. "I'll mail your cancelled contract. But remember, if that couple who saw your home three weeks ago buys it through another agency, I'm still entitled to the full commission. I don't imagine another agent is going to want to sell a property that can't make them any money."

"I'll take my chances, Mrs. Gordon. After all, I have my safety to think about."

"I'm sorry. I don't follow you."

"I'm a client just like that Mr. Humphries. What's to say I won't turn up dead as well."

Mags held the phone away from her ear, in an effort to escape the insanity. Finally, when she knew she had to terminate the conversation, she returned the phone to her ear. "I'm certain then that my assurances that your life is safe will mean nothing, so I'm going to end this conversation because I have other things to do. You'll have your contract in the mail in a couple of days."

Mags ended the call and began to pace the office, then realized how dark it was inside. She moved quickly to the windows to open the blinds, only to be rewarded with blinding sunlight and many inquiring faces.

"Something tells me that all of you aren't here to buy property, so what can I do to help you?"

The group, some standing in the yard and others on the porch, totaled about fourteen, Mags noted. At her greeting, some dropped their heads and wouldn't look her way. A few actually began to move toward the gate, and left the yard completely. In the end, three ladies and one man remained.

"How may I help you?" Mags asked again.

"Is it true about Carole?"

Mags couldn't help but wonder which question the man was posing. "It's true that she's been arrested. But there's no truth to the story that she killed Mr. Humphries. I'd stake my life on it."

"You may be doing just that," one of the women volunteered. "From what I heard, you're liable to be arrested next. 'cording to the sheriff, it's just a matter of time."

"I'm not guilty of anything and neither is Carole."

"Oh, we know Carole's innocent. She's one of us," another woman announced. "Grew up here. And we don't appreciate you getting her in this kind of trouble."

Mags recognized the "come-here" philosophy espoused by

many natives, and knew she was helpless to fight that mindset. To them, anyone who wasn't born in Crabapple Cove was subject to suspicion.

"I'm sorry you feel that way," she said. "No one is more upset about Carole's arrest than me, and I am working to clear her name." She hesitated, wanting to say more, and knowing all the while that she was spitting in the wind. She felt like Annie Darling in *Dead by Midnight*. In the newest Carolyn Hart mystery that Mags had finished only a few weeks before, Annie fights when everyone is pitted against her, to prove that Elaine Jamison didn't murder her own brother.

The group, apparently having said their piece, began moving slowly toward the street. With his hand on the gate, the man turned back to Mags. "We don't believe for one minute that Carole killed that man. And if she did, it was because you made her. If she's found guilty, we'll always hold you responsible."

As she watched them reach the sidewalk and head toward the business district, Mags had no doubt they had spoken the truth. If Carole went down, so would Mountain Magic Realty by Mags. Wouldn't Franklin love that?

The remainder of the afternoon was occupied by angry and troubled clients fearing the negative publicity would hurt their chances for a sale. Mags was able to convince a few of her callers to remain under contract but, at the end of the day, she had agreed to cancel contracts for close to a dozen homes; deals she'd depended on to generate income for the agency.

In the midst of all the insanity, Mags grabbed the phone without checking the Caller ID, and was rewarded with Doreen's screeching voice on the other end.

"You haven't brought me my check. I told you to bring me that check. You owe me two million dollars and I'm not going to just forget that. Now I hear you're about to be locked up for murder. I want that check. Today, Missy."

At that point, feeling that she had very little to lose, and suddenly not caring if she lost everything, Mags unloaded her own volley on her irritating caller. "Look, Doreen, let me make this as clear as I can.

I don't owe you one dime, so if you're waiting for me to cut you a check, you're going to be waiting a very long time. It ain't happening in this lifetime."

"Why… why… why you're trying to cheat me. And why not? If you're a murderer, well I guess you wouldn't hesitate to con a poor old lady out of her life savings!"

"I've told you before. The agreement you think you had with Mr. Humphries wasn't legal. In fact, he put contracts on three more houses after he saw yours, and backed out of all of them. He had no intention of buying your house."

"Says you. He was the nicest man."

Mags knew that her patience was wearing dangerously thin; knew that she was hanging on by her very fingernails. "That's your opinion, Doreen, and you're welcome to it." She ran a hand through her hair. "I happen to think otherwise. And since it's obvious that we've agreed to disagree, I don't see any reason to continue this conversation."

"If you don't bring me that check today, before you get yourself arrested, I'm going to sue you."

Suddenly the thought of appearing before an unbiased judge with common sense and knowledge of the law was very appealing. "Why don't you do that, Doreen? I think you should. In fact," she checked the office clock, "it's only three-thirty. I'll bet if you called your attorney right now, he could get on it today."

"Harrumph!"

There was that sound again that was, to Mags, more excruciating than fingernails across a chalkboard.

"I'll just do that, Missy. I'll see you in court!"

"Goodbye, Doreen."

Mags dropped into the nearest chair, unable to stand another minute. Her legs felt like rubber bands, as if she'd just run a marathon, and her brain was clicking away on overload. I've got to get out of here, she told herself. She switched the phone to automatically answer on the second ring, gathered up her tote bag, knocked the thermostat to a higher reading, and made for the door.

Getting away from the office hadn't been easy. Mags was stopped no less than seven times between her front door and where her car was parked just outside the fence. Thirty feet and seven unpleasant encounters. At long last, however, she was on her way out of town. Then came the question of where was she going. She wasn't ready to go home, and didn't want to go anywhere public.

Carole! Mags realized she needed to see about Carole. But a call to the sheriff's office offered little encouragement.

"She hasn't seen the judge yet, and I'm not going to let you visit her. Besides, we're still questioning her and you're sure not going to sit in on that."

"But what about clothes, Malcolm? Toiletries? I need to bring those to her."

"She's got a jail uniform and we have toiletry items here. Forget it."

"Have you called her dad? Does he know his daughter is in jail?"

"He's in Montana hunting and there's no cell phone signal."

"But Malcolm…"

"Skip it, Margaret. Now you're bothering me. Get off the phone and let me get back to something more important."

Feeling it was useless to argue further, Mags put her phone down, as she drove around, aimlessly, unsure of where to go or what to do. She only knew she had to have refuge and some relief.

Three hours later, as the sun began to finish its mission for the day, Mags reluctantly returned the book she'd been reading to her tote bag and prepared to head home. She'd spent the afternoon far away from Crabapple Cove, in another picturesque mountain community in the pacific northwest. To say that she identified with amateur sleuth and newspaper editor Emma Lord, who saw her paper about to be snatched away, was an understatement. How could she have known when she purchased Mary Daheim's *The Alpine Traitor*, that her personal life would so soon imitate fiction?

But dark was obscuring the native beauty that surrounded the little mountain top grove, where she had spread the blanket and pillow that she always kept in the Jeep in case she were ever stranded. No longer could she clearly see the green of the hemlocks, or make out the shoreline of the lake far below. Even the birds, it seemed, had packed it in for the day, and she knew that she must do likewise. Besides, Delilah would be waiting for her at home.

Mags had found the little paradise when she got lost trying to find a piece of property shortly after opening the agency. She had always vowed to come back and enjoy what she had ultimately discovered was part of the national forest. Until today, she hadn't had time to do so; or perhaps she hadn't made time. At any rate, the remote little point, where she could be totally alone and relax, had served her well. Now it was time to get back to the real world. Emma Lord had triumphed and she would as well.

Mags hadn't been on the road long when it became necessary to use her headlights. A glance at the clock told her it was almost eight o'clock. Delilah would be worried, and would probably have her back legs crossed as well, since it was past time for her to go outside. Mags mashed the accelerator a little harder, while knowing that sharp curves and night darkness didn't mix well.

By the time she was on her road, Mags had no choice but to slow down and take her time. Suddenly there was an urgency within her, one she couldn't explain; she just knew she had to get home.

The Jeep made its way down the gravel drive at The Slop Bucket, jolting and bouncing from the roughness of the road. Yet out of the darkness, as she approached the lodge and the headlights played on the end wall as she swung into the parking area, Mags was startled to see what appeared to be a person. He was running away from the property.

"Hey, come back here," she screamed, as she shoved the gearshift into park and jumped from behind the wheel. "Whoever you are, come back. Now!"

The shape, which by this time had disappeared into the darkness beyond the trees surrounding the lodge, didn't heed her commands. Wondering why anyone would have been there, Mags made her way around to the entrance, where another surprise awaited. The side door closest to the car park, was standing wide open. Her first thought was Delilah who, when Mags called her name, came ambling out.

Mags grabbed for her phone. "Let me speak to the sheriff. Now. Please!" To her surprise, in only a matter of seconds, she heard his voice.

"What is it now, Margaret?"

"Malcolm, I've had a prowler at The Slop Bucket. As I was pulling into the drive, I saw someone running away. When I got here, the end door was standing wide open."

"Did you see who it was?"

"No. Of course not. It was too dark."

"Are you sure you saw anyone at all? Like you said, it was dark."

"I know what I saw, Malcolm."

"Is there any damage? Vandalism? Is anything missing?"

"I don't know. I haven't been in the house because I'm afraid to go in alone. Will you please come out here?"

"Can't turn loose, Margaret. We're short-handed."

"But Malcolm, I'm reporting a possible crime. Aren't I entitled to a visit from your office to investigate?"

"You're entitled. I'm just telling you that I'm pinched for manpower tonight and that, unless your life is in danger, or the lodge is trashed, you'll have to wait until tomorrow."

"By tomorrow whoever it was will have gotten away."

"Sounds to me like they've gotten away as it is."

"Malcolm...!"

"Look, Margaret. You walk up on the porch, reach inside the door, flip on the lights. You can tell immediately if there's vandalism. I'll stay on the phone while you check things out."

Unhappy, but knowing this was as close to cooperation as she was going to get, Mags did as directed. Her reward was to find the great room and kitchen-dining area just as she had left them that morning.

"So far, everything looks normal."

"Good. Now walk on through the house, turning on lights ahead of yourself."

Mags complied, and soon had to report nothing out of order; no apparent vandalism or burglary.

"See. Now I'd have wasted a man for nothing."

"But Malcolm. I know what I saw. How do you explain the door standing open?"

"Did you come out that door this morning?"

"You know I did. It's the one closest to the car."

"Then you failed to pull it completely shut, and the wind blew it open."

Mags had to admit his theory made some sense. As she was searching for a rebuttal, Delilah nuzzled her hand, her way of saying, "I'm hungry. Feed me, please." That's when the light bulb came on.

"But if the door has been open all day, why was Delilah still inside when I got here?"

"That's simple. She may have been in and out all day, and just happened to be inside when you arrived home. Besides, at her age, she's not going to wander far and she's comfortable at home."

As much as it bothered her to admit, everything the sheriff was saying made sense. So why wasn't it calming her fears?

"I still say someone was here," she insisted. "I saw someone running away. Now who would be out, on foot, at this time of night? Explain that one."

"Do I look like I've got a turban on my head and can see all, know all?"

"Don't be crass, Malcolm. A crime has been committed here, and I need you to take me seriously."

"What crime? You just told me everything is in place. Nothing is missing. You're okay. Even Delilah's fine. So tell me, Margaret. What crime are you reporting?"

Margaret racked her brain. "Trespassing," she blurted at last. "He was trespassing."

"You're sure it was a he?"

"No."

"You're certain it wasn't a she?"

"Uh… no."

"Do you have your property legally posted against trespassing?"

"What does that have to do with anything?"

"Unless there is damage of some description, even if you know who the person was, you can't prosecute for trespassing unless you have posted signs displayed."

'Well that's a fine thing."

"And it sounds like you're fine as well, Margaret. I don't think you really saw anyone, but then we'll probably never know, will we?"

"Malcolm, you make me so angry!"

"I do have that effect on people. Now I suggest you lock your doors this time, chill out and get some rest, and let me get back to real crimes. Like murder."

The sheriff's mention of murder reminded her once again of Carole. When she asked about her friend, the sheriff's response was both arrogant and dismissive.

"How do you think she is? She's in jail, looking at a pre-meditated, first degree murder charge. How would you be?"

"You know, Malcolm. Somebody hit you with a mean stick somewhere back down the line. Talk about crimes, you ought to go arrest those people, because what they did to you was criminal."

"Thanks for your assessment. Now good night. I've got work to do."

Yeah, Mags thought. Torturing innocent people.

Since she didn't know what else to do, Mags walked through the house for a second time, then secured all the doors and double-checked the windows. The sight of a motion sensor on one of the windows triggered a panic attack. Regardless of when the door was opened, why didn't the security system sound? Why didn't the company call her? A quick check of the control panel showed that several phases had malfunctioned.

Mags grabbed for the house phone, only to discover that the line was dead. She knew then, without a doubt, that an intruder had been there. The only questions were who, when, and most importantly, why?

Using her cell phone, Mags called the security company.

"We're so glad you called in, Mrs. Gordon." The voice belonged to a young man, who immediately added, "The sheriff's office had been alerted and they should be there shortly."

"But why didn't you call me?"

"We couldn't. The only number we had for you was your land line. It wasn't working. We verified it."

Mags thought quickly. "What time did you get the alarm?"

"Seven thirty-two."

Mags knew that it was roughly seven forty-five when she arrived home. So there had been a visitor on the premises. As Margaret was giving the gentleman her cell phone number, plus the number at the office as secondary contacts, she saw the red flashing lights of a sheriff's car outside.

"The sheriff's office is here. Let me go and deal with them."

It wasn't Malcolm, but at least he had sent a deputy. Obviously Malcolm had prepped him on how to act, Mags told herself, because it was obvious that he was only there because the security company had called.

"Come inside and see what I discovered." The officer followed her and observed the control panel. Then Mags handed him the phone.

"It's dead."

"Obviously somebody cut the wires."

"Where's the lead-in to the house for all these services?"

Mags flipped on outside lights and led the officer around the corner of the house where, when he shined his light where she pointed, it was clear that someone had been up to no good.

"Sheriff Wiley believes that I accidently left my door open this morning. And I do make mistakes." She pointed to the cut cables. "But I don't disable my own alarm and phone. Whether he wants to admit it or not, someone was here."

"Yes, ma'am, it looks like there was. I'm going to radio the sheriff." He left and went to the patrol car, where Mags could see him talking, at times very animatedly, to someone she assumed was Malcolm. In a few minutes he was back.

"We're going to write up a report."

"That's all?"

"Yes, ma'am. There's not much more we can do. Whoever was here is obviously long gone."

After the officer left and Mags had secured and double-checked all the doors and windows yet again, she headed to the bedroom. In her mind was the worry that she was sleeping without an alarm system, and that she had to call the next day to arrange for repair of both systems. Hopefully the technicians could get her back in business quickly. She would call first thing, on her way in to the office.

That's when it hit her. She had bigger fish to fry. Like an appointment in Atlanta with the man she hoped would be Carole's attorney. And the sheriff had already forbidden her to leave town. How was she going to get out of town and get back in, without being seen? This was definitely a time to ask forgiveness rather than permission. As exhaustion from the day from hell consumed her, a plan began to form in Mags' head.

Chapter Six

SHE'S IN DEEP TROUBLE, ISN'T SHE?

A tlanta traffic was worse than Mags remembered. Unforgiving. It didn't help that she was driving Carole's mini-pick-up, and it was a stick shift. None of this was how she had planned it.

The realization the night before that she would have to sneak out of town, in order to avoid the sheriff's wrath, had required that Mags revamp her plans. It was critical that her Jeep be in a prominent location in town, in order to give the impression that she was somewhere around. That left the question of how she would get to Atlanta without wheels.

Mags was up long before the clock buzzed, having spent the entire night sleeping with first one eye open, then the other. During those periods of wakefulness, she had crafted a plan. She would park her Jeep in front of the office, put a note on the door saying she was showing property, then walk to Carole's house and borrow her friend's truck. She knew where Carole hid a door key, and she knew where a spare truck key would be.

It worked, too, except for the clutch in the little truck. It had been years since she'd had to shift gears, and it took a while to remember how to depress the clutch pedal and move the stick at the same time. She finally made it to the attorney's office none the worse for wear.

"So you see," she explained to the man on the other side of the massive desk, "there's just no way Carole's guilty. She did not kill that man, but the sheriff is going to bury her under the jail and call the case closed, if I don't do something."

The attorney, Wyatt Fulton, who had been one of Mags' sometimes tennis partners in her previous social life, sat quietly in his high-backed executive chair. His hands were arranged tent-style under his nose, and he said nothing, as Mags laid out the problem.

"Divorce evidently agrees with you. Either that, or it's that backwoods place you're living."

"Believe me, Wyatt, it's both. But why do you say that?"

He straightened in his chair, dropped his hands, and said, "It's written all over your body. Contentment. Looks to me like you've found the nirvana we all crave."

"It has been almost perfect, at least it was up until the past few days." She wrung her hands. "But when it went south, it went in a hurry. And now this. With Carole."

"So what are you asking of me?"

"Come to Crabapple Cove and represent Carole."

Her attorney friend fiddled with his pen and regarded Mags intently. "You don't have lawyers in this paradise of yours?"

"There are several." She got up from the client chair and picked up a piece of pottery from a side table. Turning it over and over in her hands, she studied the design embossed into the clay. "Of course we have lawyers. More than we need, probably. But there's not a one I'd trust to go toenail to toenail with Sheriff Malcolm Wiley."

"A cross between Buford Pusser and Boss Hogg?" he asked, referring to a legendary Tennessee sheriff and a corrupt fictional TV lawman.

Mags laughed. "More or less." She sobered quickly. "Maybe now you understand why Carole's only hope is to have outside representation." She looked him directly in the face. "She needs you."

The attorney reached for his calendar, then picked up the phone and asked, "Ramona? Do I have any appointments for this afternoon or in the morning that we can't reschedule?" Mags could see the wheels turning in his head. "Good. Shuffle those two around, and put me out of the office for the remainder of today and all day tomorrow." He looked at Mags and flashed her the "OK" sign with his hand. "I'll be in Crabapple Cove in court."

"Oh, Wyatt, thank you. Whatever your fee is, I'll pay it, because I know Carole doesn't have that kind of money."

"You must think very highly of her to risk incurring the sheriff's wrath, and then be willing to pay the freight."

"She's my best friend and," she paused to reflect, "she's like the sister I never had. So, yes. I'd do anything for her." She felt her face harden, and she continued, "Besides, if it weren't for me, she wouldn't be in this jam."

While she was talking, the attorney had been gathering his materials and stuffing them into a fine, tooled-leather attaché case. "There's one thing I need to do before we leave."

"Of course! You need me to write a check."

"We'll get to that. First, I need to put your local sheriff on notice that Carole has an attorney. What's his name again?"

Mags told him, and supplied the sheriff's phone number. Even as she was telling him, he was fingering the phone keys.

"Sheriff Wiley. This is Wyatt Fulton an attorney in Atlanta, and I've been retained as Ms. Carole Pickett's attorney. I believe you have her under arrest in your jail?" The expression on his face hinted as to what was happening back in Crabapple Cove. "That's right. No, Ms. Pickett doesn't know me, but I have been retained by a third party to represent her, and I will be there shortly after lunch to confer with her."

He winked at Mags and flashed a high sign.

"Now Sheriff, I've been doing this lawyer business for a while, and I've never heard that I'm required to reveal the identity of Ms. Pickett's benefactor. In fact, I'm under specific instruction not to tell anyone, including my client, who retained me."

Mags watched as a myriad of expressions crossed the attorney's face.

"Sheriff... Sheriff! Does Ms. Pickett have representation that you know of?" He grinned. "Well she does now. I will be there within three to four hours, and I am specifically requesting that you do not question her further until I've had a chance to talk with her. What's more, I will be present for any interrogation that takes place."

He hung up the phone. "This guy thinks he's Buford Pusser but he's actually more like Boss Hogg, with a side of Roscoe Coltrane thrown in."

Mags knew he meant two characters from the long-canceled TV series "Dukes of Hazard". "That he is."

Margaret left within just a few minutes, knowing she was AWOL. It had been one thing to leave town under cover of the pre-dawn darkness. It was another to sneak back in broad daylight. But there was no other way. She and Wyatt had agreed they would not appear to know each other until after he had spoken with Carole. Then... if he should decide to visit his client's employer, they might be introduced.

Mags found she was more than glad to leave the hustle and bustle and confusion of the big city behind her. She was even getting accustomed to the stick shift and considered how she would look in a small, low-slung, two-seater sports car, zipping around the hairpin curves in Crabapple Cove.

Back in town, she drove carefully, so as not to attract attention; parked Carole's truck in its accustomed space, and set off on foot. She would replace the keys later. There were more urgent matters at hand. Such as how to pop back into her office without making a noticeable production out of the deal, for one. Plus she was hungry. Suddenly she knew just what she'd do. By cutting through yards and crossing a couple of back streets, Mags soon found herself down the block from the "Eat and Greet."

"Let's see," she told Maudeann. "Iced tea, of course..."

"With plenty of lemon!"

Mags laughed. "You know me too well. Yes to the lemon, and I'll have the country fried steak, mashed potatoes and gravy, fordhooks, cole slaw and two rolls."

Mags saw the server's eyebrows go up. "You alright? What happened to your diet?"

"I'm hungry. Showing property is hard work, and today I've got an appetite. To heck with some dumb diet."

"You got it."

"Oh, by the way, Maudeann. Many thanks for bringing the Edwards couple up to speed on all my activities the other day. I mean, how many people can say they bought their house from a person of interest in a murder investigation?"

The server colored, then mumbled. "You're welcome. I guess."

Mags sipped her tea and looked around the café, making eye contact with several people. She even spoke with a few. Should she ever be questioned, she could definitely provide several names to substantiate her presence that day.

Back at the office, fed and feeling far more than just fat, Mags yanked the note off the door and slid her key into the lock. There was plenty she needed to be doing, but her concern for Carole was foremost in her mind. It occurred to her that she should check on her friend.

"Malcolm. How's Carole?"

"She's not cooperating," he growled. "I'm about at the end of my rope with her."

"You mean she's not rolling over and playing dead."

"Don't be a wiseass."

"When can I see her? You can't hold her forever. You can't keep me from visiting her."

"She's in my jail and I can do anything I damn well please. Besides, she's got an appointment with her lawyer this afternoon."

"Her lawyer? Who? How'd she get an attorney?"

"Damndest thing. He's some feller from Atlanta. I don't have the first clue how she got him."

And it's killing you not to know, Mags told herself. "What's his name?"

"He told me, but I don't remember. He ought to be here any time now."

"So when can I see your prisoner, Malcolm? I've been patient about as long as I'm going be."

"You know, you're one giant pain in the..."

"Don't say it, Malcolm. Just don't even go there. Now about my friend..."

"Call me back late this afternoon. I'll see what we can do after she talks to the lawyer."

The clock said two-twenty-seven. The next time Mags looked, after busying herself with several clerical chores, it was two-thirty-three. It was going to be a long afternoon.

Mags was actually dozing at her desk when the office door opened. The jangle of the bell interrupted her siesta. It was Wyatt.

"Did I wake you?" He grinned and came around behind her chair.

"Yes, thank goodness, you did. I'd hate to think of what kind of impression I might have made on a client." She grinned. "Not that we have too many of those these days."

"It's been rough, hasn't it?"

"You don't know the half of it. But I'll survive. What about Carole?"

The attorney helped himself to a seat in the reception area, and Mags joined him. She should have been embarrassed by her poor hostess skills, but she was so tired and worried, she simply didn't care that she could visualize her mother's disapproving stare.

"Your friend is in a bad situation."

"But she didn't kill that miserable little man. I'd stake my life on

104

it."

'I'm right there with you." He reached into his case and pulled out a yellow legal pad covered in writing. "There's no way this woman is guilty. But because she has no way to prove she's innocent, she's already given up the fight."

"She told you that?"

"Verbally, and with her body language. She's already laid down on the table, waiting for them to inject the execution chemicals."

Mags jumped from her seat. The mental image of her friend about to be executed was too real and very uncomfortable. "Wyatt, we can't let this happen."

"I couldn't agree more. But it's very difficult to help someone who won't even meet you half way."

"Can I talk to her?"

"That's up to the sheriff."

"Can you go back to see her and take me with you?"

"Sure. But…"

"But nothing. Let's go." She grabbed her purse, fished in her pocket for the door key, and locked up. They were soon on their way, walking, to the jail.

"Did you get back into town without arousing suspicion?"

"So far, so good. But I'm still waiting for the other shoe to drop."

"That's a shame, especially when you live in such a beautiful place."

Mags had to agree. The sky was so perfect, she felt as if she could reach up and touch the blue dome. Even in mid-afternoon, the sun was delivering just the right amount of heat and light, and the birds were united in concert. Out on the lake several water craft could be seen, and the downtown was bustling and jiving with visitors and townsfolk alike.

"I may have to buy a house here." The attorney had stopped walking and was turning around to get a panoramic view.

"Say what?"

"This place is great. I'm going to have to bring Christine back. She'll be in love. I guarantee it."

"I know a real estate agent who could help you. That is, if you don't care that she's reputed to have difficult clients wiped out." Mags blushed at her brashness. "I'm sorry. You can tell how this has torn me out of the frame." She pulled herself up to her full five-feet-five. "Besides, I'm sleep deprived."

"Not to worry. I'm a lawyer. I'll match my background with yours any day."

The two soon arrived at the jail, where the first face they saw was Sheriff Wiley's.

Does he ever leave the office, Mags wondered?

"You back already?"

"Yes, Sheriff, I am. And I need to talk with my client again."

The lawman turned to Mags. "I told you to call me later this afternoon." He fingered his chin. "But I don't think you're gonna be able to see Carole today."

"Oh, yes she is, Sheriff. Mrs. Gordon is going in with me to talk with my client."

"Huh?"

"You heard me. Mrs. Gordon is here with me, at my request."

With visibly poor graces, the sheriff instructed a deputy to bring the prisoner back to the visiting area. "You two can go through this way," he directed. "Mrs. Gordon, you need to leave your purse here." He exaggerated the words and stretched Mrs. into three syllables. "I'll have to go through your case again, Mr. Lawyer."

The sheriff was being extremely condescending, and it was clear that he understood what he was doing. Without complaint, however, both Mags and the attorney submitted to his demands.

As they were led down the hallway, Mags was horrified at the filth and the desolate air of defeat that screamed from every corner. No wonder Carole was so depressed. There was nothing to inspire confidence or hope. But nothing had prepared Mags for the sight of her friend in the drab olive jumpsuit, either. Her face wore no make-up, and the normally tidy, shoulder-length red hair was sticking out in all directions.

"Mags!" Carole cried, when the two caught sight of each other. "What are you doing here?"

"I'm worried about you, so I came to see what's going on." It killed Mags not to be able to embrace her friend, but Wyatt had already warned her that no touching could happen, or they would be escorted out.

Carole fell back into the chair across the visitor's table, and put her head down on her arms. Defeated, Mags thought, didn't begin to describe her friend's attitude.

"Carole. Mags and I need to talk to you."

"Look. Like I told you before. I can't afford a lawyer. Besides, the deck is stacked against me."

"The deck is not stacked against you, Carole. You've got to believe that."

The prisoner raised her head. "My gun killed him. They found my gun hidden on your boat within feet of where his body was."

"But you didn't kill him. And you didn't put the gun there."

"Prove it."

"Look, Carole," Wyatt said, and Mags was amazed at the gentle nature of his voice. "There's no evidence to connect you with the murder. It was your gun, but they cannot put that gun in your hand. They can't prove that you pulled the trigger."

Carole's eyes blazed, the first sign of fight Mags had seen. "And I can't prove that I didn't kill him. So we're at a stand-off."

"That's the beauty of the whole deal, Carole. They have to prove that you killed HJH. You don't have to prove that you didn't."

"But Mags, Malcolm says they CAN prove it."

"How?"

"I don't know," she wailed. "But he told me I might as well confess, because it would make things go so much faster and easier."

"Easier for him," Wyatt interjected. "Now listen, Carole. You've got to work with me on this, or you will be railroaded." The attorney leaned across the table, so close, the deputy standing nearby had actually moved so he could be certain no contact was occurring.

Carole spread out her hands on the scarred, laminate table top. "I appreciate what both of you are trying to do, but like I told you, Mr. Fulton, I can't afford you. I just wish I understood who sent you here."

"It doesn't matter, Carole. He is here, and you've got to have an attorney. In the morning you'll go before the judge, and we've got to try to get you out on bail. Don't worry about the Good Samaritan who's paying the bill."

The prisoner's eyes brightened. "Do you think there's a chance I can get out? You don't have a clue how bad this is."

"We're going to ask for bail. How much can you raise?"

Carole's face fell. "Not much," she confessed. "So I guess we're right back where we started. I'm going to be living here for a while."

The prospect of her friend literally being held prisoner in such surroundings bothered Mags more than she could explain. "Don't give up before we even know where we're going. Let's get the judge to set bail, then we'll see how we can raise it." She glanced around the depressing space. "We're going to get you out of here if it's the last thing we do."

"Carole, let's talk about the gun." The attorney had seized control of the conversation.

"What about it?"

"When's the last time you saw it? Now think. The very last time, when was it?"

Carole didn't answer at first, but her face betrayed the depth of confusion that plagued her. Finally, "Like I told Mags and the Sheriff, the last time I saw it was when my father brought it to the office.

That's when I stuck it up in the cabinet out of sight. I'm afraid of guns," she wailed.

"You're positive you didn't take it down at some later date?"

"That's what I told you. What, you don't believe me?"

"I'm not doubting your honesty. I just need to be sure there wasn't a time, later, that you've forgotten."

"So if you never took it out again, how did it get on board the *One True Love*?" Mags decided to get back into the game. The stakes were too high and the consequences of failure too great.

"I don't know," Carole wailed. "You have to believe me. I... don't... know!"

"We do believe you," Mags reassured her friend, and physically held herself back to keep from touching her. "But somehow, some way, that gun got out of the office."

"Has anything happened out of the ordinary at the office in the last few weeks?" Wyatt asked. "Something that maybe didn't seem that big of a deal then, but in hindsight might be significant?"

Carole's hands went to her head in a gesture of frustration and resignation, her fingers kneaded her scalp. Finally, in a voice heavily laced with resignation, she said, "There was that morning the back door was unlocked." Her face mirrored uncertainty. "But that couldn't have anything to do with this." Mags watched the grief in her friend's body language relax a little. "Could it?"

"Can you think of anything else, any other time?" The lawyer's tone was kind, yet probing.

Again, the look of confused panic swept over Carole. "There's nothing else that comes to mind."

"Then that almost has to be when it happened. When was that?"

"Not that long ago, say maybe a week, maybe a little longer, before Mags discovered HJH's body."

"Carole," Mags exclaimed. "You never told me about that."

"Didn't think it was important. I just figured when we put the trash out the evening before, we failed to flip the deadbolt home.

We've done it before. Besides, this is Crabapple Cove."

Mags knew her friend was right. In fact, forgetting to secure the back door had become a running joke in the office. "Still, that has to be when it happened. So the question is, did we leave the office vulnerable or did someone break in?"

"Someone went into that office specifically to get Carole's gun," Wyatt volunteered. "I'd think it too much of a coincidence that you left the door unlocked on the same night they planned to burgle the office. They broke in, alright."

"But who knew the gun was there?" Carole begged. "Who knew? Even I'd forgotten it until all this came up."

"And why Carole's gun?" Mags asked. "If you want a gun to kill someone, there are much easier ways to get one than by breaking into our office. We sell real estate, not firearms" She felt completely flummoxed and ran both hands through her hair. "So who? And why?"

"Yeah," Carole volunteered, "just answer those two simple questions and we'll know everything."

"Okay, Carole. I see that deputy giving us the eye, so we'd better cut this short."

Carole's face fell and Mags' heart split in two.

"Before we go, I need to hear from you."

Carole's eyebrows rose, but she said nothing.

"Do you want me as your attorney? Despite the fact that you aren't paying me, do you want me to represent you in the preliminary hearing tomorrow?"

"I don't have much choice, do I?" Her face colored. "I'm sorry, I don't mean anything against you." She appeared to fight for composure. "Yes, I want you by my side, and I don't care how you're getting paid."

"Great! That's all I needed to know."

"But you also have to know that I didn't kill him. I didn't!" Tears puddled in the corner of her eyes, and panic was written over her entire body.

Her outburst was so loud the deputy took several cautious steps toward the table. Wyatt waved him off. "Everything's okay," he said quietly, in an effort to further appease the guard.

"Now you leave all of this in my hands, and I'll see you in court in the morning," he assured her. He and Mags rose to leave, then Wyatt turned back. "One more thing, Carole. Regardless of how hard they question you, I don't care how badly you want to proclaim your innocence, say nothing. Absolutely nothing, unless I'm with you, and only then if I give you the go ahead to speak."

"I understand," she said in a small, quiet voice. Her shoulders slumped and, when she responded to the guard's touch and waited to be escorted back to her cell, Mags could see defeat written all over her friend's body.

Neither of them said anything until she and the attorney were safely outside the jail, on their way back to Mags' office. The sun was dipping into the west, making beautiful saffron highlights that peeped in and around the various mountain peaks. Only Mags didn't see any of the beauty that normally helped her bring each day in her new life to a close. "Carole's in deep trouble, isn't she?"

"Yes, and no." Wyatt pulled off his suit coat and flipped it over his shoulder. "It's like I told her… they absolutely cannot put the gun in her hand, much less prove that she pulled the trigger. That means they have, at best, a circumstantial case."

"And that's in her favor, right?"

"Right. What works against her is that we don't have any stronger circumstantial evidence to prove otherwise. She was at home. Alone. It's her word against theirs."

"Meaning?"

"Meaning it's all going to come down to how the jury sees everything."

Mags felt sick to her stomach as she fitted the key into the front door lock and let them back into the office. As she made her way over to her desk, she noticed the message light blinking on the phone console. In the meantime, Wyatt wandered into the back hallway, where he examined the door that seemed to figure so prominently in Carole's defense.

"After all this time, there's no need to have this door dusted for prints. But what I do see immediately is that this door was not jimmied or forced open."

"You're saying somebody used a key to come in?"

"Either that, or they had someone with professional locksmith skills to open it."

"They wanted to get in mighty bad."

"It looks that way."

Mags turned to her computer to put it down for the night and realized she had several new e-mails in her box. She knew if she let them wait until morning, she'd wonder all night if there was something important. A flick of her mouse and she was quickly into her new mail. Several were obviously junk and she made quick work of trashing them. Two of the three remaining messages related to upcoming closings, and were status reports from the mortgage brokers. As she opened the final e-mail, she realized she didn't recognize the sender's address. What's more, there wasn't anything in the subject line. She clicked to open the message.

You're as guilty as Carole. Both of you killed that man. Don't think you're in the clear. Sooner, rather than later, they'll catch up with you. Enjoy your jail cell. Bet you've never peddled prison property before.

Mags couldn't hold back the rapid intake of breath. Wyatt heard it, and asked, "What's wrong? You're white as a ghost."

"Come... here...," she managed to stammer. "Look at... look at this." She swiveled her chair out of the way, as the attorney bent to look at her monitor. Mags saw his entire body do a double-take.

"Wow! Who sent this?"

"I don't have a clue," Mags admitted. She would have said more, but the events of the past few days had finally exacted a toll greater than she was able to pay. "What can happen next?"

"Unfortunately," Wyatt admitted, "several possibilities come to mind." He looked again at the e-mail still open on the screen and read it aloud. "This is no accident. It was sent with a mission in mind."

"What should I do? I mean..." Mags couldn't make everything connect.

He didn't answer. Instead, his fingers began to pound the keys and, when he had finished, he said, "Look at this."

Mags pulled her chair back into position to read what he had typed.

Your threats will do you no good. They are harassment and will be treated as such. Your e-mail has been forwarded to the authorities, who will be able to identify you.

"Can they really?"

"Really what?"

"Did you send this to someone? Is there a way to track down this scumbag?"

Mags could feel her temper rising, and was encouraged that she hadn't lost her mettle.

Wyatt turned around and braced himself against the edge of Mags' desk. "There are ways to trace an e-mail back to its sender. But, no, I didn't send this message to anyone. At least, not yet."

"So you think we should reply?"

"Do you have a problem with it?"

In response, Mags reached over, grabbed the mouse, and clicked "send". "This whole thing just gets more and more bizarre."

"I'll admit, this does change the color of a few things and further convinces me that this whole deal is a gigantic vendetta against Carole and you."

"What'd we do?"

"I guess this is just one more question we need to answer. How close are you to being ready to leave? Dinner's on me."

"Let me check the answering machine and switch to the night

message and put my computer down, and I'm more than good to go." At the same time she was punching the message retrieval button.

You have three new messages.

The first call was from yet another listing client wanting to cancel. "They're going to cancel me right into the poor house." The next message was a request for information from an out-of-state potential client. "Or maybe I won't go to the poor house just yet."

She and Wyatt were laughing about Mags' latest aside, when the third message began to play.

You're as guilty as Carole and, because of you two, a man is dead. How can you live with that? Your days of freedom are numbered.

It was a man's voice speaking, but Mags had already lost what little starch remained in her body. "Oh, Wyatt, this is all getting too ugly, too confusing. It's crazy…"

"Check your Caller ID. See if it shows where this call originated. Do you recognize the voice?"

"There's the handset. You check. I'm too wiped out to even think straight."

He inspected the phone. "Blocked. It came from a number that was programmed as unknown."

"I've never heard that voice before."

"Slide out of the way." Wyatt Knelt in front of Mags' computer that was still to be put to bed. He called up the offending message, clicked forward, and typed in an address and a quick message. He hit send.

"I've sent that e-mail to a private detective who does technology-related work for me from time to time. Let's see what he can uncover."

"How long will that take?"

"Could be several days, so don't sit here holding your breath."

"You got any better suggestions."

"Yeah, dinner. I'm starved."

Mags had to admit she was feeling some hunger pangs herself, despite the fact that her eyes were drooping fast and furious. "I just hope I can stay awake."

Wyatt was closing down the computer. "Bring one of the real estate catalogs with us. We'll find Christine a weekend house while we eat."

They went in two vehicles to one of the more popular restaurants in the area. After they'd enjoyed salad and chicken marsalla, followed by generous slabs of homemade key lime pie, the two parted company.

"I'll be at the courthouse before nine o'clock in the morning. Carole's appearance before the judge is set for nine-forty-five. But I want time to talk to her first," Wyatt explained as he slid behind the wheel of his Mercedes.

"I'll see you there."

"And Mags, try to get some sleep tonight. I know that's easier said than done."

"Ordinarily, it would be. But between no rest last night, plus all that I've just eaten, I hope I can get home before sleep kicks in."

"See you tomorrow."

Mags pointed her vehicle toward The Slop Bucket, and tried to concentrate on the now-dark roads that challenged her safe journey home. There's something weird going on, she told herself. In the back of her mind, something so minute she couldn't put her finger on it, kept rising to the surface and taunting her. But try as she might, she couldn't bring it into focus. She believed in her gut if she could zero in on what was bothering her, many of their questions would be answered.

Only it wouldn't happen that night. Her brain was dead and her body was close behind.

Sleep. It was, she decided as she snuggled down into her covers, one of the sweetest words in the English language.

Chapter Seven

THERE'S SOMETHING CROOKED IN THERE

"No bail," the judge had announced. Despite eloquent arguments from Wyatt, and very little substantial evidence to the contrary, the defendant would stay in jail indefinitely. Mags saw Carole's face drop and watched her friend's body sway, nearly falling. Had her attorney not quickly placed his arm around her waist, Carole would have hit the floor. Mags knew that her own heart hit hard. It was a curve she hadn't seen coming.

As the deputy led her friend away, Mags mouthed the words, "I'll see you soon. Keep your chin up." When Wyatt joined her in the back of the courtroom, she demanded, "What just happened here? Carole doesn't deserve to be locked up."

Wyatt grabbed her arm and bent his head toward her ear. "Don't say anything until we're outside." He propelled her through the hallways, out into the parking lot. The skies were gray and overcast, and there was a feel of rain in the air. But the skies couldn't come close to the black mood that had captured Mags' emotions. She was about ready to turn on the waterworks herself.

"Why, Wyatt?" she wailed "Why isn't Carole out here with us?" If she had been a child, Mags was certain she would have thrown herself to the ground and pitched the grand champion of all tantrums.

As it was, she tried, with only limited success, to control herself.

"There's something crooked in there and it smells to high heaven."

"You mean...?"

"That judge had his mind made up before Carole's case was ever called. He didn't even consider anything we had to say."

"What do you mean?"

"Sheriff Wiley. Is he honest? Does he have a private agenda?"

Mags debated how to answer the questions and, in the end, decided Carole's welfare demanded that she share with the attorney everything she knew. She eyed the western horizon and noted that the sky was turning still darker. "Let's go back to my office. It looks like it's going to rain. Besides, we'll have more privacy there."

Once settled on the loveseats in the reception area, Mags began to explain. "I wouldn't trust Malcolm Wiley any farther than I could throw him, but then I have good reason to be biased."

"You and the sheriff have a past?"

"We do. Only not in the way you're imagining. Get comfortable."

When she finished explaining how Malcolm Wiley had been in her life since before she and Franklin married, and how the two men had aided and abetted each others' extra-marital activities, Wyatt looked at her and said, "My hat is off to you. I never knew the details of your divorce, but that's some more story."

"So you see, Malcolm holds several grudges against me. I can only assume that he might transfer some of that hatred onto Carole. Even though they both graduated together from Crabapple Cove High School, I don't think they belong to a mutual admiration society."

"But would the good sheriff go so far as to buy a judge or bribe a juror?"

Mags had to think about that one, so she held up one finger to ask for indulgence. She didn't want to allow her own emotions to unfairly convict the sheriff. "I don't think that Malcolm believes there's anything wrong with whatever he does. So, yes, bribing a juror or paying off a judge for a verdict he needed would be right down his alley."

"But…"

"Hang on. I'm getting there. I do think that he sees himself as the high sheriff and that whatever he does, whatever he wants to do, is okay, because he says it is."

"That's an interesting take."

"Malcolm is an interesting man, and it's only been in the last year or so that I've come to understand just how many different facets there are to his personality."

"So, in answer to my question, you think it's entirely possible that our judge this morning was "persuaded" to rule the way he did."

"I'm afraid so."

The dark skies outside had finally turned loose their burden, and Mags got up to open the door to watch the rain come down. Somehow, it matched the mood of the moment, she thought.

Wyatt came to stand beside her. "I've got to hit the road back to Atlanta, but I want to go back by the jail and talk to Carole before I leave. I'm sure she needs some encouragement right about now."

"Are you going to be able to get her out of this?"

"It's definitely going to be more difficult, but knowing the nature of the creature we're fighting will help tremendously. I just wish I'd known before we got into court this morning."

Shame consumed Mags. "I should have told you everything. Only it never occurred to me that Malcolm would go to such lengths."

"And we don't have any proof that he did. Just like he doesn't have any concrete proof that Carole murdered that man."

"But you do believe that Malcolm messed where he had no business?"

"There's no other explanation for that judge's behavior."

"So what now?"

"I'll have to mount a full-fledged investigation and hire private detectives."

"Then do it. I don't care if I have to liquidate this agency. I will not sit by and watch my best friend be railroaded for something she didn't do."

"I thought you'd feel that way."

"Now," Mags told him. "You're going to need some money. How much and I'll write you a check?"

Wyatt tossed an amount into the air and Mags agreed. "Let me get my checkbook."

While she was digging in her purse for her money market account book, Wyatt excused himself to call his office. When he returned, Mags could tell he was talking to his wife. "I'm telling you, honey, you'll fall in love with this place. One of my clients here is a real estate broker, and she's already shown me listings for several houses I think you'll love." He gave Mags a thumbs-up sign. "Hey, maybe we can schedule it where you come with me the next time. Then we could look at property together."

He put his hand over his phone. "Christine loves the idea." He returned the phone to his mouth. "I love you honey. I'll try to be home by six. I've got to go by the office when I get back to town."

"She's excited. Christine has been begging for a second home for quite some time, but I've not found any place I cared to invest my money. Something tells me that's about to change."

Mags handed him the check she'd written. "Remember, we have to do whatever it takes, whatever it costs, to get Carole out of this."

"I understand." He bid her goodbye and dashed out into the rain that continued to fall. Mags stood at the door and watched until his car's red tail lights disappeared out of sight. The sound of the falling rain made her want to lock the door and sack out on one of the couches. It was the perfect day for sleeping. Then she remembered her friend, who was stuck in a small, dark and smelly cell, whose days ahead would be far from perfect if Wyatt wasn't able to negotiate her release on bail.

There was no business to handle, and the rain, which looked like it had set in for the long haul, meant there would be no one wanting to look at property. Mags decided to make better use of her time. After setting the phone and turning out the lights, she posted the closed sign and locked the door.

Her first stop was the drug store where she bought magazines and candy bars. Then she went to Carole's house, where she collected toiletries and other personal items that she placed in the bag with her purchases. On the list beside her friend's kitchen phone, she searched until she found Carole's father's cell phone number. Praying there would be a receptive signal in Montana or Wyoming, or wherever it was he was hunting or fishing, or whatever he was supposed to be doing, she entered the number and was rewarded with the first ring. Mags also prayed that her friend would forgive this intrusion into her personal life.

"Hello. Who is this calling?" a man's voice on the other end demanded.

"Mr. Pickett?"

"That's right. But who are you? Talk quick, I'm going in and out of range."

"This is Mags Gordon, Carole's employer."

"Oh, Mags. Why didn't you say so? I didn't recognize your number."

"Can you get stationary so we can be sure the signal holds? I've got to talk to you about Carole."

"Carole? Is something wrong? Is she sick?"

Mags hesitated. How did you break news such as this? She finally decided that quick and sure was the best course of action. "I'm sorry to tell you this, but Carole is in jail."

"Jail? Whatever for? She's never even gotten a parking ticket."

"I'm afraid it's much worse than a traffic citation. Carole's been charged with murder."

"Murder?"

"I'm afraid so."

"I've never heard anything so ridiculous. Carole wouldn't hurt anyone. Who's she supposed to have killed?"

Mags hesitated. "Mr. Humphries, our client that was such a pain in the neck." She recalled that Mr. Pickett had left on his trip before their lives had been turned upside down. "He was killed with the gun you bought Carole almost two years ago."

"Carole didn't kill him."

"Sheriff Wiley thinks otherwise."

Silence reigned from the other end, and Mags feared they'd been disconnected. Finally a defeated voice asked, "What proof do they have that my little girl murdered that man?"

"Ballistics tests prove that the fatal bullets came from her gun. Carole's prints were on the gun. And they found the gun hidden on board my boat, the *One True Love*, which is where I found Mr. Humphries dead body."

"That's all? They can't place her at the scene of the crime? Or you?"

"Neither of us have alibis, but neither can they put us there, or prove that Carole pulled the trigger."

"If that don't take all!"

"According to the sheriff, Carole tried once to call you, but you were evidently out of signal range. She thought she could deal with this herself. Only I'm afraid she's in over her head."

"Maybe she tried, and maybe Malcolm's lying. Either way, she needs a lawyer, but I don't know who to get."

"I've taken care of that." She went on to explain what had gone down in court earlier that morning. "I agreed with Carole that we shouldn't interrupt your trip, since we all thought she'd be out on bail this morning. After it became clear she wouldn't be released, I made the decision to find you."

"Carole doesn't know you're calling me." It was a statement and not a question.

"No sir, she doesn't. Although I'm going to tell her that I've talked with you. I'm going to the jail as soon as I leave here."

"You tell her we've talked, and you tell her I'll be there sometime tomorrow. Just as soon as I can get a plane out of here."

"Thank you, Mr. Pickett. I think Carole needs you worse than even she realizes."

"Thank you for calling me. Now tell me one thing, and give it to me straight. Do you think she's guilty?"

"Definitely not. But I fear she's going to become Malcolm's easy-out resolution to a murder."

Mags heard what sounded like a snort, and wondered if their connection was breaking up. "Malcolm Wiley wouldn't have enough gumption or expertise to pour piss out of a boot with the instructions written on the heel."

While she realized she wouldn't have expressed it in just that way, Mags was forced to agree fully with his assessment. She filled in a few more details, then ended the call with her assurances that she would contact him again if anything changed. In return, he promised to call her as soon as his travel details were confirmed.

She locked Carole's house and headed to the jail, where she had to fight with the sheriff to get permission to see her friend. Despite his protests that it wasn't regulation visiting time, she stuck to her guns. After having her purse confiscated, enduring a more intrusive pat-down than she really thought necessary, and having her purchases and the toiletry items inspected, she was finally escorted into the visiting room. It was more than fifteen minutes before Carole was brought through the door on the other side. Mags was shocked at her appearance.

"Are you alright?" she queried before Carole was even settled in the prisoner's chair. Her friend had aged twenty years in just the span of a few short hours, and Mags heart ached. "We're going to get you out of here. I promise."

"It's hopeless," Carole mumbled, her head hung low. "I'm never going to get out."

"Don't say that. Wyatt is working right now on a new strategy."

In a broken, quiet voice, she said, "A new strategy isn't going to do any good when it's the same old Malcolm Wiley."

Mags pondered what her friend had said, and had to admit, but only to herself, that there might be a malignant nugget of truth in those words. "I'm sorry that my problems with Malcolm have ensnared you. In a million years I could never have imagined this."

Neither could she have ever imagined she'd be sitting in a filthy, drab jail visitor's room, talking to her best friend who was accused of a murder she didn't commit. There was nothing cheery about the place, Mags decided. From the grime-coated windows to the broken floor tiles, not to mention the accumulated dirt in the corners, the entire place had an air of neglect and abandonment. And every time the door to the cell block opened, Mags caught the very distinct odor of diluted, urine-laced disinfectant. The stench made her nauseous. She could only imagine how much more potent it was back in the cell area. How could Carole tolerate such, she wondered? Then she took another look at her friend and realized, with sadness, that Carole was deteriorating right before her eyes. Between the emotional and the physical, her friend was down for the count.

She was forbidden to touch her friend, but if ever a person needed a hug, or at least a pat on the hand, it was Carole. "I have something to tell you, but you have to look at me. Hold your head up and look at me."

At first there was no response, then, slowly, Carole raised her head. Her eyes were red and swollen; her face was tear-stained. But what squeezed Mags' heart the hardest was the tiniest flicker of hope that she saw in her friend's eyes.

"Promise you won't be mad, but I talked to your dad."

"My dad? How did he happen to call you?"

"He didn't. Carole, I called him. He needs to be here."

There was an unmistakable bolt of lightning that shot from the prisoner's eyes. "I didn't want him to know."

Mags struggled to maintain her equilibrium. "This has gone far beyond what it should, and we need all the allies we can get. Besides," she said in a voice that was rapidly heading toward pleading, "don't you think he would be furious to get back and find out that all this went down, and no one called him?"

"He'd get over it."

"I'm sorry if I over-stepped my bounds, but I've never seen you so determined... so angry. Why?"

Carole's head dropped again. "It's a long story."

"I've got all day. What's more, I'm going to sit here until you tell me what's going on."

She had begun to think her friend had taken a vow of silence when, at last, Carole's mouth began to move. Mags had to lean in to hear the words, and she soon understood why her friend was talking so softly. She didn't want anyone to overhear.

"You know Malcolm and I were in school together. My dad was the football coach. There was an incident between Dad and the sheriff that has never been resolved. I didn't kill HJH, but I'm afraid if my dad gets involved in this, he'll be sitting in here for killing Malcolm."

"Surely it can't be that bad? What was that? Twenty-five years ago?"

"Dad hates Malcolm Wiley with a vengeance."

"But your dad is so laid-back."

Carole shrugged her shoulders. "About most things, he is. When it comes to our good sheriff, that's another matter entirely."

Mags remembered Mr. Pickett's rather crude assessment of the sheriff's intelligence during their conversation. "So what happened?"

"I'll give you the down and dirty details later. You know Malcolm thinks he's a stud; he was that way in school, too. Thought the girls ought to fight over him. I didn't see it that way, so he retaliated by trying to trash my reputation. Dad caught him red-handed."

"I imagine your dad was one unhappy man."

Carole snickered. In her eyes, Mags could see that she was reliving that time. "That's putting it mildly. Dad was livid, and it got even worse when Malcolm was elected sheriff. Dad literally has no use for the man."

Mags hesitated before she spoke, analyzing the new facts she'd just been given. "I didn't know any of this," she confessed. "But I still think it's time we brought your dad into the loop. Most especially since Malcolm appears to have an axe to grind with the both of us."

Her friend sighed, and Mags took the long and labored emission as agreement. "Look, I've got to go. Your dad will call me later to let me know when he's getting in."

When Carole raised her head again, Mags saw that fresh tears were carving new tracks on her friend's face, as she said, "Thank you. I don't know what I'd do without you." Then she signaled the deputy that she was ready to leave.

Mags retrieved her purse from the front desk and quickly made her escape from the jail that had taken on more dungeon-like qualities the longer she remained. It was not, she decided, once they finally gained Carole's freedom, a place she would ever visit again.

Outside the jail, the rest of the day showed promise of being one of bright sun and gentle breezes, indigo skies and let-your-hair-down opportunities. Or perhaps, Mags thought, looking at the world through jaundiced eyes, the dismal jail was making the outside world and freedom look that much better. Either way, she decided, she would choose the outside world.

Back at the office she checked e-mail and phone messages. Only spam showed up in her incoming mailbox, and she thought once again about the harassing message she'd received the day before. After scanning all the new messages a second time, there was no response to the reply Wyatt had sent the anonymous mailer. A quick listen to the messages revealed no new threatening calls. Mags breathed a cautious sigh of relief.

Unable to concentrate on business, and only too-painfully-aware there was basically no business awaiting her, Mags decided to invest her time and energies elsewhere. The flowerbeds around the office demanded attention. She needed something to do, to keep herself from going stir-crazy, so she headed to The Slop Bucket to change into work clothes and get her gardening tools.

Several hours and one late lunch delivered from the Eat and

Greet later, Mags shoved herself up from the squatting position. Every muscle in her body was screaming in protest, but the beds had never looked better. What's more, she'd been able to use the time while she worked to re-process all that she knew about HJH, and how he had used her agency for some nefarious game she had yet to understand.

"Margaret! What are you doing?"

At the sound of an unfamiliar male voice, Mags twisted to look in the direction of her visitor. When she did, her lower back muscles seized, and she toppled over.

As she struggled to right herself, she heard, "Here. Let me help you. Didn't mean to startle you." In a matter of seconds she felt strong hands on her shoulders and she was upright, looking up into the face of Dwayne Watkins, a not-too-distant neighbor to The Slop Bucket.

"You took quite a tumble there. You okay?"

How graceful I must have looked, Mags thought. "Here. Give me your hand. Help me up."

Her visitor complied, and in a moment, Mags was standing, but not without some discomfort.

"Thank you. I guess I overdid it today, but once I got started, it felt so good to have my hands in the dirt."

"I know what you mean. I raise daylilies. I'm always at peace when I'm playing with them."

"Mags liked the way he used the word play to describe what most would consider work. She told him so.

"To me it is play. I just wish I could get someone to pay me."

"I love to garden; I just don't get many chances to do it. But today I was in the mood." She rubbed her back. "Unfortunately, my body wasn't as ready as my mind was."

His laugh was comfortable. Contagious, too, Mags realized. "Say. What are you doing tonight?"

"Tonight? Something tells me I've got a date with a giant tube of pain cream." She was immediately wary, wondering what this man's motive was. After all, she didn't know him THAT well.

"I wondered if you'd like to have dinner with me. Nothing fancy."

Mags considered. She had not dated at all since her divorce, and had been surprised to discover that she was able to feel complete without a man in her life. Still… there was something about the prospect of going out on a gentleman's arm that was still enticing.

"Sure," she said. "I'd love to have dinner with you. Provided you'll wait until I get cleaned up and presentable, and don't object if my perfume smells very similar to old-age rub.

"It's a deal." He looked at his watch. "Seven-thirty work for you? That gives you about three hours."

"I'm moving slowly, but seven-thirty should work fine."

"Great. See you shortly."

I've just agreed to go out on a date, she reminded herself. I never thought I'd be on that merry-go-round again.

Mags finished the last of the weeding, gathered her tools and loaded them into the Jeep. After checking the office back door, she pulled the front door closed behind her. Then she unlocked the same door to re-enter the office. She knew if she didn't check both the phone and the computer, she'd lay awake all night wondering about more threatening messages. To her relief there were none. She re-locked the office and left.

"You look nice," her date said when she opened the door to admit him. "In fact, you clean up exceptionally well."

Mags shared the laugh with him and didn't take the joke personally, knowing that he had seen her at her worst. While she turned on the outside lights and prepared to lock up, Dwayne played with Delilah, who responded with enthusiasm.

"She usually doesn't take to strangers, especially men," Mags told him. "You should be honored."

"I'm a dog person and she can tell. I've got two cocker spaniels. I imagine she probably smells them."

"Aren't dogs wonderful?"

"Hey." He spread his arms apart and opened his hands. "I love my dogs better than I do some two-legged members of my family." He laughed again, and Mags truly felt it catching. She also remembered that her neighbor was a widower, whose wife had died with cancer about the time she got her divorce.

"I imagine your dogs are good company for you." She bent to scratch Delilah's ears. "I don't know what I'd do without this little lady in my life."

"Same here. After Delores got sick, our two were her constant companions. So I kind of feel like I've still got a little piece of her here with me."

"It must have been rough."

"It was. But then I don't imagine divorce was any piece of cake."

"It wasn't. If I'd known how much it would hurt, I wouldn't have had the guts to do it." She tossed a treat to the dog. "It felt like deliberately walking in front of a firing squad and begging, 'shoot me!'."

"I can only imagine." He extended his arm to her. "But there's nothing either of us can do to change the past, so how's about we head out in the present, for what I hope will be an enjoyable evening with good company and good food?"

"Lead on." Mags turned out the overhead light in the great room. "I'm looking forward to both."

It was a good evening. Dwayne had selected a small, home-grown eatery on the banks of Lake Boyard, where fresh-caught lake trout, dredged in pecan dust and the restaurant's special mix of seasonings, found its way to both their plates. In between bites of fish and fresh-baked sweet potatoes and Cole slaw with an extra twang that Mags couldn't identify, their conversation was spirited but low-key. They talked about Dwayne's daylilies and Mags' full-time transition to the mountains. He explained how his background in management had allowed him to retire to the mountains early, while continuing to work from home as a consultant. She confessed that real estate had just been a parlor game among her social set in Atlanta, but when she was finally divorced, it had proven to be her only means of support.

The evening couldn't be going much better, Mags thought, admitting silently to herself that she was enjoying Dwayne's company much more than she would have thought possible. That's why, when things went south, they went south in a hurry. It all began so innocently.

"So what's this I hear about you finding a body on your boat? Man, this bread pudding is fantastic, but there must be a half-pint of bourbon in this one bite." He laughed. "If we get stopped by the law going home, I hope you have some magic pull. I'll test over the legal limit for sure." There was that laugh again.

"Then you better stop eating right now, because if they see that I'm with you, those daylilies of yours will be blooming again next year before you see freedom."

"You're kidding. Right?"

"Afraid not, my friend." She proceeded to give him the condensed version of all that had gone down since the morning she first found the body. "What's worse, the sheriff has tunnel vision. He's not even looking for the real killer. It looks like it's going to be up to me to solve his case for him."

"You? You're a real estate agent. Not a detective." He looked at her quizzically, and Mags suddenly felt as if she were under a microscope. She felt herself shrinking, so as not to be so vulnerable. "Besides, don't you have to have a license to be a detective?"

Mags flushed, but held her tongue, which was no easy matter. "You don't have to be licensed to unofficially investigate a case. Besides, the professionals don't seem to be doing a very good job. They're going to hang my friend and she didn't do it."

"But how can you be so sure?"

Mags fought for control. She glanced around the room and decided that when the old structure had been a lakeside home, the space they were in had probably been a bedroom. The master bedroom perhaps, since it opened onto an outside deck? The restaurant owners hadn't done much in the way of decorating, which made a minimalist statement in and of itself. She might not be a licensed PI, but she'd always done all her own decorating, and to rave reviews at that.

"I know my friend. She's no murderer. That's how I'm certain she's innocent. But the sheriff thinks otherwise. It's going to be up to me to prove him wrong, and clear her name."

Mags could see that her dinner companion was making a herculean effort to keep from laughing. When he could contain his mirth no longer, he burst out laughing so loudly, diners at nearby tables stopped eating and looked on in alarm.

"What's so funny?" Mags demanded. "Are you laughing at me?"

"I'm just trying to picture you with a deerstalker hat on your head, wearing a trench coat and smoking a pipe." He snickered again. "It just doesn't compute."

"Dwayne, you've just insulted me!"

"Aw, come on. You're going to solve a murder case? Let's face it, you're way too old to be playing Nancy Drew, and you're far too beautiful to be Miss Marple."

"Don't try to be cute, Dwayne."

"Margaret. You're the one who's trying to be cute, what with this playing detective routine. You need to leave this to the sheriff and his officers. That's their job."

Mags realized it would be a waste of time and words to continue the argument. Instead, she said, "I'd like to go home, Dwayne. Now, please." Her mother, she decided, would definitely approve of her manners.

"Well, uh. Sure." A look of confusion contaminated the face Mags had found so friendly and comfortable just a few minutes before. "Look, I didn't mean to imply…"

"Just take me home. Please?" She didn't want to discuss the matter further and decided she should have followed her first gut instinct when he asked her out and said "no."

"Whatever." He stuck cash in the payment folio and moved around to pull out her chair. Mags beat him to the draw, and was already standing by the time he got to her side of the table. She allowed him to open the car door for her, because it was his car, but there was no conversation between the two all the way back to The Slop Bucket. To his credit, Dwayne attempted to initiate conversation more than once. Mags never answered the serves.

"I'm terribly sorry if I offended you," Dwayne said again, as he pulled the car to a stop at the base of Mags' side steps. "I hope you'll accept my apology."

Feeling her dead mother's eyes boring holes in her back, Mags replied, "I accept your apology. Thank you for a…" How did she want to describe it? "Thanks for a great meal and great atmosphere."

"I get you." Mags was certain that he did. "Let me get the door for you." He deftly slid out from behind the wheel, came around, opened her door, and extended his hand. Such a gentleman, Mags thought. Franklin never did this, even when we were dating, and he was trying to impress me with what a catch he was.

"Thank you, Dwayne. Now I really must get in the house. Tomorrow promises to be a hard day."

"Good-night Margaret." The sound of sadness in his voice almost made Mags reconsider her position. The memories of how Franklin had belittled her, undermining her self-worth, gave her the rocket boost she needed to stand firm.

"Good-night Dwayne." She let herself into the house and locked the door, dropped onto the sofa, and submitted to Delilah's love kisses. Sometime later she heard Dwayne's car start up and slowly leave the drive. "So much for dating, Delilah." She rubbed the dog's stomach. "I know I've always got you."

Mags wasted little time getting ready for bed and plumped up the pillows behind her, planning to watch TV for a while. Only she couldn't find a program that interested her and, after several minutes of channel-surfing, she finally hit the power button. The screen went black.

When her cell phone rang, the quiet was so loud, she barely managed to hear its soft ringtone. "Hello?"

"Mags. It's Joe Pickett. I'm cleared out of Helena at seven-oh-five in the morning. I should land in Atlanta about twelve-forty-five Georgia time."

"Do you need me to meet you?"

"That's taken care of. A buddy in Atlanta will be there to drive me to Crabapple Cove. I hope we'll be there by five o'clock at the latest."

"What about your truck and all your gear? Didn't you drive out?"

"There are enough guys on this trip, one of them will get it home for me, when the trip is over in another week. I can use Carole's truck."

Mags had never returned the key from her trip to Atlanta. She told him so.

"Just hold on to it. You can hand it to me when I get there."

"Carole doesn't know I took it. She doesn't know that I got Wyatt Fulton to represent her, and please don't tell her."

"Whatever you've spent, I'll pay you back."

"We'll hash that out later. If it weren't for me, she wouldn't be in this jam."

"You mean, if it weren't for Malcolm, don't you?"

"Carole finally told me about the bad blood between the two of you."

"More on his side than on mine. He was wrong and I did my job the way I was supposed to."

Mags detected a note of confidence and peace in his voice. "Malcolm is a piece of work. Was then and hasn't changed any today. That doesn't say much for a man, does it?"

"You have a safe flight and let me know when you get into town."

"Will do. And Mags?"

"Yes?"

"Thank you for looking after my little girl. I couldn't bear to lose her."

Mags choked, and it was a minute before she could say, "You don't owe me any thanks. She's my friend."

"And fortunate she is to have you." Mags thought she detected a sob on the other end. Then he continued, "I apologize for calling so late, but it took some doing to get all the details arranged. I just got everything finalized a few minutes ago."

"It's not too late. Don't worry. Just get here because Carole needs you more than she wants to admit."

"She's always been that way. I'll see you late tomorrow afternoon."

"Goodnight, Mr. Pickett."

She was wide awake with no hopes of going to sleep any time soon. Instead of fighting the bed, she took herself back to the great room, where she crawled up on the couch and called Delilah to her. Once the old dog was settled up against her, and was snoring again, Mags allowed her thoughts to roam.

Her eyelids were drooping, and sleep was beginning to claim her. Mags looked at the clock. It was almost two o'clock. She'd been out of her bed for almost three hours. But she had accomplished something very significant in the time she'd been chilled out on the couch. For starters, she had traveled back over the timeline from the day Horace J. Humphries first darkened the agency's door, up through the previous afternoon. There were too many dovetailing incidents, way more points of similarity for everything to be coincidental. But first and foremost, there was something crooked about HJH, a fact that Sheriff Wiley was conveniently overlooking.

Horace J. Humphries, dead or not, was a fraud. His duplicity had led to his death, she believed. It was obvious that she alone would have to follow that trail. Deep in her gut, she knew if she found the deceased's true identity, she would also find his killer. That was the only way Carole would ever be exonerated.

Mags went to bed with a mission and a plan. It began with getting a good night's sleep. At least out of what remained of the night. And it involved sneaking out of town. Again. Hopefully without Sheriff Wiley being any the wiser.

In her dreams, she wore a trench coat, a deerstalker hat, and carried a pipe. She refused to consider putting the pipe in her mouth, but she was confident that even carrying the smelly thing, no one would recognize Mags Gordon. Mr. Holmes himself should have been so invisible.

Chapter Eight

OUT OF TOWN IN PLAIN SIGHT

Mags rose before dawn, energized and determined, despite the short amount of sleep she'd gotten. In fact, when the alarm sounded, she initially slammed the snooze button and burrowed deeper into the covers. Then she remembered her mission for the day, and her eyes were wide and her body was ready.

Retracing her modus operandi of two days earlier, she parked her Jeep in plain sight and hung the "showing property" sign on the locked office door. Then openly and proudly, with her head held high, she walked up past the café, hung a left and strolled two more blocks, before cutting through several yards to arrive in Carole's back yard, where the truck was parked. Along the way, she met several individuals out jogging during the early-morning cool. She had acknowledged their waves, and even exchanged pleasantries with a couple. All in all, she was well satisfied with how she was about to slip out of town, all the while being in plain sight of so many potential witnesses.

As she backed out of the driveway, she noted the truck had only a quarter of a tank of gas. She would have to fill up before she got to Atlanta, but there was enough fuel to get her well out of Crabapple Cove, before she had to call attention to herself at a gas pump.

The trip down was uneventful. She had stopped for gas some forty miles away, grabbed herself a doughnut and a soft drink, and didn't stop again until she pulled into an alleyway deep in an older, downtown portion of Atlanta. It had been years since she'd been in that part of town.

At the office, before she left, Mags had pulled the folder of information on HJH and copied down the address he had provided. On-line she had searched for directions. What she expected to find, since the area hadn't been residential in many years, was an office building. But try as she might, once she'd gotten her bearings, she couldn't find the address. She found Pryor Street. She circled the area several times, and even found street numbers climbing toward the 9176 location their client had listed on his data sheet. She also found buildings numbered higher than that, but the number she sought simply wasn't to be seen.

In the middle of the block, about where Mr. Humphries' address should have been, a multi-level parking garage that had definitely seen better days slumped back from the street. Thinking perhaps someone there might point her in the right direction, she pulled the truck up almost on the sidewalk, got out and made her way to the toll booth, just inside the structure on the ground level.

"You can't park that truck there, lady," a burly guy with dreadlocks barked as she walked up. You wanna park, you gotta pay."

"I'm lost," she told him. "If you can help me, it won't be there but a minute." As she spoke, she looked around at the almost skid row appearance of the garage. The only thing missing was a couple of winos leaned up against the wall, panhandling. Should she be afraid?

"We sell parking, we ain't no information booth."

"I'm trying to find 9176 Pryor Street, and I don't intend to pay for the information or for the parking."

"Look. Don't get mouthy with me. If the boss man comes by here and sees that truck like that, it's my ass gonna get reamed out."

"Then just point me toward 9176 and I'll move it. With pleasure."

She walked a couple of steps closer, as if to drive home her point. "You've already wasted more time being rude, than it would have taken to answer my question."

"Well, lady. I don't know how to answer you, because you're standing at 9176 right now. What part of that don't you understand?" He pointed to a grimy, faded sign posted above the booth. "Do you even know who you are, 'cause obviously you don't know where you're at?"

Mags recoiled because the sensation of being slapped was that strong. THIS was 9176. She'd found HJH's address, just one more indication that the man wasn't what he claimed to be. What's more, she realized she'd found something she wasn't hunting. Below the street number, which could only be read up close and personal, was a smaller line that read, "These premises owned and operated by Ophelia, Inc."

"Ophelia." That name rang a bell with Mags, who wracked her brain. The explanation was so close, she could feel it, yet she couldn't make the connection.

"Uh… uh, thank you," she managed to stammer. The garage employee stood looking at her like he couldn't decide whether to fear for his safety or her sanity. "They must have written the address down wrong. I'm looking for an office building."

"Yeah, okay lady. Whatever. Now either move your truck or pull it up in here and pay me for parking."

"I'm gone," she mumbled. "I'm gone right now. Sorry." Mags made quick work of getting back behind the wheel. She cranked up and drove off, but her head was reeling. She'd found his address. HJH had used the old vacant lot trick. As she drove, keeping one eye on the clock, she threaded her way out of the downtown area, headed for the expressway. She needed to get back to Crabapple Cove as quickly as possible, before Sheriff Wiley figured out what she was doing.

Traffic was heavy, especially congested for a late weekday morning, and a haze created primarily by exhaust fumes hung over the city for as far as Mags could see. As she negotiated the entrance ramp onto Metropolitan Parkway, the light bulb popped on so suddenly and so brilliantly, she almost drove off the road. Ophelia had been her late mother-in-law's middle name. But of greater importance, it was also the Gordon family's corporate name. All of Franklin's various ventures were subsidiaries of Ophelia, Inc. She had occasionally seen it while they were married.

Question was: how, and why, was Mr. Humphries connected to property that belonged to her ex-husband? Especially when that location was a parking garage, and not an office building or even an attorney's office? The more she learned, the more confused she became. What made it even more difficult, she didn't have anyone to share with, who could bounce it back and forth.

In Crabapple Cove she took back streets to reach Carole's house. It wouldn't do for the sheriff or any of his deputies to see her driving that little red pickup truck, while her own vehicle was parked in front of the office. So far, as best she could tell, no one was aware that she had left town. Again.

As she was pulling into the drive, the sound of Jimmy Buffett singing "Margaritaville" began issuing from her purse. She braked to a stop. "Hello?"

"It's Joe Pickett," the man's voice announced. "We've just left the airport headed that way."

"You don't know how good that is to hear. I'll be at the office when you get to town."

She made quick work of returning the truck to its accustomed space, lest anyone come nosing around, then set off on foot to the center of town. It was more difficult to look cool, calm and collected when you were guilty as sin, and the temperatures had soared to mid-day highs. Still, she managed to appear as nothing more than one of the town's business people out walking.

At the office, she knocked the air conditioning down a couple of notches to help her get cool, kicked off her tennis shoes and pulled on a pair of sandals, and turned on her computer. There were no phone messages. That was good and bad, but she was glad there were no new threats. The e-mail box was full, but most of it was junk. Again, there were no mysterious messages.

While she was on the computer, she decided to Google "Ophelia, Inc." After a few minutes of searching and reading, Mags pushed her chair away from the keyboard. "Man oh man," she said aloud to the empty room. She knew Franklin's family had money. She just never knew they had so many different corporations beneath the Ophelia umbrella. If she knew her ex-husband, there was a shady reason for each one of those companies. But, still, how did that tie in to HJH? Nothing made sense.

It would be at least two more hours before Carole's father arrived, and Mags needed to kill time. There certainly wasn't any work to do. With a sigh of resignation, she went to the supply closet, dragged out the vacuum, the window cleaner, and the furniture polish. For the rest of the afternoon, she attacked all the dirt in the office. Finally there wasn't a speck of dust where none had been before. At least that's what she told herself just before the door opened, and Mr. Pickett walked in.

"Am I ever glad to see you," she told the tall, thick man with a shock of white hair crowning his head. "Carole will be, too."

"How is my girl today?"

"I don't know. I had to sneak into Atlanta this morning, and I've only been back a little while." She went on to explain where she had gone, and why. "Sheriff Wiley refuses to even investigate the matter of Mr. Humphries' true identity, but he does admit that the man was not who he claimed to be."

"Malcolm Wiley doesn't have the sense God gave a goat."

"So just what did go down between you two? Carole was afraid to call you because of that long ago incident." She indicated the couches in the reception area, and he dropped into one of them. She followed suit on the other sofa.

The man scratched his head. "I was head football coach and Malcolm was my quarterback his senior year. He just barely stayed eligible academically, but he fancied himself the campus stud, his and God's gift to women. Most any girl he wanted was only too glad to melt into his arms and… some of them definitely melted into the backseat of the fifty-five Chevy he drove. He wanted Carole bad. I even heard him boasting in the locker room that she would be the biggest notch in his belt. Only Carole wanted nothing to do with him. She told him that, in front of witnesses."

"I'll bet that didn't set well."

He grinned. "Not much it didn't. Anyway, his pride was wounded and he vowed revenge."

"But what could he do? He was just a high school boy with a greatly inflated opinion of himself."

"Never mind that. He carried through with his threat and the next thing I knew, I was being investigated by the high school athletic association."

"For what?"

"For allegedly participating in a gambling operation with the coach of our rival team, where he and I supposedly were paying our players to throw the games."

"You're kidding."

"Wish I were. But I was there." He scratched his head. "It got really ugly."

"So how'd it play out? Obviously you didn't lose your job."

"I thought there for a while that I might, but in the end, we prevailed. Malcolm was shown up for everything he was."

"And…?"

"Malcolm was kicked off the team in the middle of the season, and was expelled from school. Because of that, he didn't get to finish his senior year, and he didn't graduate."

"You're telling me this county's sheriff is a high school drop-out?"

"That's right. I heard he did go later and take his G.E.D., but he never walked with his classmates, and he never got his senior football letter."

"So Malcolm's bitter?"

"Was. I suppose he still is. He vowed then that he would get even with me, if it took him the rest of his life. It felt like the sucker punch of all blows when he was first elected sheriff."

"And now you think he's making good on his threat?"

"From what you tell me has gone down, I'm forced to believe he is."

"Do you think Malcolm would try to buy a judge or a jury?"

"In a heartbeat, but then my objectivity may be warped pretty bad." He grinned again. "Now, I want to go see my little girl. You coming?"

"Thought you'd never ask. I'm right behind you." She turned off the lights, raised the thermostat setting, and locked the door behind them. "I wouldn't miss this for anything in the world."

Mags had braced herself for fireworks and she wasn't disappointed. Once in the sheriff's outer office, a deputy denied them the right to see Carole, claiming it would upset the jail routine. It wasn't an excuse that Joe Pickett bought.

"Now you look here," he thundered. "I didn't fly over two thousand miles to have some two-bit, tin-horn stooge of a deputy tell me I can't see my daughter."

The deputy, clearly unnerved, nevertheless stood from his seat behind the desk and moved his hand to his service revolver, as he said, "You can't talk that way to an officer of the law."

"Th' hell I can't," Mr. Pickett thundered. "Now you just move your hand away from that gun and get the high sheriff out here, before I come across this counter and do it for you."

All the color left the deputy's face and, without moving from where he stood, the officer yelled, "Sheriff! Sheriff Wiley! I need you out here. Now!" Panic was clearly evident in the high squeak of his voice. In a matter of seconds, a closed door at the rear opened and Malcolm Wiley emerged. He definitely lacked the requisite chamber of commerce expression of warm welcome.

"Yeah, what is it?" he asked the deputy, totally ignoring both Mags and his former coach.

"This man, here. I told him he couldn't see Ms. Pickett, and he threatened to come across the counter and take care of me."

Mags saw Malcolm puff up. When he turned to confront them, the sneer on his face was far from pretty. "Well, well, well. Coach. To what do we owe the pleasure?"

"It's Mr. Pickett to you, Malcolm. And I'll tell you like I just told your little puppet here. I've traveled over two thousand miles and I intend to see my daughter. Now."

"Sorry, Coac... er... Mr. Pickett. But that's not possible. The jail is on lock-down right now. Nobody allowed in or out."

"That's crazy, Malcolm," Mags blurted out. "You've only got three prisoners back there, and two of them are habitual violators."

"It's on lock-down and nobody goes in," he barked.

"Then I guess I'll have to take matters into my own hands." Mr. Pickett's voice was so quiet and low, Mags had to strain to hear him. It was the steel in those words, however, that caused her the most concern. She reached out and put her hand on his arm.

"Wait a minute, Mr. P. There's another way to do this." To her relief, she felt the tension in his body lessen, although he never indicated he'd heard anything she'd said. "Okay, sheriff. You're on lock-down. When can we come back to see Carole?"

"The sheriff scratched his chin and made a production out of answering her question. Behind him, a couple of deputies snickered, until they caught Mr. Pickett staring at them, and they quickly stifled their mirth. "I'd say about three forty-five in the morning. We can probably get you in then."

"Why you two-bit shyster, I'll..." Carole's dad bellowed. "I'll..."

"You'll what, Joe?"

"He'll take that visiting time," Mags injected. He and I both will be back here at three-thirty tomorrow morning, in plenty of time for that three forty-five time slot." Then she literally pushed one angry former football coach from the building.

"That sawed-off bastard, I'd like to mop the floor with his fat ass, like I should have done back there in high school." The man, Mags saw, was consumed with rage, and she didn't much blame him. It was only too clear that Malcolm was operating with a personal agenda. "If I'd taken care of him then, all this might not be happening now."

"You're partially right. What just happened is a direct result of that incident years ago. But you didn't have anything to do with Mr. Humphries. For certain, you didn't have anything to do with his death. All of this is connected, only I can't figure out how."

"Still, I come all this distance and now I've got to get up in the middle of the night to see my daughter. Lock-down my ass. The only thing locked down back there is Malcolm Wiley's brain!" Again, he was sputtering.

Mags reached for his arm. "Mr. P, you need to calm down. You won't be any good to Carole if you're laid up with a stroke."

"You're right, and I know that. But I've put up with so much grief out of that idiot, it just tears me a new one that he can call the shots. He's no more qualified to be sheriff than I am to be the Pope."

Mags knew the Picketts were staunch Baptists, and she couldn't help laughing. Fortunately, the sound of her chuckle broke the tension and, soon, he was laughing as well.

"So what now?"

"Tell you what," she suggested. "I know you're tired and probably would like to get a shower."

"Man would I ever. I didn't sleep any last night, then I had to change planes three times, and now it looks like I'll lose another night's sleep." Then, apparently fearful he'd given the wrong impression, he added quickly, "But I'll gladly sacrifice rest to see my daughter."

Mags knew that and quickly reassured him. "Look," she said, "let me drive you to Carole's house to get her truck." She produced the key from her pocket. "You go on home. Get that shower and sack out. I'll call you about two o'clock. We can meet out at the all-night diner on the four-lane and get something to eat, before we go to the

145

jail."

As he got out of Mags' Jeep, he said, "Thank you again for all you've done and for saving my hide back there. I have no doubt Malcolm would have arrested me, and I'd be prisoner number four in his jail."

"Glad to be of service." She grinned. "I need you on this side of the bars, because there's more going on here than meets the eye."

"Malcolm Wiley is eyebrow deep in the middle of all of it."

"That's what I think," she said, all traces of humor missing from her voice. "I'm convinced there's a plot here with more tentacles than an octopus. Only I can't figure out where the starting point is."

Back at The Slop Bucket, Mags and Delilah spent some time outside, before she fixed the dog's evening bowl and stuck a frozen pizza in the oven for herself. She had eight hours before she had to wake Carole's dad, and those hours stretched long and lonely. Again there wasn't anything on television and not even M.C. Beaton's newest Hamish McBeth mystery could hold her attention. She had, she knew, her own mystery, and for once, a fictional whodunit paled alongside the real thing.

In the end, she decided to grab a few winks of shut-eye herself, and set not one but two clocks to awaken her, should she sleep past two o'clock. It proved to be a wise move, because when exhaustion claimed her, she knew nothing until the shrill air raid siren belonging to the biggest clock began to scream. Fighting her way out of sleep, Mags finally got oriented, remembered what had to happen, and grabbed her phone.

It rang almost forty times, before a groggy voice answered. "Mr. P," she said loud and with as much authority as she could muster. "Wake up. I'll meet you out at the diner in about forty-five minutes."

Mags showered, mostly to wake herself up, dressed and, after assuring Delilah that everything was okay and watching the dog go back to sleep, pointed her Jeep toward the highway that funneled all the tourists in and out of Crabapple Cove. In the distance, she finally saw the tall sign for the twenty-four-seven establishment. Less than five minutes later, her breakfast partner drove in to join her. Over waffles, eggs and sausage, the two compared notes. Feeling the need to be proactive and prepared, they planned their strategy at the jail.

To their surprise, when they showed up just before three-thirty, they received no static, and were even escorted to the visiting room a few minutes before their appointed time. Almost at the same time, a very sleepy Carole was brought through the door by a deputy, who barked at all of them, "Remember. Absolutely no touching, or this visit is over."

Mags could tell that Mr. Pickett was aching to fold his little girl into his arms and make everything right. Unfortunately, that wasn't an option for a number of reasons. Before either of them could say anything, Carole asked, "Why are you visiting me at this ungodly hour? I was sound asleep for a change." She yawned as if to emphasize her groggy state, then stared at her dad as if she were seeing him for the first time. "You're here," she said finally, as if she thought she was dreaming.

"Carole, honey. Why didn't you call me? Or at least let Mags or someone get word to me?"

"Oh, Daddy," she sobbed, "I wish now I had. I never expected this to go so far." She looked at him with undisguised hope in her eyes. "Now I'll probably never get out of here."

"Carole," Mags interrupted, getting back to her friend's initial question. "Was there a lock-down going on here about five o'clock yesterday afternoon?"

"A lock-down? I don't understand."

"You know. You go to the movies. All the prisoners are locked in their cells and the guards are usually searching each cell for contraband or whatever."

"No. Why are you asking? There's just me and Simon and Oliver, the tequila twins, back there. Those two were sawing logs all afternoon. It about drove me crazy. No one was searching my cell."

Mags and Mr. Pickett exchanged knowing glances and Carole saw their expressions. "Why? What?"

It was her father who spoke first. "When we came yesterday

afternoon, Malcolm wouldn't let us see you. Said the jail was under a lock-down. That we'd have to come back at three forty-five this morning. So here we are."

"That jerk!"

"That he is, darling. But I'm not worried about him. I just want to get you out of here."

"The judge wouldn't give me bail. Said I was a flight risk, a danger to the community."

"Now that's a load of BS if ever I heard it."

"I'm doomed, Daddy. They can't prove I killed him, but I can't prove that I didn't."

"We're going to prove your innocence," Mags broke in. "I'm still not sure how, but we're going to get to the bottom of all this." She told Carole about her discovery in Atlanta. "No legitimate person would list a parking garage in a seedy part of town as their legal address. There's something here that smells worse than fish. Then there's the connection to Franklin's family business. Nothing is that coincidental."

"You mean you think your ex-husband is messed up in all of this?"

"That's what's so crazy. There is absolutely no way he's connected, so why is there is a link between the two?"

The two continued visiting with Carole until the guard made moves to indicate that he was tired of standing in the corner, and probably wanted to go get a doughnut, Mags figured. "We're being given the old heave-ho," she told her friend. "But we will be back. Don't give up, because we aren't."

Outside, where they felt free to talk, Mags glanced at the clock in the courthouse cupola. Four-twenty-seven. Too early to stay up and too late to go back to bed. Except she was wired. Possibly it was because of two cups of black diner coffee she'd consumed earlier, or it could be the injustice and insanity that was going on.

"That about killed me in there," the old man said. "I've never seen Carole look so defeated."

"If I had any doubts that Malcolm is playing fast and loose with all this, his lie about the lock-down convinces me. What's more, he's involved in this killing somehow."

"He's one stupid oaf, but is he even smart enough to get himself involved in something like this?" Mr. Pickett rubbed his cap back and forth across his head in confusion. "I mean, he is the sheriff, whether he's qualified or not."

"That's right. He's the sheriff. In his mind, that gives him carte blanche to engage in anything he pleases. He thinks he's untouchable."

"So what's next? How do we go about getting Carole released?"

"I'm going back home and go though all my notes again. There is something I'm overlooking, and it's probably as big as the proverbial two-thousand pound elephant. Only I'm not seeing it."

"Want some help?"

Mags started to decline, then had a change of heart. This gentle man needed to feel like he was doing something to help his daughter. "Sure," she told him. "A fresh set of eyes may be exactly what this deal needs."

Back at The Slop Bucket, she spread all the documents out on the huge dining table that was never used any more. After she'd reassured Delilah that it was okay to go back to sleep yet again, she and her guest attacked what evidence they had, one piece at the time. It was well after sunrise when she placed the final document back into the folder.

"I'm like you. There's a key hidden in all of this, but I can't see the one element that ties everything together; something that shows us what happened." Mr. Pickett scratched his head. "But I'm with you. The fact that Mr. Humphries wasn't who he claimed to be is proof that something evil is afoot."

"Knowing it is one thing; proving it's another."

"I agree. I need the name of Carole's attorney. I'd like to have a talk with him today to see if there's any way we can force this bail issue."

"Sure. I had wondered that same thing." She went for her purse, dug in its depths, and produced Wyatt's business card. "Here. That's his number and that's his mailing address." She handed the card across the table. "You'll like him," Mr. P. He's a nice guy, but he's also very astute. He and I used to play tennis doubles in my other life, so I got to see him in a different light from most of his other clients."

"If you think he's the man for the job, I'm not going to rock the boat. I just want Carole out of that hell-hole." He jammed his Atlanta Braves cap back onto his head. "She should never have been put there in the first place."

The two agreed to touch base in the late afternoon, and he took himself back to town. Mags, on the other hand, couldn't decide what her next step should be. Part of her wanted to crawl back in the bed and sleep until whenever she woke up. But the practical little angel on her right shoulder insisted that she should freshen up and head to the office. In the end, the practical argument prevailed.

Think positive, she told herself. It will make all the difference in the world.

And the little angel on her right shoulder smiled, and stuck out her tongue toward the horned creature on Mags' left shoulder.

Chapter Nine

DON'T GO BACK TO PRYOR STREET

Mags arrived in the office where she adjusted the thermostat to better cope with the approaching heat of the day, opened all the blinds, turned the door sign to open, and spoke to her beloved African violets. A check of their soil indicated they needed a drink of water, and she grabbed the red, plastic pail from the kitchenette and took care of that task, before the demands of the day caused her to forget.

Then she approached her desk, where she saw the red message light on the answering machine blinking. Settled in her chair, she pushed the power button on her computer, then turned her attention to the phone console. With pad and pen at the ready to take notes, she pushed the message retrieval button.

This is your last opportunity to secure vinyl siding for your home…

She hit the skip button.

Hi, Mags, this is Tony Edwards from Florida. Just wondering how things are coming on that end for our closing. We haven't heard from you so we just wanted to be sure everything was still on go. Please call us.

Mags was overrun with guilt. She hadn't been dealing with her

153

real estate business, because her private investigations agency had been thrown into overtime. As she made notes, she also made herself promise to change that scenario. She couldn't afford to antagonize what few paying customers she had.

Margaret Gordon. I want my check and I want it now. You're trying to swindle me and I know the real estate commission won't like it if I have to take my case to them. You owe me two million dollars, less what would have been your commission, of course. I'm not a greedy person. But I want my money, and I want it now. You've got until the end of the day Thursday to pay me, or my attorney will be making some calls. You know, I ought to charge you for my attorney's fees, but I'm not that kind of person.

By the time Mags finished listening, her hands were doing a number big time through her hair. Why, she wondered for the umpteenth time, couldn't this woman get it? And today was Thursday. The last thing she needed at this point was a complaint registered with the state charging that she was trying to play fast and loose with a client. Between that and HJH's murder, she'd lose her license for sure.

Unsure of what to do for the best, yet painfully aware that she had to take some kind of action, Mags shoved the notepad aside and turned her attention to the computer. She logged into her e-mail and was rewarded with thirty-seven new messages. Since most were junk, it took only a minute to whittle the number down to a more manageable eleven. That's when she saw it. The e-mail with no subject identified sent a chill over her body. She wanted to ignore it, but the curiosity factor was too great. She clicked on the message.

Thought you were smart going to Atlanta yesterday, didn't you? But what good did it do you? You're wasting your time and you're putting yourself in danger.

Don't go back to Pryor Street.

Mags had to grab hold of the desk to keep from losing it. How did anyone know she'd gone to the parking garage? What's more, exactly who was keeping tabs on her? For the first time, she felt as if she were losing control. It was "Twilight Zone" time, a place where the unusual and unexplainable were the norm. That definitely described how things were at Mountain Magic Realty by Mags at that moment.

Mags grabbed her phone and punched in a number. When the attorney's receptionist in Atlanta answered, she said, "This is Margaret Gordon. I must speak with Mr. Fulton immediately. It's an emergency and it has to do with the Carole Pickett case he's representing.

"I'm sorry, Mrs. Gordon. "Mr. Fulton is in court this morning. I'll be glad to take a message for him, but it will be the noon recess before he'll get it."

Mags consulted the clock. It was only ten-oh-nine. Two hours. Yet this seemed so terribly urgent. "There's no way an assistant could take a note to him in court, just hand him the note, so that he knows I have to talk with him."

The receptionist laughed, somewhat condescendingly, Mags thought, before she said, "I'm sorry, Mrs. Gordon. But the judges frown on such as that. It really isn't the way it's depicted on "Boston Legal" or "L.A. Law". But I will be glad to make certain he knows you need to speak with him. I'm sure he'll call you back while they're recessed for lunch."

Mags didn't like to admit defeat, but short of driving back to Atlanta and hunting him down in the courtroom, she knew of little else she could do. In the end, she asked that Wyatt call her ASAP. "Be sure to put on there that this is urgent and underline it five or six times."

"Yes, ma'am, Mrs. Gordon. I've got the message right here, ready to give to him when he calls in."

"When he calls in? You mean someone isn't going to meet him and hand him my message?"

"No, ma'am. He'll check in with the office as soon as they adjourn. I'll give him your message then."

"But what if he doesn't call in?" Mags felt as if she were standing on shifting sands.

"Please, Mrs. Gordon. I've got to deal with another matter. I assure you, Mr. Fulton will call me as soon as he's free. I will give him your message. Now you have a great day."

The line went dead. I could have a better great day, Mags thought, if I could talk to Wyatt.

Unable to concentrate on anything else, Mags wandered aimlessly around the office, watching the clock hands crawl around in slow motion. There was work she needed to do. Phone calls that needed to be made. Messages that required replies. And most desperately, she needed to find out who was aware of her every move.

The clock registered twelve-seventeen when the phone rang and Mags finally got a measure of relief. The last seventeen minutes had been the longest of the morning. Mags had truly begun to wonder if the attorney and her S.O.S. had connected.

"What's wrong, Mags? My lady at the front desk said you sounded absolutely frantic. That's not like you."

"Let me read you the e-mail that was in my box this morning, and you'll understand." When she finished, her reward was dead silence. "Wyatt, are you there?"

"I'm here. Just trying to digest the whole thing."

"What am I going to do? Somebody is stalking me."

"You may be right, but I don't understand all that's going on here. What's that reference to Pryor Street?"

Mags explained her early-morning run to Atlanta in search of HJH's address. "Don't you see? No one who was on the up-and-up would give the address of a parking garage as their legal address. This, combined with the bogus or out-of-date phone numbers he gave us, proves to me that this was one gigantic con job."

"I'm not arguing with you on that."

"But, why? Why me?"

"Mags, I'm going to throw something out that may or may not be on target."

"I'm ready to hear anything that will shed some light on all this."

"I'm not sure you'll want to hear what I'm about to say, but is there any chance your ex-husband's involved in this in any way?"

"Franklin?"

"Yeah. It just seems that his fingerprints are in several different places here. I noticed it before when you were sharing your file with me. But this latest deal, if you know for certain that parking deck belongs to him, seems to me to be a direct tie-in."

Mags massaged her hair again. Much more of this and she would be bald. "Gosh, Wyatt. Franklin is a womanizer, and he's a cold-hearted individual. But it's taking quite a leap for me to think he could be involved in murder."

"I could be wrong and, remember, I said you might not want to hear my thoughts. Just think about it. Meanwhile, send me that e-mail and let me get it to the investigator."

Mags hit the send button before she ended the phone conversation and, in the hours that followed, she did exactly as Wyatt had instructed. She thought about Franklin. She pondered what she knew for certain, and she tried to objectively evaluate what she suspected or surmised. In the end, she had to agree that Franklin appeared to be involved in all that had gone on. Yet she knew that it was all circumstantial evidence. The same kind of evidence that had Carole behind bars for a crime Mags knew her friend hadn't committed. Unfortunately, her ex-husband's past behaviors didn't inspire the same degree of confidence. All she needed was yet another angle, another mystery within the big mystery, to further muddy the waters.

To say she was confused was an understatement, and to be a prisoner there in the solitary confines of the office, unable to bounce her fears and concerns off anyone else, was getting to her. She needed someone. But who? Then it hit her; Carole knew more about the case than anyone. Question was, could she get in to see her friend? And could they talk without being interrupted or overheard? After this morning's e-mail, Mags was beginning to think that someone was standing over her, watching every move she made.

She encountered little resistance, and the sheriff approved her visit with only a modicum of harassment. What troubled Mags was the wink he gave her when he approved her request. She didn't know how to read it. Or even if she should read it.

"Am I ever glad to see you," Carole exclaimed, as she caught sight of Mags on the other side of the table. "I'm about to go crazy back there." Her face was lined and gray, and her eyes, always bright and sparkly, were instead dull and lifeless. She was definitely not the Carole that Mags knew and loved. Jail was taking a toll on her.

"Listen, we've got to put our heads together. There are things going on here I'm not certain about."

"I don't know what good I can do you from in here."

Mags was once again struck by the sheer nastiness of the jail complex. The smell of the place was something she carried out with her following every visit. It remained in her nostrils for hours afterward, a constant reminder of what her friend was enduring around the clock. She couldn't imagine what it would be like to contend with all that, plus the knowledge that she couldn't walk out whenever the mood struck her.

"You can listen. You know more about the background than anyone else. Don't let this jail get to you."

"Face it, Mags. It's hopeless," she wailed, as the tone of her voice became more scratchy and frantic.

"It is not hopeless," Mags hissed, aware that the guard she could see in the background was moving their way.

"Is there a problem here?" the uniformed deputy asked. His hand hovered near the grip of his service revolver. "We can end this visit right now if there's going to be dissention."

Carole's averted her eyes and wouldn't even look in the man's direction. Mags saw her visibly withdraw and build a shell around herself.

"She's despondent, as anyone in her position would be, and I'm trying to encourage her. You're interference isn't helping any."

"Look, little lady. I'm the one in charge here and I say what goes and who stays. One more problem and you go."

"I'm not your 'little lady'," Mags charged. "You may address me as Mrs. Gordon."

"Yeah, I know who you are. You were Franklin Gordon's old lady. Him and the sheriff are good friends."

Mags gripped the table edge trying to prevent her anger from boiling over. "I am Franklin Gordon's ex-wife. I am not now, nor have I ever been his 'old lady' and I resent that remark."

"Ain't no skin off my nose," he replied, as he turned to walk away. "But I can put you out any time I get ready, so you two keep it in control, or I'll have to get rough."

"You might as well go," Carole suggested in a deflated whisper. "We're not going to be able to talk and, besides, I don't know anything that can help you."

"How do you know you don't know? Give me a chance here."

"Whatever. Anything's better than sitting back there in that cell staring at those green and gray walls."

"Good. Now listen closely, because I'm going to have to talk low." She glanced around the room, accidentally made eye-contact with the guard, then quickly dropped her eyes back to Carole's range. "After all that's happened, I wouldn't put it past Malcolm to have this table bugged somehow."

"You mean we're being recorded?" Carole's exhausted eyes grew large and alarmed. "Why?"

"I'm sorry, Carole. I didn't mean to frighten you. There's so much going right now, until I don't put anything past the good sheriff."

"Don't keep me in suspense."

Mags began by telling her about the e-mail she'd received that morning.

Carole's eyes grew again. "You're not serious? Somebody knows you went to Atlanta and found the parking garage? But who? How?"

"That's what I'm talking about. At this point, I'm suspicious of almost everyone."

"It makes my skin crawl to think somebody out there is plotting against us."

"It's not doing my skin any favors, either." She hesitated, because once the words she was about to say were out of her mouth, there would be no taking them back. Taking a deep breath, she plunged ahead, "Now, consider this: are you seeing any indications that my ex-husband could somehow be involved in all of this?"

"Franklin?" Carole's expression turned pensive. "That's pretty far-fetched, isn't it?" She drummed her fingers on the tabletop.

When Mags spotted the guard's radar honing in on them, as he began walking their way, she muttered, "Stop the finger noises. You're upsetting his nibs back there."

Carole clinched both her hands into fists. "You can't even think loudly in here without getting reprimanded."

"So you don't think there's a connection with Franklin," she asked, returning the conversation to its original topic.

Carole was quiet and Mags could see the wheels turning in her head. "First, HJH's address is a parking garage. To me, that proves he was a fraud. But when you tell me that Franklin's corporation owns that garage, it's just crazy. It doesn't make sense."

"So far we're on the same page."

"Did anyone know you were going to Atlanta? Did you mention it to any of our clients, or maybe someone at the Eat and Greet?"

"Absolutely not!" There were few aspects of all that was ongoing that Mags could be definite about, but on this question, she had no doubts. "I didn't even decide that I would go until I was already in bed. And I waited 'til I was forty miles away before I stopped for gas." She drew circles on the tabletop with her index finger. "I didn't want to take any chance on meeting anyone I might have to talk with, who might remember seeing me away from Crabapple Cove."

"Then maybe Franklin has risen a couple of notches on the suspicion scale. If no one knew you were going, I'm inclined to take a second look at your ex-husband."

Mags eyed her friend cautiously. "You're not saying that because I planted the idea in your mind?"

"Well..." Carole fingered her chin. "I have to admit I would never have gone down that road if you hadn't asked, but at the same time… there are so many coincidences."

"That's how I felt, too."

"So what's the next step?"

Mags saw the deputy making fidgeting motions and understood their time was about to come to a close. "Gotta talk quick. Godzilla approaches." She dropped her voice to a loud whisper. "If we're right, there's no way Malcolm will ever agree to investigate his best friend." The guard was almost upon them. "So it's up to us."

"But how?" Carole hissed.

"We'll have to…"

"Alright, ladies. This tea party is officially over. I've got other things to do."

"Just another minute? Please?"

"No can do, Mrs. Gordon. It's time for the prisoner to go back to her cell, and for you to go. Wherever it is you go."

Mags didn't have to have a ton of bricks fall on her to know when she wasn't wanted. "I'll check into things and get back to you," she said to Carole's retreating back." A nod of her friend's head told her the message had been received, while the slump of her shoulders was mute testimony to her friend's mental state of mind.

For lack of anywhere better, Mags went back to the office. Once again, she had put investigative work ahead of her paying job, and that had to come to a swift and productive halt. She returned several phone calls. Updated files to get ready for several closings that were imminent, and answered a number of e-mails. While there was no walk-in traffic, a mainstay during the tourist season, there were e-mail requests for information. She responded in what she hoped was a very positive and encouraging manner. Lord knows she didn't feel that way. She was sure the town's grapevine was responsible for the lack of clients, but also knew she was helpless to change the situation.

It was almost four o'clock when Mags felt her stomach rubbing up against her backbone, and realized she hadn't stopped to have lunch. "I'm hungry," she announced to the empty office. Without waiting for a response, she locked the door and made her way to the Eat and Greet, where she proceeded to throw caution to the wind and ordered a Reuben sandwich and fries. She would, she knew, have to compensate somewhere for the indulgence, but right at that moment she needed comfort food. The last time she had retreated big-time into excess fat and calories had been when she was divorcing Franklin. He was the common denominator then, and it appeared that he might be at the bottom of this latest foray as well. But how? It simply made no sense.

While she waited for her food, Mags noticed the café was almost empty of customers. Not uncommon at four o'clock in the afternoon. What was uncommon was her server. She knew she was seated at Maudeann's table, and she'd seen the server on the other side of the room, but it was someone else who took her order. Was Maudeann avoiding her? Why? Somehow, given the woman's years as a major commentator on the town's grapevine, it wasn't like her to be ashamed of her actions. Just one more question with no easy answer. And did it have anything to do with HJH's death, or was it strictly a coincidence? Of which there were already too many.

The sandwich was as good as she had imagined, and Mags managed to bury her paranoia somewhere between the corned beef and the sauerkraut. Fresh cut fries dipped in catsup helped to shove all her concerns into the background. She left cash on the table, included an ample tip, then made her way back to the office. It was time to lock up and go home.

Mags adjusted the thermostat, grabbed the mail that needed to be dropped by the post office, and sat down to put her computer to bed, when she noticed that three more e-mails had arrived while she was out stuffing her face. She had made so much headway on work tasks, until it seemed almost sacrilegious to let those three hold over 'til the next day. Besides, she told herself, they're probably junk mail. The better to get them out of the way.

Her fingers clicked over the keys and the in-box opened to reveal two pieces of spam. Before she could delete them, Mags' eyes landed on the third message and she felt a chill invaded her spine. The e-mail had no subject, just like the first two harassing notes she'd received.

The sender's address wasn't familiar, so it was with trembling hands that she opened the message.

You can't do anything that we don't know about it. You're being watched by many eyes. You can be smart about this and keep your nose out of what doesn't concern you. Or you might lose that nose. It's your choice.

Mags fought to hold herself together, knowing if she caved even a little, she would totally crumble. She was unsure how long she sat there, but finally, as darkness and shadows grew to proportions inside the office that couldn't be ignored, Mags roused from the protective emotional cocoon that had been her temporary shelter. It was clear. Someone was stalking her; watching her every move. For all she knew, her office was bugged, and she was afraid to utter a single word or commit anything to paper that might be discovered. Forget the Internet, for sure.

Mags put the computer down, grabbed her tote bag and purse, and escaped the office. It was such a relief to lock the door behind her, although she knew her fears weren't totally rational. Neither was anything else that was happening. She was several miles out of town before she remembered the outgoing mail in her bag. The peace and security of The Slop Bucket was very enticing, and she could think of nothing but getting home, locking all the doors, and turning on the security system. But she also knew that the mail needed to go to the post office, so she made a u-turn and headed back to town, where she dutifully deposited her outgoing letters in the slot.

After making her detour, Mags' commute to The Slop Bucket seemed longer than the Christmas Eve nights when, as a child, it had seemed that morning's first light would never come. She was certain someone had inserted a few extra curves in the road. Patience was eventually rewarded as the old lodge she had come to love so much came into view. Be it ever so humble...

Mags wasted no time getting into the house, dealing with Delilah's needs, then locking the doors behind them. All she really wanted was bed, but knowing that hunger would wake her before morning, she popped a frozen dinner in the microwave and prepared to dine. It might not be five-star cuisine, but it was quick. On a night like this when exhaustion threatened, it was the only way to go.

As she forked into the somewhat tough chicken and quickly emptied the small serving of rice, Mags thought again about that last e-mail. She was being stalked. There could be no doubt about it. So what if whoever was sending them decided to get physical? Perhaps she should file a report so there would be a record? Without bothering to reconsider, she dialed the sheriff's office and was soon speaking to Malcolm Wiley.

"This is the third harassing e-mail I've gotten. I'm starting to get uncomfortable."

"So what do you want me to do about it?"

Excuse me! "I want you to investigate and find out who is stalking me. I want this on the record."

"Stalking? Are you serious?"

"That's what it is."

The sheriff was laughing. "That's not how I see it, and I'm the sheriff."

"Malcolm, how can you be so cavalier?"

"Look, Mags. Face it. You've made some enemies around here. Now that you're involved in this guy's death, one of these jokers has decided to take advantage of your situation to have a little fun."

"So why am I not laughing?"

"You just need to lighten up." She could hear him whistling. "Besides, there's no way to find out who's sending those e-mails. It's all that Internet stuff."

"There is so a way. You can trace e-mails back to their source."

"Do you know how to do it?"

She fingered the fork she'd used to eat her dinner. "Well... well, no."

"Neither do I. End of discussion. Now curl up with one of those mystery books you find so interesting, and let me get back to real police work." The line went dead.

Well, I guess that was a whole lot of wasted effort for nothing, she thought. And, yes, I will curl up with a good book and read until I fall asleep. But tomorrow morning I'm going to find out who's sending those messages. Then I'll show Malcolm Wiley just how incompetent he is.

Chapter Ten

YOU READY FOR COURT?

When the first rays of sun crept through Mags' bedroom window the next morning, it roused a soundly-sleeping seller of real estate, who still clutched the copy of *Last Lessons of Summer* she had been reading when fatigue claimed her. Even the investigative skills of Judge Deborah Knott hadn't been compelling enough to fight exhaustion. Upon awakening, she lay for a few minutes, unwilling to abandon her comfortable bed but, in the end, her feet hit the floor and her morning routine began.

At the office Mags put in a call to Wyatt at his Atlanta office. "This is Margaret Gordon calling for Mr. Fulton."

"I'm sorry, Mrs. Gordon. He won't be in until noon. He had a doctor's appointment this morning."

As she talked, Mags was opening blinds, watering violets, and running the carpet sweeper. Just because there was no business was no excuse for letting the dirt pile up. "Would you please ask him to call me as soon as possible? It's very important."

"I'll put your request with all his other messages, and I'm sure he'll call you when he can."

She's a lot of help, Mags muttered to no one in particular, as she returned the phone to its cradle, thankful she wasn't dying.

Determined to be productive, she spent the morning cleaning, straightening and throwing away. As she was emptying and re-arranging the contents of the wall of cabinets she and Carole had searched earlier, while looking for the pistol, Mags fantasized that she would find the gun that had eluded them. She wasn't sure how to explain the murder weapon, but she didn't have to.

The office line rang. A customer? Or was it a harassing call? Caller ID indicated number unknown. Her hand was shaking as she lifted the phone to her ear. "Mountain Magic Realty." She braced herself.

"Mags?" It was a man's voice. "Hey, it's Grant Lewis. You ready for court tomorrow?"

"Court? Wha… why?"

"Your petition to the judge to get your boat out of impound." He stopped and Mags could feel awkwardness between them. "You did ask that I take steps to get your boat back?"

Mags could imagine the attorney feared he'd gone out on a limb, so she was quick to reassure him. "No… I mean, yes, I did send you that request. I just hadn't heard that we had a court date." Besides, with no business, she hadn't needed the boat, so out of sight, out of mind.

"Just got the word that we can see Judge Beecham at ten-thirty in the morning. You can be there?" There was a real question mark in his voice.

"I'm writing it on my calendar as we speak. Do I need to bring anything?"

"Nope. Just leave it all to me. Should be pretty cut and dried." Yeah, she recalled, that's what we thought about Carole's bail hearing, too. Look how that one went south.

After assuring the attorney that she would see him the next morning, Mags finally took the step she'd been avoiding all morning. At her desk, her heart in her throat, with shaking hands, she powered up her computer and clicked on e-mail. Nothing there from her mysterious correspondent, and she breathed a quick sigh of relief.

Knowing that she didn't have to deal with yet another message from her unknown stalker, Mags was immediately more at ease, able to deal with the other e-mails that needed attention.

Her stomach was protesting loudly, so Mags closed the office and wandered down the street to the Eat and Greet, struck yet again by how lonely she was without Carole. Somehow, some way, she had to prove that her best friend was innocent, because she couldn't envision not having that beautiful person in her life.

Throwing caution and good sense to the four winds, she ordered country-style steak and gravy, mashed potatoes, fried okra and a pear salad. This is sooo good, she thought, savoring a bite of the fork-tender steak, when her cell phone rang. It was Wyatt. She swallowed quickly and punched the talk button.

"Sorry it took me so long to get back to you. I spent half the morning sitting in the doctor's waiting room, and the rest of the morning sitting in the exam room. He was with me for all of ten minutes."

Mags laughed. "Been there, done that. You'll live, I assume?"

"Yeah, not planning to check out yet. So what's up? This note says urgent, with question marks. What does that mean?"

Mags hated to complain, but believed she'd never get a better chance. "Let's just say your receptionist is totally immune to the hysterical pleadings of a client. Those question marks mean she didn't take me seriously."

Wyatt laughed. "I'm sorry. Ramona is very dedicated. I'll speak to her."

"I don't want to get her in trouble," Mags was quick to explain. "But it is really frustrating when the word urgent doesn't move her."

"Don't worry. She's not in trouble. But I will tell her that if you call, it's important. Now, tell me all about urgent."

Mags, fork in hand, toyed with the remainder of the mound of fresh mashed potatoes. "I got another e-mail late yesterday."

She related the message, and confessed that she had reported the harassment to the sheriff. A move that, by the new day's light, didn't look quite a smart as it had the evening before.

There was silence on the other end. "Wyatt?"

"Sorry. I'm here. Just thinking. I really wish you hadn't brought him into the loop, but what's done is done."

Mags put down the fork. Suddenly she had no stomach for the remainder of the good food still on her plate. "I had doubts when I was talking to him, but I was in too deep to back out. Not that he believed me."

"He didn't believe you?"

"Let me clarify. He didn't doubt that I'd gotten the e-mails, but he thinks they're from someone I've angered around here. And, he said there was no way to trace them."

"Well, he's wrong. And I've got some information on your first two e-mails. They were sent from public libraries in the greater Atlanta area."

"Libraries. With an S?"

"Two different libraries about thirty miles apart."

"Well, we know whoever it is has transportation. Now what do we want to bet this third one is from yet another public library?"

"I'd be very surprised if it wasn't. But send it on to me anyway, so we can be sure."

Mags promised to forward the offending message as soon as she returned to the office. "I've got to go up against the sheriff in the morning, when we try to get the *One True Love* sprung. I hope I have better luck with it than we had with Carole." She made a mental note to visit her friend before heading back home.

"Speaking of your friend, I had a nice conversation with her dad this morning. I wish he'd been in the picture when all this went down."

"He was out west fishing or hunting or something, and Carole deliberately didn't involve him. You know, because of the bad blood between him and Malcolm."

"Yeah, he told me that story. Somehow, it's not hard to see Malcolm morphing into the sheriff we're dealing with today."

"You talked to Mr. Pickett this morning?"

"That's right."

"What time?"

"It was about ten-thirty, I guess. I was in the doctor's office. Waiting."

Mags was doing some quick calculations. "Let me get this straight. I called and had to leave a message, but he called and somehow was connected with you?"

"Ramona texted me that he needed to speak with me and gave me his number. I called him back. So what's your…? Uh-oh…!"

"You've got that right."

"Like I said, I'll speak with Ramona." Mags sensed she'd really embarrassed him. "Now shall we talk about Carole?," he asked.

"Please tell me some good news. And Wyatt, I didn't mean to imply that I thought you were avoiding me."

"I didn't take it that way. But as far as Carole is concerned, we're going back into court to request bail again. Only this time her dad will be there, and he will have an opportunity to speak."

"That's great," she enthused. "Does Carole know yet? I'm going to see her later this afternoon. If I can get in."

"Do me a favor and let her dad tell her. They need to come together on the same page on this."

Mags smiled. The visual image of those two coming together – one with flaming red hair and the other a former red-head – was rich. Still, she would have loved to be a fly on the wall. The server was at Mags' elbow with her tea pitcher, but Mags shook her head, smiled, and covered the top of her glass with her hand. "I need to get back to the office. I'll forward that e-mail but I won't be surprised at what you find. There's an orchestrated effort going on here to harass and stalk me."

"I fear you're right on the money. My man is still working on all of this, but we're getting few leads that can be connected. Just be careful. Watch your step and watch your back."

"Will do." The connection severed and Mags returned her phone to her purse, policed her table, and left the café. Wyatt had given her a lot of think about and little to work with. Still...

She made short work of her time back at the office and was soon standing in the reception area at the jail. Once again, excuses were manufactured, seemingly out of thin air, about why she couldn't visit her friend.

"Look," she said to the deputy who was almost as wide as he was tall, "I've not visited with Carole today, and I have no intention of being put off."

"The sheriff gave strict orders that she couldn't have visitors today, so I can't let you go back."

"Call him out here. I want to talk to Malcolm. He's just trying to be difficult."

"He's not here, ma'am."

"Well where is he? Call him on his cell phone or get him on the radio."

"He's not where he can be reached."

The words echoed in her head. "...not where he can be reached." Questions flooded her brain like a mountain stream after a spring storm. Did that mean he was with a woman? Where, she wondered, did he take them now that The Slop Bucket wasn't available? Or was he up to some other kind of dirty work? How could the high sheriff be out of communication?

She asked as much.

"He's entitled to time off," the uniformed face replied, but it was his body language that provided the deputy's real response, which Mags interpreted loosely as something like, "Up yours, lady."

"So you're not going to let me visit my friend."

"That's right."

Unable to budge the man, Mags retreated, although not with good graces, hoping that the lawman wasn't as skilled as she at reading body language.

Back at the office, as she dealt with a few clerical tasks and confirmed closing dates on a couple of deals, Mags was struck once again with how lost she was without her friend. It wasn't Carole's office management skills, as much as it was the bond that had developed between them. A bond she hadn't realized existed. As an only child, she had entertained herself, and had been happy as a loner. But not any longer. She needed Carole in much the same way that Mr. Holmes had relied on Dr. Watson. She shook her head, as the thought of the erstwhile British detective without his equally famous sidekick flittered through her mind. There was no doubt about it, she and Carole were a team... to sell real estate, she quickly clarified to herself.

When there was no more work she could do, or manufacture, Mags closed the office, even though it was only three-thirty. A quick stop by the jail was met with the same refusal as before, and the sheriff was still out. Mags gave up and drove home as quickly as the curves and the congested traffic allowed. She put Delilah on a leash and the two went for a walk along the lake. The wild Canada geese were flying in for their nightly layover, as the sun's rays reflected off the placid lake waters. A symphony of insect sounds and bird chatter soothed Mags' fractured mind, and relaxed her tortured soul.

Back at the lodge, she fed and watered Delilah, fixed herself a couple of deli meat sandwiches, and curled up on the sofa with "Catering to Nobody." Dianne Mott Davidson's very first book was about Goldy Bear Schulz, a caterer turned detective out of dire necessity. Mags had read the book many years before, but found it comforting to visit with an old friend again. She soon found herself right in the kitchen beside Goldy, prepping for the wake that almost killed the new caterer's fledgling business. It also set her on the road to revealing who the real killer was and saving the situation. Not unlike my situation, Mags reassured herself.

The hour was late before she returned from the mountains of Colorado, where the book's heroine lived, to her own mountains in northeast Georgia. Yikes, she thought, when she spotted the clock, an acknowledgement that she was long overdue for bed. She let Delilah out one last time and began securing the house for the night. It wasn't until she was snuggled beneath the covers, under the slowly oscillating ceiling fan, that she remembered her date in court only a few hours away. How could she have forgotten about that, Mags wondered. What's more, she realized, she hadn't thought about Carole once that evening. Then sleep claimed her.

Because of the time set for her case in court, Mags went directly to the courthouse the next morning, where she met her attorney on the steps. They walked in together, talking in easy, comfortable terms. Mags had a great deal of respect for the young, blond lawyer who, despite his excessive height, couldn't manage to dribble a basketball. They had met when Mags began to need real estate closings, and the Lewis firm, it seemed, handled the lion's share in Crabapple Cove. But a criminal trial lawyer, he wasn't, which was why she hadn't even considered him for Carole's defense.

His Honor, Judge Beecham, informed the parties that due to the nature of the case, and the fact that no jury was present, he intended to make the proceedings as simple as possible. Then he asked Mags' attorney to state his client's case.

"Your Honor, this is a simple matter, so we don't plan to waste the court's time with a lot of extraneous information. Basically, Margaret Gordon, a well-known real estate broker here in Crabapple Cove, markets real estate from her boat, the *One True Love*. I have here one of her brochures that clearly illustrates that the boat is her own unique marketing hook." He held up a printed, four-color pamphlet, then delivered the evidence to the judge. As he returned to his place, he continued, "Recently Mrs. Gordon discovered a man dead on board her boat and called the authorities. Sheriff Wiley and his deputies responded and, ultimately, the sheriff seized the boat, which would have been standard procedure. He has now impounded it indefinitely."

The judge held up his hand. "If it was standard procedure, why are we here? What is your objection?"

Mags sneaked a glance around the courtroom. There were few others in the room, most of them connected with the court in some manner. She did spy one gentleman sitting all the way in the back, who looked somewhat out of place, for reasons she couldn't immediately identify. She turned her attention back to her attorney who had begun speaking again. That unknown man was probably connected with another case, and had arrived early. She realized that she felt very out of place, herself, and wondered if it showed on her as much as it did on him.

"Simply this, Your Honor. Sheriff Wiley still has the boat impounded, and refuses to release it. Instead, he has deferred judgment on the matter to this court. We're asking you to order the boat's release. The sheriff has examined the craft in detail, he has photos. There's no other evidence to obtain, and there's no reason to deny Mrs. Gordon's petition. She needs the boat for her business, and we're asking you to return it to her today. That's our petition. Thank you, Your Honor." He sat down and patted Mags' hand.

The judge appeared to be studying the brochure. When he spoke, his remarks were addressed to the sheriff, who sat alone at the neighboring table. "Sheriff Wiley. Where is the county attorney? Do you still have Mrs. Gordon's boat impounded?"

"That is correct. There's no need to bother the attorney for something like this."

"Very well," the judge replied. "The record will show that the sheriff is not represented by counsel." He fixed the sheriff with another inquiring gaze. "So where is the boat? And why are you refusing to return it to the owner?"

"It's in a secure area at Davis Marina."

Mags could feel the fury moving up her backbone. Malcolm was, she knew, being deliberately difficult.

"For what reason?" the judge asked.

"I'm not through examining the boat."

"What else is there to examine?"

Mags saw the sheriff's chest expand ever so slightly, before he spoke. "This is an on-going murder investigation, Your Honor." The buttons on his shirt were straining. "There are still many unanswered questions. If I release the boat before we finish the investigation, and we need to examine it again, any evidence that might still be on board will have been destroyed or contaminated."

"Sheriff Wiley." The judge leaned forward in his chair and looked over the top of his glasses, directly at the lawman. "What else could possibly be there that you haven't found? Have you thoroughly gone over the boat?"

"Yes, Your Honor. Several times. And each time we've found something new, something we didn't know about, didn't have before."

Grant Lewis rose slowly from his chair. "Your Honor?" He interrupted. "This appears to be a deliberate stall tactic to deny my client the use of a tool she needs in order to earn her livelihood. In short, Mrs. Gordon needs her boat. The sheriff needs to conclude his investigation and return it to her."

"I'm inclined to agree with Mr. Lewis," the judge told the sheriff. "Do you have anything else to add?"

"Just this, Your Honor." The sheriff fingered the knot of his tie. "I'm not a psychic, and I'm dealing with a case that still has many loose ends. I don't know if I'll need the boat again, but if I do, I want to protect the integrity of any evidence that might still be there. If Mrs. Gordon gets the boat back, I lose that option." He glanced at Mags and, while the judge might have been fooled by the smile he gave her, she had seen it too many times. She clearly saw the insulting smirk behind it. "Besides, from what I hear around town, Mrs. Gordon doesn't have much business these days, so the loss of the boat shouldn't be that big of a deal."

Mags felt the sucker punch and would have reacted, had Grant's hand not exerted a tremendous amount of pressure on her shoulder.

"Your Honor, I must object to that last remark by the sheriff."

"I have to agree, Sheriff Wiley. That was unnecessary," the judge ruled.

"I'm sorry, Your Honor." He winked at Mags again, before turning his attention back to the man in black behind the bench.

"Mr. Lewis," the judge said at length, after studying Mags' brochure again, "I'm in total sympathy with Mrs. Gordon. It's obvious that to deny her the boat makes her advertising appear to be misleading, and it would force unnecessary expense on her to lease a replacement boat."

Is he going to give me back the *One True Love*, Mags wondered, daring to get her hopes up.

"However…"

Mags' heart fell. However's were rarely good news.

"…to jeopardize evidence-gathering in a murder investigation could place the sheriff and the court in a compromised situation. My first responsibility is to the investigation. For that reason, and for the moment, I'm denying the plaintiff's request. I need to study the matter and I'll rule in a few days."

Mags felt the room spinning around her. First Carole was refused bail, now she was being denied her boat. What was it about her and courts?

"Mrs. Gordon," the judge said, breaking through her pity party. "I sympathize with you, but this is more involved than it might appear. I'm sorry I can't return your property today."

"Thank you, Your Honor," Grant Lewis said. "We'll wait for your ruling."

Mags knew what the ruling would be. Malcolm held all the cards. She knew, or at least felt like she knew, that there was no true need to continue to hold her boat. It was just one more instance when the sheriff was using the power of his office to further a private agenda. She vowed silently that she would peel back the protective façade his badge provided for his less than savory actions.

"I'm sorry, Mags," her attorney was saying. "I truly thought this one was a slam dunk."

"Never underestimate the good sheriff," she told him, and hoped her voice didn't reveal the depth of revulsion she had for Malcolm. "There's a history you don't understand. I should have told you, but

I gave the sheriff credit for having too much integrity to allow his personal feelings to dictate professional actions." Her grin reflected her discomfort. "Obviously I was too generous."

The young attorney's face was a study in chagrin and uncertainty. "Maybe some day I'll let you tell me the whole story. But not today." He wiped his hand across his forehead. "Whatever happened, I still came up short. I'm sorry."

Mags patted his arm. "Don't lose any sleep over this. What you don't truly understand is that this was a done deal before we ever got to court this morning."

"What are you saying? That Sheriff Wiley influenced the judge?"

Mags knew she had to be cautious in how she answered. "Do I think Judge Beecham was bribed? No. I don't. Do I believe our sheriff is capable of buying a judge if it suits his purpose? You bet I do, and you're the second attorney to ask me that question this week. But I'll tell you that story another time as well."

"Suddenly this all seems so much deeper than it did before we got to court this morning."

"That's because it is much deeper than any of us can comprehend."

"What do you mean? What do you know that I don't?"

Mags hesitated. Would this man demean her intuition as others had? "It's not so much what I know, as what I suspect." She hesitated, grinned self-consciously, and continued. "I hesitate to call it woman's intuition, but it's at least a gut feeling I've got, based on what all I know at this point. Malcolm's determined to hold on to my boat, only his reasons go far beyond possible evidence contamination."

He put his hand on her arm. "Come on, they're about to call the next case. Let's get out of here."

As they two made their way out of the courtroom, Mags was already plotting what her next step should be.

"Margaret," said a man's voice behind them. She and the attorney both turned around. "I'm sorry I had to fight you over the boat."

Suddenly all of Mags' resolve to behave as her mother would

have preferred flew right out the window. Her mother had never met Malcolm Wiley, and would have forbidden Mags to play with him if she had.

"Come off it, Malcolm. You're not the least bit sorry. You knew when you were spewing that bilge back there, that you were giving the judge the one and only reason that would keep him from ordering the release of my boat. You knew exactly what you were doing, so don't come around acting all apologetic now."

"You need to talk some common sense into your client, Mr. Lewis."

"Thank you, sheriff. I'll study that suggestion and make up my mind in a few days, if I think such action is warranted."

The naturally port color of the sheriff's face turned a little darker and, before he could speak, Mags grabbed the floor. "Since you're out of the office every time I come by, I'm going to take advantage of this chance to say something that needs to be said."

"I... I beg your pardon?" Confusion was obvious on his bulldog face.

"You've got the wrong person in jail for that murder. You know it and I know it."

His red face was quickly assuming a more purple hue. Mags held up her hand, and hurried to make her point before she was stopped.

"Carole Pickett didn't kill that man any more than Mr. Lewis here did. But you've got your mind made up that she's the murderer, and you're not even looking for anyone else. That's wrong!" she protested, and pounded her left hand with the fist of her right hand.

"Now look, Margaret. You don't have access to the evidence we've amassed, so you're making an assumption without all the facts."

"I know Mr. Humphries was a total sham, operating under an assumed name, a fact you overlook far too conveniently," she countered, the temperature of her voice warming with every word.

"His identity has nothing to do with his murder. Like I said, you don't have all the information we have. Quit going off half-cocked."

"How do you know there isn't a connection? Just tell me how you can conveniently overlook that aspect of this whole deal? It doesn't make sense."

"Again, Margaret. You don't know what we know. If you did, you'd see how damaging the evidence is for your friend."

"Malcolm Wiley, I'm telling you one last time. Carole Pickett didn't pull that trigger and you've got the wrong person locked up. Meanwhile, the real killer is getting away."

"I've got the real killer. Give it a rest, Margaret. Go peddle real estate."

"I'll go alright," she replied hotly. "But it won't be to peddle real estate. I will not rest until I prove that Carole is innocent. And when I do, Sheriff Wiley, you'll have egg on your face." She put her face right up in his, at least as close as she felt safe in going. "You're going to regret not keeping an open mind about all this."

The purple in the sheriff's face was rapidly being replaced by black. Coal black, Mags thought. "And you're going to regret sticking your nose in where it doesn't belong." He raised his hand, extended his forefinger, and wagged it in Mags' face. "Don't mess with me, Margaret, because I won't hesitate to arrest you as well for obstructing justice and interfering with a criminal investigation."

"Get your finger out of my face, Malcolm, before you draw back a bloody, broken nub."

"Add threatening a law enforcement officer to that list of charges I can haul you in for," the lawman threatened. His voice had risen to a level that passersby were overhearing, causing them to stop and gawk.

Grant Lewis poked Mags in the back. "Let's leave the sheriff to his rat killing," he suggested quietly, as he shoved her toward the closest exit door.

"You're not kidding about the sheriff," he said, once he and Mags were outside, where they could stop and talk.

"There's so much more going on here than any of us can understand, but you mark my words, Malcolm Wiley is eyebrow deep in something he shouldn't be."

"Whether he is or not," the attorney advised, "you need to keep your cool. Unfortunately, if the sheriff feels threatened by you, he can manufacture those charges and slap you in a cell." He examined Mags with quizzical eyes. "If you're serious about investigating this case, and proving your friend innocent, you can't do that from behind bars."

Mags knew he was right. "I know, but Malcolm just pushes my buttons."

"He knows that. Why do you think he does it?"

"Huh?"

"If he can push your buttons, causing you to react exactly the way he knows you will, then he can keep you off base, off center, and you're much less of a threat to him."

The light bulb came on. "Damn him! He's playing me. He knew exactly what he was doing when he pretended to apologize."

"You got it. Now that you know his game, it doesn't matter why he's doing it. You don't want to further empower him by falling for his tricks."

Her attorney spoke fact, Mags knew, and she would be a fool not to heed his warning. "You're right. Thanks for straightening me out."

"The pleasure is all mine. Especially in this situation." He glanced at his watch. "Oops, got to run. Got an appointment in five minutes and I'm not ready."

"Go!" Mags urged. "And send me a bill for this morning in court, as well as the advice you just gave me. It's worth its weight in gold."

"Will do," he called over his shoulder, and he took off in the direction of his office on the other side of the square.

Mags, on the other hand, didn't run anywhere. Instead, she stood for the longest just thinking about all that had gone down. What did it add to what she already knew? Did it change any of the impressions she had already formed? Once she had processed everything a second time, she began to move slowly toward her office. No running this time. That had been one of her shortcomings, she realized. She'd been running so frantically in her efforts to get Carole off death row, she literally hadn't been able to see the real story in the forest for all the trees of confusion that had gotten in her path.

That, she vowed, was about to change.

Chapter Eleven

WHO ARE YOU?

S he was too fractured to sit and deal with clerical tasks. After her third lap around the small office, Mags knew she had to escape. Pacing simply wasn't the answer. She felt helpless to save her friend, and she knew in her gut that the dead man's real identity had everything to do with why he was killed. But knowing and proving were two distant concepts. What's more, the absence of new clients looking for their own mountain getaway weighed heavily on her mind, and served as a constant reminder that she could easily lose all that she had worked so hard to build. There wouldn't be anything she could do.

Proof that she wasn't imagining things, Mags watched couples walking by her office. No one even came up the walk onto the porch to look at the board filled with photos of listed properties. It was like the building itself had a gigantic scarlet M for murderer painted on it. By way of reassurance, she examined herself to be certain she wasn't wearing a similar symbol of exclusion. The Crabapple Cove grapevine was thriving and functioning.

Pacing the room wasn't the answer to her problems; neither was running away. In the world of common sense, she knew it would be impossible to escape. Nevertheless, Mags believed she would literally lose her mind if she had to sit in the empty office and continue to void listing contracts. That had been the bulk of her work for the past few days, and was a constant, painful reminder of how quickly circumstances could change.

Fueled by an inspiration born out of desperation, Mags grabbed her purse and didn't even take time to set the phones. Once out the door, she sprinted for her Jeep and was soon on her way out of town. She might not be able to truly escape all that was going on, but she knew where she could have a short time of peace, a sanctuary away from the chaos that had become her daily existence. A mountaintop hideaway, in the edge of the national forest, was exactly what she needed, she knew, as she edged the accelerator closer to the floor. She would make her escape short, and quick.

The cocoon of green greeted her with the peace and serenity she craved. Through the trees, she could hear the thunder of a majestic waterfall that was one of the area's major tourist attractions. It didn't take long for her to spread her blanket, grab a pillow and the book she was reading. She got comfortable and dived back into caterer-turned-PI Goldy Shultz's exciting life. As she was reading, Mags pondered all the static that had rained on her parade, especially whenever she mentioned working undercover to discover who really murdered HJH. Why, she asked herself, couldn't she be a detective? If a caterer could do it, it should be a piece of cake for a real estate broker.

Mags was alongside Goldy, elbow-deep in preparation for the party the book's main character was catering later that evening when, out of the corner of her eye, a sudden movement grabbed her attention. She mentally laid down the paring knife she was using and looked around. Sun was filtered through trees, and a gentle breeze moved the shadows that resulted with a gentle rocking motion. Birds unseen sang their songs, and Mags could hear scampering of the woodland creatures. So what had she seen? She studied her surroundings, and could find no explanation for the motion that had brought her back to reality. Her initial fear that it might have been a deer or, even worse, a bear, soon disappeared. Either of those animals would have already shown themselves.

With questioning reluctance, she abandoned her search and

returned to Goldy's kitchen, glad to see that her absence hadn't slowed the production. After all, she reasoned, it took a lot of coordination to cater events like the dinner Goldy was serving. As she followed the cooking sleuth, Mags could sense unseen eyes following her. She feared to turn around or to react suddenly and, instead, forced herself to continue reading. Finally, when the words on the page had lost all their relevance, and the hair on the back of her neck was standing at attention, Mags dropped her book. She swung her head in an uncomfortable arc, desperate to locate the unknown what, or whoever, was nearby. Again, she saw nothing, but she was unwilling to chalk it up to either nerves or imagination. Someone or some thing was out there.

Mags twisted and turned, peering into the lush, green undergrowth and the spread of green that was the forest beyond. Nothing. Reluctantly, she reclaimed her book but was unable to re-immerse herself in the activities ongoing in the kitchen. Miss Goldy, Mags decided, would have to finish this gig without her assistance. She put down the book and lay down on the blanket, pulling the pillow under her head. A person in the trees, anyone who was there innocently, enjoying nature, would have introduced himself or herself, she reasoned.

She didn't have long to wait. Laying so as to give the impression that she was napping, Mags had her eyes almost closed. She became aware that the birds had stopped their concert, just before she sensed movement out of the slits formed by her almost-closed eyelids. It was a man. Her breath caught in her chest, and she thought her breastbone would shatter. The man, who now stood not more than fifty feet from her, was the same man she'd seen in the back of the courtroom that morning. Strong was the urge to bolt and run.

She knew she was being stalked, and now she had a clear look at the man who was following her. But why? Who had put him on her tail? Had he followed her to Atlanta? Mags lay there for the longest, wondering whether to continue playing possum, or if she should jump up and confront him. In the end, she elected to call his bluff, figuring that she might have to lay there the rest of the day if she chose the other option.

Once the decision was made, she wasted no time. In one motion, Mags leapt up from her pallet and, before she was even on her feet good, she charged her unwelcome visitor. "Who are you?" she screamed, as she lunged toward the startled figure dressed in camouflage. "Why are you following me? WHY?"

Her unwelcome visitor didn't answer, but turned instead and disappeared quickly into the forest that closed its doors of greenery behind him.

Mags was suddenly alone, but she was far from comfortable. The magic of the secluded promontory in the clouds, within hearing range of a lyrical mountain waterfall, had lost all its allure. Suddenly, she was a woman alone in the wilderness of the national forest, with no means of self-defense. What's more, no one knew she was there. The Slop Bucket had never looked so good. Mags quickly scooped her blanket and pillow into her arms, and grabbed for her book. Pausing only to survey her surroundings once again, she dashed for her Jeep, running as fast as her sandals would allow. When she was safely inside the vehicle, even before she allowed herself a deep breath of relief, Mags locked the doors and cranked the engine. Only then did she give herself the luxury of enjoying a good case of shakes and hysteria.

It wasn't until she had navigated the rough and remote mountain road and was back on the populated ribbon of pavement that would lead her home, that Mags really began to relax. The entire time she had been picking her way slowly down the two-mile long twisting road, her eyes had been in constant motion, fearful that someone would jump out from the trees. By the time she reached the bottom, Mags was aware of two things. First, there could be no doubt that she was being followed. She even knew what her shadow looked like. Second, as she had picked her way down the rutted roadway, she had seen no sign of any other vehicle. So how had her stalker gotten to the top of the mountain? Was it possible that more than one person was following her?

There were many more questions than she had answers, but she couldn't wait to call Wyatt to bring him up to speed. It was, she promised herself, the first thing she would do once she reached The

Slop Bucket. After locking the door and setting the security system, of course.

Finally, thankfully, she was home, where she unlocked the door and stepped inside, relieved to feel once again the welcome and safety the lodge always offered. From the huge stack-stone fireplace that took up almost an entire end wall, to the bank of windows that looked out onto the lake and literally brought the outside indoors, it was a diamond that never lost its sparkle.

"Delilah. Come here, girl. Let's go out right quick, I've got to call Wyatt."

Only the beloved corgi didn't appear as she usually did, and Mags called again. Louder this time. Her companion was getting older, she reminded herself. Still no dog was to be seen, and Mags's stomach did an uncomfortable flip-flop. Something wasn't right.

Mags began walking through the house, calling. She looked in all her dog's favorite places. It wasn't until she reached the end of her emotional endurance, at the master bathroom door, that she found the lovely tan and brown dog she'd first brought home as a puppy. Delilah was sprawled out on the tile floor, in a most uncomfortable looking position, surrounded by puddles of noxious-smelling vomit.

"Delilah!" What's wrong, baby?" She knelt by the dog, stroking her head. Instead of the usual excited kissing, her pet's only response was a moan that tore Mags' heart to pieces. "Baby? What happened?" she asked again, as if she expected the dog to explain. She knew had to get her companion to the vet, so she scooped the corgi into her arms and headed back through the house, pausing only to grab her purse.

With Delilah laid out on the back seat, Mags drove as fast as the curving roads allowed. She didn't have a clue what was wrong, but she knew she couldn't imagine her life without Delilah. Somehow, some way, her dog had to get well. She told the veterinary technician as much when she surrendered her beloved Delilah's almost comatose body.

"Tell Dr. Sanders to do whatever he has to do."

"I'll tell him, Mrs. Gordon." She turned with her burden and headed to the back, and Mags watched the woman's retreating back, praying harder than she had in a long time. There was too much ugliness going on, and somebody had to get to the bottom of things. Only how could Delilah's illness be connected to stalkers in the woods and bogus clients being murdered? Nothing made any sense, and there were too many loose pieces.

The clock, Mags was certain, was taking its own sweet time counting down the day. She studied the room where two other people, a man and a woman, sat nearby. The worried expressions on both their faces hinted at the angst they, too, were evidently feeling. Bags of pet feed were on a pallet in the far end of the room. Overpowering the cool air in the room was the unique fragrance of animal, poop and disinfectant that tickled her nose and reminded, once again, that this was a special place for special needs. Mags recalled other, less stressful visits to the various vets she had used over the years, and decided that animal clinics were much more embracing than human care facilities. Hospitals could take a lesson from the vets.

"Mrs. Gordon?"

Mags' head jerked to attention and she leaped to her feet. It was the wonderful Florence Nightingale who had taken Delilah from her. Oh, please, Mags prayed, don't let this be bad news.

"Yes? Delilah… How is…?"

The woman put her hand on Mags' arm. "It's okay. Dr. Sanders just wants to talk with you."

Mags followed robot-like, numb to all that was happening, unable to decide if she was going to hear good news or the verdict she didn't want to even consider. The technician led her into a treatment room, where Delilah was stretched out on her side, on the exam table. Standing over the dog, wearing a lime green smock decorated with cartoon figures of various Disney characters, was a bald-headed man with a stethoscope looped around his neck. He was stroking the dog and talking softly to her.

"Dr. Sanders," Mags blurted, "what's wrong with Delilah? I've never seen her like this. Please tell me she's…." The remainder of the words stuck in her throat and refused to vacate.

"We've got a very sick girl here," he volunteered, coming to her rescue. "I think we'll be able to pull her through. But you and I need to talk. Delilah has been poisoned."

"Poisoned!" Mags leaned against the wall to keep from falling. "How? I don't understand."

"Judging from her symptoms, from the stomach fluids we withdrew, I strongly suspect rat poisoning."

The room continued to tilt. Rat poison! But how?

"That's impossible," she told him. "I'm not questioning your expertise," she hastened to explain. "But I don't even have any rat poison at home. And she's been inside all day." She waved her hands, helpless to further explain. "I… I found her like this when I got home. Is there some other kind of poison that could have caused this?"

The doctor scratched his head. "She's got all the classic symptoms of poisoning. It's a textbook example." He paused. "From the smell of the stomach contents, it has the faint smell associated with ingested rat poison. But there wasn't very much there, especially for her to be so compromised."

Mags remembered the bathroom. "There were several puddles of vomit in the bathroom where I found her."

"That explains it. Somehow she knew she needed to get it up and out. That's probably what saved her life."

"And you really think it's rat poison that did this?"

"I'm ninety-nine percent certain. We should know for sure in about five more minutes. My lab is testing what we withdrew."

"But she is going to live." She had, Mags realized, phrased her words as a demand rather than a question.

"It'll be touch and go for the next twenty-four hours. I've already given her an injection of antidote for rat poison, to get it into her system. It won't hurt her, but if I'm right, it gives us a head start."

As the doctor spoke, he continued to fondle the corgi's head, never breaking the human to animal connection, Mags realized. A different uniformed technician entered the room bearing a piece of paper. The lab results, she assumed. The vet studied the report, then looked straight at Mags.

"There's no question about it. Rat poison." He rattled off a long, technical-sounding name that totally escaped Mags' comprehension. She was too much in shock, because the doctor's findings had much larger implications than even he could appreciate. The full impact of it all was still settling about Mags uncomfortable shoulders.

"So what do we do?" she asked at length.

"I'll need to keep her here for the next day, maybe two. If she makes it through this time tomorrow, I suspect she'll pull out of this. Between the medication I gave her and the body's natural elimination process, what little is left in her system should be gone within twenty-four hours."

"Rat poison?"

"I'm afraid so. You say you don't keep any at home. Are you absolutely certain there's none stuck back somewhere that you might have forgotten about? Somewhere that she might have gotten into it out of boredom or mischief?"

"I've never had rat poison in the house. I'm afraid of it." I really am, now, she told herself. "And Delilah doesn't plunder or get into things she shouldn't. She never has."

"Then I'd say you've got a mystery on your hands. A fairly dangerous one at that."

He doesn't know even a tenth of the mystery that has been my life of late. But all of this is connected. Of that I am convinced.

"I'm going home and search the house, just to be certain," she told the vet. She felt like she was expected to say something along those lines, and she complied. "I've only been there about two years. I suppose someone before me could have hidden some. I'll make sure."

"Do that," he agreed. The vet left Delilah who, Mags realized, was snoring, and came around the table. "We don't want this to happen again."

"No, we certainly don't."

"Let me buzz for someone to move her to a kennel in the back."

"Please," Mags asked, hoping her voice didn't sound as desperate as she felt. "May I say goodbye to her first?"

"Sure. Take as much time as you like."

Mags moved around to her pet's head and leaned close, burying her face in the fur. "Delilah, I love you. I don't know what I'd do if anything happened to you." She raised her head and realized she was crying. "Leaning close again, she whispered in Delilah's ear. "Somebody did this to you deliberately and, if it's the last thing I ever do, I'm going to find out who, and they are going to pay." She felt the enormity of the situation welling up in her throat. "When I do," she vowed to the sleeping dog, "when I do, they will pay and pay big time. They went too far when they involved you."

The technician arrived to move the dog back to her kennel, after Mags bade her one last, reluctant goodbye.

"We'll take very good care of her, Mrs. Gordon. Thanks to you, for getting her here so quickly, she stands a good chance of recovery. Another hour or two would have meant just the opposite."

Mags felt a cold chill invade her. If the man in the woods hadn't spooked her, she might not have gotten home until it was too late. "Thank you, Dr. Sanders. You will call me if there are any complications?"

"We will," he promised, and patted her on the shoulder. "But don't panic if you see our number on your Caller ID. We're also going to call you, probably tomorrow morning, to let you know how she made the night."

"So a phone call isn't automatically bad news?"

He smiled. "That's about the size of it."

Mags made her departure, sick at heart, and fearful to leave Delilah behind, even though she knew it was for the best. At least at the vet's, she reasoned, her pet was safe.

She grabbed her cell phone and dialed Wyatt's office. When Ramona heard Mags' name, her voice assumed a much warmer tone than she had exhibited before. "Mr. Fulton's on another line, and I've got yet another call holding for him. Let me hand him a note asking that he call you back as soon as he's free."

Mags told her that would be fine, and hung up. Evidently, she told herself, Wyatt had spoken to the receptionist, just as he promised. She would wait for his call. In the meantime, she turned the Jeep toward The Slop Bucket. While the vehicle's wheels were turning toward home, her mind was turning and turning with all that she knew, plus everything that she didn't understand. Which was a lot.

Somebody, she realized, had killed Mr. Humphries. For reasons totally unknown to her, Delilah had become the next victim. Most frightening of all, was the sudden realization that she might be the next target? It was not a prospect she could entertain. Somehow she had to find them, before they got her.

It was a daunting assignment, since she had not the first clue who "they" were.

Chapter Twelve
COULD I BE NEXT?

F or the first time ever, Mags hesitated as she unlocked The Slop Bucket door. Even when she had been forced to acknowledge that Franklin used the place as a love nest, she had never been fearful of opening the door. But that was then. This was now.

As she fitted the key into the lock and turned the knob, her cell phone burst forth with a reprise of Jimmy Buffett's famous tune. Mags grinned. A margarita would taste good. Talk about timing. She got into the house, grabbed the phone from her purse, and checked the display screen.

"Hello, Wyatt. I thought you'd never call back."

"Ramona said you sounded very distressed. What's wrong?"

Mags found her favorite chair and allowed her legs to buckle. Not very gracefully and her mother definitely would not have approved. But then Mags didn't approve of attempted murder, either.

"I saw my stalker this morning and again this afternoon. What's more, somebody tried to murder my dog."

"You've got my complete attention."

Mags walked him through the morning's court appearance, and

explained about the man who sat in the very back. Then she told about seeking out the mountain sanctuary, where she literally came face to face with the same man, except in different clothes.

"This is an organized operation," she stressed. "Wyatt, somebody is following me. They know everything I do, only I don't know why." She waved her arms around her, forgetting that he couldn't see. "For all I know, they're right here, outside The Slop Bucket. What's to say somebody doesn't have my house bugged?"

"Unfortunately, all of the above are possibilities," he said very quietly. "But what's this about your dog?"

"She was asleep when I left her," she said, after she finished recounting the frightening discovery of her sweet Delilah and the race to the vet. "He said if I hadn't gotten her there when I did, she probably would have died."

"That's hitting pretty low."

"Tell me about it."

"But she's going to pull through?"

"There's a good chance." She sobered. "Which means there's also a chance she won't."

"Think positive."

"Believe me, I am. But beyond Delilah, I'm thinking about me. It hit me coming home. HJH was murdered. Obviously, his death is tied to me in ways that I simply do not understand. Now someone tries to kill my dog, and would have succeeded, if I had stuck to my normal schedule." She stopped, knowing what she wanted to say, but searching for words that didn't frighten quite so badly. "Wyatt... could I be next on their list?"

The attorney's first answer was silence. Then, finally, when Mags felt she would explode, he said, "I'd be less than honest with you if I told you I thought there was no danger."

Thanks, I think, Mags said to herself. "So you think I'm at risk?"

"Do you?"

"I'm scared to death. As of an hour or so ago, I had a complete change of attitude. Somebody tried to kill my dog. These people mean business."

"Looks that way."

"And why? Why, Wyatt? What have I done?"

"I can't answer that, Margaret. I'm totally scratching my head."

While they talked, Mags' eyes were searching all areas of the lodge she could see from where she was sitting. Instead of seeing the massive, hand-hewn beams in the great room, or the wormy chestnut paneling on the walls, she saw instead darkness and shadows. What if someone was hiding in those once-friendly nooks and crannies.

"I'm frightened in my own home," she confessed again. "I never thought that could happen. Not here." Then it hit her. Delilah was staying at the vet's clinic. She would be at home totally alone that night, without even the company of a dog to reassure her.

"I'd like to say you were safe as long as you're at home, but Delilah was at home, and she almost died."

"My point exactly!" She fiddled with her hair. "I'd clear out and go to a motel, but what good would that do? Somebody… maybe several people… seem to know every move I make."

"I was about to suggest the motel myself, but you're spot on. You'd probably be wasting your money."

"What am I going to do, Wyatt? I can't go around terrified to breathe."

"I've got an idea."

"Okay?" Mags wondered what his solution might be and, more importantly, how effective would it be?

"Christine went through the homes catalog from front to back the night I brought it home. She likes the ones you and I selected, but she's spotted a few more she'd like to see."

"That's great, Wyatt! Whenever you two can get back up here, it'll be my pleasure to show you as many houses as you'd like." It's not like I've got any other clients clamoring for showings, she reflected sadly.

"That's what I'm suggesting. Tomorrow is Saturday. How about if we drive up early tomorrow morning and stay through Sunday evening. That should give us enough time to see several places."

Mags knew Wyatt's offer was intended more to reassure her, than it was to look at property, but she was too relieved to protest. "That would be fantastic. You can stay here at the house."

"We wouldn't want to impose."

"You're not," she vowed. "I've got plenty of room and I won't take no for an answer."

Their conversation ended and Mags realized, once again that she was all alone at a remote lodge, miles from town. As much to kill time as to reassure herself, she made the rounds in the house double-checking that every window was latched, and that all of the outside doors were locked. She examined the security system's control panel, and determined no greater level of protection was available. Thank goodness the technicians had gotten repairs made to both systems. That led to another check of the windows and doors. She realized she was acting a fool, but she also knew genuine fright when she encountered it.

The evening stretched long before her and with it, the emptiness of the lodge and the night. Delilah contributed more to the emotions of home than she had ever realized, and she even shed a few tears as she recalled finding her beloved dog so near death's door. A TV dinner for her evening meal and a long, lonely night of mind-numbing shows on the idiot box finally got her to bedtime. She checked the security system again and even called for Delilah to go out one last time, before she remembered that her dog lay in a kennel at the vet's. Mags wished she'd remembered to tell them that her dog was cold natured, to please put a blanket in with her.

Convinced she wouldn't sleep a wink in the empty house, Mags tossed and turned a few times to prove herself right. The next thing she knew, morning light was streaming through the window over the bed, and Mags realized it was Saturday. She had survived.

Knowing she had guests coming gave her motivation to begin the day. While her hot tea brewed, Mags showered. She popped a couple of frozen biscuits into the oven and had her breakfast ready to enjoy on the screened porch overlooking the lake, when she remembered she was being stalked. She opted instead for one end of the massive dining room table. It was safer, although not nearly as picturesque.

After she'd cleaned the house, taking special pains in the guest suite with the adjoining bath, she felt her house was ready for guests. Unfortunately, her pantry and her refrigerator were severely lacking.

She would have to meet Wyatt and his wife in town, since he'd never been to The Slop Bucket. Mags made her grocery list, changed clothes, and made ready to head to town. She would buy groceries, then kill time at the office until her company arrived.

As she left the house, Mags found herself looking over her shoulder, checking the Jeep's back seat to be certain no one was hiding there. In the road that normally gave her so much enjoyment and reward, she found herself keeping one eye on her rearview mirror. Was someone following her? The few cars she met, she scanned the faces inside, hoping all the while she wouldn't see the man she'd confronted in the woods.

Groceries bought, Mags swung through the post office to get the mail, then drove to her office and stowed the perishables in the break area refrigerator. Got to remember to get all that out when we leave, she reminded herself. Then she tackled the mail by thumbing through the envelopes and circulars she'd pulled out of the post office box, committing most of it to the trash can. Two statements that remained, the only viable pieces in the day's delivery, went into the "to-be-paid" basket, to be dealt with next week. It was Saturday, for a change she had guests coming for the weekend, and Mags vowed to play and not worry about work. So strong was her vow, she didn't even turn on her computer. She considered going to visit Carole, but decided to wait until Wyatt arrived, in case Malcolm was his usual charming self. Wyatt could get them in where she might fail. Instead, she settled down in the reception area to read the Atlanta daily paper.

There, on page three, the headline screamed: Murder Victim Was a Fraud; is the Real Killer Still Running Loose?

Ernestine Shelby's article!

So much had transpired over the past few days Mags had all but forgotten about the interview.

Crabapple Cove, GA: There's a town in northeast Georgia where the inhabitants believe they're in paradise. Just ask anyone in the small, picturesque town of Crabapple Cove. They'll confirm there's definitely something special about this small, mountain hamlet. But even paradise, it seems, is subject to darker forces. This fact of life and death was revealed when the body of one Horace J. Humphries was found murdered a couple of weeks back. Now a woman sits in jail, charged with his murder. It only took the sheriff's office about a week to make the arrest. Case closed.

Or is it? Should this case really be chalked up as resolved?

Consider this... the deceased was discovered to have been operating under a false identity. The woman who allegedly pulled the trigger can't be directly tied to the crime. It was her gun, but no one saw her commit the killing and, unfortunately, corpses don't tell tales or identify their murderers. What makes this murder even more suspect? So far, no one, including the local sheriff Malcolm Wiley, has been able to learn the dead man's true identity. Or why he was in Crabapple Cove under false pretenses. The sheriff has proclaimed his disinterest in investigating the man's background. "A man is dead, murdered. It doesn't matter what name he died under."

In the meantime, emotions are...

Mags shifted in her seat, and raised her eyes from the tapestry of words the writer had woven to tell the story of one Horace J. Humphries, who met his demise under questionable circumstances. Her admiration for Ernestine Shelby's expertise rose several notches, the further she read, as she discovered inconsistency after inconsistency the writer had brought to light. If anything could affect public opinion in the community, this would do it, she believed. There was still more to read, and she wasted no time getting back to the article.

"We're here," a voice rang out, as the bell on the front door signaled the arrival of a visitor, and yanked Mags from her reading.

"Wyatt," she exclaimed. She made her way across the room to greet the attorney. To the attractive, willowy blond standing beside him, she said, "And you must be Christine." She extended her hand. "I'm so glad to meet you."

Mags immediately liked the laugh that accompanied her guest's reply. "No happier than I am to meet you. I understand I may finally get that second home I've been begging for, thanks to you. I'll never be able to adequately repay you."

"And I'll never be able to repay your husband for all he's doing for Carole," Mags confessed. "Why don't we make it easy on everyone and just consider all the debts paid? Except for Wyatt's professional fees, of course," she added hastily, lest the attorney think she was trying to evade his bill.

"How is Carole?" Waytt asked. "I need to see her while we're here."

Mags was scurrying about closing the office. "I wanted to visit her this morning, but I decided to wait until you arrived. You may have more power over Malcolm than I do."

"Then let's go. The sooner the better."

Wyatt ran into initial resistance, but soon persuaded the deputy to allow a short visit, and he and Mags were escorted into the now-familiar prisoner visiting area. Carole arrived a short time later.

"Oh, thank goodness you've both come," she cried, when she was brought from the back of the complex. "I've about lost my mind for somebody to talk with. Daddy can't look at me without crying, and I don't want to hurt him."

"Are they treating you alright?" Mags asked, alarmed by her friend's generally unkempt appearance. Did Carole have an opportunity to bathe, she wondered.

"They're not mistreating me, if that's what you mean. But they keep me locked in my cell, unless I'm getting out to shower or to come in here."

"You do get to bathe?"

"Yeah, such as it is. They only have one shower area. This jail wasn't designed for ladies, so I have to shower in the men's area, under the very prying eyes of a female deputy. Talk about feeling violated." Her face reddened. "That's just loads of fun. I don't exactly feel like taking my time to enjoy the soothing waters." She laughed, but Mags didn't detect any humor in her voice.

"Listen, Carole," Wyatt interrupted. "I don't know how much time we'll have, but you need to keep your chin up. I've prepared a petition that will be filed on Monday morning, before I go back to Atlanta, asking that your request for bail be reconsidered."

"Do you think it will work? I can't stand much more of this. It's not just the loneliness. The food absolutely isn't fit to eat, and the cell block has roaches and mice for sure. I'm afraid to consider what else might be crawling around back there."

Mags' mouth dropped open. "That's inhumane! Wyatt, you've got to do something. Malcolm shouldn't be allowed to..." She stopped talking, as she saw laughter lines at the corners of his mouth.

"Hate to burst your bubble," he said. "What Carole's describing is typical for jails, whether they're in small towns or big cities. I don't know of a jail anywhere that's anything like the Mayberry Jail."

Mags remembered the two-cell courthouse on the old Andy Griffith TV sitcom, where the prisoners had rocking chairs and trays of Aunt Bea's home cooking. "I didn't imagine it would be that way, but decent people deserve better than mice and roaches and inadequate facilities."

"I'm afraid what Carole's got is as good as it's going to be. But I am going to do everything in my power to get her released on bail, even if we have to stipulate to house arrest and an ankle monitor."

The two ladies exchanged shocked expressions before Mags broke the silence. "You mean she'd still be in prison? That's what it would be like if she couldn't leave home. She's not guilty and she shouldn't be treated like she is."

"Sorry, Mags. We're fighting an up-hill battle here. If I'm successful in getting her out of here, there are going to be conditions attached, I'm almost certain. Take your choice."

"Just get me out of here," Carole pleaded. "I'll stay at home and never even open the door to look out. Just get me out of this jail. I'm about to lose my mind."

The three talked for a few more minutes, while the attorney explained what would be happening over the next few days. When the deputy who was always at the rear of the room began to fidget, Wyatt called a halt.

"I'll be back to see you soon," Mags promised, as the guard led her friend from the table. "Please stay strong for a few more days."

They returned to the real estate office where Mags collected her perishable items and called the vet to learn that Delilah was holding her own. Then she led her guests west, out of town, toward the lake and The Slop Bucket.

"Margaret, this place is beyond words," Christine Fulton offered, after Mags had given the couple the full tour. "I'd rather have this lodge any day than some mansion in Buckhead."

"Gee, I wish you'd told me that before we bought our last house," Wyatt quipped. "I could have saved half a million dollars."

His wife punched his arm. "There's no way you'd ever leave Atlanta full-time."

"No, because that's where the job is that's going to pay for your new house here in the mountains."

"Oh, you!"

Mags watched the interaction between them, consumed by a moment of envy. She couldn't recall a time when she and Franklin had engaged in such lighthearted banter. Not even, she realized, when they had been newlyweds.

"I've got cold cuts for sandwiches. It'll be quicker to fix a bite here and eat, then we can head straight for the marina. I've got a boat rented for today and tomorrow."

"You didn't need to do that," Wyatt protested. "We wouldn't have held you to your marketing promise to sell us our house by boat."

"It's got nothing to do with integrity," she informed him. "It's all about time. We'll never be able to see all the listings you've selected if we have to go overland. Trust me." She headed for the kitchen. "Lunch will be ready in five."

"Let me help you," Christine volunteered.

It wasn't much more than five minutes later that the three gathered on the porch for sandwiches and a selection of salads, chased with tall glasses of icy, cold sweet tea. For dessert, Mags had picked up a lemon icebox pie.

"We're not even going to take time to wash the dishes," she informed them when they were finished eating. "Let's stow what needs the refrigerator and pile the dishes in the sink. We're wasting sunlight."

Some forty-five minutes later, Mags piloted the same boat she had used a few days earlier out into the lake. Christine had ten homes on her wish list, and they were scattered in various places on the three conjoined lakes. It would take all the time the weekend would afford to see them.

It was well after seven o'clock and a very full afternoon later, before she brought the boat back to the marina dock.

"I'm worn out," Christine volunteered, as Wyatt helped her from the boat. "I never knew house-hunting was such hard work."

"You ought to have to work to make the money to pay for these houses we've seen today."

"And you aren't tired?"

"Whether he is or not," Mags interjected, "I am. And I do this for a living."

"How many did we see?" Christine asked. "I'm so tired I can't remember."

"Five," Mags replied. "We saw five and went back to look at one house twice, so technically I guess we saw six. Trust me, that's quite an afternoon's work, even for me."

"What do you ladies fancy for dinner?" Wyatt asked. "It's on me."

"That's not necessary, Wyatt. I've got steaks and fresh shrimp at home, and a big grill that rarely gets used. That is, if you don't mind playing grill master."

"Let me take us out tonight. We're going to stay over until Monday morning, and we can do your steaks and shrimp tomorrow night. They'll keep, won't they?"

"Well, sure. No problem there. Where would you like to go?"

Mags realized he wasn't familiar with the area. "There's a fantastic place down on the lake. You dine in elegance and comfort, out over the water."

"If you like it, I'm sure we will."

"Sounds perfect," Christine agreed.

Mags handed Wyatt the keys to the Jeep. "He who pays, drives," she informed him. "I'm bushed!"

They were enjoying after-dinner drinks, when Christine said, "I wish we had this place in Atlanta." She was almost purring, Mags thought. "That Argentine steak was to die for, and the view is just as fine as the food."

"If you buy a home here, you'll always have this place right in your own back yard. More or less."

"That's settles, it Wyatt. Now we have to buy a house. Which one do you like the best."

"The one nearest this restaurant. It'll cut down on mileage and gasoline. Something tells me we'll be dining here every trip up."

"Thank you, dearest. Now I won't have to connive and scheme. You make it so easy."

Again, Mags was struck by the beauty and the safety of their give and take. That they each adored the other went without saying. But it went much deeper. Underneath all the fun and lighthearted quips, was a genuine sense of respect that could clearly be seen. That was what had been missing from her own marriage, she realized. It also turned out to be the fatal flaw. Seeing another marriage in action demonstrated with painful clarity where her own relationship had come up short.

"We'd better be headed back," Wyatt proposed. "It's getting late, although I'll admit, I could sit here looking out this wall of glass, watching the twinkling lights imposed against the darkness forever. It's so tranquil."

Wyatt piloted the Jeep and Mags provided the directions. Before she realized it, he was pulling up beside the lodge. Getting out and getting into the house was nothing to be feared, she realized. It was because she wasn't alone. That night in bed, which came shortly after their arrival, she found sleep without effort and rested soundly, until the first warm, bright stabs of morning light awakened her.

"Coffee's on the sideboard and I'm working on breakfast," she informed her guests who appeared, still wiping the sleep from their eyes. "Hope you like French toast and fresh fruit."

"Sounds wonderful." Christine fetched a cup from the mug tree and poured a cup of the hot, fragrant liquid. "I can't wake up without my coffee," she volunteered. "Otherwise I'm an absolute bear."

"Tell me about it! You ought to try to live with you when you miss your caffeine fix."

"Like you're a gold-wrapped package with a big floppy bow."

Wyatt saluted his wife with his raised cup of coffee. "Touché."

"You two, do you always go on like this, or is this your special kind of a hostess gift?"

The couple exchanged uneasy glances before Wyatt spoke first. "We're not doing anything here that we don't do at home. Perhaps we should be on better behavior?"

"Perhaps we should..." Christine said, her voice trailing off.

I've offended them, Mags feared. "You misunderstand," she hastened to say. "I love it. It's like a breath of fresh air." Fearing she was about to embarrass herself, she turned back to the toast that was ready to take up. "I have to wonder if Franklin and I might have lasted if we had engaged in such give and take."

"We've just always been this way," Christine confessed. "I have to admit, I'd never thought that much about it."

"It's a rarity in the marriages I know," Mags explained, thinking of all her friends back in Atlanta, for whom marriage was a social status rather than a relationship. "Let's adjourn to the porch, breakfast is ready."

The threesome enjoyed their food, rather than bolt the meal and run, the way they had the day before.

"That was delicious," Christine said, when she finally shoved her chair back from the table. "You simply have to give me your recipe for French toast. Mine is always so soggy. Yours was custard-like in the center."

"It's the bread. Mine used to be soggy as well, but I was watching a cooking show one day that showed me why. First you have to choose the right type bread. Then you toast it ever so slightly before dipping it in the egg and milk mixture."

"Whatever it is, I want the recipe. I'll never, ever be able to eat my version again." She flashed her husband an intimate grin. "From here on out, Mags' French toast is my French toast." She raised her arm in salute.

"Listen, you two. It's just been so nice to have someone to cook for. I didn't realize what a loner I've become since I moved here. I rarely cook for myself, and I can't remember the last time I had guests."

You may have to remedy that situation, you know, the little voice behind her left ear observed. Mags didn't feel like arguing. It wasn't becoming for someone who had become far too much of a hermit.

"We've got five more houses to see," she reminded her guests. "How are you feeling about those we saw yesterday?"

The couple exchanged glances. "We like them all," Wyatt said. "That's the problem."

"But the third one, the one we went back to see the second

time, is still at the top of our list so far. Who knows where it'll be by tonight?"

"Indeed." Mags echoed. "We'd better get underway."

The lake was smooth and the winds were teasing as Mags set course for the first house of the day. They didn't linger long there, after it was quickly apparent whoever had written the description of the property, had taken very liberal license.

The next four houses were relatively close together and by two o'clock, Mags was pulling away from the last dock. "You've seen them all. What say ye?"

"I don't know about Wyatt, but I didn't see anything today that I liked nearly as much as the third one yesterday. There was just nothing about that one that I didn't like."

Mags looked at Wyatt with a question mark on her face.

"Hey, I liked them all. But I have to agree with Christine. That house just seemed over the top in so many ways."

"Could we go back and see it again?"

Mags thought Christine's request to be a sound one, and said so. "I'm famished and I know you both must be as well. It's been a long time since this morning's French toast."

"I'm with Mags," Christine agreed. "Where can we get a sandwich or something quick?"

Mags was already headed back to the Fultons' dream house. "There's a little lakeside café on down a ways. We can get something there, then go back to look at the house. Food is on the way."

True to her word, Mags soon brought the little boat alongside the dock behind what had once been a service station, now masquerading as a sandwich shop. Over burgers and fries, the three talked about the property they were about to see for the third time. Soon she was nosing the craft into the boat slip.

"Oh, Mags. This house is almost perfect." Christine whirled around the great room, her arms clasped to her chest. "I promise I'll live in Atlanta and not complain, if I know I can come here every

Friday and not have to go back until Monday morning."

"Can I get that in writing? Preferably notarized," Wyatt asked with mock seriousness.

"No, you may not," his wife replied. "Besides, once I decide I want to live here year-round, I don't want something I signed in a moment of euphoric stupidity to come back to haunt me."

"So you're ready to make an offer?"

The couple exchanged glances. "What the hey, why not? It's just money."

Christine brushed her husband's cheek with a kiss.

"Mags, what kind of deal can we make on this place?"

She turned out the lights and locked the house, then joined her friends outside on the deck. "I've been thinking, Wyatt. The asking price here is one million six, but it's been on the market for a while. In fact, I think it was listed, withdrawn and then relisted. I need to see what I can find out about the history. It could help us decide what to offer."

"I'm leaving it all in your hands," he said. "Just get it for us."

The three re-boarded the boat and Wyatt untied the mooring rope. Mags cast off and in a matter of minutes, they were back at the marina. Wyatt tied up while Mags returned the key, and they were soon on their way to The Slop Bucket.

"I am absolutely exhausted," Christine lamented as she fell into one of the rockers on the front porch of the lodge. "I never thought I'd see the day I wouldn't want to look at houses, but I think this weekend has cured me."

"Gosh," Mags said. "I hope I didn't push you too hard. I don't guess we had to do it all in one weekend. It's not like you couldn't come back again."

"Careful, good wife. Don't ever let your friends hear that two days of looking at high-priced property wore you out. They'll blackball you. Then you'll have no choice but to move to Crabapple Cove full-time, to live out your years in shame."

"Blackballed," she mumbled. "It might be worth it to be a social outcast."

The rest of the day was low-key and uneventful. The three friends lazed around, grilled the steaks and shimp, and enjoyed them by the waning rays of sunlight. Conversation covered many topics but not, Mags realized once she'd settled down for the night, anything about HJH, people stalking her, or even Carole. That omission caused Mags to suffer pangs of guilt. Her best friend was spending yet another night in a filthy, stinking jail, on a hard bed with no frills. Yet, she was forced to admit, it had been nice to put all the mess down for a few hours. She also realized, as sleep claimed her, just how much an unknown man's death had altered her entire life.

Following breakfast the next morning, the three friends made their way into town in both vehicles. Christine rode in with Mags, who was going to the office to work on an offer for the house, while Wyatt was headed to the courthouse to file the petition for a new bail hearing. He would meet them back at the office later.

"Come in and make yourself at home." Mags was turning on lights, adjusting the thermostat, powering up her computer, opening the blinds and sticking her finger in the African violet pots, while she talked. "I'm going to pull up the listing on your house and see what I can find before we make a decision on price."

"That would be great. Wyatt really wants to have an offer on the table before we leave today." She walked over and stood by Mags' chair, watching the moving images on the computer screen. "Can you imagine what it must have been like to sell real estate before computers?"

Mags had to laugh. She had been in real estate before technology; she just hadn't been serious enough about her job to have any basis for comparison. She confessed as much.

While she was reading the listing details on the house, Mags noticed the "you've got mail" icon in the lower right corner of the screen illuminate. Out of habit, and without really thinking, she clicked on it. Her reward was a page full of new messages. But the one that caught her attention, the one that had triggered the alert, was the newest one at the top of the list. The one with nothing in the subject line, and a sender's address she didn't recognize, sent fear coursing through her.

"What's wrong?" Christine cried with alarm. "You've turned white as a sheet."

For Mags, the room was whirling. "It's… it's this." She pointed to the still-unopened message. "I've been getting some very harassing anonymous e-mails. This looks like it might be the latest."

"Does Wyatt know?"

"He does." Mags could feel her insides reacting like an earthquake. "We've been able to trace them to libraries in the Atlanta area, but that's as far as the investigator could go."

"Are you going to open this one?"

"I… I'm afraid to," she confessed. Then despite Mags' intense dislike for women who cried, she began to sob, unable to contain the tears. "It's been so long… so long since the last one. I had decided whoever it was had gotten tired of their little game." She grabbed a tissue from the box on her desk and poked at her eyes.

"I'm calling Wyatt." Christine fished her phone from the depths of her purse and hit a couple of keys. "Wyatt? How soon will you be here?" She listened to her husband. "Mags thinks there's another one of those e-mails and she's too upset to open it." She listened again. "Okay. Get here as quick as you can. She needs you."

"He'll be finished at the courthouse in about fifteen minutes. He said to sit tight. Don't open it until he gets here."

"He has nothing to worry about. After all that's happened in the last few days, I'm almost afraid to open any of my mail." Mags stared at her hands, unable to think or reason. All she wanted was for someone to tell her that everything would be okay.

Wyatt, unfortunately, wasn't that person. When he arrived, Mags slid away from the computer and allowed him use of her keyboard. He quickly opened the troubling message. "Your gut feeling was spot on," he told her. "Here's the latest."

Mags hung back. "I can't, Wyatt. I just cannot deal with anything else. Read it aloud. We've got no secrets here." Even though she had braced herself for its contents, the message nevertheless hit her hard.

> *Horace Humphries was killed because of what he knew, and you can be killed, too. Remember... dead bodies don't talk.*

"But Wyatt," she wailed, "I don't know anything. I don't have anything to talk about. This is insane!"

The attorney had begun to pace the small room. "But that's just it. Don't you see? You do know something. Something that's making someone else very uneasy. You just don't realize what it is."

"And that's making me very uncomfortable. It's one thing to be killed because I could implicate the shooter. But it's another to think that I could accidentally spill the truth, and never even know it."

"This thing just gets more and more confusing. Meanwhile, we've got the good sheriff marking the murder solved, and an innocent woman's going to be hung out to dry."

Wyatt's last comment hit her hard, and Mags jerked around to look the attorney in the face. "Level with me. Carole's not here. Are things really that bleak?"

He didn't hesitate with his answer. "No. And yes."

"You wanna explain?"

The attorney dropped into a sitting position across the arm of one of the loveseats. "Look at it this way. The case, at best, is circumstantial. It was Carole's gun. Her prints were on it. Big deal. There were no other viable fingerprints, but some of her prints, like one on the trigger, for example, were smudged. Someone else handled that gun, being certain to leave enough good prints to implicate Carole."

"This was a planned crime."

"That, it was."

"So why can't you prove that?"

The lawyer mopped his head with his hand, creating a tousled nest of brown hair. "If only we could prove where Carole was the night this guy was killed, we'd be home free."

"So? Sheriff Wiley can't place her at the marina, either."

"But he can place her gun there. It was even found on board the *One True Love*."

"And...?"

"It's going to come down first to the grand jury. Will they indict her? My guess is they will. All they have to have is reasonable cause. Her gun was there, she can't prove she wasn't."

"That seems so unfair," Mags cried. "She's innocent. I'd stake my life on it."

"Try proving that to a jury."

"So this is hopeless? Is that what you're saying?"

"Not hopeless. Not even impossible. It's all going to come down to the jury that hears the case."

"Then we're sunk."

"How do you figure that?"

"You don't know how well-liked Malcolm Wiley is here. If he tells the public he's confident he got the killer, that's all a jury will need to hear to find Carole guilty. It won't matter what kind of evidence you put forth, the verdict is going to be whatever has the good sheriff's endorsement on it. The locals are not going to make their lawman look bad."

"I fear you're right," Wyatt confessed. "But I do disagree on one thing."

"You've lost me."

"It's not respect people have for the sheriff. It's fear. The undercurrent of intimidation that runs rampant in this place is off the charts. And it all comes from the very top. Sheriff Malcolm Wiley."

"Interesting you should pick up on that."

"It's easier to see if you're an outsider."

"I always felt that way, but then I've had Malcolm thrown in my face since Franklin and I started dating. I didn't really like him then, but I tolerated him. He was my husband's best friend."

"Ugh. Poor you."

"You don't know the half of it, Christine. After I arrived here to live full-time, I found out the sheriff had a key to my house, and used it for years as his private love nest."

"You're kidding?"

"I wish I were. Nothing you could tell me about Malcolm or his actions would ever be a surprise."

Wyatt pulled himself up and came back to Mags' computer. "We need to send this message on to the investigator." He was rubbing his chin. "But before we do, scroll down through the rest of the new e-mails. Are there any others you don't recognize, that don't look familiar?"

Mags did as he asked, and quickly pronounced that everything else appeared legitimate. "A lot of it's spam, but I don't see anything that might be another message from our mysterious sender."

"Then let's get this one on its way." The attorney clicked a couple of keys and stood up. "It's gone."

"I wish it really were gone." Her hands found their way to her head, where they began massaging her hair. "I'm scared, Wyatt. I'm afraid to even sneeze."

"You've got good reason to be frightened. The thing is, I don't know what…"

The ringing of Mags' cell phone interrupted. She held up one finger as she grabbed for it and checked Caller ID. *The vet!* Then she remembered the doctor's reminder, that not all calls were bad news. "Hello?" she answered cautiously.

"Mrs. Gordon?"

"Yes, how is Delilah?"

"Dr. Sanders wanted me to give you an update. Your little girl is showing slow progress. She's stable, but she's just not bouncing back as quickly as he'd like."

"But she is going to pull through?" Please, she begged silently for her dog to live.

"Delilah is a fighter, which is why we're concerned. Rat poison affects the heart, so she's had a double strain. Dr. Sanders has her in a drug-induced, semi-coma to lessen the load right now."

"Coma?"

"It's not as frightening as it sounds, Mrs. Gordon." Maybe not to you, Mags thought. "It's more like a heavy twilight sleep. It just means her heart and her body don't have to work so hard."

"So what are you telling me?" Mags braced for the worst.

"Simply this. Delilah is holding her own and gaining strength. Dr. Sanders would like to keep her here for another day or so, to give her as much rest and recovery as possible. Do we have your consent?"

While her heart screamed agreement, her head was shouting: You'll be home alone again. No Delilah waiting for you!

"Of course. Whatever the doctor thinks is best."

"Thanks, Mrs. Gordon. We'll keep you posted. And if you'd like to come by and visit her, feel free. If she even knows you're here, she probably won't respond the way you'd like, but family visits never hurt."

I can go visit her, Mags told herself. That was something she hadn't thought about.

"Good news, I hope?"

"The best we can expect, Christine. At least I guess it is. Whoever poisoned my dog meant to kill her. She's still very sick. But how does she fit into this miserable little man getting killed? He never even saw her."

"When we find the real killer, we'll also understand why Delilah was such a threat."

"And how do we find that killer who so far has…"

For the second time, Mags cell phone interrupted their conversation. It was Grant Lewis. "Mags," he said, "Judge Beecham is ready to rule on our petition. Can you meet me in his chambers in twenty minutes?"

Although she knew in her gut what the outcome was going to be, Mags told him she would be there.

"Great. See you."

She clicked the phone's disconnect key and shared the news with the others. "I'm sorry, y'all, it doesn't look like we're going to get an offer together this morning."

"This is more important," Wyatt advised. "Besides, I'm really curious to see how this judge sees the situation."

"We should know pretty soon, although I'll be very surprised if I get my boat ."

"Don't think negatively."

"This is Malcolm we're talking about."

"You may be right at that."

Mags reached for her purse and stood up. "I'm going to head on up to the courthouse. You two feel free to stay here and be comfortable. I won't be long. It shouldn't take the judge but a minute to say 'no'."

Chapter Thirteen

THAT'S WHERE THE GUN WAS

B y the time Mags was shown into chambers, the sheriff and her attorney were already seated. Everyone, it appeared, was waiting on her.

I'm sorry," she said, as she took the only remaining empty chair. "I was working with a client." She looked toward the judge expectantly, being especially careful not to glance toward the sheriff, who sat to her right.

"We'll come to order," the judge intoned, and noted that a court reporter would be transcribing everything that was said. "This is a legal proceeding, we're just not in the courtroom," he explained to Mags, who cast a quick, questioning glance at the woman the judge had indicated.

She nodded that she understood.

The judge began to speak. "I've spent a great deal of time researching this issue, and applying various scenarios, in an effort to reach a decision that is, in itself fair, but what's more, one that is equitable to both parties. I've come to conclusion that such an outcome isn't possible."

Mags had known getting the *One True Love* back was a long-shot.

Still, the judge's words were just the latest sucker punch inflicted.

"…to do anything that might compromise the sheriff's complete investigation, especially as long as there are still unanswered questions, and thus unwittingly aid in a murderer going unpunished, is something this court cannot do."

Mags realized her mind had been wandering, and she'd missed the first part of what the judge said. Still, she'd heard enough to know that Malcolm had won.

"Mrs. Gordon? Are you with us?"

"Wha…? Oh, yes, Your Honor. I'm listening." Evidently she had zoned out and it showed.

"I was saying that while I cannot return the boat to you at this time, I am not without sympathy for your situation. Therefore, I am ordering that Sheriff Wiley may continue to impound your boat for as long as he deems necessary, or until someone is convicted of this man's murder."

Her intake of breath must have been audible, Mags realized. Everyone was looking at her. She couldn't believe what she'd just heard. The judge had just given the sheriff carte blanche to hold her boat forever.

Mags realized he was looking at her and she just wanted to shrink into the chair. The judge continued. "However, I'm ordering that the sheriff will permit you on board the boat as soon as it is convenient for you, so that you may remove any documents or other possessions that you need. He will go with you, and you may also take along a witness, if you wish. This is to be done today, if possible."

It had been so long, Mags couldn't remember what might be on board. It sure wouldn't hurt to go look.

"Furthermore," the judge intoned, "I've checked and the sheriff is paying standard, daily boarding rates to the marina for storing your boat. If he can pay that, then he can compensate you out of his investigation budget, for the "use" of your boat." The judge used two fingers on each hand to emphasize the word use.

Malcolm bounced to his feet; his face beginning to darken. "But

Your Honor, I don't have that kind of discretionary money."

"I'm sorry, Sheriff. But Mrs. Gordon is not going to be denied the use of her property indefinitely, and not be compensated. She is NOT the defendant."

Don't give him any ideas, Mags begged silently. But she kept her mouth shut. It was clear that Malcolm had been thrown a curve he hadn't seen coming.

"Any time you need a boat to show property, rent it and present the sheriff with the receipt for reimbursement within five business days. Is that clear, Mrs. Gordon?"

"Yes, Your Honor. It is. And thank you."

"As I understand it, you've already had to rent a boat the day the sheriff first refused to return the *One True Love*?"

"That's right. And I had to rent one again Saturday and yesterday."

The judge fixed her with a stern stare. "Get those bills in to the sheriff today, and he'll have you a check by Friday." The jurist swung his gaze to the obviously irritated sheriff. "Isn't that right, Sheriff Wiley?"

Malcolm didn't answer the judge but asked, instead, "When do you want to go on board? I need to plan my day." And he didn't ask it very willingly, Mags observed.

Mags consulted the clock on the wall. "It's already eleven-thirty. Why don't we say one-thirty? My witness and I will meet you at the marina."

"I'd say we have no further business," the judge intoned. "Court adjourned."

As Mags and her attorney left the courthouse, he said, "I didn't say anything back there, but I've got appointments all afternoon. I can't go with you to the marina."

"Don't be offended," she replied. "But I was going to take Wyatt Fulton, Carole's attorney." She stopped in the middle of the sidewalk. "Who knows? It might somehow help him with his case." She grinned. "Besides, he's accustomed to mixing it up with Malcolm."

"No offense taken. As long as you don't feel like I'm running out on you."

"Not in the least. Thanks for all your hard work. This actually went down better than I had expected."

The lawyer was the one to grin this time. "Let's just say the judge saw that the sheriff was pushing a valid point for invalid purposes."

"That's a nice way of saying private agenda."

"It was, wasn't it?" Then he punctuated his agreement with another grin.

The two parted company, he to his office and Mags headed back to her office. It was another one of those chamber of commerce-perfect mountain days, and Mags yearned to lay out and feel the sun's rays, worship the blue sky, and sip on lemonade and read a good book. There was the new M. C. Beaton book, "Death of a Chimney Sweep", that was just begging to have its cover opened. For a change, she didn't care if she sold any real estate or not.

Real estate! Oh my gosh, Mags realized, Christine and Wyatt were waiting back at the office. Meanwhile, she was mooning along like a love-sick teenager. What was she thinking? They want to buy a house!

"I'm sorry, you two. It took longer than I anticipated and now, I'm about to inconvenience you even more."

"How'd it go?"

"Better than I had hoped. I didn't expect to get my boat back, but Malcolm didn't get the ruling he expected, either." She explained what had gone down. "So I sort of drafted you to go on board the boat with me. As a witness. But I also thought it might help you to see where it all happened," she hastened to add.

"It can't hurt," Wyatt agreed.

"Only thing is," Mags said, pointing to the large clock over Carole's desk, "it's almost noon. We need to eat and be at the marina by one-thirty. Perhaps I should have said two-o'clock, but I knew you needed to get back to Atlanta." She spread her hands. "And we still haven't bought you a house."

"Not to worry," Christine informed her. "Wyatt and I are going to stay over another night. If your guest suite isn't already reserved. He called his office and told them."

"Gee, I'll have to check the reservation log, but I don't think we have anyone else in that suite tonight."

"But we will have to leave first thing in the morning. Early," Wyatt explained. "Now, let's go eat. But where?"

Mags was collecting her purse and punched the answering machine activation. "The Eat and Greet, of course. It's where everybody who is anybody takes lunch."

"The Eat and what?"

"The Eat and Greet, Christine. Just wait, you'll see."

Mags was glad the eatery lived up to the billing she'd given it. After they had placed their orders, she and her guests watched all the socializing.

"Looks like to me they ought to call this place the 'Greet and Eat'," Wyatt observed. There's much more visiting going on than there is eating."

"This is going to become another of my favorite haunts, once we get a place here," Christine volunteered. "Their sweet tea is to die for."

"Maybe I should buy you a restaurant instead of a house," her husband suggested. "Save you the commute."

"Cute. Not great, but definitely cute."

Maudeann served their plates, openly curious about the identity of Mags' guests. She dropped several pointed hints, but neither Mags nor the Fultons took the bait and, in the end, the server left clearly disappointed and definitely miffed.

"I hated to do that to her," Mags told her company. "No, on second thought, I loved it." She went on to explain the other woman's penchant for gossip, while the three of them forked up fresh vegetables and salads. They finished eating and headed in Wyatt's

Mercedes to the marina, where Malcolm Wiley waited.

"I've been here almost twenty minutes. Where've you been?"

Mags consulted her cell phone. "It's only one-twenty-nine," she informed the sheriff. "We said one-thirty."

"Yeah, but I thought you'd be anxious, so I got here early."

"Not at my request, you didn't. Now let's get this show on the road."

The sheriff led the way back to a restricted part of the docks. "What's he doing here?" he asked, pointing at Wyatt. "Where's young Mr. Lewis?"

Mags wondered if young was Malcolm's way of saying green and inexperienced? "He had commitments this afternoon, so I brought Mr. Fulton along."

"But he's not your attorney."

"The judge didn't say my witness had to be my attorney."

"Is there a problem with me going on board," Wyatt asked. "If there is, we need to notify the judge and let him clarify this issue for us." Mags saw the steel in his stature, although his voice was low-key and easy-going. "I'm certainly willing to abide by his decision."

"Uh... uh, no, there's no problem. You still in town?"

For some reason, Wyatt's presence was rattling the sheriff, and Mags didn't know how to interpret his actions. Clearly he had been thrown off balance, only Mags couldn't decide why!

"Let me go aboard first," Malcolm said, when they reached the dock side of the *One True Love*. He stepped over into the boat, then held out his hand to assist Mags. As much as she hated to even touch the man, she relented and allowed him to steady her. The last thing she needed was a broken leg. Wyatt followed quickly behind her.

Mags headed toward the wheelhouse, only to be brought up short by the sight of dark, dried blood. HJH's blood, she thought. Obviously none of the crime technicians had thought it necessary to clean up the mess. Now it had dried to the point there would be no cleaning. Replacement would be the name of the game.

"I can see I'm going to have to put down new carpet," she said aloud to no one in particular. "That is, if I ever get my boat back."

Mags went on into the wheelhouse, where she began to open doors and lift the lids of floor compartments. For the most part, she removed nautical maps and atlases, legal registration papers and a lot of trash. None of it was truly critical and it wouldn't have mattered if it stayed on board. But she wasn't about to give Malcolm Wiley the satisfaction. She would, she vowed, take anything that wasn't nailed down.

"That's where the gun was," Malcolm volunteered, when Mags pulled back the floor carpet near the captain's seat, and popped the latch on a small doorway. "Carole stuck it in there, thinking we wouldn't know about that little hidey-hole."

Mags knew that was where Franklin had always hidden the illegal liquor he bought from the moonshiners around the lake. She remembered seeing him stash it there, before heading back out into the lake, where the patrols might stop him. "How in the world do you think Carole knew about this little space?" She inspected the compartment again. If it had once been connected with murder, there was nothing there now to betray that fact.

"Don't know," the sheriff replied, his manner conveying clearly how bored he was. "But that's where she put the gun after she killed Mr. Humphries."

Mags' temper flared. "I keep telling you, she didn't kill that man. And his name wasn't Humphries. How you can conveniently overlook that aspect is more than I can comprehend."

"The facts speak for themselves."

"The facts, Malcolm, say what you want them to say. Carole did not kill that man. Why can't you at least entertain that idea?"

"Because I've got my killer, plus I've got enough evidence to convict. So she must be guilty."

"There are none so blind as those who will not see," Mags mumbled.

"Beg pardon?"

She was sure the sheriff had heard her. "Nothing, Malcolm. I was talking to myself."

"Yeah, just like you talked to that newspaper lady from Atlanta. You didn't paint me in a very good light," the sheriff complained. "She made me look like an idiot."

"She called 'em like she saw them, I'm sure," Mags replied. "She's got a pretty good reputation."

"Are you calling me an idiot, too?"

"Malcolm. How long have we known each other? Would I do that?"

The sheriff didn't answer, but instead turned his attention to Wyatt. Mags, thankful for the reprieve, continued her search with little success.

"So how long you in town for?" Malcolm asked the attorney. "I figured you'd already be back in the big city. Little ol' place like this must be pretty tame for a fellow like you."

"For a fellow like me?"

"Yeah, you know." Mags noted that the sheriff was getting all folksy and shuffling his feet. It was a trait she'd identified years before, as something Malcolm did whenever he was uncomfortable or compromised. "We roll up the sidewalks here pretty early. You're probably used to that Atlanta night life."

"Believe me, sheriff. Crabapple Cove holds all kinds of attractions for my wife and me. We plan to come back. Often."

Seeing that he wouldn't be able to BS the lawyer, either, the sheriff returned his attention to Mags. "You about finished? I've got other things to do this afternoon."

Mags had brought a large shopping bag with her, and had crammed it with everything she found. "Yeah, I guess I'm about ready. I need to get back to town, so I can get those boat rental receipts over to your office." She gave him her most endearing smile. "So I can get my check on Friday."

"Yeah, whatever. Judge Beecham shouldn't have saddled me

with that. I'm just trying to do my job and preserve evidence."

Mags didn't bother to point out that their foray through the boat had automatically compromised any evidence that might still remain. Not that she believed there was anything.

In short order she wrapped up her search and the three of them rejoined Christine, who had remained on the dock. As the sheriff escorted them back to their vehicles, his cell phone rang. He took the call, listened more than he talked, then jammed the phone back into his pocket. He didn't even bother with the niceties of saying goodbye, but jumped instead into his cruiser and scratched off, leaving Mags and her guests standing in a cloud of dust.

"I'd say he was in a hurry."

"I'd agree, Mags. And I'm willing to bet it was that phone call that built the fire under him."

Back at the office Mags copied the two boat rental receipts and made a deliberate trip back to the sheriff's office. "You two sit tight. Let me get this over to sheriff and when I come back, we're going to buy a house. I don't care what else comes up to distract us."

"The sheriff wasn't in his office. The deputy said he hadn't been back since he left to meet us at the marina," Mags reported, as she came back in the office door. She had run from the courthouse and was panting so hard, she had to stop to catch her breath.

"With Sheriff Wiley, there's no telling. The man definitely operates on a private agenda." Wyatt looked at Mags, gasping, standing in the doorway. "Sit down. You shouldn't have tried to break any speed records."

"I wasn't," Mags gasped. "All of a sudden I didn't feel safe in the courthouse."

"Just so long as you weren't running because of us," Christine said. "We can wait."

"No you can't," Mags vowed. "You've already delayed long enough." She moved to her computer and brought it out of its sleep mode. "Let's see what we can find."

For the next few minutes, Mags flipped from site to site, and from screen to screen, occasionally making notes on a pad at her right hand. Finally, she turned from the computer, pad in hand, and said, "Okay. Here's the dope. Let's see what we think about this."

"Lay it on us," Christine offered. "I'm so excited. I just want that house."

"The house is on the market now for one million, five ninety-nine."

"One million six," Wyatt observed dryly.

"Exactly." Mags grinned. "Oldest real estate ploy in the book. Makes it sound so much cheaper."

"What else?" Christine asked. "You've got more on your pad."

"Here's where the crunch happens," Mags explained. The house has been on the market for over two years altogether."

"That really explains the musty smell," Wyatt observed. "What do you mean 'altogether'?"

"It went on the market twenty-six months ago on a year's contract. Original price was one million, seven hundred fifty-thousand. The contract expired and about eight months ago, it went back on the market for the current listing price."

"It ain't moving. But why?" Wyatt asked. "It's a nice house. Or at least it looks to be a nice house. A little dated, but it's got good bones, as you real estate folks say."

"You may have noticed that I left one of my business cards at every house we saw. That's what all agents do, only there was no pile of cards at this house. Just one other card and then mine."

"Which means the house has only been shown once since it went back on the market?"

"It would appear that way," she told Christine. "But I'm about to see what else I can learn. She lifted her office phone, doubled-checked her notes, and dialed. A few rings later, she was talking to the listing agent. When she ended the call, a broad grin was plastered across her face.

"Here's the dope. There have been several people interested in the house. They couldn't get financing."

"We can get financing, can't we, Wyatt?"

"We're pre-approved," he assured his wife. "I took that step before I ever offered to buy you a lake house."

"That pre-approval is going to play greatly in your favor," Mags promised. "But here's the really important part. That house appraised about three months ago for a deal that fell through at the last minute, for one million, six-hundred, ninety thousand."

"So it's already priced below appraisal?"

"It is, Wyatt. But I think we can do even better than that. I get the impression from the way the other agent's voice was squeaking by the time we finished, they're desperate to sell."

She rolled back to her computer. "Let me check one other thing." Her fingers began to play the keyboard, then she turned back to her clients. "I just love having all the county's real estate records on-line." She fingered her notes. "The sellers bought this house fifteen years ago and paid nine-hundred and twenty-two thousand dollars. They took a twenty year mortgage, so they still owe about..." she turned to her keyboard again. "They probably need two hundred thousand to pay off the mortgage."

"Are you going where I think you are?"

"I don't know, Christine. Are you thinking about a low-ball offer that would put their purchase price back in their hands, but little more?"

Her friend grinned. "It's a good starting point. I imagine we'll have to pay a little more than that."

"Here's what I think we ought to offer," she proposed. "Let's go in at one million, one hundred, eighty-nine thousand, and stress that you are pre-approved for a mortgage."

"You don't honestly think they'll let it go that cheap?"

"I get the sense they're desperate, Wyatt, but I figure they'll counter. Then we'll get a better idea of what they're thinking."

"Let's do it then."

Mags moved to Carole's computer and soon had the appropriate template on the screen. She made quick work typing in the specifics, printed out the forms, and led her clients to a table in front of the window.

"Here it is," she told them. "Here's our offering price. We're putting in a contingency to void the contract if the home inspection shows any major problems. You can also get out of it if financing should fall through. And they're paying their full share of the closing costs, plus the agents' commissions."

The couple exchanged glances. "Where do I sign?" Christine crowed.

Mags pointed to the applicable spaces, and one after the other, each of them complied.

"Now," Mags intoned, "comes the really fun part. I need an earnest money check, and we can get this show on the road."

Wyatt pulled a checkbook out of his attaché case. "How much do you need?"

"Ten thousand ought to be sufficient to show good faith, especially since you're pre-approved for the mortgage."

While the attorney was writing the check, Mags picked up the phone and re-dialed the last number. When the agent answered, she advised her colleague that she was about to fax an offer, and asked for a response as quickly as possible. "My clients are from out of town, and have to leave in the morning. They'd like to wrap this up while they're here." She gave the agent her cell phone number, and invited her to call, even if it was after hours. The she walked to the fax machine behind Carole's desk, inserted the pages and hit the necessary keys. In a moment, the sheets began to disappear into the machine.

"Now we wait."

"That's the part I hate the most," Christine groused. "I guess I'm not very patient, am I?"

A loud snort was Wyatt's only response.

Mags consulted the clock. "Hey, folks, it's almost quitting time."

She began scurrying around, closing down the office. "We don't have to stay here. They'll call me on my cell phone. We can go home."

"You're sure we're not an imposition for another night?"

Mags had to laugh, but she tried to temper her mirth by placing her hands on her hips and adopting a stern look. "Really, Christine. Have you noticed anyone else lined up outside my door seeking lodging? Of course you're welcome." More than welcome, she thought, because it meant she wouldn't be alone.

"Okay," Wyatt agreed, "but dinner's on me. Where shall we go?"

"Back to that wonderful place on the lake," Christine proposed. "I could eat there every night."

Mags chuckled. "Let's go in a different direction tonight. Literally. I want to show Christine another great place to eat."

Both she and Wyatt looked expectantly at the third member of their party. "You'll love it just as much," Mags promised. "It's different, but just as good."

"Okay. What the hey? Let's do it."

As Mags was closing the office, Wyatt wondered aloud. "What if we call Joe Pickett and see if he'd like to join us?"

"That's a wonderful idea," Mags agreed. "I know he has to be feeling pretty low."

"Besides that, I really need to touch base with him while I'm here."

A quick call from Mags' cell phone to Carole's dad, while they all stood on the covered front porch of the real estate agency, produced quick acceptance. "We'll pick you up about seven o'clock," Mags assured him. "Dress code is casual." He promised to be ready and waiting.

"I feel bad," Mags told her friends. "I've neglected him, but there's just been so much going on."

The threesome drove quickly to The Slop Bucket, changed into more comfortable clothes, got back into Wyatt's vehicle and headed back to pick up the fourth member of their party. Mags consulted the digital clock inside the Mercedes and saw that it was not yet six o'clock.

"Since we're a little ahead of time, could we swing by the vet and let me check on Delilah?"

"Sure," Wyatt agreed. "You should have said something sooner."

"I just thought of it, but it would make me feel better if I could see her." She gave Wyatt directions and, in a matter of minutes, they were walking into the veterinary clinic. Mags spoke with the employee behind the front desk, and they were quickly escorted to an empty exam room.

"Someone will bring Delilah to you in just a minute," the friendly face informed her. "She's a real darling, you know."

"I do know, believe me."

It was only a couple of minutes before the door opened, and a uniformed technician entered with Mags' dog in her arms. While she had been expecting a groggy dog, what she got was something else entirely. Her baby was awake and alert, and even began to wag her tail when she saw the face of the one she loved most.

"Oh, my sweet one," Mags crooned. "I've missed you so badly."

The technician placed the dog in Mags' outstretched arms. "She's doing much better." Delilah's tail was beating a tattoo rhythm, and she stretched her head and neck to reward her mother with a big, wet kiss.

"But… but I thought she was in a coma. That's what they told me this morning." Mags buried her face in the dog's fur, and could feel the tears that welled up in her eyes. She was getting her dog wet, but she didn't care.

"Dr. Sanders decided to let the medication wear off, so we could get a better assessment. This," the technician said, making a great show with her hands, "is what we got."

Mags continued to hug the dog close to her, aware once again just how close she had come to losing the one source of unconditional love in her life.

Christine stepped over to pet Delilah. "Hello, girl. I'm Christine and we are so glad to see you feeling better." She smiled at Mags, "No wonder you two are so attached. She's not only beautiful, she's so loving."

Wyatt, too, was gently scratching the dog behind her ears, although Mags thought him unnaturally quiet, and wondered why.

"I'd better take her back to her kennel," the technician said, interrupting the reverie. "It's almost closing time, and I need to get her situated."

"It breaks my heart to have to walk off and leave her again," Mags cried out, as she handed the dog back. "What must she think of me?"

"You'd be surprised how intuitive dogs are. And I won't be surprised if you get to take her home tomorrow," the girl in the purple smock volunteered.

"Really? You're not just trying to make me feel better?"

The technician rubbed Delilah's head. "She's really doing very well. We're going to lightly sedate her for overnight, but if she's still doing this well tomorrow, we've done all we can do."

Mags hugged the corgi once again, and watched with tears in her eyes, as the dog disappeared through the door. "I can take her home tomorrow," she told her friends. "You're my witnesses."

"That's wonderful, Mags." Wyatt put his hand on her shoulder. "We'd better be going if we're going to collect Mr. Pickett on time."

She had forgotten all about dinner and Carole's dad, Mags realized, and felt just a little bit guilty for the omission. "By all means, let's get out of here."

Back in the car, on the way into town, Mags asked Wyatt, "Was anything wrong back there? You were very quiet, you know?"

The attorney and his wife exchanged glances, but it was Christine who spoke. "Wyatt had to put down his golden lab about three months ago, and he hasn't… well… we haven't been able to convince ourselves to get a new puppy."

"Oh, I'm so sorry, Wyatt. I hope seeing Delilah didn't upset you."

"On the contrary. I'm a dog person. Seeing you and Delilah showed me that I have to get another dog. Soon. Like maybe this coming weekend!"

"She means everything to me. Rattling around in that mini-mansion in Atlanta, her love was the only love I knew. And here, The Slop Bucket is so remote. She's been practically my only company."

"Whoever poisoned her meant to kill her," Christine volunteered.

"They almost succeeded, too," Mags replied, unable to keep the bitterness she felt from showing in her voice. "I wonder if we'll ever understand why?"

The three soon claimed the fourth member of their group and, under Mags' direction, Wyatt headed deep into the mountains to a rustic lodge of cedar and glass that straddled the headwaters of a massive waterfall. The weather was nice, and the group dined on Chateaubriand and smoky-flavored glasses of Beaujolais. Conversation around the table ranged from the lighthearted, to probing questions and answers about Carole's case.

In bed later that night, Mags remembered again how wonderful it had been to hold her dog, to find her recovering. Someone had tried to kill Delilah, she knew, probably because of her investigation of HJH's murder. The real killer, she now understood, was desperate for Carole to take the fall. He, or perhaps it was another she, it appeared, would stop at nothing to ensure that Mags couldn't upset the plans. She knew she couldn't abandon her investigation, any more than Mac Smith would have dropped his search for the killer in Margaret Truman's "Murder at the Opera". At the same time, she couldn't leave Delilah vulnerable, either. If the killer found out the dog was still alive, would there be another attempt?

Mags dropped off to exhausted sleep soon afterward, and dreamed of Delilah in disguise, making it impossible for the killers to know who she really was.

Chapter Fourteen

Taking Delilah Home

Mags unlocked the office door with a greater spirit of enthusiasm than had been the case of late. She and her houseguests had left The Slop Bucket to have breakfast at the twenty-four hour diner on the four-lane. When they parted company, the Fultons were headed back to Atlanta. She, on the other hand, was on her way to the office. Real estate work beckoned. For one thing, they'd heard nothing from the agent on her friends' offer. And for a change, there was going to be some money-making business. She had two closings scheduled for the afternoon. It would be nice to have money in the house again.

"I'm calling the other agent as soon as I get to the office," Mags assured her friends. "I'll call you as soon as I know anything."

The office line began ringing before Mags could even deposit her purse and tote in their accustomed place. She grabbed for the phone without verifying the caller's identity.

"Mrs. Gordon. This is Phyllis Marshall. I'm sorry I couldn't get back to you last night. My client was out of town and I had to track him down. Are your people still in town?"

Mags explained that the Fultons had already left, but assured the other agent that she could contact them.

"To be honest with you," her caller explained, "my client felt the offer was a little low."

"It is lower than the asking price," Mags agreed. "But the house has been empty and deteriorating for more than two years. It doesn't show well, and there's work that will have to be done to make it a viable home again."

"Will your clients entertain a higher price, or is this offering price their max?"

"Within reason, I believe we could look at increasing our offer. What did you have in mind?"

The other agent hemmed and hawed for a minute or so. Mags, who had other work to do, finally cut her short. "Make us a counter-offer and I'll convey it to my clients."

"We'd take one million, three hundred thousand."

"That may be more than my people would pay. Before we waste time putting everything to paper, let me call them and see what they think."

"Let me know and we'll go from there."

"It may be later today before you hear back from me. I've got two closings today and I'm not sure exactly where my clients are."

"Two closings. Lucky you. I haven't had one in over three months. The economy is killing me."

She doesn't know how long it's been since I had a closing, Mags thought, but chose not to divulge that much information. Instead, she ended the conversation by promising to call as soon as she had an answer. Then she reached for her cell phone and dialed Christine's number. "I've heard from the other agent," she crowed when her friend answered.

"Did we buy a house? You mean they took our offer?"

"Not exactly," Mags explained. "They countered. Are you ready for this? One million, three hundred thousand."

Mags could hear Christine relaying her message to Wyatt.

"Wyatt wants to know if you think they'll go any lower."

"They're desperate to sell. Even the agent just told me she hasn't had a closing in forever. But I don't think we'll get them much lower. This is exactly the target I was shooting for."

"Let me talk to Wyatt."

Again, Mags heard the couple having a conversation.

"Do you think we could get them down to one million, two hundred ninety thousand?"

Mags scratched her head. "That's just ten thousand dollars. Is that what you meant?"

Christine snickered. "Wyatt's trying to be a bad boy."

"Is he serious?"

Again, there was conversation.

"Apparently he is. He doesn't want to pay one million three. He says see what you can do."

"Will do. I know you're not a patient waiter, but I'm not calling her back immediately. Let's let them feel impatient as well."

"Oh." Christine's voice dropped. "Okay, call us when you know something."

Mags busied herself for the next couple of hours reviewing files for the two afternoon closings, double-checking with Grant Lewis' secretary to be certain everything was in order, and placing calls to both her clients to reassure them that everything was on target. "By tonight," she told each of them, "you'll be homeowners.

Finally, as the clock climbed past eleven, Mags dialed the listing agent on the Fulton offer. "Okay," she said, when she finally got the other woman on the phone, "here's how it shakes out. My clients are willing to go higher, but not a penny more than one million, two hundred seventy-five thousand. They've crunched the numbers and that's their top dollar offer."

"Would they walk over just twenty-five thousand dollars?"

"I get the impression they would."

"Let me get back to my client and I'll be in touch."

"I'll be waiting. Unless, of course, it's this afternoon. I'll be tied up in those closings. It may be tomorrow before we can conclude this, even if it falls through."

The other agent ended the call promising a quick turn-around. Mags busied herself re-filing paperwork she'd pulled out, and getting the documents she needed for both the afternoon closings. Among the contents of her tote bag was a deposit ticket, so she could get both commission checks into the bank as soon as possible.

Ten minutes later the phone rang. Caller ID, she noted with satisfaction, displayed Phyllis Marshall. "Mountain Magic Realty by Mags."

"Mrs. Gordon, I've heard back from my client."

"And...?"

"He has accepted your clients' offer, but he has to have a thirty-day close. Is that feasible?"

"Let me call my clients and I'll get back with you."

Mags understood the short closing stipulation. The seller probably didn't have the money for another payment, and she explained as much to Christine a couple of minutes later.

"Wyatt," Christine squealed, "Mags got it for fifteen thousand less than we told her to offer." Then Mags could hear her explaining about the closing contingency. There was conversation between the two.

"Wyatt is grinning from ear to ear," his wife reported. "Closing isn't a problem."

"Great. I'll revise the contract and e-mail it to Wyatt's office in the next thirty minutes. It should to be there by the time you all are."

"Thanks, Mags. We owe you!"

"I'm as happy as you are," Mags assured them. "We'll be talking."

As she ended the call and moved to Carole's computer to amend the contract, Mags also called the other agent, who answered on the first ring. "My clients can close in thirty days. I'm about to send a new contract to their office in Atlanta. They'll sign and fax it back this afternoon."

"We have a deal?"

"We do. I'll have the new contract for your client's signature before five o'clock today. But as far as we're concerned, it's a deal. I'll order the home inspection and the termite check later this afternoon."

"I'll call the seller. He'll be very happy."

Mags detected a note to relief in the agent's voice and understood. Real estate was, she knew, anything but a guaranteed paycheck.

The next five hours where a blur, as she transmitted the Fultons' contract, grabbed a bite of lunch, attended the two closings, and made several necessary phone calls in the forty-five minutes between the appointments. She managed to scoot through the bank drive-through to deposit her two sales commissions, and was positive she heard her account breathe an audible sigh of relief.

As she walked back into the office, her cell phone rang. It was the vet's number, but this time she didn't panic.

"Mrs. Gordon? Dr. Sanders wonders if you'd like to take Delilah home this afternoon?

Having her dog back at home where she belonged meant Mags wouldn't be alone. It was, she knew, how it was supposed to be. "You better know I'd like to have her back where I can love on her."

"Well, she's ready to go any time you can get here. The doctor does need to talk to you. She's going to have to be on a very bland diet for the next few days. That poison really messed up her stomach lining."

Mags checked the clock and her to-do list. "I can see you in about an hour. Does that work?"

"We'll be here."

Wyatt had returned the signed contracts. They were waiting in the fax machine tray, and she quickly sent them over to the other agent. "I've just hit send," she told her colleague, when she called to give her a heads-up. "It should to be there in a minute or so."

Then she placed her closing documents into the appropriate files, and locked the file drawers. Taking one final look around the office, she went through the shut-down procedures, locked the door, and edged over the speed limit on her way to the vet.

"She's doing remarkably well, considering all she's gone through," the kindly vet explained, as he went through the items in the discharge packet. "The main thing is her food. We need to give her stomach plenty of TLC and time to heal."

Mags was studying the directions. Scrambled eggs. Mashed potatoes. Rice. Bland custard. "How much time?"

"I'd think a week, ten days at most. But be sure to call us if she doesn't continue to improve."

"Whatever she needs, of course I'll do it." It was, she knew, the least she could do, since her actions had almost cost an innocent dog her life.

In a few minutes' time Mags had been duly instructed, had paid the bill, with a silent word of thanks for the afternoon's commission checks, and was reunited with her beloved corgi.

"Come on, girl, we're going home," she told the happy dog that was about to wiggle out of her arms. With the help of a technician, Delilah's leash was attached, and she walked out of the clinic in much better shape than she had gone in.

On the ride home, Mags kept glancing into her rearview mirror, checking on her dog, almost as if she were afraid she'd find her gone. Once home and off her leash, Delilah made a great production out of exploring the entire house. Mags couldn't decide if it was the lingering scent of her weekend guests, or something more sinister that the dog was fixated on. Either way, it had been a long time since she'd seen Delilah so active and animated.

Deciding if you couldn't beat them, you ought to just join them, Mags scrambled a big skillet of eggs for the both of them, gave Delilah an overly-generous helping, then added Canadian bacon and freshly-baked, frozen biscuits to her plate, before she sat down to enjoy a night at home.

By bedtime, Mags had made several decisions concerning her dog's welfare. For starters, or at least until the real killer was found, Delilah would no longer go out without a leash. No more just opening the door and turning her out. Instead of being banished to a bed in the laundry room, she would now occupy the master bedroom. Heck, Mags vowed, she could share the bed if she wanted, but she would bring Delilah's familiar dog bed into the bedroom as a back-up. And she would take the dog to work with her. It was her business, so she had the freedom to make that call. Otherwise, she knew, she'd be tied in knots all day, wondering if her precious companion was safe.

Even though a killer was still out there somewhere running lose, Mags fell into bed and into one of the best night's sleep she had enjoyed since the nightmare began. When morning woke her, and she realized that she'd slept the night through, she couldn't decide whether it was having Delilah back, or the previous day's full and productive agenda. Either way, it was time to start all over again.

Mags pulled on her robe, put Delilah on her lead, and the two went out for a long walk by the lake. On their return, Mags showered, fixed breakfast for the both of them, then she dressed for the day. Delilah, who usually loved to travel, was hesitant to get in her accustomed seat in the Jeep. Perhaps, Mags considered, her dog now associated car travel with her traumatic stay at the vet. She hoped not, cranked up and drove off toward town.

A chance look at the fuel gauge brought her up short. She was running on empty. A quick detour led her to The Tank-up, the convenience store where practically every local bought gas. It was pump-your-own, and Mags did just that; another skill she had acquired, thanks to her divorce decree. After telling Delilah she'd be right back, she scooted in to the register to pay. Behind her she could hear the dog barking. She wasn't accustomed to being left in the car, Mags realized.

"That'll be eighty-two twenty," the clerk she knew as Marian, told her. "You must have been on fumes today."

"I guess I was," Mags admitted, and laughed self-consciously. "Glad I realized it before I ran out."

The clerk handed her change across the counter. "Is your ex-husband living here now?"

"My ex-husband? Franklin?"

"Yes'um. He was just here. Him and the sheriff. You didn't miss him by even five minutes."

Franklin. Here? For reasons Mags couldn't totally understand or explain, the knowledge that her ex was so close totally unnerved her. If he was in town this early, he almost had to have spent the night. But where? The motel? With Malcolm and his wife? It was troubling.

"Well lucky me," she said at last, because the clerk seemed to expect some response. "I'm glad I missed him."

As she drove into town, the revelation she'd just received continued to haunt her. It would have been too much to expect Franklin to break his ties with Malcolm. Nevertheless, she found the news that he was close enough to reach out and touch somewhat unnerving.

While Mags was opening the office, Delilah was making herself at home sniffing into every corner and testing out the couches. She had only been to work once before, so it was a new experience.

It was another day of real estate grunge work. Two more closings were imminent and, surprise of surprises, there were several e-mails requesting information about different properties on the company's web site. Maybe she could hold her business together after all.

When lunch came, Mags was hesitant to leave Delilah alone. Would she still have an intact office when she returned? There were more aspects to bringing your dog to work than were obvious in theory. In the end, she ordered a plate delivered and cancelled her plans to visit Carole afterwards. Where could she find a pet sitter? Perhaps a dependable doggie daycare?

By three o'clock, she'd attended to everything that needed her attention, and was twiddling her thumbs. There was still no walk-in traffic. So why was she keeping the office open? On that note, she made the executive decision to hang up the closed sign, turn off the lights, and go home.

As she wound down the curvy, tree-shaded drive to The Slop Bucket, Mags' heart was light and she was actually humming an inane little tune. All was right with the world. Then she saw the end of the lodge, the side nearest the parking turn-around. Painted in white against the dark green shingle walls, in letters about five feet tall, was the message: *"You could be next"*.

Mags slammed on the brakes and sat, numb and dumbstruck. Who? What? How? Why? Questions assaulted her brain, but she was too horrified to try to find any of the answers. In the end, she left her Jeep exactly where it had jerked to a stop. She got out, opened the back door, put the leash on her dog, and the two made a hasty entry into the house. Mags dropped the leash and dropped herself into the closest chair. It was a hot, mountain afternoon outside, but the chills that ran up and down her spine were definitely of the sub-freezing variety. How long she sat, zoned out, she couldn't be certain. It was Delilah's loving ministration, licking and pawing, punctuated with low whines, that finally brought her back to the reality that her brain had tried to escape.

She knew what she had to do. At the same time, she realized that her action plan would result in less than she desired. Reaching for the land line phone, she placed a call to the sheriff's office where, to her surprise, the head man himself answered the phone.

"I need a deputy out here. There's been more vandalism, Malcolm."

"How can you be sure?" The question was immediate and piercing.

The edge of doubt that embroidered his words sent a fire up Mags' back, in effect melting the frozen spine that was hobbling her. "The five-foot tall letters spelling out a death threat were a pretty good first clue," she snapped. "Don't give me a hard time, Malcolm. It's time you stepped up to the plate and started being a sheriff to all the county's taxpayers. Now send somebody out here." She slammed down the phone, but continued to mutter her disgust, while she moved about the house checking for other possible violations. Finding none, she returned to the great room, where she soon was rewarded with the sound of tires in the drive.

"Any idea who did this?" the uniformed deputy asked. "What could you be next for?"

Mags ground her teeth. "A man was found dead on my boat. Somebody tried to poison my dog. I can only assume they mean that bad things come in threes, and I'm up to bat next." She planted her hands on her hips and stepped closer to the officer, who seemed to have no clue. "Of course I don't know who did it. That's your job!"

"Oh...?"

"Oh, what?" she demanded. "What does that mean?"

"You're Franklin Gordon's wife. I heard his boat was involved in a murder."

"Ex-wife. I'm his EX-wife, and that's my boat."

"That's not what the sheriff says."

Mags wanted to tear the man apart piece by piece, but she reasoned it was really Malcolm that her anger was directed toward. No need to take it out on this guy. Besides, from what she'd seen so far, he was dumb as a stump. No need trying to reason with him.

"Never mind what the sheriff says. Are you going to make a report on this? Someone has come onto my property and defaced my home, and threatened my life. Your office needs to investigate."

The tan-uniformed man was staring at the message that had obviously been created using white spray paint. "I can make a report and take a picture of the damage. But there's nothing else I can do."

"You can investigate. That's what you can do."

The man was clearly confused. His face showed it, and his voice confirmed it. "There's nothing to investigate."

"You can't check the stores and see who bought white spray paint?" She knew that's where Paul Drake would have started if Perry Mason had given him this case.

"You watch too much TV, lady. It don't work like that in the real world."

"You mean it doesn't work that way in Sheriff Malcolm Wiley's world. Especially when the complainant is named Margaret Gordon."

"Huh?"

"Never mind. Take your pictures and write out your report. You're not leaving here without doing at least that much."

Back in the house, Mags was still seething. Unfortunately, the service and concern she received from the sheriff's office was no less than she had expected. She also realized, more strongly than ever, that a successful resolution to all the problems would depend on her.

The deputy had gone, but the evidence of a troubling visit was still prominent on the gable end of the sprawling, rustic lodge. It would have to be painted over, and she knew it couldn't happen that night. The message was simply one more symptom of a bigger, more deadly problem. Painting over the words might hide them from sight, but there was still a killer out there.

That same killer was in the back of Mags' mind, when she attached the leash and took Delilah for a walk. The woods and serenity of her backwoods sanctuary had been violated, and she no longer felt comfortable and carefree walking along the lake. Delilah, she could tell, didn't like her loss of freedom, either.

For supper she fried steak, fixed okra and creamed corn and mashed potatoes and gravy. Thinking her patient might like a change of taste, she peeled extra potatoes and filled her dog's bowl with an ample serving.

While she was eating, Mags realized she could barely taste her favorite comfort foods. Something had to be done. As the snowy pile of mashed potatoes on her plate dwindled, an action plan emerged and by the time her plate was empty, she was ready to put wheels under her ideas. She piled her dirty dishes in the sink and left them. Her mother would scold, but it wasn't her parent who had been threatened with death.

She picked up the land line phone and, before she lost her resolve, called the one person she believed could guide her in the right direction. "Wyatt," she said when he answered. "You've got to listen to me and you've got to help me. Something's got to give."

"Well, sure, Mags. I'll do whatever I can. You sound super upset. What's happened?"

"Get comfortable, because this is going to take a few minutes." Then, heeding her own advice. Mags settled into her favorite chair. "You'll never believe what I found when I got home this afternoon." She explained about the message on the wall, and she started at the very beginning, the first time Horace J. Humphries came into her office. She didn't stop until she had laid every fact, every fear, every idea and every theory out on the table."

"Man, oh man," was the only response she got initially, followed by a silence so quiet, Mags finally had to ask, "Wyatt? Are you there?"

"Sorry, Mags, while I already knew most of this, there's something about hearing it all in one sitting, in chronological order, that's kind of overwhelming."

"Tell me about it. And please tell me what to do about it."

"I don't have a magic lamp, my friend. I don't know what to say."

The shadows in the room were darkening and they matched Mags' mood perfectly. She made no move to turn on any lights in the house, preferring instead to shine light on the issue of one man who died violently, under an assumed name, and for which her best friend was the prime suspect.

"There has to be something I can do, Wyatt. I'm just a real estate agent and a former social bigwig, but I am willing to do whatever's required to really investigate all of this. That's what's lacking; the sheriff isn't investigating. He's taking the easy way out. But still, how does all of this connect with me and Delilah, and why would someone leave a threatening message on my house?"

"You are spot on; the sheriff hasn't even begun to investigate this man's death. But please don't take offense when I say, you are nowhere near able to adequately dig through all the muck to find the truth, either."

"But somebody has to do something. It's obvious Malcolm Wiley doesn't plan to pursue it. So where do I go from here?" She hesitated. "And don't tell me to lock my doors and let the justice system work."

"I would never suggest that. No, I have another proposal for you."

"Let's hear it."

"You need a good private investigator. Emphasis on good."

"A private investigator?"

"The people paid by the taxpayers obviously aren't going to do their jobs. What this case needs is another investigator qualified to do the job. You aren't qualified and you don't have the luxury of learning those skills on-the-job."

"Wyatt, I wouldn't have the first clue about how to find this person you're describing, either."

"But I do," he replied. "Hang on and let me see where I've got that contact info."

In a moment he was back to the phone. "Her name's Jennifer Masterson. Here's how you reach her." He gave her the details, then his voice took on a serious tone. "Call her. Don't e-mail her. For some reason she never checks her computer regularly."

"This investigator is a woman?"

"Yeah. Is that a problem?"

"And she's one of the best?"

Wyatt was laughing, she realized. "You're not discriminating because she's female, are you?"

"Of course not. What do you take me for?" He's right, she quietly told herself. That's exactly what I am doing. "It's just that I somehow expected a man. I can do anything another woman can do."

"Think about it again, Mags. This woman is a trained detective. It's not like you see it on TV, or what you've read about in all those mysteries you love so much."

"I know that," she protested. "But still…?"

"But still nothing. Call her, Mags. Trust me. You'll be glad you did."

"I will, I promise. Now, let's change subjects." She brought him up to speed on the status of the house deal, explained that the property inspection would be two days hence, and advised him to go ahead and bring his lender into the loop. "With that thirty-day close, we don't have a lot of time."

They chatted about the house and Mags suggested several contractors he might want to consider for the renovations. Then, before she was really ready to be robbed of the sound of another human voice, Wyatt ended the call.

"It's just you and me, Delilah," she told her roommate. "Let's go out again, then we're going to adjourn to the bedroom. I'm bushed."

Mags didn't allow the dog to explore and sniff as much as she might have liked, and soon the two had secured the house, set the alarm, and were piled up on the king size bed. Delilah, who had always been discouraged from getting on the bed, was clearly confused, and kept moving from one place to another. It was almost as if she was tempting her mother to order her off. But Mags had other things on her mind. The last thing she could recall the next morning, was questioning Wyatt's suggestion that she hire a detective.

Surely she could do the job herself.

Chapter Fifteen
YOU DON'T LISTEN, DO YOU?

M ags was running late by the time she'd tidied the house, and she and Delilah got to the office. One of the things delaying her was the raging internal debate over whether she should call the investigator. While she was washing the breakfast dishes, it seemed to be a no-brainer. She should call the woman and employ her. The sooner the better. But when she got to the other end of the house, and was making the king size bed, it seemed a total waste of time and money to pay someone else to do what she could do herself. After all, she had the time. Real estate wasn't selling that well, and there was no one more motivated than she was.

As Mags unlocked the office door, the phone was ringing. Adding to the hue and cry was the alarm bell on the fax machine, letting the entire world know that it was out of paper, demanding to be fed. Mags tackled the phone first, only to have the caller ask if she could speak to Mr. Moses. By the time she had made the woman understand she had dialed a wrong number, the high-pitched protest emitting from the fax machine was almost over the top. She literally dropped her purse and tote bag in the middle of the floor, grabbed paper from the supply rack, and satisfied the machine into silence.

What a way to start the day!

Mags retrieved her possessions, stowed them in their usual place next to her desk, dropped into her comfortable office chair, and booted up the computer. The "you have mail" icon illuminated immediately and, since she was expecting several messages pertaining to deals in progress, she quickly opened her mailbox. Forty-one new arrivals since yesterday, she saw. Most of them, she knew, were junk, and she quickly went about the task of eliminating those first, leaving her with a more manageable lot of nine. She spotted a couple of messages she had been anticipating, and opened and dealt with them first. A quick first glance had shown that none lacked a subject line. Which was why, near the end, when she opened a message referencing , "Details on what comes next", she suddenly dropped her mouse as if it were white hot.

> You don't listen, do you? We missed on your dog, but we won't miss on you, unless you take your nose out of where it doesn't belong. You have been warned about what comes next.

Mags gripped the arms of her chair and prayed that she wouldn't totally lose control. It was definite. They were after her. But who were "they", and why? WHY? In her head, she knew that some action was demanded, but to do anything would mean losing her grip on the chair arms… and possibly her grip on reality. She had never been so frightened.

It was the ache in her hands that provided a means of escape from the trance into which she had retreated. Sometimes pain could be a good thing, because it forced her to release her death grip. Once loose, she had to do something to keep her hands occupied, and grabbed for the phone.

"Ramona. I absolutely must speak with Wyatt. This is an emergency."

"I'm sorry, Mrs. Gordon. He's in court in Macon this morning, and I truly don't have any way to reach him until he checks in with me over lunch."

"There's no way?" Mags had visions of being marooned on a ocean knoll, with no way to communicate with the rest of the world.

"There's not. I'm sorry. But I'll be glad to ask him to call you. And I'll tell him that you're very upset."

"I guess… yes. Please ask him to call me." What other option did she have?

Mags ended the call and stared at the office walls that had once been so friendly and welcoming. Not any longer. There was no place, it seemed, where she was safe. Without stopping to debate the wisdom of what she was about to do, she was on the phone again, dialing another number.

"This is Margaret Gordon. I have to speak with Sheriff Wiley. Now!"

The officer who had answered said nothing in response, and all Mags heard was background conversation. She had to wonder if he had deliberately laid the phone down. Was he ignoring her? Fearing to put her phone down, Mags continued to clutch it to her ear and finally, the gravely voice she knew so well, greeted her.

"What is it this time, Margaret? You got another idea on how we can find who sold the spray paint?" She heard a definite snicker. "Do you have any idea how stupid you look trying to act like one of your storybook detectives?"

"Malcolm, you've got to come down here. I've gotten another e-mail. They're threatening to kill me."

"Who is 'they'?"

"That's just it. I don't know," she wailed, finally allowing her raw nerves to surface.

"Then what do you expect me to do about it? Arrest everyone in town?"

"Of course not, Malcolm. But my life is in danger. You need to come read this message. Find out who sent it."

There was a long, loud discharge of breath on the other end. "And what am I going to do after I read it? I've already told you, there's no way to find out who sent it."

"But Malcolm, there is a way. Authorities do it all the time."

"In those mysteries you read, maybe."

"Malcolm! I need help." Mags didn't know what else to do. It was obvious the sheriff had no intention of coming to the office. "Will you at least listen? I'll read it to you."

"Whatever. You aren't going to give me any peace if I don't."

Mags read the message aloud, which to her, only made the threats more sinister.

"Like I told you before. You've made somebody angry and they're venting their frustration."

She remembered the man in the courtroom, the one she saw later in the forest. "Is that someone you?" she charged. "Are you having me followed?" She went on to explain her encounters from a few days before, encounters she'd forgotten after discovering her beloved Delilah at death's door.

"I don't have enough manpower to handle all the cases we have. Why would I waste a man keeping you under surveillance?"

"That's what I'm asking you. Somebody is following me."

"You really do read too many of those books. You're living in la la land."

"So you aren't having me followed?"

"I already answered that question. What part of 'no' don't you understand?"

"He was tall, I'd say close to six feet. Blond hair and a weathered complexion."

"You want to come inspect my crew? You won't find one guy who comes close to that description. I told you, somebody is venting."

"Were they venting when they poisoned Delilah? They've taken credit for almost killing my dog. It's right here. Surely there's something you can do."

"Tell you what, Mags. You investigate the matter. Because you're going to anyway." He chuckled. "If you get any solid leads, let me know. Then we'll see what I can do."

Mags knew when she was defeated, and ended the call without even saying goodbye. She doubted Malcolm would even notice, let alone care. She might not be a licensed private investigator, but she knew when she was getting a run-around. She also knew deep in her gut, that everything that had happened from the first moment HJH walked into her life, was part of a very organized plan. It appeared that plan was targeted at her. But who hated her that badly?

The dog had heard her name and got up from her resting spot in the corner of the room. She nuzzled Mags' hand, and her owner responded with a vigorous head and ear massage.

Her only hope was that Wyatt would have some suggestion when he called back at lunch. If he called back. Would Ramona really give him her message? Mags busied herself around the office, cleaning what wasn't dirty, reorganizing the files that were already in good order. Anything to coerce the clock's hands to keep moving. Finally, at ten after twelve, her phone rang.

"Wyatt! Thank you for calling me. I'm absolutely frantic." Her words tumbled out, running all over each other.

"Whoa… whoa. Slow down. I can barely understand you."

"I'm sorry."

"Something's got you spooked big time bad."

"Listen." She read the words from the morning's threatening mail. "This was waiting for me when I pulled up mail this morning."

"Wow! That's really over the top. Thank goodness Jennifer Masterson's in the game now. She could find a worm under a rock from ten miles away."

Mags was immediately flooded with guilt. "Uh… Wyatt, I didn't call her."

"You what?"

"From the way you described her, it just seemed like she was a bigger gun than I needed."

"Do you still see it that way?"

Mags played with her hair, then the paper clips in the little bowl on her desk. "No," she said finally, "no, I don't guess she is."

"Call her, Mags. Hang up and call her right now." His voice softened. "These people are serious, my friend. You desperately need somebody in your corner."

"Okay. I'll reach out to her." Internally, she was still struggling with the concept. "Thank you for being there... for being so concerned."

"It's more than concern, Mags. You're in danger, whether you realize it or not."

"Let me get off this phone so I can reach out to this detective."

"I'll call tonight."

"Thanks, Wyatt."

Mags was beginning to feel the defection of her morning's bowl of cereal. It must be lunch time. But she would keep her promise and call Ms. Masterson. Only it wasn't that simple. Before she could call, she needed the investigator's phone number. It wasn't in her planner, where she thought she'd placed it the night before. Desperate, she dug in her purse and came up empty again. She went through the contents of her tote bag, before finally finding the number in her planner, right where she'd thought it should have been.

Before she could lose the contact information again, Mags picked up her phone, took a deep breath, and entered the number. When she thought it was going to be a lost cause, the person on the other end answered. Or at least her answering machine did. "Hello. Jennifer here. Leave me a message and I'll call you back as soon as I can. Don't forget to leave me your number. I'm not psychic, you know!"

Mags complied, and added that Wyatt Fulton had referred her. Might help, might not. But what did she have to lose? What more could she do? Then she turned her attention to her complaining stomach. Again, the dilemma of Delilah's presence was the source of angst. Should she leave her, or order lunch in again. After much gnashing of teeth and mental ping-pong, Mags decided to chance leaving the dog alone. After all, what could happen?

At the Eat and Greet, the dining room was almost filled. She found a small table for two near the back and settled in. It wasn't her first choice location, so close to the kitchen, but it was either compromise or wait. Deciding to be good, Mags ordered a Cobb salad, with lite vinaigrette dressing, and her usual sweet tea with plenty of lemon.

Things were so busy, Maudeann didn't even take the time to pick Mags for anything she could convert to gossip. For that, Mags was thankful, and concentrated instead on finishing her meal. She was forking up the last of the succulent salad when she heard a man's voice speaking right around the corner. What she heard made it impossible to swallow that last bite.

"I gotta to eat quick and get back. The grand jury has indicted that Pickett woman for murder. Sheriff Wiley and the D.A. are going to hold a news conference on the courthouse steps at two-thirty today. Sheriff wants everyone on hand, in case things get out of control."

As she listened to the men talk about her friend's perceived guilt, Mags was paralyzed with fear. What should she do? What could she do? At that moment, all she could think about was getting back to her office to call Wyatt. Yet she dared not walk out through the restaurant, where she'd have to pass the deputy who had just spilled his gut. She rose from her chair, spinning around, physically and emotionally, and almost fell into a heavily loaded server returning dirty dishes to the kitchen.

The kitchen!

It was, she decided, the lesser of all the evils, so before she could lose her nerve or anyone could stop her, Mags charged through the door marked "in", through the kitchen, and out the back door. Heads had turned and eyes had followed, but Mags hadn't slowed down long enough for questions, answers and especially explanations. Instead, she concentrated on reaching her office three blocks away, without getting caught or killed.

"Ramona, somehow we've got to get word to Wyatt." Her voice was a high-pitched screech, but she didn't care. "Wyatt needs to know that Carole Pickett has been formally indicted for murder. They're announcing it at a news conference in a little more than an hour."

"Calm down, Mrs. Gordon. Now start over again. I couldn't understand half of what you were saying."

Mags made a concerted effort to calm her nerves and slow her speech. After she had repeated the original message, she added, "This is going to kill Carole. Wyatt really needs to know, so he can do damage control."

"Yes ma'am, I agree. Let me see what I can do. I'll call you back."

"Please hurry," Mags urged. "This mess has gone too far."

Unable to just sit in her office and watch time pass, Mags found Delilah's leash, snapped it on her, and the two of them left for a walk around town. According to the clock in her phone, it was only about forty-five minutes before the sheriff's upcoming fifteen minutes of fame. She made up her mind to be in the group at the courthouse.

They walked along the lakefront, up one side of Main Street and back down the other side. She was saddened at the number of her fellow downtown merchants who appeared to turn their backs when they spotted her. Then, the more she thought about it, she realized she didn't care that she was looked upon as the source of trouble in paradise. A few people did stop and speak to Delilah, who clearly enjoyed the attention. They were on their third big loop of the town when Mags' cell phone rang.

"Hello?"

"It's Wyatt. I'm calling on a borrowed phone, so talk quick. What's happening there?"

She related the conversation she had overheard. "You've got to do something. Carole's already at the bottom of the heap. Once she finds out she's an indicted murder suspect, I'm afraid she'll spiral out of control."

"There's nothing I can do to stop them. Especially not from here, although I'll be back in Atlanta tonight."

"You might need to be in Crabapple Cove tonight."

"Something tells me I probably will be there sometime tomorrow."

"I'm going to that news conference. Call me when you get a chance later and I'll bring you up to speed."

She and Delilah continued to kill time until it was almost two-thirty, then she directed the dog toward the courthouse, where a crowd had already begun to form. Several TV cameras and people with note pads told her the media was in attendance. Where, she wondered, did all the people come from? More importantly, how did they get the word? If invitations had been issued, her's must have gotten lost in the mail, she decided. She held back at the rear of the crowd, not because she was uncomfortable being seen, but because she didn't know just how Delilah would react in what could be an excited crowd of strangers.

At the time Mags had understood an announcement would be made, the courthouse doors opened and the sheriff along a second man she didn't know, appeared and took their places on the main portico. The sheriff, she noticed, was so proud he was about to pop the buttons on his uniform jacket. Without meaning to, her eyes caught his, and the expression of surprise that appeared in his eyes was quickly replaced by a look that clearly said, "gotcha... again". She dropped her eyes, then made sure she didn't look his way a second time.

The strange man introduced himself as Stanley Bankston, the district attorney. He wasted little time telling the crowd that he held in his hand a formal grand jury indictment of Carole S. Pickett. She was indicted, he said, for the premeditated murder of one Horace J. Humphries, and he was reserving the right to pursue the death penalty once the case got closer to trial.

The death penalty! They had all talked about that possibility, but it had been in a half-joking, gallows humor manner. This man was serious. Her friend could die.

"... without Sheriff Malcolm Wiley's diligent, dare I say bulldog tenacity, this case might never have progressed to a conclusion so quickly. He and his staff are to be commended for their professional attitude and determination, leaving no stone unturned. Thank you, Sheriff." The two exchanged congratulatory handshakes.

Mags watched the sheriff's chest expand even more as he stepped to the microphone. "Good afternoon," he pronounced with a joviality Mags recognized as his ego voice. "It is a pleasure to appear here today with the honorable Mr. Bankston, to officially bring to a close the investigation into the death of Mr. Humphries. This man died a gruesome death that no one should be forced to endure. I don't mind telling you; forensics tests show that he lived for possibly an hour after he was shot, while he lay there, helpless, with the life ebbing from his bullet-riddled body."

Oh good grief Gertrude, Mags thought. Let's add a little drama here. But she understood what was happening. The sheriff, with the D.A.'s unspoken blessing, was doing a little missionary work in advance of jury selection. This was serious, she realized. They planned to convict Carole. Unless someone or something intervened, their plans would go forward and Carole would be executed. Never mind that she was innocent.

Mags had no desire to return to work. She and Delilah made their way back to the office, where she secured everything, locked the door, and the two of them returned to The Slop Bucket, where they stayed for the rest of the day.

It was almost six o'clock when Wyatt called. She had almost given up hearing from him.

"I'm sorry, Mags. Court ran over. It became apparent to the judge that we could finish today, provided we stayed late. Since the judge calls the shots, we stayed late. Tell me what went down."

Mags complied, giving him a play-by-play of the news conference, complete with commentator color profiles and sidebars. "I'm sure you can catch it on the evening news."

"I'll have a little conversation with Mr. Bankston. Professional courtesy dictates that he would have given me a call, to let me know what was going to happen before he made the public announcement. This shows me how they're going to play the game."

"What can you do?"

"For starters, I'll be in Crabapple Cove by mid-morning tomorrow. And I'm going to call Mr. Pickett as soon as we hang up. You mean he wasn't there?"

"I didn't see any sign of him. He probably didn't even know. I wouldn't have if I hadn't been in the right place at the right time, and overheard." She slammed her fist against the table by her chair. "But I can tell you this much; there were more than three dozen people gathered around. They found out somehow."

"I'll touch base with you when I get to town in the morning."

"I'm going to see Carole, to reassure her that you're coming."

"Won't do you any good," Wyatt informed her. "Now that she's under indictment, no one but her attorney, her clergyman, or her physician can get in to see her. Even her dad is going to be turned away."

"That's not going to set well with him."

"Likely not. But that's how it'll be. I'll have to see if I can get him in with me."

Mags told him goodbye and replaced the handset. Following a sandwich for her and scrambled eggs for Delilah, she retired early and actually watched TV in bed, desperate for something to take her mind off what had happened. Anything to pass the time until she could fall asleep.

There were, she understood, so many aspects of this story that didn't dovetail or even make sense. But at that moment, she felt too helpless to even know what to do. Instead, she crawled into the safe space that was her king size bed, and pulled the covers up over her head. It was all she was capable of, and even the realization of that shortcoming sickened her. But it was what it was.

Chapter Sixteen

CAROLE DIDN'T KILL THAT MAN

The shrill sound of a bell roused Mags from sleep. It was too early to get up. Through barely-opened eyes, she could see it was still dark outside. But why was the alarm clock sounding off so early?

Slowly the light bulb in her brain began to glow, and she realized the noise was the landline telephone, not a clock alarm. She scrambled in the dark to reach the bedside lamp, then grabbed for the handset. "Hello!"

"Mags, it's…"

"Wyatt! It's not morning. Why are you calling? What's wrong? It's…" she glanced across the room where her digital clock stared back. She squinted. "It's three-forty-nine. Why are you calling?"

"I'm sorry, but I knew you'd want to know…"

"Know what?" she demanded, interrupting his explanation.

"Carole tried to take her own life tonight."

"She what?"

"Mr. Pickett just called me. They found her unresponsive in her cell and rushed her to the hospital in Jonesborough."

Mags knew he meant the regional medical center in the next county.

"But why? What?"

"We don't know. Only that she was unconscious when they found her. Her dad's at the hospital, but they aren't telling him anything."

"That's a good hospital, Wyatt." She said it as much to reassure herself as him.

"That's well and good, but Mr. Pickett says cops are crawling all over the place, actually interfering with the doctors doing their jobs."

"I'm going to the hospital!" She was already throwing back the covers. Delilah, who was asleep on the foot of the bed, roused up to protest the disturbance, then lay her head back down and resumed snoring.

"I was hoping you'd say that. I'm leaving here within the next thirty minutes, but it'll take me two hours or more."

"I'm on my way. I'll call you after I get there."

True to her word, Mags was soon in clothes, had kissed the top of Delilah's head, armed the security system, and was on her way through the mountain darkness to the next county. The trip took almost half an hour and soon, the hospital was a brilliant, blinding glow in the night sky. She found the ER entrance, parked in the first available space, and set off at a run toward her friend. Inside was the typical trauma setting, complicated by the presence of more uniformed officers than she could count. She didn't see Malcolm, and she wasn't looking for him. Instead, her attention was focused on finding Joe Pickett, whom she soon spotted in the crowd near the far end of the room. He was seated in a small waiting area, with his head buried in his hands, looking less like a football coach than Mags would have thought possible.

She hurried over to him. "Mr. P, what happened?" She scooted into the seat next to him, and recoiled with shock, when the man she knew raised his head. Never had she seen anyone so depleted of soul. His eyes were red and swollen, and tears still trickled down his pale cheeks.

"Is Carole…?" Mags couldn't bring herself to finish the question.

"She's still alive. I guess. They won't let me see her."

"What happened?" She took his hands in hers. Icy skin was all she felt.

"I got a call from the jail saying they were transporting her here. I got here as quick as I could. They tell me she tried to kill herself."

"Not that I believe that for one minute," Mags charged, trying to keep her voice down. She didn't want to attract attention. "She was in jail, for gosh sake. How could she do that?"

The old man shook his head. "I don't know," he said finally. "I don't understand any of this."

Activity continued to swirl around them, but when the sun was finally strong in the early morning sky, Mags and Mr. Pickett were still sitting, wondering, but most of all, still uninformed. Mags had tried twice to get additional information, only to be threatened with removal if she continued to interfere.

"Mr. Pickett. Mags. Thank goodness I found you."

"Wyatt!"

Mags leaped to her feet, but the older man remained seated. She motioned for the attorney to take her seat.

"Mr. Pickett. I'm here. What can you tell me?"

Mr. Pickett gave no indication he heard the question, but continued to stare at the floor. Finally, in a voice barely audible, he mumbled. "My little girl didn't try to kill herself. I don't care what they say."

"They won't tell us anything, Wyatt. I've tried, but all they do is threaten me."

"I'm her attorney. They can't threaten me. I'll be back." He rose and made quick strides to the other side of the room, where a football team of law enforcement blocked the double doorway.

Mags watched as he waded through the melee, pushing aside those whose bulk would deny him passage. Then he disappeared, and the cadre of testosterone closed ranks again. He was gone so long, she had begun to wonder if he'd been arrested. This was, after all, Malcolm Wiley's turf away from home.

Finally, when she felt she'd explode if she had to wait much longer, Wyatt elbowed his way back through the officers.

"She's stable," he said, before even sitting back down. "Here, Mags, you sit, too. I need to talk to both of you." Mags moved into her old seat, while the attorney knelt in front of them. "We need to make this quick."

"Did you see her?" Joe Pickett asked. "How is my little girl?" Then sobs began to attack his body.

"She's alive, she's awake, and she's talking," Wyatt informed the older man. "She's going to make it, but not because she has any fight left in her."

"What do you mean, Wyatt?"

"She's given up."

"That doesn't sound like Carole."

"She's totally beaten down, Mags. She even told me there was no need for anyone to pay me, that she would just throw herself on the mercy of the court, and take her chances."

"You're not...?"

"Of course not," Wyatt asserted. "I'm in this for the long haul. She needs representation now, worse than before. She's her own worst enemy."

"My little girl didn't kill that man."

"No, Mr. Pickett. She didn't." He put his hand on the old man's shoulder, and gave it an encouraging pat. "We're going to clear her."

"Wyatt? What about their claim that...?" She was fearful to complete the question in Mr. Pickett's presence. She nodded instead, in his direction.

Wyatt picked up the thread. "Carole doesn't know anything about trying to commit suicide. In fact, she's flabbergasted."

"What does she say?"

"She awoke feeling like she had a stomach virus, but she couldn't get anyone to answer her calls for help. The next thing she remembers is waking up here."

"I don't like the looks of this, Wyatt." There was a scenario playing through Mag's mind that absolutely defied belief. Yet, to her dismay, it was also the only theory that made any sense. But would these people be daring enough to try and kill Carole while she was behind bars? How did they get to her?

"You're thinking the same thing I am," the attorney replied, his face sober. "And I don't want to go there. But we may have to."

"I want to see my daughter," a voice from the other side announced. "If Malcolm tries to stop me, I'll break his sorry neck. Should've done it a long time ago."

Mags and Wyatt exchanged troubled glances over Mr. Pickett's head. "Sit tight," he told the older man, "let me see what I can arrange."

He was back in a few minutes. "Come with me. They're going to let you go back with me, but just like at the jail, no touching or hysterics." He took the older man by his arm, and guided him through the mob of uniforms. Mags wondered what was going on, but didn't attempt to break the ranks. Better that Mr. P saw his daughter. Wyatt would fill her in.

A short time later, the two men reappeared in the waiting area. Mr. Pickett's face was ravaged by a fresh onslaught of tears. "She's pitiful," he told Mags, as he hugged her to him. "She's totally given up."

"But she's adamant she didn't try to take her own life. That's the only time I saw a spark, and I believe her."

"So what do we do now?"

"Did you call the lady in Atlanta?"

Mags realized he didn't want Mr. P to know everything they were doing. "I called her at lunch yesterday, but had to leave a message. She hasn't gotten back to me."

"We need her. Let me see what I can do." He pulled his cell

phone from his pocket, as he stepped to the other side of the room. Mags saw his lips moving.

"Why'd he go over there?"

"It's so noisy in here, Mr. P. I imagine it's easier for him to hear over there." The older man seemed to buy her off-the-cuff explanation, and Mags breathed a sigh of relief.

"Ramona is going to work on it," he told Mags quietly, when he returned. "Mr. Pickett," he addressed the other man. "They're going to keep Carole here for a day or so, until the doctor says she's out of danger. But you're not going to be able to see her. I'm sorry."

The other man raised his face to look at them both. "At least she's not in that nasty jail." He rubbed his hands back and forth. "It don't seem fair, and I don't like it that I can't sit in the room with her, but if I can't, well… then I can't."

"You might as well go on back home. I'm going through Crabapple Cove to the courthouse, then back to Atlanta. I've got appointments this afternoon that can't be canceled. But I'll be checking on things by phone, and I'll call you."

Mags had an idea. "Tell you what, Mr. P, I'm ready to head back. Why don't we meet out at the diner on the four-lane? We can get a late breakfast." She patted his shoulder. "I don't know about you, but I'm famished."

Mr. Pickett agreed, and the three of them left the ER together, then split once they reached the parking lot. Mags watched until she saw Carole's little truck headed toward the highway; she pulled in behind it. Half an hour later, the two of them were seated in a booth at the diner, sharing breakfast and information.

"Carole didn't kill that man, and she certainly didn't try to kill herself. You'll never make me believe otherwise."

"Wyatt doesn't think so, either. He's working on everything." She was working on things, as well, but elected not to share everything that she knew. Mags was even less willing to divulge all of her suspicions, because she wasn't sure she even believed it all.

Breakfast over, the two separated. Mags promised to keep in touch, then headed back to The Slop Bucket, where an anxious Delilah was waiting. With the dog on a leash, the two enjoyed a leisurely walk around the property, before returning inside where Mags prepared her dog's breakfast. While Delilah ate, Mags jumped into the shower for a long-delayed jump-start on the day, then dressed in old clothes and returned to the living area. She would not to go to the office. Instead, she intended to try to find the missing piece from the puzzle that had started with nasty little Mr. Humphries. She wished fervently he had never darkened the door. But he had. What's more, it was clear to Mags, even if no one else saw it, that everything that had happened was part of a gigantic scheme to ruin her. It would be left to her to discover both the why and, more importantly, the who.

Mags spread out all the documents one more time. Somewhere in those papers was the loose string she needed to pull in order to unravel all the confusion. But first, in a move not unlike Annie Darling, one of her favorite modern-day amateur sleuths, she began to list what little she did know about the case.

While it was still to be proven, there obviously was a connection between HJH and her own past. She didn't kill Mr. Humphries, but she understood that she would have to find that connection in order to learn who the murderer was. Slowly her list began to take shape. With it, small lights started to illuminate, as she was finally to connect a few of the dots.

1. The murder weapon was stolen from her office

2. It was found, hidden, in a compartment on board the *One True Love*, a secret compartment where Franklin had hidden jars of illegal moonshine

3. HJH's stated address was actually a parking garage belonging to her ex-husband's family business empire

4. The night she had a visitor to The Slop Bucket, her dog hadn't barked

5. Someone had intentionally fed Delilah rat poison, when ordinarily the dog wouldn't have taken food from a stranger

6. In listing business affiliations on his client information

form, HJH included Ophelia Corporation, the corporate name
of Franklin's family business empire

Mags didn't understand how, but she understood that each one
of the items on her partial list of clues pointed to her ex-husband,
Franklin Gordon. Only how could HJH and Franklin be connected? If
she didn't unravel the mess of loose ends, that connection threatened
to definitely kill any possibility of her future. She also realized that if
her ex-husband was implicated in any way, Sheriff Wiley would do
whatever he had to do to keep his best friend safe. Or had he already
done that? Mags could but wonder... and worry.

The ring of her cell phone brought her back to the present. It was
Wyatt. "Hello. Where are you?"

"I'm back in my office. Ramona managed to track down Jennifer.
She's ready to meet you and go to work on this case."

"You've got to listen to what I've discovered this morning." She
began to read the contents of her list. "Wyatt? Do you realize what
this means? Do you see the common thread that I see?"

Mags could hear him breathing, so she knew her friend hadn't
ended the call. Finally, he said, "Franklin. On items two through six,
I definitely see his fingerprints. Number one is iffy in my mind, but
those last five can't be discounted."

"That's how I see it, too."

"But what is the connection, Mags? Are you telling me you
suspect Franklin is behind all of this? Surely you don't think he's a
murderer?"

"I don't want to think that, but what choice do I have? This should
have hit me sooner, but Delilah was so sick, I couldn't see anything
but how close I came to losing her."

"You mean the unknown visitors you've had to The Slop Bucket
had to be someone she knew?"

"Exactly. Delilah doesn't socialize very much outside this house.
Besides Carole and a couple of other friends I've made, no one here
in Crabapple Cove knows my dog. If they invaded this space, she
would go berserk. Franklin and Delilah had a good relationship.

Probably better than Franklin and I had," she explained sheepishly. "He's the only one I know who could come in here, and Delilah not react. If he offered her food, she would take it without hesitation."

"Franklin is your ex-husband, and I hate to dump this on you, but I'm afraid you're closer to the truth than any of us are comfortable with."

"I suspect and surmise, but I can't prove it. Not with what I have now."

"That's where Jennifer can pick up the ball and run with it. You've gone about as far as you can go."

"I feel so disloyal. Franklin cheated on me with many women; some of them were friends of mine and yours. But there's a world of difference between cheating and murder. I wouldn't want to throw him to the wolves unless we could be certain."

"Jennifer can give us that clarification. When can you meet with her?

"The sooner the better, I'd say. What about tomorrow morning?"

"Do you think it's wise to have her show up in Crabapple Cove? You never know who might be able to overhear."

Inspiration hit. "Wyatt. She can come here as a potential property buyer. I'll take her out by boat, where we can talk in the middle of the lake if we have to. It'll all look perfectly normal, and there won't be any danger of being overheard."

"Sounds like a plan. I'll get hold of Jennifer and share the specifics. Call you back before bedtime."

"Wyatt?" The words stuck in her throat. "Do you think Carole tried to kill herself?"

"What do you think?"

"I don't believe it, but if she didn't… that means someone tried to kill her."

"That's exactly what it means, and that's what I fear really happened."

"But, Wyatt. That means the attempt on her life originated right there in the jail."

"It does, doesn't it." There was no question mark at the end of his statement.

Mags didn't want to consider the implications, and said as much.

They ended the call, and Mags spent the remainder of the day totally at loose ends. There wasn't that much housework to be done, and she wasn't in the mood to dust and clean bathrooms anyway. A stack of unread books, most of them mysteries, stood beside her chair, but suddenly someone's imagination couldn't compete with the reality that had come home to her a few hours earlier. Her brain was fuzzy, a victim of too little sleep and too much stress, but when she lay down to nap, her eyes refused to shut. The late afternoon talk shows on TV couldn't snag her interest. Even the beauty of the mountains that always recharged her batteries didn't deliver.

The one fear, the one question in her mind replayed on a loop. Had she been married to a man capable of murder? Had he murdered before? Was her Buckhead and Piedmont Driving Club lifestyle bankrolled with blood money? And the one that troubled her most? Was her own life ever in danger? Would Franklin have killed her, or purchased her death? She had slept beside this man. Supposedly infidelity was his biggest character flaw. She hadn't been able to forgive his sleeping around, so how was she supposed to handle murder?

Sunlight became twilight which soon became darkness. She scrambled the last of the eggs for Delilah, and made a mental note to pick up more at the store. Mags ate nothing. The rough mass of concrete in her belly wouldn't have welcomed any competition. But it didn't matter, because she wasn't hungry.

It was almost bedtime when her phone rang.

"Jennifer will be at your office around eleven tomorrow morning. She's about five feet tall, and wears maybe a size two. Dark, long, shoulder-length hair. You'll love her."

Mags thanked him and promised to report in following investigator's visit. Then she put herself to bed where, contrary to her expectations of another sleepless night, she was unconscious by the time her head hit the pillow. Stabbing rays of morning sunlight pouring in through the window over the bed summoned her back to the real world the next morning, and Mags complied.

She had little time to lose, between breakfast for the two of them, showering and getting ready for the office. After making her bed and straightening the room, she worked around the dining room table organizing the paper trail she had to share with the detective. By ten o'clock, she was at the office, where she spent the next half hour copying all her paperwork. This way they both could have the same files.

Right on time, the door opened and the very person Wyatt had described walked in. "Hi, I'm Jennifer Masterson. Call me Jennie. You must be Mags. Love that name."

Mags couldn't help smiling. Her guest's elevator speech had been flawlessly delivered, although there was much emotion evident. This woman was far from walking dead, she decided. What's more, she looked the least like a private detective of any PI Mags had ever known. Fictionally or otherwise. She said as much.

"One of my most potent tools of the trade. By the time the other side figures out there's more to me than meets the eye, they've usually made the fatal mistake that's going to hang them. By that point, there's no redemption."

"I'd never take you for anything to do with investigations or law enforcement." As she spoke, Mags couldn't stop studying the woman who was supposed to unravel the mystery, and save Carole's life. Dressed in a buttery-yellow pants outfit, with red, open-toed sandals peeping out from beneath the hem of her pants, the woman looked like she was next up on a fashion runway.

"Don't get too hung up on the law enforcement end of my deal. Sometimes I have to live dangerously and cut a few select corners that could cost me my license, so I stress investigation more than enforcement."

I like this woman, Mags thought. She's sharp and then some. "So tell me," she said, "what kind of property are you interested in seeing?"

The comeback was swift and sharp. "Anything that will give you a chance to fill me in on all the down and dirty details. The more you can give me, the better job I can do. Faster, too."

"I've got just the place in mind. Shall we go?"

At the marina, Mags rented a boat and they set out for the middle of the lake. One of her listed properties was a mini-compound on six acres. The house had no lock box and could be shown by appointment only. No one had contacted her to get the key, and she knew the owners were in Europe. They should have plenty of privacy. Conversation was difficult in the open boat, so little was said until Mags had docked and unlocked the kitchen door. "Let's sit over here at the breakfast table," she invited. "We might as well get comfortable."

While her companion got settled, Mags removed the two folders of papers from her tote bag, and laid one in front of each of them. "How do you want to begin?"

Jennie reached into her purse and removed a small tape recorder. She flicked the power button and smiled at Mags. "I assume you don't mind being recorded?"

Mags indicated her agreement.

"Great. All this paper trail is valuable, but right now I want to hear everything you know. I'll probably interrupt to ask questions, but don't let me intimidate you."

"Where should I start?"

"How about when the dead man first contacted your office? Go from there."

For the next twenty minutes, Mags led the detective through the different encounters with the man she had known as Mr. Humphries. When it came to the part where she found his body, she had to stop for a minute. The memories were overwhelming.

True to her promise, Jennie stopped her several times to clarify points, or to ask questions, the answers to which caused Mags to have to dig even deeper into her memory bank.

Then she completed the story of the past few days, and went over the points on her list that caused her to suspect her ex-husband.

"I've got your story here, where I can listen to it as many times as I need. I can go over the paper trail back at home. But I have to say, if your ex isn't involved in this to some extent, I'm going to be the most surprised person around. This is just too much coincidence to be believable."

"How long do you think it's going to take to do your investigation?"

"That's hard to answer. You've done much of the groundwork for me." She picked up the folder and held it aloft. "This right here will probably save me a week of work, and it also gives me an idea of which trails are hot and which ones would be a waste of time."

"Time is slipping away. My office manager's life is literally on the line, and I'm not just talking about executing her for murder."

"I understand. Wyatt filled in many of the blanks."

"Speaking of Wyatt, as we head back to the marina, I'll make a little detour and show you the house he and Christine are buying."

"He told me all about it. Said I ought to pick up something here while the market is depressed." She grinned. "He seems to forget I'm just a lowly PI. My income level doesn't match his."

"Neither are self-employed real estate agents. So why don't us poor folks be on our way?"

True to her word, Mags swung by the property that would soon be Wyatt's and Christine's, and pulled up to the dock. They didn't get out, but instead sat in the boat, talking about property in the mountains.

"I'd love to have something here. Never mind that I can't afford anything costing more than two dollars and ninety-five cents. But even if I had the financial ability to buy it, I wouldn't have time to use it and enjoy it. So why bother?"

Mags soon set course for the marina and, in quick fashion, had turned in the key and signed the charge slip. Then she and Jennie headed back to town. Conversation was once again about HJH, as Mags tried her best to remember every detail about the oily little man and his business. Back at the office, Jennie didn't come in, but said she needed to head back to Atlanta. "Ordinarily, it would have taken me a week or more to get up here, but when Wyatt explained the circumstances, I knew I needed to come on. That cheating husband or the guy trying to scam the insurance company with his bogus bad back can wait a day or so."

Mags shook hands with her. "I really appreciate you coming so quickly. If you need anything else, you know how to reach me."

Mags bid her guest safe travel back to Atlanta. "Then, in case anyone was listening, she said in a louder voice. "It was a pleasure to meet you. Talk to your husband, show him the listing sheets on the houses we toured. If you need to see any of them again, just give me a call and I'll make it happen."

The two women grinned at each other as the detective got into her gunmetal gray VW Jetta and backed out of the parking space. Mags returned to the office, double-checked everything and locked the door behind her. She'd left Delilah at home, and was anxious to get back to her. No more real estate work, imaginary or otherwise, would happen today.

Nothing happened over the next few days, and Mags tired of waiting for the other shoe to drop. She usually drove into town once a day to check messages and the mail, but her confidence had been shattered. The Slop Bucket had been her safe house during the years when marriage to Franklin had gone so horribly wrong. The beautiful old lodge had been her refuge in those dark days after her divorce, when she'd come to the mountains to reinvent herself. Despite its remote location, the familiar, comfortable old house was once again her fortress against the world, and all the evil in it. Safe inside, with the locks engaged and the security system activated, Mags couldn't manage to lose her fear of everything that moved, of every tree that creaked and swayed.

The stack of whodunits dwindled during that week. She ate and exercised Delilah. Once a day she'd call Mr. P to check on him and get an update on Carole. It hurt that she couldn't visit her friend, but even her father had only seen her twice and then, only for a couple of minutes.

On the fourth day, he told her that Carole had been returned to the jail, but that his access to her was still limited. She was very depressed, he explained, and still wasn't willing to fight to save herself. Mags hung up fairly depressed herself, and loudly cursed Franklin Gordon for all the trouble he had caused. In her mind, it didn't matter what Jennie found, the blame lay squarely at his feet.

Then the call she had been anticipating arrived just as she was getting ready for bed on the fifth night. "Hope I'm not calling too late."

"In this situation, there is no too late." Mags plopped down on her bed. "So spill it. And don't leave out one single detail."

"I'll give you the high points. Then I'll forward the complete report."

"I'm all ears."

"Your Mr. Humphries was actually Donald Hamilton Watkins, an officer with Ophelia, Inc. He was single, never married, no known children, a loner in every respect. One sister in Cincinnati that he hadn't talked to in more than ten years."

"In other words, a man whose absence wouldn't easily be noticed?"

"That's how I read it. Anyway, he and Franklin were golfing buddies outside the office. Speaking of your husband, did you know he's bought a place there in Crabapple Cove? About six months ago."

"Franklin has a home here?"

"Hate to break it to you, but he's living not more than two miles on past you by car. Probably only several hundred yards on foot around the edge of the lake."

Mags felt the freeze of panic attack her body. Suddenly the security she'd made for herself evaporated, and she felt extremely vulnerable. "Something tells me there's more."

"Franklin has been in residence there almost every day since about a week before Mr. Humphries, or Mr. Watkins, take your pick, first visited your office. And… Mr. Watkins' bank account suddenly began to grow much fatter, starting about a month before he died. As far as I can tell, your ex-husband knew they were one and the same person."

"So Franklin could easily have been involved in breaking in to The Slop Bucket and all the other crap that's gone down."

"He definitely could. What's more, for a few days there, neighbors saw a car that matches the description of Mr. Humphries' Lexus at Franklin's house at all hours. Then, suddenly, it wasn't there. Didn't anyone question what happened to the dead man's car after he was dead? Or where he was staying? How about what he did when he wasn't making your life miserable?"

"None of that ever crossed my mind," Mags had to admit. Some kind of detective she was. All those books she'd read, but she couldn't manage to question even a few basics. "So it does look like Franklin is implicated in this somehow."

"I'm afraid it does. The authorities are going to have to be told about all of this."

Mags digested what she had heard. "If you think the sheriff is going to take down his best friend, think again. We're going to have to blow the lid off this mess in such a way that Malcolm can't dodge his sworn responsibility."

"We? What do you have in mind?"

"Remember when you told me you concentrated more on investigation than enforcement? Well, you and I are going to have to do this sheriff's job, so that the law will be enforced."

"How so?"

"You didn't know it, but you're coming up for the weekend. Stay here with me. I'll have a game plan by the time you get here tomorrow afternoon."

"I can do that, but there's one thing I haven't told you. I strongly suspect that your sheriff is involved in this case, at least as an accessory."

"I'd be very surprised if he weren't. Malcolm's almost besotted with Franklin. They've been joined at the hip since childhood."

"Just so you know, this may get ugly."

"It will get ugly. Wear your army boots."

The two compared notes and Mags gave the detective directions to get to The Slop Bucket.

"I'll be there by four o'clock."

"Drive safely. Call me if you have any problems."

If she's here by four o'clock, by bedtime we should have a plan devised to rip the covers off this sordid mess. Franklin Gordon has underestimated me again. She couldn't wait to see his face when he realized his mistake.

Chapter Seventeen

IT WAS BLACKMAIL

"**N**o offence meant, but are you a good enough actress to pull this off?"

Jennie's question involved Mags' plan to cozy up to her ex-husband and get him to expose, then implicate himself in the murder." Mags still wasn't ready to believe that Franklin himself pulled the trigger, but she had to agree that, at the very least, he had hired the job done.

"I've done my share of little theater stuff and Franklin's ego is big enough to hide any imperfections in my acting skills. He'll be so puffed up because I've to come crawling back, begging for his help, he won't stop to second-guess the situation."

"But if he is the killer, you could be in big trouble."

"Not as long as I only meet him in a public place. If you're nearby, within earshot, so much the better."

"So where do we begin?

The detective had arrived shortly before the appointed time, smiling and enthusiastic. Mags, on the other hand, was down in the dumps. She'd gotten up that morning and done her housework.

Then it was in to town, to check things at the office. She had to buy groceries. It wouldn't do for the two of them to be seen together in public, so that meant eating at home. By lunch time, Mags was out of patience, waiting for the investigator's arrival. It depressed her to realize that what happened in the next few days would forever change her life. She was no longer married to Franklin, but his actions were still affecting her. Would it never end?

Jennie had brought with her the complete report which, Mags was shocked to see, showed that her husband had been paying sums exceeding one hundred thousand dollars a week to Mr. Watkins, aka Mr. Humphries.

"Blackmail?" she asked.

"Look at the big picture," Jennie urged. "For six weeks the guy was getting five thousand dollars transferred from one of the Ophelia accounts into his account. Always an even amount of money; no few cents dangling, as it would have been with a payroll payment subject to withholdings. Then, three weeks before the murder, suddenly we have two hundred thousand from one of Franklin's personal accounts. A week later there's another one hundred thousand, followed by a third payment."

"It was blackmail. I can almost smell it."

"So how, exactly, do you think we can expose all that's going on here?"

"By making a phone call. That's how we get the ball rolling."

"A phone call. To whom?"

"To the man of the hour. My ex-husband." She retrieved her cell phone and searched for the number that had shown up when he called her a few days before. "He called to offer me his help. I'm just going to be a helpless, clinging female and ask him to do his big, strong man thing." As she spoke, Mags' voice had gotten definitely more southern in drawl. Jennie was in stitches, laughing but was trying not to lose control.

Mags waited until they both had recaptured their composure, then she made the call. A man's voice answered on the fourth ring.

"Franklin?"

"Mags? Is it really you?"

"I'm not calling at a bad time, am I?" Like I hope you're not in the middle of bedding another one of my friends? Mags forced the mental image from her mind, and concentrated instead on the image she wanted to create in Franklin's mind.

"Nonsense. Any time's a good time to talk to you. But I have to admit, I'm somewhat surprised. You made it pretty plain the other night that you wanted nothing more to do with me."

"I was rude, wasn't I? It had been a bad day." She mimed a retching action, then continued. "I hope you'll forgive me."

"Well, of course. We've got too much history to let a little thing like that be a sticking point."

"Thank you, Franklin. Because… well, you offered your help when you called the other night. I hope that offer's still open."

"Sure. I mean, yeah. If I can. I'm no miracle worker, you know."

"I don't want to go into this on the phone." She paused. "If only you were up here, we could have breakfast tomorrow."

"But I am here. Staying at the Mountain Manor Lodge. I drove up this afternoon."

"2M", as the hotel was known locally, was the most expensive place in town, but how like Franklin, even in his lies, to select only the most exclusive.

"Gosh, that's great. Did you come up for something special?"

"Just needed to get away from the corporate rat race. I've been so busy I haven't been up in… let's see, it's been over two months."

LIAR, Mags thought, but bit her tongue to refrain from yelling it through the phone.

"Okay, then. You're here. Great! How about we meet for breakfast tomorrow at the diner on the four-lane at… say, nine o'clock?"

"I'll be there, Mags." There was silence. "Thanks for calling me back. It's nice to be needed. Maybe someday we can work on rekindling what we had together."

"See you in the morning, Franklin. Good night."

Jennie, who was sitting on the comfortable, over-stuffed sofa, close enough to hear Mags' end of the conversation, applauded. "That, my friend, was a masterful piece of acting."

"Was it masterful acting or just an exceptionally dumb audience?"

"Huh?"

"Franklin thinks he's charmed me to the point that I want a reconciliation. I'll guarantee you right now, he's already moved back into this house, and he's on his way to take out the *One True Love*. Which means I'm left sitting out in the cold. Just like old times."

The two went to bed shortly after they walked Delilah who, to Mags' relief, was really showing her recovery. The clocks were set and the plans were made. Mags, who was still having attacks of doubt, had figured she wouldn't sleep. No one was more surprised than she, when the morning sun interrupted her slumber even before the alarm went off.

The plan called for Jennie to already be at the diner, just a regular tourist who had pulled off the highway for breakfast. Mags would arrive a few minutes later, and the two would have no contact. Jennie left The Slop Bucket ten minutes before Mags, so she could be in position.

When Mags arrived, Franklin was already in a booth and, she was surprised to see Jennie in the booth directly across the aisle. Good. She'd be able to hear and see everything.

Franklin rose as she made her way to their table. "Mags. You don't know how good it is to see you." He kissed her on the cheek. "It's been too long. I've missed you."

Mags had to steel herself not to flinch when his lips touched her. She believed he missed his money, his boat and his lodge much more than he did her. But she didn't say that. "We did have some good times, didn't we?" Once she had settled into her seat, Franklin attempted to take her hand in his, but Mags resisted. She could endure only so much.

The two ordered breakfast then, over coffee, Franklin made small talk about some of their friends in Atlanta, especially those at the club he saw regularly. "I'm usually there every Friday and Saturday. Just can't rattle around by myself in that big old house."

Their food was served and both had made a decent dent, when he asked. "So what is it you need my help on?"

"It's Carole. My office manager."

"The one who killed that guy on my... er, your boat."

"She's the one who's charged with murder. But she didn't kill him."

"I've been following the story in the papers. Looks pretty open and shut to me."

"But it's not. You see, Carole knows who really killed Mr. Humphries. But locked up in jail, she can't do very much about it."

She noticed that his body jerked ever so slightly in reaction to her announcement.

"So where do I come into the picture?"

Mags leaned across the table, forced herself to place one of her hands on his, then in a low, conspiratorial voice that she hoped sounded helpless enough, said, "Carole has proof of the killer's identity. I'm not sure how it happened. She couldn't tell me much what with all those visiting restrictions at the jail. According to her, the killer better hope this evidence never surfaces. She swears it'll convict them. That's why she hid it on the boat, just until she could come back for it. Then Malcolm arrested her before she got a chance."

She watched as Franklin's face lost then quickly regained its color. She definitely had his attention.

"So why doesn't she just tell Malcolm? He can get the evidence and she'll go free."

"She's tried. He won't play ball."

Franklin lowered his voice. "Where on board did she hide it? Malcolm went over that boat from one end to the other. Several times. He told me so."

Mags forced herself to giggle. "Remember, you built that secret compartment inside the captain's seat? I showed it to Carole one time. She stuck the evidence in there."

"Malcolm must have overlooked it."

"You did such an excellent job of hiding that little canister, no one would ever suspect."

"Yeah, that was pretty swift of me." He appeared to grow larger from pride.

Mags wanted to puke. Just get this over with. Don't lose it now, she kept reminding herself. "So here's what I want you to do..."

"Now let me get this straight. I ask Malcolm for permission to go on board, I find Carole's proof, and give it to Malcolm?"

"Simple. See?"

"Well... I guess."

"Look, Franklin. Malcolm won't even think twice about letting you on board. For some reason, he doesn't like me any more. He must not, he sure does give me a lot of grief."

She was positive she saw the light of revenge sparkle in his eyes.

"So will you do it? Please? As soon as possible? I don't care who killed him. He was an obnoxious little man. But Carole didn't do it, and she's having a really rough time emotionally. We've got to get her out of that jail." Mags mentally donned her Scarlett O'Hara gown for the barbecue at Twelve Oaks. "Why Franklin, have you ever been back there in that jail? It's awful. It stinks to high heaven, there's filth everywhere, and the colors are so drab and lifeless. You really ought to suggest to Malcolm that he needs to call in a cleaning crew." She started to add... and a decorator... but decided that might be a little over the top, even in the dumb, blond, socialite department.

Franklin was counting out money for the check. "It's a jail, Mags, not the Ritz Carlton." He recounted the bills he laid down. "Let me talk to Malcolm and I'll call you back. But what excuse am I going to use for wanting to go aboard"

"Nostalgia? Old times sake? I've told you I might sell it, and since

290

you don't know when you'll be here again, you want to say goodbye." Did she really have to paint him a picture?

"Okay, I guess that would work." He extended his hand and helped her up. "I'll talk to you later today."

"Oh, thank you, Franklin. I knew I could count on you."

He leaned in for another brush of her cheek. "You know you can always count on me. I've never been one to hold grudges."

Yeah, and the Democrats and Republicans have decided to unite and form one party! But she managed to keep her mouth shut.

She and Franklin walked out together, he put his head near hers once again, as he said goodbye. She watched him drive off toward town in his new Jaguar, before she got into her jeep and made tracks toward the lake. A few minutes later, Jennie joined her.

"Did you get an ear full and an eye full?"

"That man's a piece of work."

"Tell me something I don't know."

"He was absolutely fawning over you. But I didn't pick up on any love or affection, or even respect."

"That's how I lived for too many years." She massaged her hair. "I really think it was the lack of respect that bothers me most."

"Knowing they couldn't be seen out and about, Mags had picked up several movie rentals at the grocery. She and her guest made sandwiches, then piled down on the couch to eat lunch and kill time, while waiting for Franklin's call.

"Do you really think he took the bait?"

"Are you kidding me? Mags, you had him. But when you told him Carole had proof of the real killer's identity, all the color drained out of his face. I saw it."

"That's the only reason I think he bit. He doesn't care anything about my wishes, and he sure isn't going out of his way to help Carole. She signed her death warrant with him when she hooked up with me."

"Makes you wonder how people like Franklin get that way?"

"That's an easy one. He patterns what he saw as a child."

"All too often, that is the case."

They were nearing the end of the second movie, when Mags' phone rang.

"I'm going on board in about an hour. I've got to make one stop on my way. Malcolm gave me the key to the impound area, and the ignition key. Even said I could take it out for a final spin if I wanted."

"Wasn't that nice of him?" Jerk, she thought. I need it for work and I can't get it.

"Mags? What, exactly, am I looking for?"

"That's just it. Carole wasn't where she could tell me a whole lot. All I got was that she stuck the evidence into that compartment in the seat. She says it's hot and totally-incriminating, and it has to be small enough to fit in that tiny compartment."

"How much stuff can be in there?"

"I'm guessing whatever you find is what she was talking about. She was pretty insistent about it. Call me when you get it, and we'll go to the sheriff together." She decided to go for broke. "Then… perhaps, we could go out for dinner? Down on the lake? We could come back here for a nightcap and… and, well you know, whatever."

"She could hear his breathing become more labored. "That sounds great. Yeah, I'll call you ASAP."

"We need to move into position," she told Jennie. "He took the bait. Every last piece of it."

"Wasn't that last bite hitting a little below the belt? No pun intended."

She shrugged. "I guess it depends on your perspective. I wanted to make sure he bit down on that bait really hard."

"But if this goes according to plan, he won't be able to call you. Or go out to dinner."

"Or whatever. Yeah. I know. Talk about frustrating."

The detective looked puzzled for a moment, then began to laugh. "You are so bad."

"Hey. I give as good as I get. But we need to get to the marina."

On the fifteen minute drive, the two women reviewed for a final time how they planned to close the trap and catch the killer.

"What's going to happen when Franklin opens that space and nothing's there?"

They were traveling in Jennie's car, so Franklin wouldn't recognize Mags' Jeep. But Mags was driving and, between the unfamiliar vehicle and the sharp curves ahead of them, she had her hands full. "He's going to be frantic," she answered finally, "because he doesn't dare let any clue surface that would point to the real killer. He has to get his hands on it, so he can dispose of it. When it's not there, he's going to pray that Malcolm has already found whatever it was. That way, he thinks he's safe, but with any luck he'll be arrested for trespassing instead."

"This sheriff must really be a corrupt lawman."

Mags laughed, although the sound lacked any hint of levity. "Wyatt says he's a cross between Buford Pusser and Boss Hogg."

"That's a dangerous-sounding six-toed hybrid."

"We're almost there. Thank goodness the marina is busy today. We'll blend right in."

They parked, and made their way along the docks, nodding and speaking to those they met. As they neared the impound area, Mags steered them into a small storage area where they could be out of sight but still have a clear view of the *One True Love*. She checked her phone. "He should be here in another twenty minutes or so."

Almost as if he were being clocked, Franklin came sauntering along the dock at the appropriate time, looking as if he had not one problem in the world. Mags and Jennie watched as he confidently produced a key and opened a gateway into the secured area. He didn't bother to close the gate, but quickly made his way to his former boat, where he boarded near the bow, and began to make his way to the wheelhouse.

Beside her, Jennie was already on her cell phone. "There's a man trying steal a boat at Davis Marina," she told the 911 operator. "It's the boat that man got killed on, and he's going to take it out into the lake and set fire to it. I heard him talking."

Mags was amazed. That last part hadn't been part of their script, but she thought it rather effective, nonetheless. She turned her attention back to the boat, where sounds of anger and frustration began to fill the air.

"Why do we think things aren't going the way he planned?"

"I'm sure I have no idea," Mags confessed. "He's getting very provoked. Do you think those deputies will get here before he gets fed up and bolts? That would ruin everything."

The noise level on board the boat was increasing.

"I started to call earlier, but then they might have gotten here before him."

"If he starts to leave, we've got to figure some way to stall. We've got to keep him here. Preferably on board."

"But how? We can't just walk up and say, 'Would you please hang around for a few more minutes? The cops are on their way.'"

Mags had to snicker. The mental picture Jennie had painted was too funny. Still, she had a valid point.

"Is there any way to set the boat free from its moorings? You know, push it out away from the dock or something," Jennie asked, as she scanned the northern horizon, looking for some assurance that help would arrive in time.

"I don't know. There are two ropes. I don't think we could get to both of them without being seen." As Mags delivered her assessment, the screams of anger and frustration became more pronounced. She could hear the boat being trashed. Franklin was one pissed guy. Perhaps Jennie's plan had potential. If one of them ran to the rope at the stern, while the other untied the bow rope, they might manage to release the boat before Franklin saw them. As for pushing the heavy craft out into marina waters, that was another concern entirely.

"Listen..."

Mags cocked her head. Sure enough, in the distance, she could hear the faint sound of sirens. Or was it wishful thinking?

"Stay there, Franklin. Take your wrath out on something else," Jennie was whispering.

Out of the corner of her eye, Mags saw an enraged Franklin approaching the side of the boat. "Jennie," she screeched, "he's leaving. Boy is he mad." She had been married to him long enough to be able to read the body language. It was very colorful and blue.

"There's nothing we can do. How can we hold him there?"

"They need to catch him on the boat,' Mags hissed. She looked around for something... anything, that she could throw to hit him in the head. It didn't make a lot of sense, she knew. But she was desperate.

In the distance, the wailing sound grew louder. On the boat, Franklin was lifting his leg over the side of the boat, and Mags was seriously considering making herself into a human cannonball. Then, for reasons she couldn't understand, he abruptly withdrew his leg, turned around, and headed back toward the wheelhouse.

"Look, Jennie! He's still aboard." As she watched, Franklin attacked something with his arms flailing in the air. She couldn't see what he was doing, but in a moment, the engine roared into life. Meanwhile, the sirens were very close and, in a matter of another minute, three uniformed deputies thundered onto the dock. As they approached the *One True Love*, the officers pulled their service revolvers, while the man in the lead yelled, "Whoever you are on board the *One True Love*, come out with your hands over your head. We're sheriff's deputies and we're armed." They assumed their trained stance.

Mags was glad they couldn't be seen, but it might be necessary for them to blow their cover. She hoped not. Franklin, she realized, was coming from the wheelhouse area and had not followed directions.

"Sir," the lead officer yelled, "your hands over your head. NOW! Hands over your head."

"Cut it out, you guys," she heard Franklin announce. "It's me.

Franklin Gordon. You know me."

"Oh, great," Mags groused. "He's playing good ol' boy with them. I should have known this wouldn't work."

"We've got an ace or two in the hole. Don't throw in the towel yet."

"Such as?"

"Shhhhh. Look. Something's happening."

Sure enough, Franklin was starting to climb over the side, and his face was all smiles. Mags was glad they were close enough to hear clearly what was being said.

"Halt, sir!" the squad leader demanded. "You will not leave the boat until ordered. Your hands over your head. NOW! I'm not going to ask you again." He raised his revolver just a little. "Your refusal to follow orders will give me no other option but to fire."

"But sir," one of the two men in back declared, "that's the sheriff's friend. Franklin Gordon." He waved. "Hey, Mr. Gordon, it's okay."

"Deputy! I'm in charge here." The spokesman addressed Franklin again. "Sir, I don't care if you're the sheriff's brother. You will follow orders. Do I make myself clear?"

"Yeah, yeah." With obviously poor graces, Franklin stood back in the well of the boat and raised his arms. He didn't, Mags noticed, extend them as high or as straight as she felt the deputy intended.

"Cover me," the leader ordered, then he stepped aboard the boat, where he proceeded to frisk Franklin Gordon. Mags was mesmerized.

"What th' hell is going on here?" Mags heard her ex demand. "What right do you have to order me about at gunpoint on my own boat? I was just about to take her out."

"911 Dispatch received a call that a prowler had been spotted on board the One True Love. "We're responding to that call."

"Oh, that explains everything," Franklin said, and his relaxed body language screamed that everyone was friends again. "Thank you for responding so quickly, I'll be certain to tell Malcolm how prompt you were. But nothing's wrong here."

"This boat is in impound. It was the scene of a murder, and the sheriff hasn't released it to its owner."

"But I'm the owner, and Malcolm gave me permission to come aboard."

"I assume you have ownership papers? The law requires you to have proof of ownership on board."

"Certainly I have papers."

Mags was doing a slow burn. How dare he pretend her boat still belonged to him? Suddenly she was very glad she had removed all the paperwork. She would enjoy watching him – the Franklin who never had to answer to anyone -- talk his way out of this.

"May I see them, please?" the deputy asked.

Franklin was clearly confused, Mags thought. "Well, sure. They're over here." He pointed toward the bulkhead.

"Let's walk over there and take a look." The officer gave Franklin a little nudge, and the two men moved out of Mags' line of sight. But she could still hear snatches of what was being said.

"I'm as surprised as anyone," Franklin said, no mistaking the belligerent tone in his voice. "Evidently when your guys were processing the boat, they removed the papers. But I'm not pointing fingers. Just call Malcolm and he'll vouch for me."

"I'm sorry, sir. But the sheriff is out of communication this afternoon."

"That's code for "he's got him a woman'" Mags whispered to Jennie. Her companion grinned.

"Then you'll just have to trust me until Malcolm can get back in pocket."

"No sir, I don't have to trust you."

"Look, I can commend you to your boss, or I can trash you. Either way, my word will carry a lot of weight. You need to stop and think about what you just said to me."

"Sir, I can already take you in on suspicion of breaking and entering. Would you like to add attempted intimidation of an officer to your rap sheet?"

Mags could feel her chest expanding with pride. Or was it a sense of "gotcha"? No one had ever stood up to Franklin and lived to tell about it. Could that be what happened with Mr. Humphries?

"I'll hang your smart ass high, you two-bit Barney Fife. I don't intend to stand here and be treated this way."

"No sir, you won't be standing here much longer." He turned to his backup officer and barked, "Cuff him. We'll transport him to the jail, then when the sheriff gets back, we'll let him straighten all this out. "By the way, Mr. Gordon, you've just added the charge of threatening to assault an officer to your other violations."

Franklin's face was contorting with rage, while his complexion was fluctuating between mottled blood red and black. He was also resisting the deputy who was attempting to get handcuffs on his wrists. In the end, the third officer had to jump on board to help subdue one angry man. The lead deputy stepped to the wheel house and suddenly the engine was silenced.

"I'll take these keys with me," they heard him say.

"What now?" Mags asked, as they watched the three extricate Franklin from the boat, which was no easy feat given the difference in height.

"Let them get gone, then we'll make our way casually out of the dock area. Franklin's on his way to jail."

"Yeah, but how are we going to keep him there? You don't think for one minute Malcolm is going to stand for his best friend being arrested?" She ran her hands through her hair. "I feel sorry for that officer. When Malcolm gets through with him, he WILL be hanging high."

"Maybe not," Jennie suggested. She punched Mags' arm and motioned for her to begin the trek to the car.

"How can you say that? You don't know how thick Malcolm and Franklin are. If we'd both been dying, and Franklin could only save one of us, the funeral home might as well have dispatched its hearse to pick up my body."

They got to the car and the ladies jumped in, anxious not to let the deputies get too far ahead of them. "Get us back to town," Jennie ordered. "They've got a head start and they can use their sirens."

"They may have the upper hand, but the curves between here and Crabapple Cove don't have any more respect for a patrol car than they have for this car. You can only go so fast. We'll be there by the time they are."

True to her word, Mags pulled into a courthouse parking space at the same time the car transporting her ex-husband pulled into the prisoner sally port at the back of the building. "Now what?"

Jennie dug in her tote bag and withdrew a bulging, business-size envelope. "You wait here. Your face is too familiar in there. But they don't know me."

"What are you going to do?"

"I'm about to walk the narrow edge of a razor blade barefooted. If I can pull this off, I can save an officer's job, and ensure that your ex-husband is investigated for murder."

Mags watched as the private detective slipped through the side door of the courthouse. In less than five minutes, Jennie came running back down the steps and quickly made her way across the lawn. Yanking open the door, she jumped into the passenger seat. Let's get out of here before anybody has time to think about what just happened."

Mags couldn't contain her curiosity. "So what did happen? What did you do?"

"I went in looking for the young man who insisted on arresting Franklin. Only I didn't reference Franklin, or the fact that he had just tangled with your ex-husband."

"What DID you do?"

"I spotted the deputy and pointed him out to the woman at the front desk. Then I asked her to please hand him the envelope. I told her it was information he had requested. I watched her put it in his hand, then I got the heck out of Dodge."

"Where are we going?"

"Back to your house, before anybody has a chance to connect this car with me."

"You got it." Mags steered the VW away from the courthouse area, and actually took an alternate route out of town, even though it took a few minutes longer to reach The Slop Bucket. The tension in the car was so great, neither woman spoke. Once in the house, Jennie collapsed on the couch. "I'm exhausted."

"So what was in that envelope you seem to think is such a hot item?"

"It's all the details of my investigation. Franklin is clearly implicated in that man's death."

"And you think Malcolm is going to roll over and play dead? You don't know that man like I do. If that deputy initiates any action because of the contents of that envelope, Malcolm will kill him. Then he'll fire him, just for good measure."

Jennie jumped up and headed to her bedroom. "We've only worked half of the plan. Come with me. I've got to change clothes before we go back to town." She quickly swapped dress slacks for a pair of jeans and a denim shirt. Digging in her suitcase, she pulled out a bandana that she tied around her head, then she popped on a pair of glasses with heavy frames.

Mags, who had been standing in the doorway the entire time, was mesmerized. "You don't look anything like you did two minutes ago. I'd never recognize you."

"And neither will anyone else in town. Which is why we go back in your Jeep."

"Tell me again, why are we returning to the scene of your crime? To gloat? Believe me, when Malcolm sees that document, he's going to shred it. Franklin will be walking out of that jail any minute, with that deputy's head on a platter."

"We're going to town to buy that deputy a little insurance."

"I don't understand."

"Surely there's one place in town that still has a pay phone?"

"Sure. There's one outside the supermarket. But why do you need a pay phone?"

"I've got an unregistered cell phone that has all identification blocked. But I'd rather use a pay phone."

The room was spinning. "You've lost me," Mags protested, as she grabbed hold of the door frame.

Jennie grabbed her arm. "Let's go. We don't have any time to waste. I'll explain on the way into town." Before she could get out of the drive, however, Mags' cell phone rang.

"Reach in my purse and get it," she instructed. "Tell me who it is."

"It's Franklin."

Franklin!

"Oh my gosh, he must be out of jail." Her hand trembled as she reached for her phone. "I better pull over. This is going to get hot."

"Hello?" She hoped her voice didn't sound as shaky as she felt.

"Dammit, Mags. What the hell did you get me into?"

"What are you talking about?" She listened, then quickly interrupted his tirade. "Calm down, Franklin. I can't understand a word you're saying."

"There was no evidence hidden on the boat. You sent me on a wild goose chase."

"Gosh, Franklin, I'm sorry. But there's no need to get ugly. So you wasted a few minutes." She grinned at the detective. "Maybe you overlooked it. Remember, we didn't exactly know what you were searching for. The important thing is, you tried, and I love you for it."

"Shut up!" he screamed. "You got me arrested."

"I did no such thing." Mags pretended to be insulted. "How in the world could I have done that?"

"It had to be you. You set me up," he snarled. "Damn you!"

"Franklin, I don't have a clue what you're talking about, but you're not going to talk to me that way. I'm hanging up. Don't ever call me again if you can't be civil."

"Wait... WAIT..." he sputtered. Don't hang up. I need to talk to you."

"Well what is it, Franklin? I don't have all day."

"There was nothing hidden on that boat anywhere. Nowhere. I took it apart."

"I know what Carole told me. She wouldn't lie. Malcolm must have gotten it."

"He says you probably found it when you went through the boat."

"Malcolm better be careful how he points his finger," she cautioned him. "But how did you get arrested? What did you do?"

"I didn't do a damn thing," he screamed. "It was some hotshot deputy who let his badge go to his head," he screamed. "He hadn't been on the job but a week."

"You're still not making sense. And lower your voice. I can't understand you when you scream."

"Somebody called 911 to say there was a prowler on the boat. I guess it was somebody at the marina. But I couldn't make the deputy who responded understand that I had permission to be there. He handcuffed me and hauled me in to the jail."

"Oh, Franklin. That must have been awful," she said, while trying not to give way the mirth she felt.

"I tried to reason with him. I was perfectly calm and tried to make him understand that he was making a mistake. He damn well understands it now."

"What do you mean?"

"They put me... ME... in a cell. Like a common criminal. But Malcolm got me out. Man, did he ever blow a gasket when he got back. There's one deputy out there who'll be looking for a new job tomorrow."

"That's terrible," Mags said. "All he did was err on the side of caution."

"Whose side are you on?" her ex-husband demanded. "If he would have listened to me, he'd still have his job."

"So what are you calling me about? What time are you picking me up to go to dinner?"

"Dinner! I've been insulted and jailed and all you can think about is food," he screamed. "Don't you care that I've been treated like scum?"

"I guess that's a no on dinner, then?"

"Damn straight it's a no. I thought you cared more about me than that."

"I do, Franklin. I do care what happens to you. More than you will ever understand."

"Huh!"

"Got to go, Franklin. I'll talk to you later." She punched the disconnect button in the middle of yet another tirade. "Yep, he's out of jail and one deputy is out of a job. We've got to do something."

"We are. Just get us to the grocery store."

"You still haven't told me what's going on here. Don't I deserve to be in the know?"

Jennie fiddled with her purse strap. "Remember when I told you that I was more concerned with investigation and less about enforcement? We're going into one of those gray areas."

"To do what?"

"Okay, it's like this. I'm going to use a pay phone to call and leave a message on the district attorney's answering machine, giving him a heads up about all that has gone down around here. He'll get it Monday morning. Then, to be on the safe side, I'm going to leave a similar message on your local newspaper's machine."

"Is that ethical?"

"Is it ethical for this deputy to be fired because he stood up for what's right? Is it ethical for your friend to be in jail for something she didn't do, because a crooked sheriff intends to use her as a scapegoat?"

"Well, no. When you put it that way."

"Yes, I'm leaving anonymous messages. But they are the truth and, if the other parties will do their jobs, we'll clean up several messes. The sad thing is, if I were to go and sit down with these people, neither one of them would take me seriously. But if I leave an anonymous message, the curiosity factor will make them take a look. And when they see even a tidbit of truth in what I've said, they'll really start digging."

"So let me get this straight," Mags said, after the detective had gone quiet. "You think these messages will be enough to tip the scales in a different direction and get Carole out of jail?"

"I'm convinced it will."

"Then go for it. I probably would have gone at it all wrong."

When Jennie came back from the pay phone near the supermarket front door, she flashed Mags a thumbs-up sign and climbed back into the car.

"Now we just sit back and wait. I'd venture to guess we'll see some action by mid-afternoon Monday. Now, if Franklin won't take you out to eat, I will."

"Are you serious?"

Jennie grinned. "Yep. There's just something about tracking down the bad guys that gives me an appetite." She fashioned her hand to look like a gun, and blew imaginary smoke away from the barrel end of her extended finger.

"You can joke all you want, but right now Franklin is out of jail, a deputy is out of a job, Carole's still doing the time for a crime she didn't do, and the real murderer is still enjoying freedom."

"Give it time. We've got a Sunday in the way here. I'll wager a year of dinners at wherever we're going, that within forty-eight hours, all of those conditions you just mentioned will be corrected."

"I hope you're right. This insanity has been going on for too long." Mags struggled to remember what life had been life before HJH, or Mr. Watkins, whichever he was, first entered the picture. She couldn't remember how, but she was convinced it had been better.

Would she even recognize a return to normalcy?

She and Jennie dined on fresh mountain trout and farm-fresh vegetables and salads at a little place Mags had been dying to try, but hadn't wanted to go alone. Neither of them was disappointed.

On Sunday, they slept in, then went out for brunch. About mid-afternoon, Jennie began loading her car. Mags wrote her a check for her services, and the two said goodbye. Mags went back inside The Slop Bucket where, for the first time ever, she found the privacy and the solitude smothering. Even a walk around the lake and a long, cold drink afterwards on the front porch didn't lift her spirits. Her entire life was suddenly a downer.

As soon as it was decently dark, which didn't come early during Daylight Savings Time, Mags and Delilah went to bed. Mags read until exhaustion finally triumphed, and she was able to fall off to sleep.

When she fixed their breakfast the next morning, Delilah turned up her nose at the scrambled eggs and looked up at Mags with the beautiful brown eyes that had first attracted her to the puppy.

"You getting tired of eggs, baby?" Throwing caution to the wind, Mags snatched up the dog's bowl and filled it with her usual food. It had been a week. If she needed validation, the way in which the corgi attacked her food was proof enough.

Mags was still afraid to leave her pet at home alone, so it was the both of them that traveled to town about mid-morning. The office hadn't gotten any attention in several days, and she did have a business to run. More than that, she knew if any of the developments Jennie had predicted came to pass, she wouldn't know anything about it down by the lake.

Mags collected the accumulated mail, opened the office, and and hung out the "open" sign. Maybe things would turn around today and people would suddenly need real estate again. And maybe the electric company would start giving away kilowatt hours. She hated to sit and watch the clock, but it took her less than an hour to go through the mail, dispose of the more than one hundred e-mails, and find and provide information that Grant Lewis' office needed for a closing coming up at the end of the week. All that was left was thumb twiddling. Mags knew if she had all her fun so early in the day, she'd really be bored by mid-afternoon.

That left watching paint dry, of which there was none, or trying to catch growth spurts on the African violet plants. It was going to be a long day, so she was slowly counting holes in the ceiling tile to pass time, when the phone rang.

What a wonderful sound, she thought. Even if it was a wrong number, perhaps she could keep the other party talking for a while. She was so desperate for the sound of another human voice, Mags didn't even check the Caller I.D.

"Hello? Mountain Magic Realty."

"Mrs. Gordon?"

"Yes, this is Mags Gordon."

"This is Ernestine Shelby. I'm calling to confirm something I just heard a few minutes ago. Do you have time to talk with me?"

"Yes, Ms. Shelby. I don't know what I can tell you, but I have time."

"I've just received a backdoor message, if you will, from your district attorney's office. Is there any truth that your ex-husband and Crabapple Cove's sheriff have both been arrested this morning on suspicion of murder?"

"Wha...? Are you serious?"

"That's the message I got. Anonymous, of course. I figured if anyone would know, you would."

"Gee, Ms. Shelby, this is the first..." The office's second line rang. Wyatt Fulton's name flashed on the Caller I.D. Almost simultaneously, her cell phone began its musical invitation for drinks and showed Jennie's unlisted number. "Ms. Shelby, I want to talk with you, but I've got two other calls coming in. Will you please let me put you on hold? I'll be right back, I promise."

Without waiting for an answer, she hit the transfer button. "Wyatt. Hold on." Then she hit the talk key on her cell keypad. "Jennie. I've got Wyatt on one line and the newspaper reporter Ernestine Shelby on the other line. What's going on?"

She could hear Wyatt yelling for her to put the phone to her ear. In the end, she cradled one phone to each ear. "Okay, you two. What's going on?

"Let Wyatt tell you what he knows," Jennie said.

"Okay, Wyatt, Jennie says for you to go first." She held her cell phone close to the landline speaker.

"All hell is breaking loose, Mags. At the request of the district attorney's office, the Georgia Bureau of Investigation has invaded the Crabapple Cove courthouse this morning with a warrant for Sheriff Wiley's arrest. I understand they have a second warrant for Franklin, and are looking for him now. I don't know how you and Jennifer did it, but you sure built a fire under somebody."

"It was all Jennie's doing," Mags explained. "But what does all this mean? What happens now?"

"I'd say you're about to see a complete reversal of situations there. I just hope they can nab Franklin before he gets wind of what's going on."

"I'm absolutely dizzy," Mags confessed. "Jennie said everything would break today."

"I've got to go, Mags. Got a client coming in the office now. I'll call you later."

"Jennie, you still there?"

"I'm here."

"Listen, let me punch back in to Ms. Shelby. I know she thinks I lied to her." She swiveled in her chair and transferred over to the other line. "Ms. Shelby, I am so sorry. But those other calls were about the same situation you were asking me about."

"Is there any truth to the rumor?"

"It appears there is. From what I understand the GBI is on the case. Supposedly the sheriff is under arrest, but they're still looking for my ex-husband."

"No... no," she heard Jennie screaming from the cell phone.

"Hold on a minute, Ms. Shelby. I think I'm getting some additional information."

She shifted her attention to the cell phone. "What is it, Jennie?"

"They've got Franklin. That's what I wanted to be sure you knew. You can relax, I don't think he'll be bothering you again any time soon. But brace yourself for the press to descend again. The Gordon name is big news in Atlanta circles."

"Thanks, Jennie. Let me call you back later today. Unless you hear something else; then you call me."

"Ms. Shelby, my ex-husband is in custody as well."

"I'm on my way to Crabapple Cove," the reporter vowed. "I'll be there before the day's out."

"I'll be looking forward to seeing you. Stop by when you get to town."

Mags put down the phone and looked at Delilah. "Great things are happening, girl. You can't begin to understand all that's going on and, if I'm honest, neither can I."

Unwilling to be a prisoner to gossip or four walls, she put the dog on her leash and the two headed out to do the town. Mags made her way up and down Main Street, speaking with merchants and tourists alike and, without planning, she ended up on the opposite corner from the courthouse. The place was swarming with uniformed people. Townspeople, who had gotten the news through the grapevine, were beginning to gather in small clusters all around the county seat of government. Mags hung back, unwilling to get caught up in the frenzy of gossip she was hearing from people she knew, her neighbors and friends. As she looked about the crowd, she saw more and more faces that she recognized. And more than one voice was familiar.

She was staring at the courthouse, trying to put herself in Franklin's shoes, having seen firsthand how rancid the jail property was. To be sure, it would be a big comedown from the Buckhead mini-mansion. Somehow, she couldn't find sympathy for him.

Then she heard the voice she would have recognized in her sleep. *Maudeann from the Eat and Greet.*

"I've told everbody. That sweet little thing couldn't have had anything to do with that awful man's death. Mags Gordon is solid in my book. As for Carole, I've known her since she was in diapers. They don't make 'em no better."

Mags couldn't keep from grinning.

"Anybody wants to say anything bad about Mags Gordon better not do it where I can hear," the waitress blathered on. "They'll have me to answer to. After all, she's one of us. It was that ex-husband of hers that did everything. He tried to frame her."

One of us. Mags realized she'd scored a real coup. By the end of the day, the grapevine would have broadcast news of her edification according to Maudeann, and no one crossed Maudeann.

Epilogue

"Ooooh, look," Carole squealed. "It's snowing. Crabapple Cove always has its first snow of the season during the first week in December. It means everything is right with the world."

Mags, who was hanging the last of the ornaments on the small tree in the corner of the reception area, raised up from where she was crouched on the floor. The landscape of the small mountain town she had come to love and call home, was inundated with large, swirling flakes of white.

"Gosh, it's coming down. If this keeps up and begins to stick, I'll have to head to The Slop Bucket. Wouldn't want to get stranded."

"You know you're welcome to bunk at my place. You and Delilah, both."

The corgi who had been napping in the corner, got up, stretched stiffly, and came to nuzzle Carole's hand, who returned the favor by scratching the dog's ears.

"I'm so glad you bring her to work with you. I think the clients like her as well."

"I started letting her come with me last summer, after she was poisoned, because I was afraid to leave her home alone."

"Let's don't even talk about last summer. I still get sick to my stomach thinking about all that time I spent in jail. I really didn't think I'd ever be free again." She wrung her hands. "I still can't believe those goons actually poisoned my food to try to make everybody believe I tried to kill myself."

"That's why Delilah comes to the office with me now. I won't have her forever, and when I'm in town and she's at home, we don't get to be together."

"Just look at that snow. It's coming on down."

"That it is. I'd say the Christmas season is officially launched."

"Wonder who they'll get to be Santa Claus this year? Carole, was working on paperwork for three upcoming closings, but she turned and looked at Mags as she spoke. The real estate broker knew what she meant.

"You know… how Malcolm could play Santa in December and help Franklin murder a man in July, just shows how twisted and sick he really was."

"Did you ever think you'd see the day Franklin Gordon would be on death row?"

"I never, ever knew him even to get a parking ticket. Not that he didn't deserve plenty, but somehow, it just always seemed like he was coated with Teflon®."

"A lot of water has gone under the bridge since last summer," Carole mused as she began putting her desk to rights. "This snow is getting harder. If you're going to the lake, you better get going. I'll shut everything down."

Mags knew a good idea when she heard it. For one thing, she didn't want to get snowed in at someone else's house. "I'm going to take your advice." She clicked her teeth and picked up Delilah's leash. "Come on, girl. Let's go home."

As she dodged some of the biggest snowflakes she'd ever seen, Mags was alone with her thoughts. Carole had been so very right. A lot of water had flowed under the bridge, and with it, many changes. Some of them sad, some of them unexpected, but all very necessary.

For starters, Franklin had been tried and found guilty of the premeditated malice murder of Horace J. Humphries, who was really Donald Hamilton Watkins. Franklin had hired him to create havoc sufficient to ruin Mags' business and force her into financial ruin. He had believed, in error, Mags was quick to point out, that she would come crawling to him begging for help. But in the end, the worm had turned. HJH was blackmailing Franklin for huge sums of money, and Franklin terminated his services. Literally. Mags finally understood that the strange man who had stalked her had been another of Franklin's low-life henchmen. It had been his job to steal the gun from the real estate office. A gun that Franklin knew about, because when Carole renewed her firearms' license a few months before, she had openly shared about stashing the gun where it would be safe.

It had all come out in court, where Mags had been required to testify. Franklin's original goal had been simply to put her out of business. But when HJH, who knew too much, turned traitor, Franklin had to deal with it, and decided if financial ruin was good, hanging a murder charge on her office manager was even better.

Franklin had enlisted the help of his life-long best friend, Sheriff Malcolm Wiley, who warped the precepts of his oath of office far beyond recognition, in order to keep his friend's crimes from being uncovered. Franklin was in a death-row cell near the state's execution chamber, while Gordon money paid for appeals. The governor's office had removed Sheriff Wiley from office, only to be replaced by the young deputy who had been so insistent that Franklin was guilty of something. He'd been elected in a landslide, bringing about an immediate attitude adjustment in the sheriff's office.

Malcolm, she knew, was serving a total ten to twenty in the state penitentiary for a variety of crimes, not the least of which was accessory to murder.

Business at Mountain Magic Realty by Mags had recovered, going on to set new sales records. All the free publicity that accompanied the fall-out of Franklin's crimes had actually been a shot in the arm for the agency. Mags had feared the *One True Love* would be tainted. Instead, potential clients were asking to see property from the boat where a murder occurred. She had replaced the carpet and bought herself a new car with the money she would have spent on another boat.

Almost to the last person, all those listing contracts she had cancelled had come back, heads bowed, deeply apologetic. She'd welcomed them warmly, without reminding them of all the ugly things they'd said.

The snow was getting heavier. Mags could feel the front wheels struggling to stay on the pavement and, without realizing it, she gripped the steering wheel harder, determined not to be stranded in the storm. All she wanted was home.

Home. It had such a wonderful sound. In part because of her new outlook on life. No longer was she a hermit at The Slop Bucket. She had begun to reach out, to make friends, to invite people to her home and accept invitations to theirs'. Many of the townspeople who had shunned her, had come around. Now they were all recommending her to out-of-towners shopping for property. Once again, a steady stream of lookers came up on the porch to peruse the big bulletin board. More often then not, they came on in to talk and visit.

One of the most unlikely alliances had been with the loud-mouthed Doreen, who had insisted that Mags owed her two million dollars over a defaulted contract. Mags had had no intention of paying the money, and fully expected a lawsuit. But after all the dirt on Franklin was made public, Doreen had cancelled the debt in a telephone conversation, during which she made certain Mags understood the sacrifice she was making. After the fact, the two had become cautious friends.

Finally, the twisting drive into The Slop Bucket was in sight, and Mags began to aim the Jeep in that direction. She still wasn't totally comfortable driving in snow, but she was learning. Just like she was discovering other things about herself that continued to surprise her. And she wasn't ready to stop. Every day was a new adventure, a new challenge. Having successfully met the challenge of getting home in the snow, Mags opened the door and turned Delilah out, without a leash on. The dog immediately began to romp in the snow, leaping into the air, attempting to catch snowflakes in her mouth. Delilah was another whose life had changed for the better. She and Mags enjoyed a much closer relationship, and at home, Delilah could now run loose, because there was no one out there to harm her. It had been Franklin who had broken in through a trap door in the basement to feed poison to the corgi. That was probably the one thing Mags would never be able to forgive. All the e-mails had been traced back to Franklin, who finally admitted he expected the harassment to frighten Mags, causing her to cave.

Mags watched her companion and finally, as the snowfall began to obscure even the trees on the other side of the drive, she reluctantly called the dog's name and the two went indoors, ready to ride out whatever the storm delivered. It was nice, Mags realized, to be able to concentrate on selling real estate and enjoying life. While she hadn't given up her love for mysteries and amateur detectives, she was content to leave the investigations to them. Her own private investigation career was in mothballs, cold storage. Suspended.

As she was taking off her coat, the phone rang. Caller I.D. showed Carole's home number. She's calling to be sure I made it, Mags told herself.

"Mags! Glad you got there. It's getting rough out outside. Did you hear that old man VanLandenham's long lost son has shown up to do the death bed gig, and collect his inheritance?" Carole was talking a mile a minute, and Mags knew she'd never get a word in edgewise. "Only Mrs. Puffery, you know, the old man's housekeeper…" Carole stopped to grab a breath, then kept going… "Mrs. Puffery says this guy's an imposter. I ran into her in the grocery store on my way home. She says there's several things that don't add up, and she begged me to ask you to take the case." There was another gasp for air. "She's afraid if somebody doesn't do something, the old man will die and this guy will steal a fortune, then never be heard from again. So I told her we'd do it."

"Excuse me?" Mags dug her finger in her ear, hoping to hear more clearly. "You told her what?"

"I told her we'd take the case and see if we can unmask this imposter."

Mags was struck speechless.

"After all, it's like she said. We found out who Mr. Humphries really was, and now people are serving time for his murder."

"You told her we would find out if this man is an imposter?"

"Yeah. Isn't that what I just said?"

"But why would you tell her that? We're in the real estate business. Remember? Besides, it was Jennie who uncovered HJH's real identity."

"But... well... you saw what she did. How hard can it be? Besides, real estate's just our day job. By night, we're like Judith McMonigle Flynn and her cousin Renee up in Washinton State."

"Excuse me?"

"You know. Private detectives working for the underdogs. Like Holmes and Watson or Peroit and Hastings."

"But Carole..."

"Hey, somebody's at the door. It's probably dad with firewood. Gotta run."

Holmes and Watson and Peroit and Captain Arthur Hastings, Mags thought. What about Coldwell Banker® and Century 21® and ReMax®. Those names were a lot safer. But, she had to admit, they weren't nearly as exciting.

She and Carole would have to come to an understanding on all this. Real estate had to come first. And they couldn't do anything dangerous. There was one other stipulation that absolutely was not negotiable. She was the owner of the agency, and she would be Mr. Holmes. Carole could be Watson, and Delilah... well... Nick and Nora Charles' dog Asta had nothing on her beloved Delilah. She would just be herself.

Coming in 2015

Gone Astray

"Why not, Mommie? Why can't we go home? I want my room and my toys. What happened to us?" The child began to sob, and the sound of his distress ripped an already bruised and bloody heart straight from Denise Mathews' chest.

What happened, indeed? Despite her best efforts, the young mother couldn't turn back the memories of all that had occurred that fateful Sunday morning. Literally, in the blink of an eye, her life and the lives of many in the congregation she led, had been forever changed. She would probably never understand all that had gone down, but one thing Denise did know: Nothing would ever be the same again.

When unspeakable tragedy lands squarely on the pulpit of a young minister's plum pastorate, she not only finds herself personally affected, but also unable to respond to the God she has pledged to serve. A journey through the wilderness of doubt and despair brings her to the other side a changed person, but not in ways you'd necessarily expect.

Coming in 2016

Out of Thin Heir

After Mags Gordon solved the murder of the man found dead on board her boat, and freed her best friend and office manager from an almost certain death sentence, she was more than content to return to peddling real estate in a pristine mountain community.

Unfortunately, a reputation earned isn't nearly as easily shed.

Town skinflint Horace VanLandenham's long lost son has shown up to do the death bed gig, and collect his inheritance. At least that's the scuttlebutt going around. Only Mrs. Puffery, the old man's housekeeper, adds a yet another element of conflict, when she vows the son is an imposter. He's there to steal a fortune, she believes. Her solution was to employ jackleg private investors Gordon and Pickett, assisted by the four-legged Delilah, of course, to prove her suspicions are on the mark before it's too late.

In this second volume of the "Slop Bucket Mystery Series", readers who met and came to admire Margaret "Mags" Gordon in **Boat Load of Trouble** can once again stalk in the tracks of this real estate broker turned detective.

About the Author

John Shivers began writing for his hometown newspaper when he was only fourteen years old. As a life-long wordsmith – some have called him a wordweaver – his byline has appeared in over forty Christian and secular publications, winning him seventeen professional awards.

Hear My Cry, his first novel, was published in 2005, and a dream of forty-four years was realized. While all his previous titles have been in the Christian inspirational fiction genre, with the publication of **Boat Load of Trouble**, he has now achieved one of his life-long goals: he's penned his first mystery novel, one of his favorite pleasure reading pastimes since he discovered "Perry Mason" in the late 1950s. He now has eight books in print.

John and his wife, Elizabeth, along with Callum, their irascible but lovable Skye Terrier, live in his hometown of Calhoun, Georgia. They are members of the Plainville United Methodist Church, where John serves the congregation as Lay Leader. When the schedule permits, he loves to slip away to heaven on earth in Rabun County, Georgia, where he enjoys the music his heart doesn't hear anywhere else.

A second title in the "Slop Bucket Mystery Series" will be released in 2016. Another Christian inspirational fiction novel, **Gone Astray**, will be released in late 2015.

47088411R00178

Made in the USA
Charleston, SC
02 October 2015